To the Land of the Living

By the same author

THE TIME HOPPERS
THE MASKS OF TIME
UP THE LINE
TO LIVE AGAIN
A TIME OF CHANGES
RECALLED TO LIFE
DYING INSIDE
UNFAMILIAR TERRITORY
BORN WITH THE DEAD
THE STOCHASTIC MAN
THE FEAST OF ST DIONYSUS
SHADRACH IN THE FURNACE
DOWNWARD TO THE EARTH
ACROSS A BILLION YEARS
CAPRICORN GAMES
THE GATE OF WORLDS
THE BOOK OF SKULLS
THE SONGS OF SUMMER
THE SECOND TRIP
LORD VALENTINE'S CASTLE
MAJIPOOR CHRONICLES
SUNRISE ON MERCURY
LORD OF DARKNESS
VALENTINE PONTIFEX
THE CONGLOMEROID COCKTAIL PARTY
GILGAMESH THE KING
TOM O'BEDLAM
STAR OF GYPSIES
AT WINTER'S END
WORLDS OF WONDER (ED.)

To the Land of the Living

by

ROBERT SILVERBERG

LONDON
VICTOR GOLLANCZ LTD
1989

First published in Great Britain 1989
by Victor Gollancz Ltd,
14 Henrietta Street, London WC2E 8QJ

British Library Cataloguing in Publication data
Silverberg, Robert
To the land of the living.
I. Title
813'.54[F]

ISBN 0-575-04461-6

Typeset at The Spartan Press Ltd,
Lymington, Hants
Printed in Great Britain by St Edmundsbury Press Ltd,
Bury St Edmunds, Suffolk

For Ralph

Who keeps track of it all, from Antigua to Zimbabwe –
dear friend, trusted adviser

Per me si va ne la città dolente,
Per me si va ne l'etterno dolore,
Per me si va tra la perduta gente.
Giustizia mosse il mio alto fattore;
Fecemi la divina podestate,
La somma sapienza ed il primo amore.
Dinanzi a me non fuor cose create
Se non etterne, ed io etterno duro.
LASCIATE OGNI SPERANZA, VOI CH'ENTRATE.

To the Land of the Living

I am he whom you call Gilgamesh. I am the pilgrim who has seen everything within the confines of the Land, and far beyond it; I am the man to whom all things were made known, the secret things, the truths of life and death, most especially those of death. I have coupled with Inanna in the bed of the Sacred Marriage; I have slain demons and spoken with gods; I am two parts god myself, and only one part mortal. Here in Uruk I am king, and when I walk through the streets I walk alone, for there is no one who dares approach me too closely.

One

Jagged green lightning danced on the horizon and the wind came ripping like a blade out of the east, skinning the flat land bare and sending up clouds of gray-brown dust. Gilgamesh grinned broadly. By Enlil, now that was a wind! A lion-killing wind it was, a wind that turned the air dry and crackling. The beasts of the field gave you the greatest joy in their hunting when the wind was like that, hard and sharp and cruel.

He narrowed his eyes and stared into the distance, searching for this day's prey. His bow of several fine woods, the bow that no man but he was strong enough to draw – no man but he, and Enkidu his beloved thrice-lost friend – hung loosely from his hand. His body was poised and ready. Come now, you beasts! Come and be slain! It is Gilgamesh king of Uruk who would make his sport with you this day!

Other men in this strange land, when they went about their hunting, made use of guns, those foul machines that the Later Dead had brought, which hurled death from a great distance along with much noise and fire and smoke; or they employed the even deadlier laser devices from whose ugly snouts came spurts of blue-white flame. Cowardly things, all those killing-machines! Gilgamesh loathed them, as he did most instruments of the Later Dead, those slick and bustling Johnny-come-latelies of the Afterworld. He would not touch them if he could help it. In all his thousands of years in this nether world, this land of dreams and spirits, of life beyond life, he had never used any weapons but those he had known during his first lifetime: the javelin, the spear, the double-headed axe, the hunting-bow, the good bronze sword. It took some skill, hunting with such weapons as those. And there was physical effort; there was more than a little risk. Hunting was a contest, was it not? Then it must make demands. Why, if the idea was merely to slaughter one's prey in the fastest and easiest and safest way, then the sensible thing to do would be to ride high above the hunting-grounds in a weapons-platform and drop a little nuke, and lay waste five kingdoms' worth of beasts at a single stroke, he told himself. And laughed and strode onward.

"If you ever had come to Texas, H.P., this here's a lot like what you'd have seen," said the big barrel-chested man with the powerful arms and the deeply tanned skin. Gesturing sweepingly with one hand, he held the wheel of the Land Rover lightly with three fingers of the other, casually guiding the vehicle in jouncing zigs and zags over the flat trackless landscape. Gnarled gray-green shrubs matted the gritty ground. The sky was black with swirling dust. Far off in the distance barren mountains rose like dark jagged teeth. "Beautiful. Beautiful. As close to Texas in look as makes no never mind, this countryside is."

"Beautiful?" said the other man uncertainly. "The Afterworld?"

"This stretch sure is. But if you think the Afterworld's beautiful, you should have seen Texas!"

The burly man laughed and gunned the engine and the Land Rover went leaping and bouncing forward at a stupefying speed.

His travelling companion, a gaunt lantern-jawed man as pale as the other was bronzed, sat very still in the passenger seat, knees together, elbows digging in against his ribs, as if he expected a fiery crash at any moment. The two of them had journeyed across the interminable parched wastes of the Outback for many days now – how many, not even the Elder Gods could tell. They were ambassadors, these two: Their Excellencies Robert E. Howard and H.P. Lovecraft of the Kingdom of New Holy Resurrected England, envoys of His Britannic Majesty Henry VIII to the court of Prester John.

In an earlier life Lovecraft and Howard had been writers, fantasists, inventors of fables; but now they found themselves caught up in something far more fantastic than anything to be found in any of their tales, for this was no fable, this was no fantasy. This was the harsh reality of the Afterworld.

The Land Rover bounced, skidded, bounced again.

"Robert – please –" said the pale man, mildly, nervously.

*

Gilgamesh knew that some thought him a fool for his conservative ideas. Caesar, for one. Cocksure coldblooded Julius with the row of fragmentation grenades tucked into his belt and the Uzi slung across his shoulders: Caesar, who represented all that Gilgamesh most despised. "Why don't you admit it?" Caesar had asked him some considerable time earlier, riding up in his jeep as Gilgamesh was making ready to set forth from the city of Nova Roma where he had lived too long, out toward the Afterworld's open wilderness, the godforsaken Outback. "It's a pure affectation, Gilgamesh, all this insistence on arrows and javelins and spears. This isn't old Sumer you're living in now."

Gilgamesh spat. "Hunt with 9-millimeter automatics? Hunt with grenades and cluster bombs and lasers? You call that sport, Caesar?"

"I call it acceptance of reality. Is it technology you hate? What's the difference between using a bow and arrow and using a gun? They're both technology, Gilgamesh. It isn't as though you kill the animals with your bare hands."

"I have done that too," said Gilgamesh.

"Bah! I'm on to your game. Big hulking Gilgamesh, the simple innocent oversized Bronze Age hero! That's just an affectation too, my friend! You pretend to be a stupid stubborn thick-skulled barbarian because it suits you to be left alone to your hunting and your wandering, and that's all you claim that you really want. But secretly you regard yourself as superior to anybody who lived in an era softer than your own. You mean to restore the bad old filthy ways of the ancient ancients, isn't that so? If I read you the right way you're just biding your time, skulking around with your bow and arrow in the dreary Outback until you think it's the right moment to launch the *putsch* that carries you to supreme power here. Isn't that it, Gilgamesh? You've got some crazy fantasy of lording it over all of us, supreme monarch and absolute dictator. And then we'll live in mud cities again and make little chicken-scratches on clay tablets, the way you think human beings were meant to do. What do you say?"

"I say this is great nonsense, Caesar."

"Is it? This place is rotten to bursting with kings and emperors and sultans and pharaohs and shahs and presidents and dictators, and every single one of them wants to be Number One again. My guess is that you're no exception."

"In this you are very wrong. It is well known to all that I have no lust to rule over men a second time."

"I doubt that. I suspect you believe you're the noblest of us all: you, the sturdy warrior, the great hunter, the maker of bricks, the builder of vast temples and lofty walls, the shining beacon of ancient heroism." Caesar laughed. "Before Rome ever was, you and your dismal sun-baked little land of Mesopotamia were really big news, and you can't ever let us forget that, can you? You think we're all decadent rascally degenerates and that you're the one true virtuous man. But you're as proud and ambitious as any of us. Isn't that how it is? This shunning of power for which you're so famous: it's only a pose. You're a fraud, Gilgamesh, a huge musclebound fraud!"

"At least I am no slippery tricky serpent like you, Caesar, who buys and sells his friends at the best prices."

Caesar looked untroubled by the thrust. "And so you pass three quarters of your time killing slow-witted lumpish monsters in the Outback and you make sure everyone knows that you're too pious to have anything to do with modern weapons while you do it. You don't fool me. It isn't virtue that keeps you from doing your killing with a decent double-barreled .470 Springfield. It's intellectual pride, or maybe simple laziness. The bow just happens to be the weapon you grew up with, who knows how many thousands of years ago. You like it because it's familiar. But what language are you speaking now, eh? Is it your thick-tongued Euphrates gibberish? No, it seems to be English, doesn't it? Did you grow up speaking English too, Gilgamesh? Did you grow up riding around in jeeps and choppers? Apparently *some* of the modern conveniences are acceptable to you."

Gilgamesh shrugged. "I speak English with you because that is what is mainly spoken now in this place. In my heart I speak the old tongue, Caesar. In my heart I am still Gilgamesh of Uruk, and I will hunt as I hunt."

"Your Uruk's long gone to dust. This is the life after life, my friend, the little joke that the gods have played on us all. We've been here a long time. We'll be here for all time to come, unless I miss my guess. New people constantly bring new ideas to this place, and it's impossible to ignore them. Even you can't do it. The new ways sink in and change you, however much you try to pretend that they can't."

"I will hunt as I hunt," said Gilgamesh. "There is no sport in it, when you do it with guns. There is no grace in it."

Caesar shook his head. "I never could understand hunting for sport, anyway. Killing a few stags, yes, or a boar or two, when you're bivouacked in some dismal Gaulish forest and your men want meat. But hunting? Slaughtering hideous animals that aren't even edible? By Apollo, it's all nonsense to me!"

"My point exactly."

"But if you must hunt, to scorn the use of a decent hunting rifle –"

"You will never convince me."

"No," Caesar said with a sigh. "I suppose I won't. I should know better than to argue with a reactionary."

"Reactionary! In my time I was thought to be a radical," said Gilgamesh. "When I was king in Uruk –"

"Just so," Caesar said, grinning. "King in Uruk. Was there ever a king who wasn't reactionary? You put a crown on your head and it addles your brains instantly. Three times Antonius offered me a crown, Gilgamesh, three times, and –"

"– you did thrice refuse it, yes. I know all that. 'Was this ambition?' You thought you'd have the power without the emblem. Who were you fooling, Caesar? Not Brutus, so I hear. Brutus said you were ambitious. And Brutus –"

That stung him where nothing else had. Caesar brandished a fist. "Damn you, don't say it!"

"– was an honourable man," Gilgamesh concluded all the same, greatly enjoying Caesar's discomfiture.

The Roman groaned. "If I hear that line once more –"

"Some say this is a place of torment," said Gilgamesh serenely. "If in truth it is, yours is to be swallowed up in another man's poetry. Leave me to my bows and arrows, Caesar, and return to your jeep and your trivial intrigues. I am a fool and a reactionary, yes. But you know nothing of hunting. Nor do you understand anything of me."

All that had been a year ago, or two, or maybe five – even for those who affected clocks and wristwatches, there was no keeping proper track of time in the Afterworld, where the ruddy unsleeping eye of the sun moved in perverse random circles across the sky – and now Gilgamesh was far from Caesar and all his minions, far from Nova Roma, that troublesome capital city of the Afterworld, and the trivial squabbling of those like Caesar and Bismarck and Cromwell and that sordid little man Lenin who maneuvered for power in this place. He had found himself thrown in among them because – he barely remembered why – because he had met one, or Enkidu had, and almost without realizing what was happening they had been drawn in, had become entangled in their plots and counterplots, their dreams of empire, their hope of revolution and upheaval and transformation. Until finally, growing bored with their folly, he had walked out, never to return. How long ago had that been? A year? A century? He had no idea.

Let them maneuver all they liked, those tiresome new men of the tawdry latter days. All their maneuvers were hollow ones, though they lacked the wit to see that. But some day they might learn wisdom, and was not that the purpose of this place, if it had any purpose at all?

Gilgamesh preferred to withdraw from the center of the arena. The quest for power bored him. He had left it behind, left it in that other world where his first flesh had been conceived and gone to dust. Unlike the rest of those fallen emperors and kings and pharaohs and shahs, he felt no yearning to reshape the Afterworld in his own image, or to regain in it the pomp and splendor that had once been his. Caesar was as wrong about Gilgamesh's ambitions as he was about the reasons for his preferences in hunting gear. Out here in the Outback, in the bleak dry chilly hinterlands of the Afterworld, Gilgamesh hoped to find peace. That was all he wanted now: peace. He had wanted much more, once, but that had been long ago, and in another place.

There was a stirring in the scraggly underbush.

A lion, maybe?

No, Gilgamesh told himself. There were no lions to be found in the Afterworld, only the strange nether-world beasts, demon-spawn, nightmare-spawn, that lurked in the dead zones between the cities – ugly hairy things with flat noses and many legs and dull baleful eyes, and slick shiny things with the faces of women and the bodies of malformed dogs, and worse, much worse. Some had drooping leathery wings and some were armed with spiked tails that rose like a scorpion's and some had mouths that opened wide enough to swallow an elephant at a gulp. They all were demons of one sort or another, Gilgamesh knew. No matter. Hunting was hunting; the prey was the prey; all beasts were one in the contest of the field. That fop Caesar could never begin to comprehend that.

Drawing an arrow from his quiver, Gilgamesh laid it lightly across his bow and waited.

"A lot like Texas, yes," Howard went on, "only the Afterworld's just a faint carbon copy of the genuine item. Just a rough first draft, is all. You see that sandstorm rising out thataway? *We* had sandstorms, they covered entire counties! You see that lightning? In Texas that would be just a flicker!"

"If you could drive just a little more slowly, Bob –"

"More slowly? Chthulu's whiskers, man, I *am* driving slowly!"

"Yes, I'm quite sure you believe that you are."

"And the way I always heard it, H.P., you loved for people to drive you around at top speed. Seventy, eighty miles an hour, that was what you liked best, so the story goes."

"In the other life one dies only once, and then all pain ceases," Lovecraft replied. "But here, where one can lose one's life again and again, and each time return from the darkness, and when one returns one remembers every final agony in the brightest of hues – here, dear friend Bob, death's much more to be feared, for the pain of it stays with one forever, and one may die a thousand deaths." Lovecraft managed a pallid baleful smile. "Speak of that to some professional warrior, Bob, some Trojan or Hun or Assyrian – or one of the gladiators, maybe, someone who has died and died and died again. Ask him about it: the dying and the rebirth, and the pain, the hideous torment, reliving every detail. It is a dreadful thing to die in the Afterworld. I fear dying here far more than I ever did in life. I will take no needless risks here."

Howard snorted. "Gawd, try and figure you out! In the days when you thought you lived only once, you made people go roaring along with you on the highway a mile a minute. Here where no one stays dead for very long you want me to drive like an old woman. Well, I'll attempt it, H.P., but everything in me cries out to go like the wind. When you live in big country, you learn to cover the territory the way it has to be covered. And Texas is the biggest country there is. It isn't just a place, it's a state of mind."

"As is the Afterworld," said Lovecraft. "Though I grant you that the Afterworld isn't Texas."

"Texas!" Howard boomed. "Now, there was a place! God damn, I wish you could have seen it! By God, H.P., what a time we'd have had, you and me, if you'd come to Texas. Two gentlemen of letters like us riding together all to hell and gone from Corpus Christi to El Paso and back again, seeing it all and telling each other wondrous stories all the way! I swear, it would have enlarged your soul, H.P. Beauty such as perhaps even you couldn't have imagined. That big sky. That blazing sun. And the open space! Whole empires could fit into Texas and never be seen again! That Rhode Island of yours, H.P. – we could drop it down just back of Cross Plains and lose it behind a medium-size prickly pear! What you see here, it just gives you the merest idea of that glorious beauty. Though I admit this is plenty beautiful itself, this here."

"I wish I could share your joy in this landscape, Robert," Lovecraft said quietly, when it seemed that Howard had said all he meant to say.

"You don't care for it?" Howard asked, sounding surprised and a little wounded.

"I can say one good thing for it: at least it's far from the sea."

"You'll give it that much, will you?"

"You know how I hate the sea and all that the sea contains! Its odious creatures – that hideous reek of salt air hovering above it –" Lovecraft shuddered fastidiously. "But this land – this bitter desert – you don't find it somber? You don't find it forbidding, this Outback?"

"It's the most beautiful place I've seen since I came to the Afterworld."

"Perhaps what you call beauty is too subtle for my eye. Perhaps it escapes me altogether. I was always a man for cities, myself."

"What you're trying to say, I reckon, is that all this looks real hateful to you. Is that it? As grim and ghastly as the Plateau of Leng, eh, H.P.?" Howard laughed. "'Sterile hills of gray granite . . . dim wastes of rock and ice and snow . . . .'" Hearing himself quoted, Lovecraft laughed too, though not exuberantly. Howard went on, "I look around at the Outback of the Afterworld and I see something a whole lot like Texas, and I love it. For you it's as sinister as dark frosty Leng, where people have horns and hooves and munch on corpses and sing hymns to Nyarlathotep. Oh, H.P., H.P., there's no accounting for tastes, is there? Why, there's even some people who – whoa, now! Look there!"

He braked the Land Rover suddenly and brought it to a jolting halt. A small malevolent-looking something with blazing eyes and a scaly body had broken from cover and gone scuttering across the path just in front of them. Now it faced them, glaring up out of the road, snarling and hissing flame.

"Hell-cat!" Howard cried. "Hell-coyote! *Look* at that critter, H.P. You ever see so much ugliness packed into such a small package? Scare the toenails off a shoggoth, that one would!"

"Can you drive on past it?" Lovecraft asked, looking dismayed.

"I want a closer look, first." Howard rummaged down by his boots and pulled a pistol from the clutter on the floor of the car. "Don't it give you the shivers, driving around in a land full of critters that could have come right out of one of your stories, or mine? I want to look this little ghoul-cat right in the eye."

"Robert –"

"You wait here. I'll only be but a minute."

Howard swung himself down from the Land Rover and marched stolidly toward the hissing little beast, which stood its ground. Lovecraft watched fretfully. At any moment the creature might leap upon Bob Howard and rip out his throat with a swipe of its horrid yellow talons, perhaps – or burrow snout-deep into his chest, seeking the Texan's warm, throbbing heart –

They stood staring at each other, Howard and the small monster, no more than a dozen feet apart. For a long moment neither one moved. Howard, gun in hand, leaned forward to inspect the beast as one might look at a feral cat guarding the mouth of an alleyway. Did he mean to shoot it? No, Lovecraft thought: beneath his bluster the robust Howard seemed surprisingly squeamish about bloodshed and violence of any sort.

Then things began happening very quickly. Out of a thicket to the left a much larger animal abruptly emerged: a ravening monstrous creature with a crocodile head and powerful thick-thighed legs that ended in frightful curving claws. An arrow ran through the quivering dewlaps of its heavy throat from side to side, and a hideous dark ichor streamed from the wound down the beast's repellent blue-gray fur. The small animal, seeing the larger one wounded this way, instantly sprang upon its back and sank its fangs joyously into its shoulder. But a moment later there burst from the same thicket a man of astonishing size, a great dark-haired black-bearded man clad only in a bit of cloth about his waist. Plainly he was the huntsman who had wounded the larger monster, for there was a bow of awesome dimensions in his hand and a quiver of arrows on his back. In utter fearlessness the giant plucked the foul little creature from the wounded beast's back and hurled it far out of sight; then, swinging around, he drew a gleaming bronze dagger and with a single fierce thrust drove it into the breast of his prey, the *coup de grâce* that brought the animal crashing heavily down.

All this took only an instant. Lovecraft, peering through the window of the Land Rover, was dazzled by the strength and speed of the dispatch and awed by the size and agility of the half-naked huntsman. He glanced toward Howard, who stood to one side, his own considerable frame utterly dwarfed by the black-bearded man.

For a moment Howard seemed dumbstruck, paralyzed with wonder and amazement. But then he was the first to speak.

"By Crom," he muttered, staring at the giant. "Surely this is Conan of Aquilonia and none other!" He was trembling. He took a lurching step toward the huge man, holding out both his hands in a strange gesture – submission, was it? "Lord Conan?" Howard murmured. "Great king, is it you? Conan? Conan?" And before Lovecraft's astounded eyes Howard fell to his knees next to the dying beast, and looked up with awe and something like rapture in his eyes at the towering huntsman.

Two

It had been a decent day's hunting so far. Three beasts brought down after long and satisfying chase; every shaft fairly placed; each animal skilfully dressed, the meat set out as bait for other demon-beasts, the hide and head carefully put aside for proper cleaning at nightfall. There was true pleasure in work done so well.

Yet there was a hollowness at the heart of it all, Gilgamesh thought, that left him leaden and cheerless no matter how cleanly his arrows sped to their mark. He never felt that true fulfilment, that clean sense of completion, that joy of accomplishment, which was ultimately the only thing he sought.

Why was that? Was it because – as some of the Christian dead so drearily insisted – because the Afterworld was a place of punishment, where by definition there could be no delight?

To Gilgamesh that was foolishness. Some parts of the Afterworld were extraordinarily nasty, yes. Much of it. It had its hellish aspects, no denying that. But certainly pleasure was to be had there too.

It depended, he supposed, on one's expectations. Those who came here thinking to find eternal punishment did indeed get eternal punishment, and it was even more horrendous than anything they had anticipated. It served them right, those true believers, those gullible Later Dead, that army of credulous Christians.

He had been amazed when their kind first came flocking into the Afterworld, Enki only knew how many thousands of years ago. The things they talked of! Rivers of boiling oil! Lakes of pitch! Demons with pitchforks! That was what they expected, and there were clever folk here willing and ready to give them what they were looking for. So Torture Towns aplenty were constructed for those who wanted them. Gilgamesh had trouble understanding why anyone would. Nobody among the First Dead really could figure them out, those absurd Later Dead with their sickly obsession with punishment. What was it Imhotep called them? Masochists, that was the word. Pathetic masochists. But then sly little Aristotle had begged to disagree, saying, "No, my lord, it would be a violation of the nature of the Afterworld to send a true masochist off to the torments. The only ones who go are the strong ones, the bullies, the braggarts, the ones who are cowards at the core of their souls." Belshazzar had had something to say on the matter too, and Tiberius, and that Palestinian sorceress Delilah of the startling eyes, and then all of them had jabbered at once, trying yet again to make sense of the Christian Later Dead. Until finally Gilgamesh had said, before stalking out of the room, "The trouble with all of you is that you keep trying to make sense out of this place. But when you've been here as long as I have –"

Well, perhaps the Afterworld *was* a place of punishment. No question that there were some disagreeable aspects to it. The climate was always terrible, too hot or too cold, too wet or too dry. The food was rarely satisfying and the wine was usually thin and bitter. When you embraced a woman in bed, generally you could pump away all day and all night without finding much joy of the act, at least as he remembered that joy from time out of mind. But Gilgamesh tended to believe that those were merely the incidental consequences of being dead: this place was not, after all, the land of the living, and there was no reason why things should work the same way here as they did back there.

In any event the reality of the Afterworld had turned out to be nothing at all like what the priests had promised it would be. The House of Dust and Darkness, was what they had called it in Uruk long ago. A place where the dead lived in eternal night and sadness, clad like birds, with wings for garments. Where the dwellers had dust for their bread, and clay for their meat. Where the kings of the earth, the masters, the high rulers, lived humbly without their crowns, and were forced to wait on the demons like servants. Small wonder that he had dreaded death as he had, believing that that was what awaited him for all time to come!

Well, in fact all that had turned out to be mere myth and folly.

Gilgamesh could no longer clearly remember his earliest days in the Afterworld. They had become hazy and unreal to him. Memory here was a treacherous thing, shifting like the desert sands: he had had occasion to discover over and over that he remembered many events of his Afterworld life that in fact had never happened, and that he had forgotten many that had. But nevertheless he still retained through all the mists and uncertainties of his mind a sharp image of the Afterworld as it had been when he first had awakened into it: a place much like Uruk, so it seemed, with low flat-roofed buildings of whitewashed brick, and temples rising on high platforms of many steps. And there he had found the heroes of olden days, living as they had always lived, men who had been great warriors in his boyhood, and others who had been little more than legends in the Land of his forefathers, back to the dawn of time. At least that was what it was like in the place where Gilgamesh first found himself; there were other districts, he discovered later, that were quite different, places where people lived in caves, or in pits in the ground, or in flimsy houses of reeds, and still other places where the Hairy Men dwelled and had no houses at all. Most of that was gone now, greatly transformed by all those who had come to the Afterworld in the latter days, and indeed a lot of nonsensical ugliness and ideological foolishness had entered in recent centuries in the baggage of the Later Dead. But still, the idea that this whole vast realm – infinitely bigger than his own beloved Land of the Two Rivers – existed merely for the sake of chastising the dead for their sins struck Gilgamesh as too silly for serious contemplation.

Why, then, was the joy of his hunting so pale and hollow? Why none of the old ecstasy when spying the prey, when drawing the great bow, when sending the arrow true to its mark?

Gilgamesh thought he knew why, and it had nothing to do with punishment. There had been joy aplenty in the hunting for many a thousand years of his life in the Afterworld. If the joy had gone from it now, it was only that in these latter days he hunted alone. Enkidu, his friend, his true brother, his other self, was not with him. It was that and nothing but that: for he had never felt complete without Enkidu since they first had met and wrestled and come to love one another after the manner of brothers, long ago in the city of Uruk. That great burly man, broad and tall and strong as Gilgamesh himself, that shaggy wild creature out of the high ridges: Gilgamesh had never loved anyone as he loved Enkidu.

But it was the fate of Gilgamesh, so it seemed, to lose him again and again.

Enkidu had been ripped from him the first time long ago when they still dwelled in Uruk in the robust roistering fullness of kingly manhood. On a dark day the gods had had revenge on Gilgamesh and Enkidu for their great pride and satisfaction in their own untrammeled exploits, and had sent a fever to take Enkidu's life, leaving Gilgamesh to rule in terrible solitude.

In time Gilgamesh too had yielded to death, many years and much wisdom later, and was taken into this Afterworld; and there he searched for Enkidu, and one glorious day he found him. The Afterworld had been a much smaller place, then, and everyone seemed to know everyone else; but even so it had taken an age for Gilgamesh to track Enkidu down. Oh, the rejoicing that day! Oh, the singing and the dancing, the vast festival that went on and on! There was great kindliness among the denizens of the Afterworld in those days, and there was universal gladness that Gilgamesh and Enkidu had been restored to each other. Minos of Crete gave the first great party in honor of their reunion, and then it was Amenhotep's turn, and then Agamemnon's. And on the fourth day the host was dark slender Varuna, the Meluhhan king, and then on the fifth the heroes gathered in the ancient hall of the Ice-Hunter folk where one-eyed Vy-otin was chieftain and the floor was strewn with mammoth tusks, and after that –

Well, and it went on for some long time, the great celebration of the reunion.

For uncountable years, so Gilgamesh recalled it, he and Enkidu dwelled together in Gilgamesh's palace in the Afterworld as they had in the old days in the Land of the Two Rivers. And all was well with them, with much hunting and feasting. The Afterworld was a happy place in those years.

Then the hordes of Later Dead began to come in, all those grubby little unheroic people out of unheroic times, bringing all their terrible changes.

They were shoddy folk, these Later Dead, confused of soul and flimsy of intellect, and their petty trifling rivalries and vain strutting poses were a great nuisance. But Gilgamesh and Enkidu kept their distance from them while they replayed all the follies of their lives, their nonsensical Crusades and their idiotic trade wars and their preposterous theological squabbles.

The trouble was that they had brought not only their lunatic ideas to the Afterworld but also their accursed diabolical modern gadgets, and the worst of those were the vile weapons called guns, that slaughtered noisily from afar in the most shameful cowardly way. Heroes know how to parry the blow of a battle-axe or the thrust of a sword; but what can even a hero do about a bullet from afar? It was Enkidu's bad luck to fall between two quarreling bands of these gun-wielders, a flock of babbling Spaniards and a rabble of arrogant Englanders, for whom he tried to make peace. Of course they would have no peace, and soon shots were flying, and Gilgamesh arrived at the scene just as a bolt from an arquebus tore through his dear Enkidu's noble heart.

No one dies in the Afterworld forever; but some are dead a long time, and that was how it was with Enkidu. It pleased the unknown forces that governed this land of the no longer living to keep him in limbo some hundreds of years, or so it seemed to Gilgamesh, given the difficulties of tallying such matters in the Afterworld. It was, at any rate, a dreadful long while, and Gilgamesh once more felt that terrible inrush of loneliness that only the presence of Enkidu might cure.

Meanwhile the Afterworld continued to change, and now the changes were coming at a stupefying, overwhelming rate. There seemed to be far more people in the world than there ever had been in the old days, and great armies of them marched into the Afterworld every day, a swarming rabble of uncouth strangers who after only a little interval of disorientation and bewilderment would swiftly set out to reshape the whole place into something as discordant and repellent as the world they had left behind. The steam-engine came, with its clamor and clangor, and something called the dynamo, and then harsh glittering electrical lights blazed in every street where the friendly golden lamps had glowed and factories arose and began pouring out all manner of strange things. And more and more and more, relentlessly, unceasingly. Railroads. Telephones. Automobiles. Noise, smoke, soot everywhere, and no way to hide from it. The Industrial Revolution, they called it. It was an endless onslaught of the hideous. Yet strangely almost everyone seemed to admire and even love the new things and the new ways, except for Gilgamesh and a few other cranky conservatives. "What are they trying to do?" Rabelais asked one day. "Turn the place into Hell?" Now the Later Dead were bringing in such devices as radios and helicopters and computers, and everyone was speaking English, so that once again Gilgamesh, who had grudgingly learned the newfangled Latin long ago when Caesar and his crew had insisted on it, was forced to master yet another tongue-twisting intricate language. It was a dreary time for him. And then at last did Enkidu reappear, far away in one of the cold northern domains; and he made his way south and for a time they were reunited a second time, and once more all was well for Gilgamesh of Uruk in the Afterworld.

But now he and Enkidu were separated again, this time by something colder and more cruel than death itself. What had fallen between them was something beyond all belief: they had quarrelled. There had been words between them, ugly words on both sides, such a dispute as never in thousands of years had passed between them in the land of the living or in the land of the Afterworld, and at last Enkidu had said that which Gilgamesh had never dreamed he would ever hear, which was, "I want no more of you, king of Uruk. If you cross my path again I will have your life." Could that have been Enkidu speaking, or was it, Gilgamesh wondered, some demon of the Afterworld in Enkidu's form?

In any case he was gone. He vanished into the turmoil and infinite intricacy of the Afterworld and placed himself beyond Gilgamesh's finding; and when Gilgamesh sent forth inquiries, back came only the report, "He will not speak with you. He has no love for you, Gilgamesh."

It could not be. It must be a spell of witchcraft, thought Gilgamesh. Surely this was some dark working of the Later Dead, that could turn brother against brother and lead Enkidu to persist in his wrath. In time, Gilgamesh was sure, Enkidu would be triumphant over this sorcery that gripped his soul, and he would open himself once more to the love of

Gilgamesh. But time went on, after the strange circuitous fashion of the Afterworld, and Enkidu did not return to his brother's arms.

What was there to do, but hunt, and wait, and hope?

So this day Gilgamesh hunted in the Afterworld's parched Outback. He had killed and killed and killed again, and now late in the day he had put his arrow through the throat of a monster more foul even than the usual run of creatures of the Afterworld; but there was a terrible vitality to the thing, and it went thundering off, dripping dark blood from its pierced maw.

Gilgamesh gave pursuit. It is sinful to strike and wound and not to kill. For a long weary hour he ran, crisscrossing this harsh land. Thorny plants slashed at him with the malevolence of imps, and the hard wind flailed him with clouds of dust sharp as whips. Still the evil-looking beast outpaced him, though blood drained in torrents from it to the dry ground.

Gilgamesh would not let himself tire, for there was god-power in him by virtue of his descent from the divine Lugalbanda, his great father who was both king and god. But he was hard pressed to keep going. Three times he lost sight of his quarry, and tracked it only by the spoor of its blood-droppings. The bleak red eye that was the sun of the Afterworld seemed to mock him, hovering forever before him as though willing him to run without cease.

Then he saw the creature, still strong but plainly staggering, lurching about at the edge of a thicket of little twisted greasy-leaved trees. Unhesitatingly Gilgamesh plunged forward. The trees stroked him lasciviously, coating him with their slime, trying like raucous courtesans to insinuate their leaves between his legs; but he slapped them away, and emerged finally into a clearing where he could confront his animal.

Some repellent little demon-beast was clinging to the back of his prey, ripping out bloody gobbets of flesh and ruining the hide. A Land Rover was parked nearby, and a pale strange-looking man with a long jaw was peering from its window. A second man, red-faced and beefy-looking, stood close by Gilgamesh's roaring, snorting quarry.

First things first. Gilgamesh reached out, scooped the hissing little carrion-seeker from the bigger animal's back, flung it aside. Then with all his force he rammed his dagger toward what he hoped was the heart of the wounded animal. In the moment of his thrust Gilgamesh felt a great convulsion within the monster's breast and its foul life left it in an instant.

The work was done. Again, no exultation, no sense of fulfilment; only a kind of dull ashen release from an unfinished chore. Gilgamesh caught his breath and looked around.

What was this? The red-faced man seemed to be having a crazy fit. Quivering, shaking, sweating – dropping to his knees – his eyes gleaming insanely –

"Lord Conan?" the man cried. "Great king?"

"Conan is not one of my titles," said Gilgamesh, mystified. "And I was a king once in Uruk, but I reign over nothing at all in this place. Come, man, get off your knees!"

"But you are Conan to the life!" moaned the red-faced man hoarsely. "To the absolute life!"

Gilgamesh felt a surge of intense dislike for this fellow. He would be slobbering in another moment. Conan? Conan? That name meant nothing at all. No, wait: he had known a Conan once, some little Celtic fellow he had encountered in a tavern, a chap with a blunt nose and heavy cheekbones and dark hair tumbling down his face, a drunken twitchy little man forever invoking forgotten godlets of no consequence – yes, he had called himself Conan, so Gilgamesh recalled. Drank too much, caused trouble for the barmaid, even took a swing at her, that was the one. Gilgamesh had dropped him down an open cesspool to teach him manners. But how could this blustery-faced fellow here mistake me for that one? He was still mumbling on, too, babbling about lands whose names meant nothing to Gilgamesh – Cimmeria, Aquilonia, Hyrkania, Zamora. Total nonsense. There were no such places.

And that glow in the fellow's eyes – what sort of look was that? A look of adoration, almost the sort of look a woman might give a man when she has decided to yield herself utterly to his will.

Gilgamesh had seen such looks aplenty in his day, from women and men both; and he had welcomed them – from women, at least. He scowled. What does he think I am? Does he think, as so many have wrongly thought, that because I loved Enkidu with such a great love that I am a man who will embrace a man in the fashion of men and women? Because it is not so. Not even here in the Afterworld is it so, said Gilgamesh to himself.

"Tell me everything!" the red-faced man was imploring. "All those exploits that I dreamed in your name, Conan: tell me how they really were! That time in the snow-fields, when you met the frost-giant's daughter – and when you sailed the *Tigress* with the Black Coast's queen – and that time you stormed the Aquilonian capital, and slew King Numedides on his own throne –"

Gilgamesh stared in distaste at the man groveling at his feet.

"Come, fellow, stop this lunatic blather now," he said sourly. "Up with you! You mistake me greatly, I think."

The second man was out of the Land Rover now, and on his way over to join them. An odd-looking creature he was, too, skeleton-thin and corpse-white, with a neck like a water-bird's that seemed barely able to support his long big-chinned head. He was dressed oddly too, all in black, and swathed in layer upon layer as if he dreaded the faintest chill. Yet he had a gentle and thoughtful way about him, quite unlike the wild-eyed and feverish manner of his friend. He might be a scribe, Gilgamesh thought, or a priest; but what the other one could be, the gods alone would know.

The thin man touched the other's shoulder and said, "Take command of yourself, man. This is surely not your Conan here."

"To the life! To the very life! His size – his grandeur – the way he killed that beast –"

"Bob – Bob, Conan's a figment! Conan's a fantasy! You spun him out of whole cloth. Come, now. Up. Up." To Gilgamesh he said, "A thousand pardons, good sir. My friend is – sometimes excitable –"

Gilgamesh turned away, shrugging, and looked to his quarry. He had no need for dealings with these two. Skinning the huge beast properly might take him the rest of the day; and then to haul the great hide back to his camp, and determine what he wanted of it as a trophy –

Behind him he heard the booming voice of the red-faced man. "A figment, H.P.? How can you be sure of that? I thought I invented Conan too; but what if he really lived, what if I had merely tapped into some powerful primordial archetype, what if the authentic Conan stands here before us this very moment –"

"Dear Bob, your Conan had blue eyes, did he not? And this man's eyes are dark as night."

"Well –" Grudgingly.

"You were so excited you failed to notice. But I did. This is some barbarian warrior, yes, some great huntsman beyond any doubt, a Nimrod, an Ajax. But not Conan, Bob! Grant him his own identity. He's no invention of yours." Coming up beside Gilgamesh the long-jawed man said, speaking in a formal and courtly way, "Good sir, I am Howard Phillips Lovecraft, formerly of Providence, Rhode Island, and my companion is Robert E. Howard of Texas, whose other life was lived, as was mine, in the twentieth century after Christ. At that time we were tale-tellers by trade, and I think he confuses you with a hero of his own devising. Put his mind at ease, I pray you, and let us know your name."

Gilgamesh looked up. He rubbed his wrist across his forehead to clear it of a smear of the monster's gore and met the other man's gaze evenly. This one, at least, was no madman, strange though he looked.

Quietly Gilgamesh said, "I think his mind may be beyond putting at any ease. But know you that I am called Gilgamesh, the son of Lugalbanda."

"Gilgamesh the Sumerian?" Lovecraft whispered. "Gilgamesh who sought to live forever?"

"Gilgamesh am I, yes, who was king in Uruk when that was the greatest city of the Land of the Two Rivers, and who in his folly came to think that there could be some way of cheating death."

"Do you hear that, Bob?"

"Incredible. Beyond all belief!" muttered the other.

Rising until he towered above them both, Gilgamesh drew in his breath deeply and said with awesome resonance, "I am Gilgamesh to whom all things were made known, the secret things, the truths of life and death, most especially those of death. I have coupled with Inanna the goddess in the bed of the Sacred Marriage; I have slain demons and spoken with gods; I am two parts god myself, and only one part mortal." He paused and stared at them, letting it sink in, those words that he had recited so many times in situations much like this. Then in a quieter tone he went on, "When death took me I came to this nether world they call the Afterworld, and here I pass my time as a huntsman, and I ask you now to excuse me, for as you see I have my tasks."

Once more he turned away.

"Gilgamesh!" said Lovecraft again in wonder. And the other said, "If I live here till the end of time, H.P., I'll never grow used to it. This is more fantastic than running into Conan would have been! Imagine it: Gilgamesh! *Gilgamesh*!"

A wearisome business, Gilgamesh thought: all this awe, all this adulation.

The problem was that damned epic, of course. He could see why Caesar became so irritable when people tried to suck up to him with quotations out of Shakespeare's verses. "Why, man, he doth bestride the narrow world like a Colossus," and all that: Caesar grew livid by the third syllable. Once they put you into poetry, Gilgamesh had discovered, as had happened to Odysseus and Achilles and Caesar after him and many another, your own real self can begin to disappear and the self of the poem overwhelms you entirely and turns you into a walking cliché. Shakespeare had been particularly villainous that way, Gilgamesh thought: ask Richard III, ask Macbeth, ask Owen Glendower. You found them skulking around the Afterworld with perpetual chips on their shoulders, because every time they opened their mouths people expected them to say something like "My kingdom for a horse!" or "Is this a dagger which I see before me?" or "I can call spirits from the vasty deep." Gilgamesh had had to live with that kind of thing almost from the time he had first come to the Afterworld; for they had written the poems about him soon after, all that pompous brooding stuff, a whole raft of Gilgamesh tales, some of them retelling his actual deeds and some mere wild fantasies, and then the Babylonians and the Assyrians and even those smelly garlic-gobbling Hittites had gone on translating and embroidering them for another thousand years so that everybody from one end of the known world to the other knew them by heart, and even after all those peoples were gone and their languages had been forgotten there was no surcease, because these twentieth-century folk had found the whole thing and deciphered the text somehow and made it famous all over again. Over the centuries they had turned him into everybody's favorite all-purpose hero, which was a devil of a burden to bear: there was a piece of him in the Prometheus legend, and in the Heracles stuff, and in that story of Odysseus' wanderings, and even in the Celtic myths, which was probably why this creepy Howard fellow kept calling him Conan. At least that other Conan, that ratty little sniveling drunken one, had been a Celt. Enlil's ears, but it was wearying to have everyone expecting you to live up to the mythic exploits of twenty or thirty very different culture-heroes! And embarrassing, too, considering that the original non-mythical Heracles and Odysseus and some of the others dwelled here too and tended to be pretty possessive about the myths that had been attached to *them*, even when they were simply variants on his own much older ones.

There was substance to the Gilgamesh stories, of course, especially the parts about him and Enkidu; but the poet had salted the story with a lot of pretentious arty nonsense too, as poets always will, and in any case you got very tired of having everybody boil your long and complex life down into the same twelve chapters and the same little turns of phrase. It had gotten so that Gilgamesh found himself quoting the main Gilgamesh poem too, the one about his quest for eternal life – well, that one wasn't too far from the essence of the truth, though they had mucked up a lot of the details with precious little "imaginative" touches – by way of making introduction for himself: "I am the man to whom all things were made known, the secret things, the truths of life and death." Straight out of the poet's mouth, those lines. Tiresome. Tiresome. Angrily he jabbed his dagger beneath the dead monster's hide, and set about his task of flaying, while the two little men behind him went on muttering and mumbling to one another in astonishment.

Three

There were strange emotions stirring in Robert Howard's soul, and he did not care for them at all. He could forgive himself for believing for that one giddy moment that this Gilgamesh was his Conan. That was nothing more than the artistic temperament at work, sweeping him up in a bit of rash feverish enthusiasm. To come suddenly upon a great muscular giant of a man in a loincloth who was hacking away at some fiendish monster with a little bronze dagger, and to think that he must surely be the mighty Cimmerian – well, that was a pardonable enough thing. Here in the Afterworld you learned very quickly that you might run into anybody at all. You could find yourself playing at dice with Lord Byron or sharing a mug of mulled wine with Menelaus or arguing with Plato about the ideas of Nietzsche, who was standing right there making faces, and after a time you came to take most such things for granted, more or less.

So why not think that this fellow was Conan? No matter that Conan's eyes had been of a different color. That was a trifle. He looked like Conan in all the important ways. He was of Conan's size and strength. And he was kingly in more than physique. He seemed to have Conan's cool intelligence and complexity of soul, Conan's regal courage and Conan's indomitable spirit.

The trouble was that Conan, the wondrous Cimmerian warrior from 19,000 B.C., had never existed except in Howard's own imagination. And there were no fictional characters in the Afterworld. If you had not lived, truly lived, in that other world of the first flesh, it was impossible for you to live again here. You might meet Richard Wagner, but you weren't likely to encounter Siegfried. Theseus was here somewhere, but not the Minotaur. William the Conqueror, yes; William Tell, no.

That was all right, Howard told himself. His little fantasy of meeting Conan here in the Afterworld was nothing but a bit of mawkish narcissism: he was better off without it. Coming across the authentic Gilgamesh – ah, how much more interesting that was! A genuine Sumerian king – an actual titan out of history's dawn, not some trumped-up figure fashioned from cardboard and hard-breathing wish-fulfilling dreams; a flesh-and-blood mortal who had lived a lusty life and had fought great battles and had walked eye to eye with the ancient gods and had struggled against the inevitability of death, and who in dying had taken on the immortality of mythic archetype – ah, now there was someone worth getting to know! Whereas Howard had to admit that he would have no more to learn from a conversation with Conan than he could discover by interrogating his own image in the mirror. Or else a meeting with the "real" Conan, if it was in any way possible, would surely cast him into terrible confusions and contradictions of soul from which there would be no recovering. No, Howard thought, better that this man be Gilgamesh than Conan, by all means. He was reconciled to that.

But this other business – this sudden bewildering urge to throw himself at the giant's feet, to be swept up in his arms, to be crushed in a fierce embrace –

What was that? Where had *that* come from? By the blazing Heart of Ahriman, what could it mean?

Howard remembered a time in his former life when he had gone down to the Cisco Dam and watched the construction men strip and dive in: well-built men, confident, graceful, at ease in their bodies. For a while he had looked at them and had revelled in their physical perfection. They could have been naked Greek statues come alive, a band of lusty Apollos and Zeuses. And then as he listened to them shouting and laughing and crying out in their foul-mouthed way he began to grow angry, suddenly seeing them as mere thoughtless animals who were the natural enemies of dreamers like himself. He hated them as the weak always must hate the strong, those splendid swine who could trample the dreamers and their dreams as they wished. But then he had reminded himself that he was no weakling himself, that he who once had been spindly and frail had by hard effort made himself big and strong and burly. Not beautiful of body as these men were – too fleshy for that, too husky – but nevertheless, he had told himself, there was no man there whose ribs he could not crush if it came to a struggle. And he had gone away from that place full of rage and thoughts of bloody violence.

What had that been all about? That barely suppressed fury – was it some sort of dark hidden lust, some craving for the most bestial sort of sinfulness? Was the anger that had arisen in him masking an anger he should have directed at himself, for looking upon those naked men and taking pleasure in it?

No. No. No. No. He wasn't any kind of degenerate. He was certain of that.

The desire of men for men, he believed, was a mark of decadence, of the decline of civilization. He was a man of the frontier, not some feeble limp-wristed sodomite who reveled in filth and wanton evil. If he had never in his short life known a woman's love, it was for lack of opportunity, not out of a preference for that other shameful kind. Living out his days in that small and remote prairie town, devoting himself to his mother and to his writing, he had chosen not to avail himself of prostitutes or shallow women, but he was sure that if he had lived a few years longer and the woman who was his true mate had ever made herself known to him, he would certainly have reached toward her in passion and high abandon.

And yet – and yet – that moment when he first spied the giant Gilgamesh, and thought he was Conan –

That surge of electricity through his entire body, and most intensely through his loins – what else could it have been but desire, instant and intense and overwhelming? For a *man*? Unthinkable! Even this glorious hero – even this magnificent kingly creature –

No. No. No. No.

I am in the Afterworld, which may be some sort of Hell, and if it is Hell then this is my torment, Howard told himself.

He paced furiously up and down alongside the Land Rover. Desperately he fought off the black anguish that threatened to settle over him now, as it had done so many times in his former life and in this life after life. These sudden corrupt and depraved feelings, Howard thought: they are nothing but diabolical perversions of my natural spirit, intended to cast me into despair and self-loathing! By Crom, I will resist! By the breasts of Ishtar, I will not yield to this foulness!

All the same he found his eyes straying to the edge of the nearby thicket, where Gilgamesh still knelt over the animal he had killed.

What extraordinary muscles rippling in that broad back, in those iron-hard thighs! What careless abandon in the way he was peeling back the creature's shaggy hide, though he had to wallow in dark gore to do it! That cascade of lustrous black hair lightly bound by a jewelled circlet, that dense black beard curling in tight ringlets –

Howard's throat went dry. Something at the base of his belly was tightening into a terrible knot.

Lovecraft said, "You want a chance to talk with him, don't you?"

Howard swung around. He felt his cheeks go scarlet. He was utterly certain that his guilt must be emblazoned incontrovertibly on his face.

"What the hell do you mean?" he growled. His hands knotted of their own accord into fists. There seemed to be a band of fire across his forehead. "What would I want to talk with him about, anyway?"

Lovecraft looked startled by the ferocity of Howard's tone and posture. He took a step backward and threw up his hand almost as though to protect himself. "What a strange thing to say! You, of all people, with your love of antique times, your deep and abiding passion for the lost mysteries of those steamy Oriental empires that perished so long ago! Why, man, is there nothing you want to know about the kingdoms of Sumer? Uruk, Nippur, Ur of the Chaldees? The secret rites of the goddess Inanna in the dark passageways beneath the ziggurat? The incantations that opened the gates of the Underworld, the libations that loosed and bound the demons of the worlds beyond the stars? Who knows what he could tell us? There stands a man six thousand years old, a hero from the dawn of time, Bob!"

Howard snorted. "I don't reckon that oversized son of a bitch would want to tell us a damned thing. All that interests him is getting the hide off that bloody critter of his."

"He's nearly done with that. Why not wait, Bob? And invite him to sit with us a little while. And draw him out, lure him into telling us tales of life as it was lived long ago beside the Euphrates!" Now Lovecraft's dark eyes were gleaming as though he too felt some strange lust, and his forehead was surprisingly bright with uncharacteristic perspiration; but Howard knew that in Lovecraft's case what had taken possession of him was only the lust for knowledge, the hunger for the arcane lore of high antiquity that Lovecraft imagined would spill from the lips of this Mesopotamian hero. That same lust ached in him as well. To speak with this man who had lived before Babylon was, who had walked the streets of Ur when Abraham was yet unborn –

But there were other lusts besides that hunger for knowledge, sinister lusts that must be denied at any cost –

"No," said Howard brusquely. "Let's get the hell out of here right now, H.P. This damned foul bleak countryside is getting on my nerves."

Lovecraft gave him a strange look. "But weren't you just telling me how beautiful –"

"Damnation take whatever I was telling you! King Henry's expecting us to negotiate an alliance for him. We aren't going to get the job done out here in the boondocks."

"The what?"

"Boondocks. Wild uncivilized country. Term that came into use after our time, H.P. The backwoods, you know? You never did pay much heed to the vernacular, did you?" He tugged at Lovecraft's sleeve. "Come on. That big bloody ape over there isn't going to tell us a thing about his life and times, I guarantee. Probably doesn't remember anything worth telling, anyway. And he bores me. Pardon me, H.P., but I find him an enormous pain in the butt, all right? I don't have any further hankering for his company. Do you mind, H.P.? Can we move along, do you think?"

"I must confess that you mystify me sometimes, Bob. But of course if you –" Suddenly Lovecraft's eyes widened in amazement. "Get down, Bob! Behind the car! Fast!"

"What –"

An arrow came singing through the air and passed just alongside Howard's left ear. Then another, and another. One arrow ricocheted off the flank of the Land Rover with a sickening thunking sound. Another struck straight on and stuck quivering an inch deep in the metal.

Howard whirled. He saw horsemen, a dozen, perhaps a dozen and a half, bearing down on them out of the darkness to the east, loosing shafts as they came.

They were lean compact men of some Oriental stock in crimson leather jerkins, riding like fiends. Their mounts were little flat-headed fiery-eyed gray demon-horses that moved as if their short, fiercely pistoning legs could carry them to the far boundaries of the nether world without the need of a moment's rest.

Chanting, howling, the yellow-skinned warriors seemed to be in a frenzy of rage. Mongols? Turks? Whoever they were, they were pounding toward the Land Rover like the emissaries of Death himself. Some brandished long, wickedly curved blades, but most wielded curious-looking small bows from which they showered one arrow after another with phenomenal rapidity.

Crouching behind the Land Rover with Lovecraft beside him, Howard gaped at the attackers in a paralysis of astonishment. How often had he written of scenes like this? Waving plumes, bristling lances, a whistling cloud of clothyard shafts! Thundering hooves, wild war-cries, the thunk of barbarian arrowheads against Aquilonian shields! Horses rearing and throwing their riders . . . . Knights in bloodied armor tumbling to the ground . . . . Steel-clad forms littering the slopes of the battlefield . . . .

But this was no swashbuckling tale of Hyborean derring-do that was unfolding now. Those were real horsemen – as real as anything was, in this place – rampaging across this chilly wind-swept plain in the outer reaches of the Afterworld. Those were real arrows; and they would rip their way into his flesh with real impact and inflict real agony of the most frightful kind.

He looked across the way at Gilgamesh. The giant Sumerian was hunkered down behind the overturned bulk of the animal he had slain. His mighty bow was in his hand. As Howard watched in awe, Gilgamesh aimed and let fly. The shaft struck the nearest horseman, traveling through jerkin and rib-cage and all and emerging from the man's back. But still the onrushing warrior managed to release one last arrow before he fell. It traveled on an erratic trajectory, humming quickly toward Gilgamesh on a wild wobbly arc and skewering him through the flesh of his left forearm.

Coolly the Sumerian glanced down at the arrow jutting from his arm. He scowled and shook his head, the way he might if he had been stung by a hornet. Then – as Conan might have done; how very much like Conan! – Gilgamesh inclined his head toward his shoulder and *bit* the arrow in half just below the fletching. Bright blood spouted from the wound as he pulled the two pieces of the arrow from his arm.

As though nothing very significant had happened, Gilgamesh lifted his bow and reached for a second shaft. Blood was streaming in rivulets down his arm, but he seemed not even to be aware of it.

Howard watched as if in a stupor. He could not move, he

barely had the will to draw breath. A haze of nausea threatened to overwhelm him. It had been nothing at all for him to heap up great bloody mounds of severed heads and arms and legs with cheerful abandon in his stories; but in fact real bloodshed and violence of any sort had horrified him whenever he had even a glimpse of it.

"The gun, Bob!" said Lovecraft urgently beside him. "Use the *gun*!"

"What?"

"There. *There*."

Howard looked down. Thrust through his belt was the pistol he had taken from the Land Rover when he had come out to investigate that little beast in the road. He drew it now and stared at it, glassy-eyed, as though it were a basilisk's egg that rested on the palm of his hand.

"What are you doing?" Lovecraft asked. "Ah. Ah. Give it to me." He snatched the gun impatiently from Howard's frozen fingers and studied it a moment as though he had never held a weapon before. Perhaps he never had. But then, grasping the pistol with both his hands, he rose warily above the hood of the Land Rover and squeezed off a shot.

The tremendous sound of an explosion cut through the shrill cries of the horsemen. Lovecraft laughed. "Got one! Who would ever have imagined –"

He fired again. In the same moment Gilgamesh brought down one more of the attackers with his bow.

"They're backing off!" Lovecraft cried. "By Alhazred, they didn't expect *this*, I wager!" He laughed again and poked the gun up into a firing position. "*Ia*!" he cried, in a voice Howard had never heard out of the shy and scholarly Lovecraft before. "*Shub-Niggurath*!" Lovecraft fired a third time. "*Ph'nglui mglw'nafh Cthulhu R'lyeh wgah'nagl fhtagn*!"

Howard felt sweat rolling down his body. This inaction of his – this paralysis – this shame – what would Conan have made of it? What would Gilgamesh? And Lovecraft, that timid and sheltered man, he who dreaded the fishes of the sea and the cold winds of his New England winters and so many other things, was laughing and bellowing his wondrous gibberish and blazing away like any gangster, having the time of his life –

Shame! Shame!

Heedless of the risk Howard scrambled up into the cab of the Land Rover and groped around for the second gun that was lying down there on the floor somewhere. He found it and knelt beside the window. Seven or eight of the Asiatic horsemen lay strewn about, dead or dying, within a hundred-yard radius of the car. The others had withdrawn to a considerable distance and were cantering in uneasy circles. They appeared taken aback by the unexpectedly fierce resistance they had encountered on what they had probably expected to have been an easy bit of jolly slaughter in these untracked frontierlands.

What were they doing now? Drawing together, a tight little group, horses nose to nose. Conferring. And now two of them were pulling what seemed to be some sort of war-banner from a saddlebag and hoisting it between them on bamboo poles: a long yellow streamer with fluttering blood-red tips, on which bold Oriental characters were painted in shining black. Serious business, obviously. Now they were lining themselves up in a row, facing the Land Rover. Getting ready for a desperate suicide charge – that was the way things appeared.

Gilgamesh, standing erect in full view, calmly nocked yet another arrow. He took aim and waited for them to come. Lovecraft, looking flushed with excitement, wholly transformed by the alien joys of armed combat, was leaning forward, staring intently, his pistol cocked and ready.

Howard shivered. Shame rode him with burning spurs. How *could* he cower here while those two bore the brunt of the struggle? Though his hand was shaking, he thrust the pistol out the window and drew a bead on the closest horseman. His finger tightened on the trigger. Would it be possible to score a hit at such a distance? Yes. Yes. Go ahead. You know how to use a gun, all right. High time you put some of that skill to use. Knock that little yellow bastard off his horse with one bark of the Colt .380, yes. Send him straight to the next world – no, he's in the next world already, send him off to oblivion until it's his turn to be plucked forth again, yes, that's it – ready – aim –

"Wait," Lovecraft said. "Don't shoot."

What was this? As Howard, with an effort, lowered his gun and let his rigid quivering hand go slack, Lovecraft, shading his eyes against the eerie glare of the swollen red sun, peered closely at the enemy warriors a long silent moment. Then he turned, reached up into the rear of the Land Rover, groped around for a moment, finally pulled out the manila envelope that held their royal commission from King Henry.

And then – what was he doing?

Stepping out into plain view, arms raised high, waving the envelope around, walking toward the enemy?

"They'll kill you, H. P.! Get down! Get down!"

Lovecraft, without looking back, gestured brusquely for Howard to be silent. He continued to walk steadily toward the far-off horsemen. They seemed just as mystified as Howard was. They sat without moving, their bows held stiffly out before them, a dozen arrows trained on the middle of Lovecraft's body.

He's gone completely off the deep end, Howard thought in dismay. He never was really well balanced, was he? Half believing all his stuff about Elder Gods and dimensional gateways and blasphemous rites on dark New England hillsides. And now all this shooting – the excitement –

"Hold your weapons, all of you!" Lovecraft cried in a voice of amazing strength and presence. "In the name of Prester John, I bid you hold your weapons! We are not your enemies! We are ambassadors to your emperor!"

Howard gasped. He began to understand. No, Lovecraft hadn't gone crazy after all!

He took another look at that long yellow war-banner. Yes, yes, of course! Those swirls and curlicues there: they were the emblems of Prester John! These berserk horsemen must be part of the border patrol of the very nation whose ruler they had traveled so long to find. Howard felt abashed, realizing that in the fury of the battle Lovecraft had had the sense actually to pause long enough to give the banner's legend close examination – and the courage to walk out there waving his diplomatic credentials. The parchment scroll of their royal commission was in his hand, and he was pointing to the little red-ribboned seal of King Henry.

The horsemen stared, muttered among themselves, lowered their bows. Gilgamesh, lowering his great bow also, looked on in puzzlement. "Do you see?" Lovecraft called. "We are heralds of King Henry! We claim the protection of your master the August Sovereign Yeh-lu Ta-shih!" Glancing back over his shoulder, he called to Howard to join him; and after only an instant's hesitation Howard leaped down from the Land Rover and trotted forward. It was a giddy feeling, exposing himself to those somber yellow archers this way. It felt almost like standing at the edge of some colossal precipice.

Lovecraft smiled. "It's all going to be all right, Bob! That banner they unfurled – it bears the markings of Prester John –"

"Yes, yes. I see."

"And look – they're making a safe-conduct sign. They understand what I'm saying, Bob! They believe me!"

Howard nodded. He sensed a great upsurge of relief and even a sort of joy. He clapped Lovecraft lustily on the back. "Fine going, H. P.! I didn't think you had it in you!" Coming up out of his funk, now, he felt a manic exuberance seize his spirit. He gestured to the horsemen, wigwagging his arms with wild vigor. "Hoy! Royal Commissioners here!" he bellowed. "Envoys from His Britannic Majesty King Henry VIII! Take us to your emperor!" Then he looked toward Gilgamesh, who stood frowning, his bow still at the ready. "Hoy there, king of Uruk! Put away the weapons! Everything's all right now! We're going to be escorted to the court of Prester John!"

Four

Gilgamesh wasn't at all sure why he had let himself go along. He had no interest in visiting Prester John's court, or anybody else's. He wanted nothing more than to be left alone to hunt and roam in the wilderness and thereby to find some ease for his sorrows.

But the gaunt long-necked man and his blustery red-faced friend had beckoned him to ride with them in their Land Rover, and while he stood there frowning over that the ugly flat-featured little yellow warriors had indicated with quick impatient gestures that he should get in. And he had. They looked as though they would try to compel him to get in if he balked; and though he had no fear of them, none whatever, some impulse that he could not begin to understand had led him to step back from the likelihood of yet another battle and simply climb aboard the vehicle. Perhaps he had had enough of solitary hunting for a while. Or perhaps it was just that the wound in his arm was beginning to throb and ache, now that the excitement of the fray was receding, and it seemed like a good idea to have it looked after by a surgeon. The flesh all around it was badly swollen and bruised. That arrow had pierced him through and through. He would have the wound cleaned and dressed; and then he would move along.

Well, then, so he was going to the court of Prester John. Here he was, sitting back silent and somber in the rear of this musty mildew-flecked car, riding with these two very odd Later Dead types, these scribes or tale-tellers or whatever it was they claimed to be, as the horsemen of Prester John led them to the encampment of their monarch.

The one who called himself Howard, the one who could not help stealing sly little glances at him like an infatuated schoolgirl, was at the wheel. Glancing back at his passenger now, he said, "Tell me, Gilgamesh: have you had dealings with Prester John before?"

"I have heard the name, that much I know," replied the Sumerian. "But it means very little to me."

"The legendary Christian emperor," said the other, the thin one, Lovecraft. "He who was said to rule a secret kingdom somewhere in the misty hinterlands of Central Asia – although it was in Africa, according to some –"

Asia – Africa – names, only names, Gilgamesh thought bleakly. They were places somewhere in the other world, that world of shadows from which he was so long gone. He had no idea where they might be.

Such a multitude of places, so many names! It was impossible to keep it all straight. There was no sense to any of it. The world – his first world – the Land – had been bordered by the Two Rivers, the Idigna and the Buranunu, which the Greeks had preferred to call the Tigris and the Euphrates. Who were the Greeks, and by what right had they renamed the rivers? Everyone used those names now, even Gilgamesh himself, except in the inwardness of his soul.

And beyond the Two Rivers? Why, there was the vassal state of Aratta far to the east, he remembered, and in that direction also lay the Land of Cedars where the fire-breathing demon Huwawa roared and bellowed, and in the eastern mountains lay the kingdom of the barbaric Elamites. To the north was the land called Uri, and in the deserts of the west the wild Martu people dwelled, and in the south was the blessed isle Dilmun, which was like a paradise. Had there been anything more to the world than that? Why, there was Meluhha far away beyond Elam, where the people had black skins and fine features, and there was Punt in the south where they were black also with flat noses and thick lips, and there was another land even beyond Meluhha, with folk of yellow skins who mined a precious green stone. And that was the world he had known when he lived in the world, that other world, the world through which he had so briefly passed before coming to this world of eternal life. But evidently there had been other places in that world, places of which he had had no inkling, or places that had come into being after his time there. Where could all these other latter-day places of the other world be, this Africa and this Asia and Europe and the rest, Rome, Greece, England? Perhaps some of them were mere new names for old places. The Land itself had had a host of names since his own time – Babylonia, Mesopotamia, Iraq, and more. Why had it needed all those names? He had no idea. New men made up new names: that seemed to be the way of the world. This Africa, this Asia – America, China, Russia – a little man named Herodotos, a Greek, had tried to explain it all to him once, the shape of the world and the names of the places in it, sketching a map for him on an old bit of parchment, and much later a stolid fellow named Mercator had done the same, and once after that he had spoken of such matters with an Englishman called Cook; but the things they told him all conflicted with one another and he could make no sense out of any of it. It was too much to ask, making sense of these things. Those myriad nations that had arisen after his time, those empires that had risen and fallen and been forgotten, all those lost dynasties, the captains and the kings – he had tried from time to time to master the sequence of them, but it was no use. Once in his former life he had sought to make himself the master of all knowledge, yes. His appetites had been boundless: for knowledge, for wealth, for power, for women, for life itself. Now all that seemed only the merest folly to him. That jumble of confused and confusing places, all those great realms and far-off kingdoms, were in another world: what could they matter to him now?

"Asia?" he said. "Africa?" Gilgamesh shrugged. "Prester John?" He prowled the turbulent cluttered recesses of his memory. "Ah. There's a Prester John, I think, lives in Roma Nova. A dark-skinned man, a friend of that gaudy old liar Sir John Mandeville." It was coming back now. "Yes, I've seen them together many times, in that dirty squalid tavern where Mandeville's always to be found. The two of them telling outlandish stories back and forth, each a bigger fraud than the other."

"A different Prester John," said Lovecraft.

"That one is Susenyos the Ethiop, I think," Howard said. "A former African tyrant, and lover of the Jesuits, now far gone in whiskey. He's one of many. There are seven, nine, a dozen Prester Johns in the Afterworld, to my certain knowledge. And maybe more."

Gilgamesh contemplated that notion in a distant, distracted way. Fire was running up and down his injured arm now.

Lovecraft was saying, "– not a true name, but merely a title, and a corrupt one at that. There never was a *real* Prester John, only various rulers in various distant places, whom it pleased the tale-spinners of Europe to speak of as Prester John, the Christian emperor, the great mysterious unknown monarch of a fabulous realm. And here in the Afterworld there are many who choose to wear the name. There's power in it, do you see?"

"Power and majesty!" Howard cried. "And poetry, by God!"

"So this Prester John whom we are to visit," said Gilgamesh, "he is not in fact Prester John?"

"Yeh-lu Ta-shih's his real name," said Howard. "Chinese. Manchurian, actually, twelfth century A.D. First emperor of the realm of Kara-Khitai, with his capital at Samarkand. Ruled over a bunch of Mongols and Turks, mainly, and they called him Gur Khan, which means 'supreme ruler,' and somehow that turned into 'John' by the time it got to Europe. And they said he was a Christian priest, too, *Presbyter Joannes,* 'Prester John.'" Howard laughed. "Damned silly bastards. He was no more a Christian than you were. A Buddhist, he was, a bloody shamanistic Buddhist."

"Then why –"

"Myth and confusion!" Howard said. "The great human nonsense factory at work! And wouldn't you know it, but when he got to the Afterworld this Yeh-lu Ta-shih founded himself another empire right away in the same sort of territory he'd lived in back there, and when Richard Burton came out this way and told him about Prester John and how Europeans long ago had spoken of him by that name and ascribed all sorts of fabulous accomplishments to him he said, Yes, yes, I am Prester John indeed. And so he styles himself now, he and nine or ten others, most of them Ethiopians like that friend of your friend Mandeville."

"They are no friends of mine," said Gilgamesh stiffly. He leaned back and massaged his aching arm. Outside the Land Rover the landscape was changing now: more hilly, with ill-favored fat-trunked little trees jutting at peculiar angles from the purple soil. Here and there in the distance his keen eyes made out scattered groups of black tents on the hillsides, and herds of the little demon-horses grazing near them. Gilgamesh wished now that he hadn't let himself be inveigled into this expedition. What need had he of Prester John? One of those upstart Later Dead potentates, one of the innumerable little princelings who had set up minor dominions for themselves out here in the vast measureless wastelands of the Outback – and reigning under a false name, at that – one more shoddy scoundrel, one more puffed-up little nobody swollen with unearned pride –

Well, and what difference did it make? He would sojourn awhile in the land of this Prester John, and then he would move on, alone, apart from others, traveling a separate path without destination or purpose, mourning as always his lost Enkidu. There never seemed any escaping that doom that lay upon him, that bitter solitude, whether he reigned in splendor in the Uruk of his ancient life or wandered in the forlorn wastes of this Afterworld.

"Their Excellencies P.E. Lovecraft and Howard E. Robert," cried the major-domo grandly though inaccurately, striking three times on the black marble floor of Prester John's throne-chamber with his gold-tipped staff of pale green jade. "Envoys Plenipotentiary of His Britannic Majesty King Henry VIII of the Kingdom of New Holy Resurrected England."

Lovecraft and Howard took a couple of steps forward. Yeh-lu Ta-shih nodded curtly and waved one elegant hand, resplendent with inch-long fingernails, in casual acknowledgement. The envoys plenipotentiary did not seem to hold much interest for him, nor, apparently, did whatever it was that had caused His Britannic Majesty King Henry to send them here.

The emperor's cool imperious glance turned toward Gilgamesh, who was struggling to hold himself erect. He was beginning to feel feverish and dizzy and he wondered if he should point out that there was an oozing hole in his arm. There were limits even to his endurance, after all, though he usually tried to conceal that fact. He didn't know how much longer he could hold out. There were times when behaving like a hero was a heroic pain in the ass, and this was one of them.

"– and his Late Highness Gilgamesh of Uruk son of Lugalbanda, great king, king of Uruk, king of kings, lord of the Land of the Two Rivers by merit of Enlil and An," boomed the major-domo in the same splendid way, looking down only once at the card he held in his hand.

"Great king?" said Yeh-lu Ta-shih, fixing Gilgamesh with one of the most intensely penetrating stares the Sumerian could remember having received. "King of kings? Those are very lofty titles, Gilgamesh of Uruk."

"A mere formula," Gilgamesh replied, "which I thought appropriate when being presented at your court. In fact I am king of nothing at all now."

"Ah," said Yeh-lu Ta-shih. "King of Nothing-at-all."

And so are you, my lord Prester John. Gilgamesh did not let himself say it, though the words bubbled toward the roof of his mouth and begged to be uttered. *And so are all the self-appointed lords and masters of the many realms of the Afterworld.*

The slender amber-hued man on the throne leaned forward. "And where then, I pray, is Nothing-at-all?"

Some of the courtiers began to snicker. But Prester John seemed to be altogether in earnest, though it was impossible to be completely certain of that. He was plainly a formidable man, Gilgamesh had quickly come to see: sly, shrewd, self-contained, with a tough and sinewy intelligence. Not at all the vain little cock-of-the-walk Gilgamesh had expected to find in this bleak and remote corner of the Outback. However small and obscure his principality might be, Prester John ruled it, obviously, with a firm grasp. The grandeur of the glittering palace that his scruffy subjects had built for him here on the edge of nowhere, and the solidity of the small but substantial city surrounding it, testified to that. Gilgamesh knew something about the building of cities and palaces. Prester John's capital bore the mark of the steady toil of centuries.

The long stare was unrelenting. Gilgamesh, fighting back the blazing pain in his arm, met the emperor's gaze with an equally earnest one of his own and said:

"Nothing-at-all? It is a land that never was, and will always be, my lord. Its boundaries are nowhere and its capital city is everywhere, nor do any of us ever leave it."

"Ah. Ah. Indeed. Nicely put. You are Early Dead, are you?"

"Very early, my lord."

"Earlier than Ch'in Shih Huang Ti? Earlier than the Lords of Shang and Hsia?"

Gilgamesh turned in puzzlement toward Lovecraft, who told him in a half-whisper, "Ancient kings of China. Your time was even before theirs."

Shrugging, Gilgamesh replied, "They are not known to me, my lord, but you hear what the Britannic ambassador says. He is a man of learning: it must be so. I will tell you that I am older than Caesar by far, older than Amenhotep, older than Belshazzar. By a great deal."

Yeh-lu Ta-shih considered that a moment. Then he made another of his little gestures of dismissal, as though brushing aside the whole concept of relative ages in the Afterworld. With a dry laugh he said, "So you are very old, King Gilgamesh. I congratulate you. And yet the Ice-Hunter folk would tell us that you and I and your Belshazzar and your Amenhotep, whoever they may be, all arrived here only yesterday; and in the eyes of the Hairy Men, the Ice-Hunters themselves are mere newcomers. And so on and so on. There's no beginning to it, is there? Any more than there's an end."

Without waiting for an answer he asked Gilgamesh, "How did you come by that gory wound, great king of Nothing-at-all?"

"A misunderstanding, my lord. It may be that your border patrol is a little over-zealous at times."

One of the courtiers leaned toward the emperor and murmured something. Prester John's serene brow grew furrowed. He lifted a flawlessly contoured eyebrow ever so slightly.

"Killed nine of them, did you?"

"They attacked us before we had the opportunity of showing our diplomatic credentials," Lovecraft put in quickly. "It was entirely a matter of self-defense, my lord Prester John."

"I wouldn't doubt it." The emperor seemed to contemplate for a moment, but only for a moment, the skirmish that had cost the lives of nine of his horsemen; and then quite visibly he dismissed that matter too from the center of his attention. "Well, now, my lords ambassador –"

Abruptly Gilgamesh swayed, tottered, started to fall. He checked himself just barely in time, seizing a massive porphyry column and clinging to it until he felt more steady. Beads of sweat trickled down his forehead into his eyes. He began to shiver. The huge stone column seemed to be expanding and contracting. Waves of vertigo were rippling through him and he was seeing double, suddenly. Everything was blurring and multiplying. He drew his breath in deeply, again, again, forcing himself to hold on. He wondered if Prester John was playing some kind of game with him, trying to see how long his strength could last. Well, if he had to, Gilgamesh swore, he would stand here forever in front of Prester John without showing a hint of weakness.

But now Yeh-lu Ta-shih was at last willing to extend compassion. With a glance toward one of his pages the emperor said, "Summon my physician, and tell him to bring his tools and his potions. That wound should have been dressed an hour ago."

"Thank you, my lord," Gilgamesh muttered, trying to keep the irony from his tone.

The doctor appeared almost at once, as though he had been waiting in an antechamber. Another of Prester John's little games, perhaps? He was a burly, broad-shouldered, bushy-haired man of more than middle years, with a manner about him that was brisk and bustling but nevertheless warm, concerned, reassuring. Drawing Gilgamesh down beside him on a low divan covered with the gray-green hide of some scaly hell-dragon, he peered into the wound, muttered something unintelligible under his breath in a guttural language unknown to the Sumerian, and pressed his thick fingers around the edges of the torn flesh until fresh blood flowed. Gilgamesh hissed sharply but did not flinch.

"*Ach, mein lieber Freund*, I must hurt you again, but it is for your own good. *Verstehen Sie*?"

The doctor's fingers dug in more deeply. He was spreading the wound, swabbing it, cleansing it with some clear fluid that stung like a hot iron. The pain was so intense that there was almost a kind of pleasure in it: it was a purifying kind of pain, a purging of the soul.

Prester John said, "How bad is it, Dr Schweitzer?"

"*Gott sei Dank*, it is deep but clean. He will heal without damage."

He continued to probe and cleanse, murmuring softly to Gilgamesh as he worked: "*Bitte. Bitte. Einen Augenblick, mein Freund.*" To Prester John he said, "This man is made of steel. No nerves at all, immense resistance to pain. We have one of the great heroes here, *nicht wahr*? You are Roland, are you? Achilles, perhaps?"

"Gilgamesh is his name," said Yeh-lu Ta-shih.

The doctor's eyes grew bright. "Gilgamesh! Gilgamesh of Sumer? *Wunderbar*! *Wunderbar*! The very man. The seeker after everlasting life. *Ach*, we must talk, my friend, you and I, when you are feeling better." From his medical kit he now produced a frightful-looking hypodermic syringe. Gilgamesh watched as though from a vast distance, as though that throbbing swollen arm belonged to someone else. "*Ja, ja*, certainly we must talk, of life, of death, of philosophy, *mein Freund*, of *philosophy*! There is so very much for us to discuss!" He slipped the needle beneath Gilgamesh's skin. "There. *Genug*. Sit. Rest. The healing now begins."

Robert Howard had never seen anything like it. It could have been something straight from the pages of one of his Conan stories. The big ox had taken an arrow right through the fat part of his arm, and he had simply yanked it out and gone right on fighting. Then, afterward, he had behaved as if the wound were nothing more than a scratch, all that time while they were driving hour after hour toward Prester John's city and then undergoing lengthy interrogation by the court officials and then standing through this whole endless ceremony at court – God almighty, what a display of endurance! True, Gilgamesh had finally gone a little wobbly and had actually seemed on the verge of passing out. But any ordinary mortal would have conked out long ago. Heroes really *were* different. They were another breed altogether. Look at him now, sitting there casually while that old German medic swabs him out and stitches him up in that slapdash cavalier way, and not a whimper out of him. Not a whimper!

Suddenly Howard found himself wanting to go over there to Gilgamesh, to comfort him, to let him lean his head back against him while the doctor worked him over, to wipe the sweat from his brow –

Yes, to comfort him in an open, rugged, manly way –

No. No. No. No.

There it was again, the horror, the unspeakable thing, the hideous crawling, the hell-born impulse rising out of the cesspools of his soul –

Howard fought it back. Blotted it out, hid it from view. Denied that it had ever entered his mind.

To Lovecraft he said, "That's some doctor! Took his medical degree at the Chicago slaughterhouses, I reckon!"

"Don't you know who he is, Bob?"

"Some old Dutchman who wandered in here during a sandstorm and never bothered to leave."

"Does the name of Dr Schweitzer mean nothing to you?"

Howard gave Lovecraft a blank look. "Guess I never heard it much in Texas."

"Oh, Bob, Bob, why must you always pretend to be such a cowboy? Can you tell me you've never heard of Schweitzer? *Albert* Schweitzer? The great philosopher, theologian, musician – there never was a greater interpreter of Bach, and don't tell me you don't know Bach either –"

"She-it, H.P. Philosopher? Musician? You talking about that old country doctor there?"

"Who founded the leprosy clinic in Africa, at Lambaréné, yes. Who devoted his life to helping the sick, under the most primitive conditions, in the most remote forests of –"

"Hold on, H.P. That can't be so."

"That one man could achieve so much? I assure you, Bob,

he was quite well known in our time – perhaps not in Texas, I suppose, but nevertheless –"

"No. Not that he could do all that. But that he's here. In the Afterworld. If that old geezer's everything you say, then he's a goddamned *saint*. Unless he beat his wife when no one was looking, or something like that. What's a saint doing in the Afterworld, H.P.?"

"What are *we* doing in the Afterworld?" Lovecraft asked.

Howard reddened and looked away. "Well – I suppose, there were things in our lives – things that might be considered sins, in the strictest sense –"

"What does sin have to do with anything?" Lovecraft asked.

"Well, isn't this place Hell?"

"Is it?"

"It sure ain't Heaven, H.P. Even if it does look a whole lot like Texas."

Lovecraft shook his head. "Heaven. Hell. Who knows? There are those who think that this place where we have found ourselves is Hell, I agree. But I'm not one of them. All we know is that it's the Afterworld, a life after life. Do you see a Devil with scaly wings and a long tail presiding over the place? Do we live in constant torment?"

"Well –"

"No," Lovecraft said. "There's no reason to think of this place as Hell, though some people do. There's no reason to think of it as anything but the Afterworld. And no one understands the rules of the Afterworld, Bob," said Lovecraft gently. "Everything's random here, completely unpredictable. Sin may have nothing to do with it. Gandhi is here, do you realize that? Confucius. Were *they* sinners? Was Moses? Abraham? Those who call it Hell have tried to impose their own pitiful shallow beliefs, their pathetic grade-school notions of punishment for bad behaviour, on this incredibly bizarre place where we find ourselves. By what right? We don't begin to comprehend what the Afterworld really is. All we know is that it's full of heroic villains and villainous heroes – and people like you and me – and it seems that Albert Schweitzer is here, too. A great mystery. But perhaps someday –"

"Ssh," Howard said. "Prester John's talking to us."

"My lords ambassador –"

Hastily they turned toward him. "Your majesty?" Howard said.

"This mission that has brought you here: your king wants an alliance, I suppose? What for? Against whom? Quarreling with some pope again, is he?"

"With his daughter, I'm afraid," said Howard.

Prester John looked bored. He toyed with his emerald scepter. "Mary, you mean?"

"Elizabeth, your majesty," Lovecraft said.

"Your king's a most quarrelsome man. I'd have thought there were enough popes in the Afterworld to keep him busy, though, and no need to contend with his daughters."

"They are the most contentious women in all the Afterworld," Lovecraft said. "Blood of his blood, after all, and each of them a queen with a noisy, brawling kingdom of her own. Elizabeth, my lord, is sending a pack of her explorers to the Outback, and King Henry doesn't like the idea."

"Indeed," said Yeh-lu Ta-shih, suddenly interested again. "And neither do I. She has no business in the Outback. It's not her territory. The rest of the Afterworld should be big enough for Elizabeth. What is she looking for here?"

"The sorcerer John Dee has told her that the way out of the Afterworld is to be found in these parts," said Lovecraft.

"There is no way out of the Afterworld," Yeh-lu Ta-shih said quietly.

Lovecraft smiled. "I'm not any judge of that, your majesty. Queen Elizabeth, in any event, has given credence to the notion. Her Walter Ralegh directs the expedition, and the geographer Hakluyt is with him, and a force of five hundred soldiers. They move diagonally across the Outback just to the south of your domain, following some chart that Dr Dee has obtained for them. He had it from Cagliostro, they say, who bought it from one of the Medici, to whom Nero had pawned it."

Prester John did not appear to be impressed. "Let us say, for argument's sake, that there *is* an exit from the Afterworld. Why would Queen Elizabeth desire to leave? The Afterworld's not so bad. It has its minor discomforts, yes, but one learns to cope with them. Does she think she'd be able to return to the land of the living and reclaim her throne? She's dead, my friend. We are all dead here, though we have the semblance of life. There is no other place for us to go. There is no throne waiting for her in another sphere."

Howard stepped forward. "Elizabeth has no real interest in leaving the Afterworld herself, majesty. What King Henry fears is that if she does find a way out, she'll claim it for her own and set up a colony around it, and charge a fee for passing through the gate. No matter where it takes you, the king reckons there'll be millions of people willing to risk it, and Elizabeth will wind up cornering all the money in the Afterworld. He can't abide that notion, d'ye see? He thinks she's already too smart and aggressive by half, and he hates the idea that she might get even more powerful. There's something mixed into it having to do with Queen Elizabeth's mother, too – that was Anne Boleyn, Henry's second wife – she was a wild and wanton one, and he cut her head off for adultery, and now he thinks that Anne's behind Elizabeth's maneuvers, trying to get even with him by –"

"Spare me these details," said Yeh-lu Ta-shih with some irritation. "What does Henry expect me to do?"

"Send troops to turn the Ralegh expedition back before it can find anything useful to Elizabeth."

"And in what way do I gain from this?"

"If the exit from the Afterworld's on your frontier, your majesty, do you really want a bunch of Elizabethan Englishmen setting up a colony next door to you?"

"There is no exit from the Afterworld," Prester John said complacently once again.

"But if they set up a colony anyway?"

Prester John was silent a moment. "I see," he said finally.

"In return for your aid," Howard said, "we're empowered to offer you a trade treaty on highly favorable terms."

"Ah."

"And a guarantee of military protection in the event of the invasion of your realm by a hostile power."

"If King Henry's armies are so mighty, why does he not deal with the Ralegh expedition himself?"

"There was no time to outfit and dispatch an army across such a great distance," said Lovecraft. "Elizabeth's people had already set out before anything was known of the scheme."

"Ah," said Yeh-lu Ta-shih.

"Of course," Lovecraft went on, "there were other princes of the Outback that King Henry might have approached. Ibn Saud's name came up, and one of the Assyrians – Assurnasirpal, I think – and someone mentioned Mao Tse-tung. No, King Henry said, let us ask the aid of Prester John, for he is a monarch of great puissance and grandeur, whose writ is supreme throughout the far reaches of the Afterworld. Prester John, indeed, that is the one whose aid we must seek!"

A strange new sparkle had come into Yeh-lu Ta-shih's eyes. "You were considering an alliance with Mao Tse-tung?"

"It was merely a suggestion, your majesty."

"Ah. I see." The emperor rose from his throne. "Well, we must consider these matters more carefully, eh? We must not come hastily to a decision." He looked across the great vaulted throne-room to the divan where Dr Schweitzer still labored over Gilgamesh's wound. "Your patient, doctor – what's the report?"

"A man of steel, majesty, a man of steel! *Gott sei Dank*, he heals before my eyes!"

"Indeed. Come, then. You will all want to rest, I think; and then you shall know the full hospitality of Prester John."

Five

The full hospitality of Prester John, Gilgamesh soon discovered, was no trifling affair.

He was led off to a private chamber with walls lined with black felt – a kind of indoor tent – where three serving-girls who stood barely hip-high to him surrounded him, giggling, and took his clothing from him. Gently they pushed him into a huge marble cistern full of warm milk, where they bathed him lovingly and massaged his aching body in the most intimate manner. Afterward they robed him in intricate vestments of yellow silk.

Then they conveyed him to the emperor's great hall, where the whole court was gathered, a glittering and resplendent multitude. Some sort of concert was under way, seven solemn musicians playing harsh screeching twanging music. Gongs crashed, a trumpet blared, pipes uttered eerie piercing sounds. Servants showed Gilgamesh to a place of honor atop a pile of furry blankets heaped high with velvet cushions.

Lovecraft and Howard were already there, garbed like Gilgamesh in magnificent silks. Both of them looked somewhat unsettled – unhinged, even. Howard, flushed and boisterous, could barely sit still: he laughed and waved his arms around and kicked his heels against the furs, like a small boy who has done something very naughty and is trying to conceal it by being overexuberant. Lovecraft, on the other hand, seemed dazed and dislocated, with the glassy-eyed look of someone who has recently been clubbed.

These are two very odd men indeed, Gilgamesh thought.

One works hard at being loud and lusty, and now and then gives you a glimpse of a soul boiling with wild fantasies of swinging swords and rivers of blood. But in reality he seems terrified of everything. The other, though he is weirdly remote and austere, is apparently not quite as crazy, but he too gives the impression of being at war with himself, in terror of allowing any sort of real human feeling to break through the elaborate facade of his mannerisms. The poor fools must have been scared silly when the serving-girls started stripping them and pouring warm milk over them and stroking their bodies. No doubt they haven't recovered yet from all that nasty pleasure, Gilgamesh thought. He could imagine their cries of horror as the little Mongol girls started going to work on them. *What are you* doing? *Leave my trousers alone! Don't touch me there! Please – no – ooh – ah –* ooh! *Oooh*!

Yeh-lu Ta-shih, seated upon a high throne of ivory and onyx, waved grandly to him, one great king to another. Gilgamesh gave him an almost imperceptible nod by way of acknowledgement. All this pomp and formality bored him hideously. He had endured so much of it in his former life, after all. Back then *he* had been the one on the high throne, but even then it had been nothing but a bore. And now –

But this was no more boring than anything else. Gilgamesh had long ago decided that that was the true curse of the Afterworld: all striving was meaningless here, mere thunder without the lightning. It was impossible to build anything that would last. It was all castles in the sand here, with oblivion rolling in on the tides no matter how hard you struggled against it. You never could bring forth sons to extol your name and strengthen the walls of your city; your friends and allies appeared and vanished again like phantoms in a dream; you yourself lived half the time in some fevered dream yourself, uncertain of your own intentions. And there was no end to it. You might die again now and then if you were careless or unlucky, but back you came for another turn, sooner or later. There was no release from the everlastingness of it all. Once he had yearned desperately for eternal life, and he had learned to his pain that he could not have such a thing, at least not in the world of mortal men. But now indeed he had come to a place where he would live forever, so it seemed, and yet there was no joy in it. His fondest dream now was simply to serve his time in this Afterworld and be allowed to sleep in peace forever. He saw no way of attaining that. Life here, or what passed for life, just went on and on – very much like this concert, this endless skein of twangs and plinks and screeches.

Someone with the soft face of a eunuch came by and offered him a morsel of grilled meat. Now that the sting of his wound was ebbing he felt hungry, and he gobbled it. And another, and another, and a flagon of fermented mare's milk besides.

A corps of dancers appeared, men and women in flaring filmy robes. They were doing things with swords and flaming torches. A second eunuch brought Gilgamesh a tray of mysterious sugary delicacies, and he helped himself with both hands. He was ravenous. His body, as it healed, was calling furiously for fuel. Beside him, the man Howard was swilling down the mare's milk as if it were water and getting tipsier and tipsier, and the other, the one called Lovecraft, sat morosely staring at the dancers without touching a thing. He seemed to be shivering as though in the midst of a snowstorm.

Gilgamesh beckoned for a second flagon. Just then the doctor arrived and settled down cheerfully on the heap of blankets next to him. Schweitzer grinned his approval as Gilgamesh took a hearty drink. "*Fühlen Sie sich besser, mein Held, eh*? The arm, it no longer gives you pain? Already the wound is closing. So quickly you repair yourself! Such strength, such power of healing! You are God's own miracle, dear Gilgamesh. The blessing of the Almighty is upon you."

He seized a flagon of his own from a passing servant, quaffed it, made a face. "*Ach*, this milk-wine of theirs! And *ach*, *ach*, this *verfluchte* music! What I would give for the taste of decent Mosel on my tongue now, eh, and the sound of the D minor toccata and fugue in my ears! Bach – do you know him?"

"Who?"

"Bach! Bach, Johann Sebastian Bach. The greatest of musicians, God's own poet in sound. I saw him once, just once, years ago." Schweitzer's eyes were glowing. "I was new here. Not two weeks had I been here. It was at the villa of King Friedrich – Frederick the Great, you know him? No? The king of Prussia? *Der alte Fritz*? No matter. No matter. *Es macht nichts*. A man entered, ordinary, you would never notice him in a crowd, yes? And began to play the harpsichord, and he had not played three measures when I said, This is Bach, this must be the actual Bach, and I would have dropped down on my knees before him but that I was ashamed. And it was he. I said to myself, Why is it that Bach is in the Afterworld, if the Afterworld is Hell, as some would have us think? But then I said, as perhaps you have said, as I think everyone here must say at one time or another about himself, Why is it that *Schweitzer* is in the Afterworld? And I knew that it is that God is mysterious. Perhaps I was sent here to minister to the damned. Perhaps it is that Bach was also, to play for our souls. Or perhaps we are damned also; or perhaps no one here is damned. That is what I finally think, that those who call this place Hell are fools. Who knows what this place is, or why we are here, eh? *Es macht nichts aus*, all this speculation. It is a mistake, or even *vielleicht* a sin, to imagine that we can comprehend the workings of the mind of God. We are here. We have our tasks. That is enough for us to know."

"I felt that way once," said Gilgamesh. "When I was king in Uruk in the other world, and finally came to understand that I must die, that there was no hiding from that. What is the purpose, then, I asked myself? And I told myself: The gods have put us here to perform our tasks, and that is the purpose. And so I lived thereafter, performing my task according to my understanding of what it was that the gods required of me, until I died." Gilgamesh's face darkened. "But here – here –"

"Here too we have our tasks," Schweitzer said.

"You do, perhaps. For me there is only the task of passing

the time. I had a friend to bear the burden with me, once –"

"Enkidu."

Gilgamesh seized the doctor's sturdy wrist with sudden fierce intensity. "You know of Enkidu?"

"From the poem, yes. The poem is very famous."

"Ah. Ah. The poem. But the actual man –"

"I know nothing of him, *nein*."

"He is of my stature, very large. His beard is thick, his hair is shaggy, his shoulders are wider even than mine. We journeyed everywhere together. But then we quarreled, and he went from me in anger, saying, Never cross my path again. Saying, I have no love for you, Gilgamesh. Saying, If we meet again I will have your life. And I have heard nothing of him since."

Schweitzer turned and stared closely at Gilgamesh. "How is this possible? All the world knows the love of Enkidu for Gilgamesh!"

Gilgamesh called for yet another flagon. This conversation was awakening an ache within his breast, an ache that made the pain that his wound had caused seem like nothing more than an itch. Nor would the drink soothe it; but he would drink all the same.

He took a deep draught and said somberly, "We quarreled. There were hot words between us. He said he had no love for me any longer."

"This cannot be true."

Gilgamesh shrugged and made no reply.

"You wish to find him again?" Schweitzer asked.

"I desire nothing else."

"Do you know where he is?"

"The Afterworld is larger even than the world, and the world is so large that it makes my head hurt to think of it. He could be anywhere."

"You will find him."

"If you knew how I have searched for him –"

"You will find him. That I know."

Gilgamesh shook his head. "If the Afterworld is a place of torment, then this is mine: that I will never find him again. Or if I do, that he will spurn me. Or raise his hand against me."

"This is not so," said Schweitzer. "I think he longs for you even as you do for him."

"Then why does he keep himself from me?"

"This is the Afterworld," said Schweitzer gently. "I think we are meant to be tested here. And so you are being tested, my friend; but no test lasts forever. Not even in the Afterworld. Not even in the Afterworld. Even though you are in the Afterworld, have faith in the Lord: You will have your Enkidu soon enough, *um Himmels willen.*" Smiling, Schweitzer said, "The emperor is calling you. Go to him. I think he has something to tell you that you will want to hear."

Prester John said, "You are a warrior, are you not?"

"I was," replied Gilgamesh indifferently.

"A general? A leader of men?"

"All that is far behind me," Gilgamesh said. "This is the life after life. Now I go my own way and I take on no tasks for others. The Afterworld has plenty of generals."

"I am told that you were a leader among leaders. I am told that you fought like the god of war. When you took the field, whole nations laid down their arms and knelt before you."

Gilgamesh waited, saying nothing.

"You miss the glory of the battlefield, don't you, Gilgamesh?"

"Do I?"

"What if I were to offer you the command of my army?"

"Why would you do that? What am I to you? What is your nation to me?"

"In the Afterworld we take whatever citizenship we wish. My nation could become your nation. What would you say, if I offered you the command?"

"I would tell you that you are making a great mistake."

"It isn't a trivial army. Ten thousand men. Adequate air support. Tactical nukes. The strongest firepower in the Outback."

"You misunderstand," said Gilgamesh. "Warfare doesn't interest me. I know nothing of modern weapons and don't care to learn. Nor do I want to be part of anybody's nation. You have the wrong man, Prester John. If you need a general, send for Wellington. Send for Marlborough. Rommel. Tiglath-Pileser."

"Or for Enkidu?"

The unexpected name hit Gilgamesh like a battering ram.

At the sound of it his face grew hot and his entire body trembled convulsively.

"What do you know about Enkidu?"

Prester John held up one superbly manicured hand. "Allow me the privilege of asking the questions, great king."

"You spoke the name of Enkidu. What do you know about Enkidu?"

"First let us discuss other matters which are of –"

"Enkidu," said Gilgamesh implacably. "Why did you mention his name?"

"I know that he was your friend –"

"*Is*."

"Very well, *is* your friend. And a man of great valor and strength. Who happens to be a guest at this very moment at the court of the great enemy of my realm. And who, so I understand it, is preparing just now to make war against me."

"*What*?" Gilgamesh stared. "Enkidu is in the service of Queen Elizabeth?"

"I don't recall having said that."

"Is it not Queen Elizabeth who even now has sent an army to encroach on your domain?"

Yeh-lu Ta-shih laughed. "Ralegh and his five hundred fools? That expedition's an absurdity. I'll take care of them in an afternoon. I mean another enemy altogether. Tell me this: do you know of Mao Tse-tung?"

"These princes of the Later Dead – there are so many of them, and their names mean nothing to me –"

"A Chinese, a man of Han. Emperor of the Marxist Dynasty, long after my time. Crafty, stubborn, tough. More than a little crazy. He runs something called the Celestial People's Republic, just north of here. What he tells his subjects is that we can turn the Afterworld into Heaven by collectivizing it."

"Collectivizing?" said Gilgamesh uncomprehendingly.

"To make all the peasants into kings, and the kings into peasants. As I say: more than a little crazy. But he has his hordes of loyal followers, and they do whatever he says. He means to conquer the whole Outback, beginning right here. And after that all of the Afterworld will be subjected to his lunatic ideas, province by province. I fear that Elizabeth's in league with him – that this nonsense of looking for a way out of the Afterworld is only a ruse, that in fact her Ralegh is spying out my weaknesses for her so that she can sell the information to Mao."

"But if this Mao is the enemy of all kings, why would Elizabeth ally herself with –"

"Obviously they mean to use each other. Elizabeth aiding Mao to overthrow me, Mao aiding Elizabeth to push her father from his throne. And then afterward, who knows? But I mean to strike before either of them can harm me."

"What about Enkidu?" Gilgamesh said. "Tell me about Enkidu."

Prester John opened a scroll of computer printout. Skimming through it, he read, "The Early Dead warrior Enkidu of Sumer – Sumer, that's your nation, isn't it? – arrived at court of Mao Tse-tung on such-and-such a date – ostensible purpose of visit, Outback hunting expedition – accompanied by American spy posing as journalist and hunter, one E. Hemingway – secret meetings with Kublai Khan, Minister of War for the Celestial People's Republic – now training Communist troops in preparation for invasion of New Kara-Khitai –" The emperor looked up. "Is this of interest to you, Gilgamesh?"

"What is it you want from me?"

"This man is your famous friend. You know his mind as you do your own. Defend us from him and I'll give you anything you desire."

"What I desire," said Gilgamesh, "is nothing more than the friendship of Enkidu."

"Then I'll give you Enkidu on a silver platter. Take the field for me against Mao's troops. Help me anticipate whatever strategies your Enkidu has been teaching them. We'll wipe the Marxist bastards out and capture their generals, and then Enkidu will be yours. I can't guarantee that he'll want to be your friend again, but he'll be yours. What do you say, Gilgamesh? What do you say?"

Across the gray plains of the Afterworld from horizon to horizon sprawled the legions of Prester John. Scarlet-and-yellow banners fluttered against the somber sky. At the center of the formation stood a wedge of horseborne archers in leather armor; on each flank was a detachment of heavy infantry; the emperor's fleet of tanks was in the vanguard, rolling unhurriedly forward over the rough, broken terrain. A phalanx of transatmospheric weapons-platforms provided air cover far overhead.

A cloud of dust in the distance gave evidence of the oncoming army of the Celestial People's Republic.

"By all the demons of Stygia, did you ever see such a cockeyed sight?" Robert Howard cried. He and Lovecraft had a choice view of the action from their place in the imperial command post, a splendid pagoda protected by a glowing force-shield. Gilgamesh was there too, just across the way with Prester John and the officers of the Kara-Khitai high command. The emperor was peering into a bank of television monitors and one of his aides was feverishly tapping out orders on a computer terminal. "Makes no goddamned sense," said Howard. "Horsemen, tanks, weapons-platforms, all mixing it up at the same time – is that how these wild sons of bitches fight a war?"

Lovecraft touched his forefinger to his lips. "Don't shout so, Bob. Do you want Prester John to hear you? We're his guests, remember. And King Henry's ambassadors."

"Well, if he hears me, he hears me. Look at that crazy mess! Doesn't Prester John realize that he's got a twentieth-century Bolshevik Chinaman coming to attack him with twentieth-century weapons? What good are mounted horsemen, for God's sake? A cavalry charge into the face of heavy artillery? Bows and arrows against howitzers?" Howard guffawed. "Nuclear-tipped arrows, is that the trick?"

Softly Lovecraft said, "For all we know, that's what they are."

"You know that can't be, H.P. I'm surprised at you, a man with your scientific background. I realize all this nuke stuff is after our time, but surely you've kept up with the theory. Critical mass at the tip of an arrow? No, H.P., you know as well as I do that it just can't work. And even if it could –"

In exasperation Lovecraft waved him to be silent. He pointed across the room to the main monitor in front of Prester John. The florid face of a heavy-set man with a thick white beard had appeared on the screen.

"Isn't that Hemingway?" Lovecraft asked.

"Who?"

"Ernest Hemingway. The writer. *A Farewell to Arms. The Sun Also Rises.*"

"Never could stand his stuff," said Howard. "Sick crap about a bunch of drunken weaklings. You sure that's him?"

"Weaklings, Bob?" said Lovecraft in astonishment.

"I read only the one book, about those Americans in Europe who go to the bullfights and get drunk and fool around with each other's women, and that was all of Mr Hemingway that I cared to experience. I tell you, H. P., it disgusted me. And the way it was written! All those short little sentences – no magic, no poetry, H. P. –"

"Let's talk about it some other time, Bob."

"No vision of heroism – no awareness of the higher passions that ennoble and –"

"Bob – please –"

"A fixation on the sordid, the slimy, the depraved –"

"You're being absurd, Bob. You're completely misinterpreting his philosophy of life. If you had simply taken the trouble to read *A Farewell to Arms* –" Lovecraft shook his head angrily. "This is no time for a literary discussion. Look – look there." He nodded toward the far side of the room. "One of the emperor's aides is calling over. Something's going on."

Indeed there had been a development of some sort. Yeh-lu Ta-shih seemed to be conferring with four or five aides at once. Gilgamesh, red-faced, agitated, was striding swiftly back and forth in front of the computer bank. Hemingway's face was still on the screen and he too looked agitated.

Hastily Howard and Lovecraft crossed the room. The emperor turned to them. "There's been a request for a parley in the field," Prester John said. "Kublai Khan is on his way over. Dr Schweitzer will serve as my negotiator. The man Hemingway's going to be an impartial observer – *their* impartial observer. I need an impartial observer too. Will you two go down there too, as diplomats from a neutral power, to keep an eye on things?"

"An honor to serve," said Howard grandly.

"And for what purpose, my lord, has the parley been called?" Lovecraft asked.

Yeh-lu Ta-shih gestured toward the screen. "Hemingway has had the notion that we can settle this thing by single combat – Gilgamesh versus Enkidu. Save on ammunition, spare a lot of warriors the bother of dying and undying again. But there's a disagreement over the details." Delicately he smothered a yawn. "Perhaps it can all be worked out by lunchtime."

It was an oddly assorted group. Mao Tse-tung's chief negotiator was the plump, magnificently dressed Kublai Khan, whose dark sly eyes gave evidence of much cunning and force. He had been an emperor in his own right in his former life, but evidently had preferred less taxing responsibilities here. Next to him was Hemingway, big and heavy, with a deep voice and an easy, almost arrogant manner. Mao had also sent four small men in identical blue uniforms with red stars on their breasts – "Party types," someone murmured – and, strangely, a Hairy Man, short of stature, big-browed and chinless, one of those curious creatures out of the deepest antiquity of the other world. The Hairy Man also wore the Communist emblem on his uniform.

And there was one more to the group – the massive, deep-chested man of dark brow and fierce and smouldering eyes, who stood off by himself at the far side –

Gilgamesh could barely bring himself to look at him. He too stood apart from the group a little way, savoring the keen edge of the wind that blew across the field of battle. Gilgamesh longed to rush toward him – toward Enkidu – to throw his arms around him, to sweep away in one jubilant embrace all the bitterness that had separated them –

If only it could be as simple as that!

The voices of Mao's negotiators and the five that Prester John had sent – Schweitzer, Lovecraft, Howard, and a pair of Kara-Khitai officers – drifted to Gilgamesh above the howling of the wind.

Hemingway seemed to be doing most of the talking. "Writers, are you? Mr Howard, Mr Lovecraft? I regret I haven't had the pleasure of encountering your work."

"Fantasy, it was," said Lovecraft. "Fables. Visions."

"That so? You publish in *Argosy*? *The Post*?"

"Five to *Argosy*, but they were westerns," Howard said. "Mainly we wrote for *Weird Tales*. And H.P., a few in *Astounding Stories*."

"*Weird Tales*," Hemingway said. "*Astounding Stories*." A shadow of distaste flickered across his face. "Mmm. Don't think I knew those magazines. But you wrote well, did you, gentlemen? You set down what you truly saw, the real thing, and you stated it purely? Of course you did. I know you did. You were honest writers. That goes almost without saying. It takes one to tell one, don't you think? And maybe I had some moments that weren't my best moments, but I tried all the time, wouldn't you say? I tried all the time!" He laughed, rubbed his hands in glee, effusively threw his arms around the shoulders of Howard and Lovecraft. Howard seemed alarmed by that and Lovecraft looked as though he wanted to sink into the ground. "Well, gentlemen," Hemingway boomed, "what shall we do here? We have a little problem. The one hero wishes to fight with bare hands, the other with – what did he call it? – a disruptor pistol? You would know more about that than I do: something out of *Astounding Stories*, is how it sounds to me. But we can't have this, can we? Bare hands against fantastic future science? There is a good way to fight and that is equal to equal, and all other ways are the bad ways."

"Let him come to me with his fists," Gilgamesh called from the distance. "As we fought the first time, in the Market-of-the-Land, when my path crossed his in Uruk."

"He is afraid to use the new weapons," Enkidu replied, casting a sour glare in Gilgamesh's direction.

"*Afraid*?"

"I brought a shotgun to him, a fine 12-gauge weapon, a gift to my brother Gilgamesh. He shrank from it as though I had given him a venomous serpent."

"Lies!" roared Gilgamesh. "I had no fear of it! I despised it because it was cowardly!"

"He fears anything which is new," said Enkidu. "I never thought Gilgamesh of Uruk would know fear, but he fears that which is unfamiliar. He called me a coward, because I would hunt with a shotgun. But I think he was the coward. And now he fears to fight me with the unfamiliar. He knows that I'll slay him. He fears death even here, do you know that? Death has always been his great terror. Why is that? Because it is an insult to his pride? I think that is it. Too proud to die – too proud to accept the decree of the gods –"

"I will break you with my hands alone!" Gilgamesh bellowed.

"Give us disruptors," said Enkidu. "Let us see if he dares to touch such a weapon."

"A coward's weapon!"

"Again you call me a coward? You, Gilgamesh, you are the one who quivers in fear –"

"Gentlemen! Gentlemen!"

"You fear my strength, Enkidu!"

"You fear my skill. You with your pathetic old sword, your pitiful bow –"

"Is this the Enkidu I loved, mocking me so?"

"You were the first to mock, when you threw back the shotgun into my hands, spurning my gift, calling me a coward –"

"The weapon, I said, was cowardly. Not you, Enkidu."

"It was the same thing."

"*Bitte, bitte,*" said Schweitzer. "This is not the way!"

And again from Hemingway: "Gentlemen, please!"

They took no notice.

"I meant –"

"You said –"

"Shame –"

"Fear –"

"Three times over a coward!"

"Five times five a traitor!"

"False friend!"

"Vain braggart!"

"Gentlemen, I have to ask you –"

But Hemingway's voice, loud and firm though it was, was altogether drowned out by the roar of rage that came from the throat of Gilgamesh. Dizzying throbs of anger pounded in his breast, his throat, his temples. This was more than Gilgamesh could take. This was just the way the dispute had begun the first time, when Enkidu had come to him with that shotgun and he had given it back and they had fallen into dispute. At first merely a disagreement, and then a hot debate, and then a quarrel, and then the hurling of bitter accusations. And then such words of anger as had never passed between them before, they who had been closer than brothers.

They had not come to blows, that time. Enkidu had simply stalked away, declaring that their friendship was at an end. But now – hearing all the same words again – stymied by this quarrel even over the very method by which they were to fight – Gilgamesh could no longer restrain himself. Overmastered by fury and frustration, he rushed forward.

Enkidu, eyes gleaming, was ready for him.

Hemingway attempted to come between them. Big as he was, he was like a child next to Gilgamesh and Enkidu, and they swatted him to one side without effort. With a jolt that made the ground itself reverberate Gilgamesh went crashing into Enkidu and laid hold of him with both hands.

Enkidu laughed. "So you have your way after all, King Gilgamesh! Bare hands it is!"

"It is the only way," said Gilgamesh. "Will you fight?"

"Most gladly I will, King Gilgamesh!"

Gilgamesh nodded. At last. At last. The rage that was rushing through him like a torrent would have an outlet. There was no wrestler in this world, or in the other, who could contend with Gilgamesh of Uruk. I will break him, Gilgamesh thought, as he broke our friendship. I will snap his spine. I will crush his chest. He summoned all his strength, and heaved, and felt the resistance of Enkidu like a wall in his hand, and heaved again. And again was resisted; and again summoned his strength.

As once they had done long ago, they fought like maddened bulls. They stared eye to eye as they contended. They grunted; they bellowed; they roared. Gilgamesh shouted out defiance in the language of Uruk and in any other language he could think of; and Enkidu muttered and stormed at Gilgamesh in the language of the beasts that once he had spoken when he was a wild man, the harsh growling of the lion of the plains.

Fury was the master now. Gilgamesh yearned to have Enkidu's life. He loved this man more dearly than life itself, and yet he prayed that it would be given him to break Enkidu's back, to hear the sharp snapping sound of his spine, to toss him aside like a worn-out cloak. So strong was his love that it had turned to the brightest of hatreds. I will send him into darkness and oblivion once again, Gilgamesh thought. I will hurl him from the Afterworld.

But though he struggled as he had never struggled in combat before, Gilgamesh was unable to budge Enkidu. Veins bulged in his forehead; the sutures that held his wound burst and blood flowed down his arm; and still he strained to throw Enkidu to the ground, and still Enkidu held his place.

And matched him, strength for strength, and kept him at bay. They stood locked that way a long moment, staring into each other's eyes, locked in unbreakable stalemate.

Then after a long while Enkidu grinned fiercely and his hard grip of battle turned subtly but unmistakably into the warm embrace of indissoluble friendship, and he said, as once he had said long ago, "Ah, Gilgamesh! There is not another one like you in all the world! Glory to the mother who bore you!"

It was like the breaking of a dam, and a rush of life-giving waters tumbling out over the summer-parched fields of the Land.

Gilgamesh too eased and altered his grip. And from him in that blessed moment of release and relief came twice-spoken words also:

"There is one other who is like me. But only one."

"No, for Enlil has given you the kingship."

"But you are my brother," said Gilgamesh, and they laughed and let go of each other and stepped back, as if seeing each other for the first time, and laughed again, and those who stood in a ring about them seemed to turn misty and vanish from view, so that in all the world there was only Gilgamesh and Enkidu, Enkidu and Gilgamesh.

"This is great foolishness, this fighting between us," Enkidu said softly.

"Very great foolishness indeed, brother."

"What need have you of shotguns and disruptors?"

"And what do I care if you choose to play with such toys?"

"Indeed, brother."

"Indeed!"

Gilgamesh looked around. They were all silent, staring – the four party men, Lovecraft, Howard, the Hairy Man, Kublai Khan, Hemingway, all astonished, mouths drooping open. They seemed stunned. Only Schweitzer appeared alert to the meaning of the moment. The doctor was beaming warmly. He came up to them and looked up at them looming far above him and said in his quiet way, "You have not injured each other? No. *Gut. Gut.* Then you must go away. Leave here, the two of you, together. Now. You have found each other: you must keep each other. What do you care for Prester John and his wars, or for Mao and his? This is no business of yours. Go. Now."

Enkidu grinned. "What do you say, brother? Shall we go off hunting together?"

"To the end of the Outback, and back again. You and I, and no one else."

"And we will hunt only with our bows and spears?"

Gilgamesh shrugged. "With disruptors, if that is how you would have it. With cannons. With nuke grenades. Ah, Enkidu, Enkidu –!"

"Gilgamesh!"

"Go," Schweitzer whispered. "Now. Leave this place and never look back. *Auf Wiedersehen! Glückliche Reise! In Gottes Namen*, go now!"

Watching them take their leave, seeing them trudge off together into the swirling winds of the Outback, Robert Howard felt a sudden sharp pang of regret and loss. How beautiful they had been, those two heroes, those two giants, as they strained and struggled! And then that sudden magic moment when the folly of their quarrel came home to them, when they were enemies no longer and brothers once more –

And now they were gone, and here he stood amidst these others, these strangers –

He had wanted to be Gilgamesh's brother, or perhaps – he barely comprehended it – something more than a brother. But that could never have been. And, knowing that it could never have been, knowing that that man who seemed so much like his Conan was lost to him forever, Howard felt tears beginning to surge uncontrollably within him.

"Bob?" Lovecraft said. "Bob, are you all right?"

She-it, Howard thought. *A man don't cry. Especially in front of other men.*

He turned away, into the wind, so Lovecraft could not see his face.

"Bob? Bob?"

She-it, Howard thought again. And he let the tears come.

Six

Without either of them saying a word they went westward, or what they hoped and thought was westward, Gilgamesh wishing that Enkidu would be the first to speak, and Enkidu, so it seemed, evidently wanting the same of him. It was a haunted land here of fire and frost, of mountains that had the shape of demons, of demons that had the shape of mountains. The sun was low on the distant horizon, but burning with a strange cold midday intensity, like a worm that was eating a hole in the sky. From time to time Gilgamesh saw some strange creature running before them, and raised his bow, and put it down again without shooting; or Enkidu it was who took aim but could not loose a shaft. It was as though the estrangement between them was not quite ended, and it was robbing them both of the will to hunt.

At last, when the silence had grown until it had the weight of a great globe of iron pressing against his back, Gilgamesh drew his breath as deep into his lungs as it would go and said suddenly, unable any longer to bear it, "Well, and will you tell me something, brother?"

"Yes?" said Enkidu, in a rush of eagerness. "Whatever it is, brother, only ask."

Gilgamesh formed the first question that came to his mind, for the sake only of ending the silence between them: "In the time that you were off by yourself, however long a time that may have been – what was the strangest thing that you saw, and where was it that you saw it?"

"Ah," Enkidu said. "The strangest thing that I saw." And he fell into a new silence so lengthy that Gilgamesh feared it would engulf them both, as the last one had, and shroud them in the chilly darkness of the soul for days to come. But then finally Enkidu said, "It was in a place in the north, beyond Cibola, beyond even Cold Sargasso. It was the doorway to the land of the living that I was seeking then, and they told me that I could find it in that place."

"The land of the living?" Gilgamesh said. "You've been looking for it also, then? For I hear that the English Queen Elizabeth has sent men in search of it, here in the Outback."

"Everyone seeks it, brother."

"Not I. Not I. It is mere fable to me, and folly."

"Be that as it may," said Enkidu. "I was off in quest of it. Perhaps I thought I would find you there, beyond that doorway in the north. But in any case there was no such doorway there, to my best awareness. Yet what I found was curious enough. I was crossing a barren plain much like this, except that there were swirls of pale blue snow everywhere in the air, and when you kicked the earth you would stir up clouds of crystals that sparkled like diamonds and gave off musical sounds. And I saw a woman before me, a fine woman with soft golden hair and heavy breasts, standing in the road and calling my name, and smiling to me."

And with that he was silent once again, as though he had finished his tale.

Gilgamesh waited, knowing there must be more, and knowing too that Enkidu had his own style in these matters of story-telling. But the moments passed, and nothing more was forthcoming. They walked on. Gilgamesh, after a time, turned toward Enkidu and said, "Did you embrace her, then?"

"Embrace her? Oh, yes, yes, that I did. I came up to her and reached for her and drew her into my arms, and quite willingly she came." He laughed. "Why would I not embrace her? She was very beautiful, brother."

"And the strangeness? What was that?"

"The strangeness, yes," Enkidu said, speaking as though from an immense distance. "I'll tell you of that. When she was in my arms, I went to stroke the smoothness of her back, as women will often like you to do. But there was no smoothness there, brother. She was a fine woman from the front, but from the back she was like a hollow tree with a rough bark."

"A demon," said Gilgamesh, and he made a gesture to invoke the protection of Father Enlil.

"A demon, yes, perhaps," Enkidu said. "But also a great disappointment, and a waste of beauty, to find that she was only half beautiful, and monstrous in the other half."

"She did you no harm, though?" asked Gilgamesh uneasily.

"Only to my sense of what is fitting and proper. A beautiful woman should be beautiful through and through, or else there should be no beauty about her at all. That is what I believe." After a pause Enkidu said, "There is more."

"Go on, then."

"I let go of her and went from her, and in a little while I came to a second woman standing beside the road, whose hair was scarlet and whose skin was white and whose face was like that of a goddess. She held out her arms to me, and I drew her close, and her far side was all bones, bare and hard and cold, not a scrap of flesh to cover them."

"How sad."

"Sad, yes, very sad. And the next woman –"

"The next? How many were there?"

"The next," said Enkidu, "had black hair and golden skin, and small breasts so lovely they would make you cry. And I turned her around and her back was all seaweed and shells. And the next after that –"

"The next after that, yes."

"Snakes and toads behind her, and the marks of leprosy. But in front she was shining like a maiden, and her eyes were blue and her hair was the color of sunrise. You would have wept, brother, at the beauty of her, and at the evil that was behind her."

"There were others after her," Gilgamesh said, "and each was worse than the last, is that not so?"

"Yes. Every hundred paces, a different one. They seemed to spring like flowers from the ground. And I went on and on, until I was running, at last, and they were waving their arms at me with a motion that was like that of the branches of the trees that grow beneath the sea, and I ran, and ran, and ran, until I came to the last of them, who was more beautiful even than any of the others, and she said, Here I am, Enkidu, I am the one. But I shook my head. I told her to keep back from me. I am the one you seek, she said, I am the one. When she came toward me I raised my bow, and put an arrow on the string, and told her I would send her to her next life if she came another step closer."

"And did she?"

"No," said Enkidu in deepest sorrow. "She turned, then, and walked very slowly away with her shoulders downcast, never once looking back. And from the other side she was lovelier yet than in front. She was perfect. She was without flaw. I watched her go until she was lost to my sight. And then I ran the other way, not stopping until the darkness came. For it seemed certain to me that the door to the land of the living was not to be found in that place. And I knew, brother, that if I had gone after her and embraced her she would have changed in my arms, and become something far more loathsome than any that I had seen earlier, and the pain of that would remain with me forever. That is so, would you not say?"

"Who can tell, when demons are involved? But perhaps you were right to flee. And in any case it is a very strange story, yes, very strange, Enkidu."

"It is the strangest one that I can tell you, of all the things that befell me while I was wandering alone."

Gilgamesh nodded.

"It is a very strange story," he said again.

"And you, brother? What did you do, in that time when we were apart from each other?"

"I hunted," said Gilgamesh. "By myself, seeking no company, though occasionally finding some, or rather being found. It was a cold time for me, brother."

"We should never have been apart."

"No," said Gilgamesh. "Never. But we were. And now that time is over."

"It was demons that came between us," Enkidu said. "It was demons that made us quarrel."

"Yes," said Gilgamesh. "I think so too."

They fell silent yet again. Then Enkidu said, "Well, brother, where shall we go now? Is there any special path through this Outback that you follow?"

"Only the path that my feet find for me, step by step by step."

"Ah. I understand. Well, that path will be my path, too," said Enkidu.

They made camp that night at a place where two dry rivers crossed in the flatlands, and jagged narrow mountains rose before them like blades, straight from the desert floor to bewildering heights. Enkidu chased a thing that was like a black gazelle, but with ropy green strands sprouting from the rim of its back and startling red horns that were curved like scimitars, and caught it and threw it down and slew it. They skinned it together, and roasted it by a fire that Gilgamesh made out of curious gray coals that were heaped in the riverbed; and afterward they sat quietly together, neither sleeping nor fully awake, saying very little. It was sufficient to be together again. From the first, from the time in lost ancient Uruk of the other world when they had met and wrestled and dropped at once into fast friendship, each had seen in the other an equal, a complement, a second half. They were nothing like each other in any way but size and strength, for Gilgamesh in that other life had been a king's son, raised in luxury to inherit power, and huge shaggy Enkidu had been born in the wilderness, a wild thing himself who ran with beasts and spoke no tongue but the tongue of beasts until he reached manhood; but they had seen at first sight that each fitted the other like two parts of a single whole, and it had been like that ever since for them, except for this time of estrangement that now was at its end.

In the moment just before first light, when souls hang suspended between eternity and oblivion, Gilgamesh sat suddenly upright, oppressed with the feeling that the sea was about to sweep down upon him with killing force. But they were far from the sea here, as far as they could possibly be.

"Brother?" he said.

"Listen!" said Enkidu, already alert.

Gilgamesh nodded. He heard foul mocking chittering sounds, like those of dung-birds or grave-jackals. His hand went to his weapon and he leaped to his feet, taking a dancing stride forward and swinging around. Just then the thin strands of first sunlight came over the low ridge behind them, and with it came a dozen creatures of the darkness, creatures with the shape of men but horridly distorted, burly short-legged things with great dangling arms that seemed infinitely long in the pale red light of the newly risen sun.

"Enki! Enlil!" Gilgamesh bellowed, and he and Enkidu went unhesitatingly toward them.

With his first stroke he cut two in half, and Enkidu another. The sundered bodies went sprawling, spilling a thick golden fluid. Gilgamesh whirled, ready to face the next that came at him; but they were backing away, making cowardly little snuffling noises. Were they frightened off by this first slaughter? A deception, only: for six more came from the side, and at least as many from the other, flinging themselves on the two Sumerians without fear. Gilgamesh plucked one from Enkidu's shoulders and hurled it far to the rear, and Enkidu, turning, sliced one free of Gilgamesh's leg, at which it was tugging in an attempt to topple him.

"Back to back, brother!" Enkidu cried.

Gilgamesh nodded. They swung about and pressed close against each other, forming themselves into a single strange being with eight limbs and two furious swords. Neither needed to give the other any further cue; they moved with one accord, now this way, now that, slashing, skewering, slaughtering. Within moments half a dozen of the ugly attackers lay dead, and the rest were circling uneasily, mewling and hissing as they looked for some way of breaking through the defenses of the two men.

Then the sun cleared the ridge entirely and its full light burst upon the scene; and the surviving creatures, making no attempt at seizing their dead, turned and went racing off toward the west as though afraid of being scalded by the newborn brightness of the day. One turned to glare back at them. Gilgamesh saw a cruel parody of humankind, a broad low dark forehead, a pair of glowering red eyes, claw-tipped hands wide outspread. He shook his fist at it and shouted in the old tongue of the Land, ordering it and all its kind to be gone. The creature fled, snuffling and hissing. The others ran beyond it, scrambling across the broken land and vanishing one by one into burrows and fissures.

Enkidu stared at the corpses that lay strewn about. With a shudder he said, "By Enlil, brother, it's a foul land that spawns such hideous beasts as those."

"Demons, do you think?"

"Mere apes, so it seems to me."

Shrugging, Gilgamesh said, "Apes or demons, it makes no difference. I would rather find myself among such creatures than in the company of fools."

"And which fools do you mean, brother?"

Gilgamesh jerked his thumb fiercely backward, over his shoulder. "Fools such as dwell in the cities that lie behind us."

"Ah. Ah. Prester John, you mean?"

"He is less of a fool than most. No, I mean such cities as Nova Roma, and the other ones of the distant east –"

"Elektrograd, do you mean? Guillotine? The cities of the Later Dead?"

Gilgamesh nodded. "Those are the ones, yes. My only purpose now is to keep myself far from those places where the little squabbling grasping ones are, the ones who yearn to be king of this, and emperor of that, and – what is the word? – president? Yes, president. Sultan, kaiser, tsar. Shah. I intend to put half the Afterworld, or more, between myself and all such people, and all such cities."

Enkidu laughed. "And to think that while I was wandering in far and lonely places I imagined that you were still living the soft life in Nova Roma, dining one night with Bismarck and the next with Cromwell, and then with Esarhaddon or Nefertiti –"

"Nova Roma!" Gilgamesh scowled. "I hated the place. I couldn't wait to be quit of it. If I never see Nova Roma again, or Bismarck, and Cromwell, and Lenin – or hear so much as their names, even –" He shook his head. "No, brother, that's a phase of my life that's over and done with. The simple huntsman's way, that's what I crave. I'll keep myself far from all the capitals where the Later Dead may lurk. Elektrograd, Guillotine, Smoketown, Hypoluxo, High Versailles – I loathe their very names! No, Enkidu, it's the Outback for me, now and forever."

"And for me also," said Enkidu. And they embraced on it.

It would have pleased Gilgamesh to spend an eternity and a half, and then an eternity more, roaming these wild unfriendly lands with no companion but Enkidu. Like hand and glove they fitted one another, so that there was scarcely any need for them to speak, but each knew the other's mind. To march on, day after day under the harsh red sun, pitting themselves against the nightmare beasts of this cruel terrain, testing eye and hand and strength of arm against the diabolical vigor and force of the hell-creatures that lurked in the Outback wastelands – ah, that was the only true joy, Gilgamesh thought! That was the one life that held pleasure and fulfilment! Gilgamesh and Enkidu, Enkidu and Gilgamesh, just the two of them alone, far from the vanities and the foolishnesses and the false strivings of the chattering city-folk!

But it was not to be.

Empty and bleak as this country was, for the most part, yet it was not empty entirely. No part of the Afterworld could be, not the ice-entombed polar regions nor the blazing midworld belt nor this parched barren Outback; for there were uncountable billions of souls to house here – the souls, so it had been concluded by those who made it their task to study such matters, of everyone who had ever lived upon the former earth. And though the Afterworld was immense beyond the comprehension of even the wisest geographers, there was no territory of it that did not have its few scattered settlers or at least its roaming nomad packs. Gilgamesh and Enkidu were hard pressed, as they made their zigzag random way across the face of the land, to maintain their solitude pure and unbroken more than a few days at a time.

Now it was some dismal farm they stumbled across, with shimbleshamble barns of unpainted wood, and rooks and vultures perched in the crook-armed trees behind it, and a family of withered gray-faced folk struggling against the miserable land. And now it was some caravan plodding from hither to thither among the far-flung cities of the plain; and now it was a wandering pilgrim, a solitary like themselves. When they could, the Sumerians generally avoided those whom they encountered. But sometimes they could not avoid without giving needless and dangerous offense, or the only route ahead lay through populated territory; and sometimes, even, pressed by hunger or thirst or the simple need occasionally to hear the voices of their own kind, they chose of their free will to break their aloofness and allow themselves a few hours of company before moving on.

Thus it was, almost despite themselves, that they fell in with these folk or these or these, and sat by their firesides and traded gossip with them and learned the names of princes and nations of the Outback, and of the vain ambitions and hollow dreams that drove them, the wars that were being fought here, the schemes and follies, the madness. Thus it was that the two Sumerians, who had dwelled for more years than they could remember among the turbulent cities that crowded the eastern coast of the great landmass that was the Afterworld, learned that even here in this wilder place that was the Outback the same lunacies held sway, the same insane attempts to replicate in this life the errors of that other one. So the truth sank home:

humans are as humans do, there is no sanctuary from their frailty, all is the same everywhere no matter what sort of clothes are worn or languages spoken. It was a somber truth to learn, and Gilgamesh, searching in the misty depths of his time-choked memory, had the uncomfortable feeling that he was not learning it for the first time.

Though they had rarely journeyed in the same direction more than three days running, they discovered that in fact they had been moving westward more often than not, and now were almost at the Outback's farther end. This they learned in a place called Vectis Minima, which was a crossroads and a hostelry of five huts presided over by a pale-eyed old man with a face more pitted and baleful than the Moon's. Here they came to take refuge from a cold black rain which fell in furling sheets that did not strike the ground, but nevertheless sent forth a chill that reached the bone. And here Gilgamesh asked, in an idle moment of curiosity, where they might be and what lay ahead.

"You are some twelve days' journey from the sea here," the shriveled old innkeeper told them.

"The sea? What sea is that?" Gilgamesh said, startled.

"Why, the White Sea, the Demon Sea. What else? What other sea would you expect?"

"To be sure," Gilgamesh muttered. "But we are strangers from the east."

"Ah, the east," said the innkeeper. "Vulking Land, you mean? Or Lord Wolfram's Domain?"

"Farther east than that," said Gilgamesh. "A thousand leagues farther. Ten thousand, perhaps. Nova Roma was our last home."

"Nova Roma," said the innkeeper, in a quiet way, as though Gilgamesh had named some other star. "Would you be of Nova Roma, then? Well, you are far from there now. Look you." And he dipped his fingertip in the grim gray wine of the place, and drew a line on the peeling wooden tabletop. "Here. The sea is here, and we are over here. This is the road to Lo-yang, and this the road to Cabuldidiri. You know of those places? No? Well, you've missed very little. Straight on here, this is the road that leads to the isle of Brasil, which surely you know."

"Brasil?" Gilgamesh said. "What is that?"

"I know of it," said Enkidu suddenly. "By report, at least. It's the famous island of wizards and sorcerers, is it not?"

"So it is, the magical isle, the haunted isle," said the innkeeper. "Where Simon Magus is king, and may all the demons preserve you from meeting *him*. Well, then, and these mountains here, these are the Mountains of the Moths" – he drew them in with stipplings of wine on the dry wood – "and beyond them we have five cities, by name Torfaeus, Gardilone, Pizigani, Camerata, and – and – well, there is a fifth, it does not come to my mind. Then here, as we proceed to the north –"

"Enough," said Gilgamesh. "You tell me more than I demand to know."

His mood had grown darker with each name the old man had rolled forth. He had not thought to come to the desert's end so soon; but he realized now that it might not have been soon at all, that he and Enkidu might have spent years or even centuries in the wasteland since leaving the court of Prester John, while thinking it was only a matter of months. The passage of time was always uncertain here. And just ahead of them now lay a coastal land that was new to him, and one that was obviously much the same as the coast he had left behind, more cities, more kings, more scheming, more folly. The thing to do, he thought, was to turn and go back, into the heartland once more. Surely they had not exhausted it all.

But that too was not to be. For they chose the road to the north, to the place that was called Cabuldidiri, thinking that from there they would cut back inland on some passable wilderness track. But they had gone no more than a league or two before the road began veering in a troublesome way toward the west, as if it were not of a mind to let them reach Cabuldidiri. They could see a valley far beyond, and a fair-sized town in it, resting upon a cleft between two slab-sided hills. Surely that town was Cabuldidiri. Yet the road would not allow them to go that way. Perpetually it swerved away. Even when they left the road and made their trek through the rough places that seemed to lead eastward, they found themselves moving before very long in the other direction.

"What is this?" Enkidu asked. "Why does the city slip away from us, brother?"

"Enlil only knows. Perhaps there's no city there at all, or no road. Or wizards move the road each night, by way of amusing themselves."

"What will we do?"

"Follow our feet," said Gilgamesh. "And our feet will follow their destiny, and so we will learn our own."

The destiny of their feet seemed to deliver them into an ever-narrowing canyon that ran, so far as they were able to tell, from east to west. Though that was the opposite of the direction they intended to follow, they had no choice but to obey, for the land rose up on both sides of them like walls of glass and they were compelled into the canyon like animals driven into a trap. Gilgamesh found this irritating, and walked along sullenly, eyeing the towering ramparts to the right and to the left in search of some opening in them. But there was none. The walls, now so close on either side that Gilgamesh could almost touch them with both hands at once, had a bright sheen, like that of polished pink marble, and the narrow path beneath their feet was of red earth marked by lines of busy green-and-black insects. In order to see the sky one had to bend one's neck far back, and look straight up.

After a time wagon tracks began to appear before them.

"We are following a caravan," Enkidu observed. "Look, do you see the fresh droppings? What shall we do, brother? Wait here until they have gone onward?"

"I think not," said Gilgamesh. "This is a dead place, very stifling to the soul, and nothing in it to eat but bugs. We'll move ahead, and overtake them, and perhaps we'll travel with them awhile, if they prove friendly."

"As you say, brother."

Three days and three nights more, and then they overtook the caravan: a dozen ragged wagons, shabby and sad, some with landsails and some drawn by gaunt and weary-looking pack animals. A dog set up a frantic barking the moment the Sumerians came into view, and the caravan halted at once. Men and a few women armed with pistols and automatic weapons jumped down, crouching in the red earth as if expecting attack.

They were all Later Dead, Gilgamesh observed with distaste. "Come," he said to Enkidu. "Let's go peacefully toward them. They must think we're scouts for a larger force coming behind us, or else they are more than uncommonly nervous."

Holding his hands raised high, he went forward.

The caravan folk were slow to overcome their suspicions. Their leader, a burly, big-bellied man named van der Heyden, who had two ammunition belts slung over his middle and a weapon jutting under each arm, questioned them for a long while, asking where they had been, where they meant to go, whether they had companions to the rear. "We are only wandering huntsmen," Gilgamesh replied, "and there are none of us but what you see."

"Hunters? Out here? What's to hunt out here?"

"We would have taken a more easterly track, but we were urged by the nature of the road into this canyon."

"Then Brasil's not your destination?"

"Hardly," said Gilgamesh. "We wish to avoid it."

Van der Heyden chuckled. "Not much chance of that now. This canyon comes out just to the mainland side of Brasil. You've got no way of avoiding it now."

"What if we turn back?" Enkidu said.

"Then you'll find yourself where you just were. And it's a long hungry walk to get there." The burly man's eyes narrowed. "You don't *look* like fools, either of you. But why would anyone want to be traveling like you are in a place like this? There's got to be more to it than that."

"What you see," said Gilgamesh, "are two men who care nothing for the life of the cities, and seek only solitude – which proves harder to find in this part of the land than we had expected. We are not spies and we plan no treacheries. If you like, we'll join you and give you whatever assistance you require until we emerge from this canyon, in return for our food and a blanket to cover us at night. If not, well, we'll move on ahead, and make shift by ourselves."

Van der Heyden considered that a moment.

"Can you fight?" he asked, at length.

"What do you suppose?" Enkidu said, grinning down from his great height.

"With what? Swords? Bows and arrows?"

"We do well with those," said Gilgamesh. "But we have mastered your weapons also. If we are not wanted, though – "

"No," van der Heyden said. "Come along with us. We can use a couple of fellows your size, I think."

"In that case," Gilgamesh said, "you should know that it is some days since last we ate anything."

"So I suspected," said van der Heyden.

The caravan was bound for Brasil out of the Outback city of Lo-yang, bearing a cargo of goods to sell in the city ruled by Simon Magus. Van der Heyden was careful not to specify the nature of the goods, nor were there any clues apparent. Plainly, from the heavy-set man's close-mouthedness and from the uneasy way that the merchants had greeted the two Sumerians, the cargo was a precious one, and there were fears of brigandry in this area. But Gilgamesh asked no questions. His plan was only to travel with van der Heyden to the mouth of the canyon, and then to turn away, whether to north or south he did not know, in the hope of finding a route back into the unpopulated areas.

It was slow going. The canyon was barely wide enough to let the wagons pass, and in places it seemed impossible that they would get through at all; but van der Heyden had a trick of tipping the wagons up first on the left-hand wheels, then on the right, and somehow maneuvering them around the jutting bosses of rock that blocked the way in the narrowest places. Gradually the canyon grew wider; and the wind was softer and more moist here, a sure sign that they were approaching the coast. Now the canyon walls sloped outward instead of rising sheerly, and there was some vegetation on them. And there was game to be caught. Though the caravan had provisions of its own, van der Heyden evidently had intended to supplement them with animals taken along the way, and the Sumerians earned the price of their transport by going out on hunting expeditions along the slopes.

Generally Gilgamesh and Enkidu hunted together. But on one occasion Gilgamesh went alone, and a great error it proved to be.

The lead wagon had thrown one of its wheels that day. It lay yawed over practically on its side, having cut a deep rut with its bare axle in the powdery red earth. Van der Heyden pounded its sides in perplexity; and then, turning toward the massive Sumerians, called out, "Here! You two, lend us a hand!"

"We're going out hunting," said Gilgamesh. "Those hills up there are rich with game."

"Well, one of you go, then, and the other give us some help. We've got to lift the damned wagon, don't you see?"

Gilgamesh hesitated. A surge of anger ran through him. Lifting wagons out of ruts was no work for one who had once been a king; and there was good hunting waiting for him. He would have replied hotly to van der Heyden, but Enkidu, as if sensing what was about to happen, put his hand quickly to his friend's arm and said to the other, "I'll help you with your wagon. My brother Gilgamesh will go to seek the game."

"Enkidu –"

"It's all right, brother. I'll put their wagon to rights, and if there's still enough light by the time I'm done, I'll follow your trail and join you in the hills. Go. Go, now, while the game's still in your grasp."

"But –"

"Go," Enkidu said again.

Gilgamesh watched, still angered, as Enkidu went to join the group straining at the wagon. Putting his shoulder to the wagon's side, Enkidu gestured to Gilgamesh to take his leave; and after a moment, scowling, the Sumerian nodded and stalked away. It was already late in the day for hunting. Quickly he clambered up the slope of the canyon wall, clinging to the twisted, gnarled trunks of the almost leafless shrubs that sprouted here. Some white-furred creature not much larger than a goat came bounding out suddenly, looked at him in amazement, and took off in frantic leaps toward the top of the wall. Gilgamesh at once gave chase, never taking his eyes from the dazzling whiteness of the beast as he ascended. The meat would be tasty, perhaps; the hide would make a splendid cloak, beyond any doubt. Up he went, and up still farther, and through a cleft in the flank of the canyon wall, and onward, and onward, tirelessly following the flash of white.

In the end he lost the creature entirely, to his great annoyance. But he prowled more deeply into the secondary canyon that he had come upon, thinking he might find another that was like it. That proved a hopeless quest, and he had to settle for smaller and less pleasing game. As the shadows began to deepen Gilgamesh retraced his steps, emerging from the little canyon into the main one, and starting downward then toward the place where the caravan had halted.

The caravan was shielded from his sight by a dip in the canyon wall. He was unable to see it until he was halfway down; but what he saw then, before any of the wagons came into view, was a plume of black smoke that somehow did not seem like the smoke of a camp-fire. Gilgamesh raced forward to the far side of the dip, and looked over the edge.

"Gods!" he cried.

The wagons lay scattered and overturned on the valley floor as though they had been tossed about by the hand of the king of the demons. Some were ablaze. All had been split open and ransacked. And everywhere about them lay the merchants, weltering in their own blood. Gilgamesh saw van der Heyden lying on his back, eyes staring rigidly. There was a great wound in his chest. Others had fallen face down, or had managed to scramble halfway under one of the wagons. No one was moving.

"Enkidu?" Gilgamesh called.

He let slip the animals he was carrying and ran in wild skidding strides down to the floor of the valley. At close range the scene was one of even more frightful devastation than he had thought. They were all dead here, the men, the women, the children, even the pack animals, all but one big brindle dog, Ajax by name, who ran up and down, barking furiously. And they had been slain with a ferocity and a vehemence that even battle-hardened Gilgamesh found repellent: a terrible butchery, a ghastly slaughter. The wagons had been ransacked and utterly destroyed.

And Enkidu? Where was Enkidu?

The sense of his absence rang in Gilgamesh's mind like the tolling of a terrible bell.

Frantically he searched behind this wagon and under that one, and with all his great strength he roared the name of his friend; but of Enkidu there was no sign at all, neither of his person nor of his weapons. That was puzzling. Had the attackers carried him off? So it would seem – unless Enkidu had not been here at all when the attack took place, unless he had set out into the hills in search of Gilgamesh, and somehow they had missed each other's path when Gilgamesh had returned from the hunt –

No. In this narrow canyon it was impossible that Enkidu would have failed to find and follow Gilgamesh's trail. And Gilgamesh's echoing cries – surely Enkidu would have heard those, no matter how far he had wandered –

"Enkidu! Enkidu!"

Gilgamesh went on bellowing his friend's name until his voice was in shreds, but to no purpose. Night was falling now. Enkidu would certainly come down from those hills as darkness approached, if he was up there at all. Gone again, then? Dead? Carried off into slavery?

Baffled, sorely troubled, Gilgamesh hauled the smoldering wagons together to form a pyre, and threw the mutilated bodies of the dead on them, and stood by, uttering the words that were proper, while the flames blazed upward. Then he turned and walked away, heading swiftly westward in the gathering shadows. He did not want to spend the night in this place of death. His soul felt empty. He had had so little time, this last reunion, before Enkidu was snatched away once more. Gods, thought Gilgamesh, are we never to be allowed to remain together?

The dog Ajax followed him. Gilgamesh waved him back, but the dog, barking in such a frenzy as if he were struggling to speak in words, would not be dismissed. Gilgamesh had no wish for a dog; and yet he realized he could hardly abandon the animal here to die. In any case sending the dog away appeared impossible. "Come, then," Gilgamesh told him, and they walked on together through the night.

When there was light enough for him to see again, Gilgamesh realized that he had come to the mouth of the canyon. The walls had opened here and were so low that they were nothing more than an embankment, far off on each side. To the north and south rose great mountains that belched flame and smoke that stained the sky. Ahead of him lay a broad plain, strangely dotted with ghostly twisted masses of pink stone something like the stalagmites one sometimes sees in caves, rising by the hundreds and seeming for all the world to be a multitude of petrified souls set close by one another. Behind these he saw a camp of tents, with people moving about them; and still farther in the distance was a shimmering body of water, and a ship with a scarlet sail riding at anchor just off shore. He had reached the White Sea of the far west.

Breaking into a steady loping trot, Gilgamesh ran forward through the field of strange stone shapes toward the place of the tents. Men in costumes that seemed Roman to him looked up as he approached.

"Who are you?" a sentry demanded.

"Gilgamesh of Uruk is who I am. I seek my friend, Enkidu by name, who –"

"Come with me."

"You know where Enkidu is?"

"Come with me," said the sentry again, impassively.

Wearily Gilgamesh let himself be led along into the group of tents, and to one that was larger than the rest, made of fabric of great richness and many colors. Within, sprawling on a sort of wooden throne, was a man of late middle years, balding, portly, fleshy-faced, his face mottled with red blotches, his eyes red-rimmed from too much wine and too little sleep.

The sentry said, "We found him wandering around near the Frozen Souls, your majesty. He calls himself Gilgamesh of Uruk, and he says that he's looking for –"

The man on the throne waved the sentry to silence. Leaning forward, he studied Gilgamesh with keen curiosity.

"Uruk?" he said. "You come from Uruk?"

"It was the city of my birth."

"Indeed. Gilgamesh of Uruk. *Uruk*, truly?"

"Of Uruk, yes," said Gilgamesh with some irritation.

"That city of great treasure," the other said, and a misty look came into his eyes. "That city so dear to my soul. How remarkable, to meet one who comes from Uruk! And have you been there lately, my friend?"

Gilgamesh stared. "How could that be? Uruk is long gone, and all but forgotten."

"Is it? No, I think not. Neither gone nor forgotten, but merely hard to find, according to the reports I hear." The man on the throne gave him a long slow look. "Yet perhaps we could find it, you and I."

"Uruk was a city of the other world."

"It is a city of this world also. With many people of your kind living there."

"It is?" said Gilgamesh, bewildered. "There are?" That was impossible. In all his years in the Afterworld he had heard nothing of that. "A new Uruk, here? Who says? Where? What are you telling me?"

"Where? Ah, that is something I hope to learn. For I would like greatly to find this place Uruk, you see. Its wealth is beyond counting. Its treasure fills storehouse upon storehouse. You and I could find it together, I think. We are in need of a grand adventure, we Brasilians, and what could be more splendid than to go in quest of Uruk, eh? Does that interest you, friend Gilgamesh, to journey with me in search of Uruk?"

In rising annoyance verging on anger Gilgamesh cried, "Who are you? What is this all about?"

"I? Did no one tell you?" The blotchy-faced man laughed. "I am the master of the isle of Brasil, Simon Magus by name. That is my ship in the harbor. We will be sailing soon for my city, which lies just across the bay. Will you come with us? Yes, Gilgamesh, come with me to Brasil." He beckoned a servant. "Some wine for Gilgamesh! Gilgamesh of Uruk!" Again Simon laughed. "Come with me to Brasil, yes. And let us speak of finding the treasures of long-lost Uruk, you and I. What do you say, Gilgamesh? What do you say?"

Seven

There was fire everywhere: red fire in the sky, blue fire in the water, green fire dancing along the rim of the shore that receded behind the swiftly moving boat. The air had the stink of sulphur about it, and worse things. The clouds here were thick and heavy, with fat gray bellies that scraped against the nearby mountains. And the mountains themselves were demons in stone: a dozen angry volcanoes that were spewing fumes and flame up and down the coastal plain as far as Gilgamesh could see. Out here on the western edge of the Afterworld, beyond the bleak plains of the Outback, it seemed to the Sumerian that the whole world must be burning, down to its deepest roots.

The dolphin-prowed vessel with the scarlet sail plunged on and on through the reef-strewn phosphorescent sea toward the island of Brasil. The boat was the royal yacht of the dictator Simon Magus, who was somewhere below decks, far gone in wine.

It sounded like madness, all this talk of finding Uruk. But perhaps not. Perhaps not. It was worth at least listening to what Simon had to say. Why not? Gilgamesh wondered. He knew nothing of this supposed Uruk; but if it was true that the city of his life had been founded anew in the Afterworld, and these Brasilians had heard some tale that could help him discover where it might be situated, why not strike a deal with Simon? What was life, in this interminable life after death, if not one long unending *Why Not*? He was again without Enkidu. Very little mattered for him now. Why not go on this quest? Why not?

The towering dark-haired Sumerian stared toward Brasil. Off in the distance the magical island glimmered in the half-darkness with a strange light of its own.

"Been here before?" a voice said.

Gilgamesh looked to his left and down, a long way down. "Are you talking to me?"

"To my shadow," the man standing beside him at the rail said. He was short and sharp-nosed, with thick curly hair and dark greasy skin. "I was trying to make conversation. It's an old shipboard custom. Do you mind?"

Gilgamesh glanced balefully at the little man. There was a soft, sleek, pampered look about him. He dressed well, a Roman-style toga and glossy Italian leather shoes, and some sort of little brocaded skullcap perched jauntily at the back of his head. A shrewd face. Bright beady eyes with undeniable intelligence in them. But something fundamentally unlikable about him, Gilgamesh thought. And pushy. Surely he ought to be able to see at a glance that Gilgamesh wasn't the sort who cared to be approached by strangers.

The big brindle dog Ajax, sleeping by Gilgamesh's side, awoke, peered, growled. Ajax didn't much care for the little man either, it would seem.

Gilgamesh scowled. "I don't know you."

"Who knows anybody in this Godforsaken place? My name's Herod. Herod Agrippa, actually. What I asked you was whether you'd been to Brasil before."

"Probably," said Gilgamesh, shrugging.

"Probably? You aren't sure?"

Gilgamesh considered tossing the tiresome little pest over the side.

"Maybe I have, maybe I haven't. You wander back and forth across the face of the Afterworld long enough and all places begin to look the same to you."

"Not to me," Herod said. "And I've done my share of wandering. More than my share. A regular wandering Jew, that's me. Anyway, Brasil's different. I know, I know, memory's sometimes a problem here, but if you'd been to Brasil before, you'd remember it. It's unforgettable. Trust me."

"A wandering Jew?" said Gilgamesh vaguely. "I've heard that story, I think."

"Who hasn't? But I'm not *the* Wandering Jew, you understand. That's Ahasuerus. He's still cruising around Upside, the way the original curse requires. Roaming Earth until the end of the world comes, which apparently hasn't quite happened yet. I'm simply a Jew who wanders. A different one. Herod."

"So you told me." Pushy little bastard, yes, Gilgamesh thought. From the pushiness alone, it would seem that the little man was one of the Later Dead. But yet there was some sort of Early Dead emanation about this man too. A borderline type, maybe. From that period when what the Later Dead called B.C. was shading into their A.D. time. Gilgamesh rummaged through his thousands of years of memories. "I met a Herod once. Some sort of minor desert prince, he was."

"King of Judaea, in fact."

"If you say so."

"Plump-faced man, bald in back, bloodshot eyes?"

"He might have been. He had a rotten look about him, that much I recall. Like fruit left out in the rain too long."

"Herod the Great, that's who you mean. My grandfather. A very nasty man, that one. A very bad piece of business indeed. Ten wives – that alone should show you how unstable he was. And other character deficiencies. A total paranoid, in fact.

Though all that ugly nonsense about Salome and John the Baptist, the seven veils, the silver platter – that wasn't him, you know. That was his son Herod Antipas, just as crazy. And it didn't actually happen anything like that. The silver platter stuff was only a fable, and as for Salome –"

"Silver platter? Salome? Little man, what are you prattling about?"

"On the other hand," Herod went on, as though Gilgamesh had not spoken, "My grandfather *did* order the slaying of the first-born. Including his own. The man was a lunatic. I'm not surprised you didn't care for him. He cut a soft deal for himself with Augustus, though. Augustus was always willing to do business with lunatics if he saw political benefits in it for himself. Which is the only reasonable explanation of how my grandfather managed to hold his throne under the Romans for so long. But I understand Augustus won't have anything to do with him now. That's Cleopatra's doing. Because Cleopatra still hates him – old Herod turned her down when she propositioned him, didn't like the shape of her nose, or something like that, but imagine carrying a silly grudge for God knows how many centuries –"

"You buzz like a wasp," Gilgamesh muttered. "Do you never stop talking?"

"I like to talk, yes. You don't, I assume. The strong silent type. A difference of style, nothing to get upset about. Oh, I say, look there – there goes Vesuvius again!"

"Vesuvius?"

Herod gestured toward the island-city. "Our volcano. It's named for the one they had back of Pompeii, in the other world. Smack in the middle of downtown, it is. You ever see anything so gorgeous?"

Gilgamesh looked off across the channel toward distant Brasil. There was new fire in the sky, a single startling point of brilliant scarlet cutting through the murky smoke-fouled atmosphere like a torch, fifty times as bright as the flames coming from the mainland volcanoes. As though driven by a giant pump the blaze rose higher and higher, climbing toward the roof of the cosmos. Under its blinding glare the towers and battlements of the city took on a dazzling mirror-bright sheen.

"And the city?" Gilgamesh asked. "Will it be destroyed?"

Herod laughed. "There's an eruption just like this every week. Sometimes more often than that. The Brasilians wouldn't have it any other way. But it never does any harm. All light and no heat, that's the deal in the contract. And never any particulate matter. You heard about Pompeii, didn't you? In Rome, that was. I mean the *real* Rome, the original one. We've got a lot of Pompeiians living in Brasil. After the way Pompeii got trashed in 79, it's hardly surprising that the Brasilians don't want an encore here. That's 79 A.D., you know. If you count your years Later Dead style. If you count your years at all. At any rate it was after my time, probably after yours. You talk to anybody who was there who lives in Brasil now, he'll tell you that it was a total nightmare, but he'll also say that he can't get to sleep at night if there isn't a decent volcano rumbling away nearby. Amazing the way some people not only adapt to danger but actually come to depend on living in the constant presence of–"

Gilgamesh was barely paying attention. He was staring at the volcano-riven night sky. In that sudden fiery illumination a host of air-borne monsters and demons stood revealed. Things that were all mouth and no body, things that were all wing and no head, things that were mere claws, things that were nothing but giant red-streaked yellow eyes borne up by jets of green gas, all of them whirling and screeching high above the sea. Ajax, barking and snarling, capered up and down the deck, leaping wildly as if to challenge the monstrosities that thronged the sky.

Herod laughed. "Simon's pets. I told you, once you see Brasil you never forget it. Demons everywhere you look. And wizards. Sorcerers, mages, thaumaturges. Simon collects them, you know. You can't walk nine paces without someone trying to turn you inside out with one of his tricks."

"Let them try," Gilgamesh said.

He drew an imaginary bow and sent an imaginary shaft soaring through the gullet of one of the foulest of the monsters overhead.

"Oh, they'd leave *you* alone, I think. Man your size, who'd fool around with you? And you look like you might have a little magic yourself. Simon hire you for his bodyguard, did he?"

"I am not a mercenary," said Gilgamesh stiffly.

"You look like you were a fighting man."

"A warrior, yes. But never for hire, except once, when I was a boy in exile. I was a king."

"Ah. A king! We have something in common, then. I was a king too, you know."

"Were you?" said Gilgamesh without interest.

"For four or five years, anyway, after Caligula finally banished my miserable uncle Antipas from Judaea and gave the place to me. Very popular with my subjects, I was, if you don't mind my saying it. I think I did quite a decent job, and if I had lived a little longer I might actually have been able to wipe out Christianity before it really got started, thereby saving the whole world six bushels of trouble, but –" Herod paused. "You aren't a Christian by any chance, are you? No, no, you don't look the type. But you say you were a king. Where was that, may I ask? Somewhere out toward Armenia, maybe? Cilicia?"

This was becoming infuriating.

Gilgamesh drew himself up to his full looming height and intoned, "Be it known to you that I am Gilgamesh of Uruk, great king, king of Uruk, king of kings, lord of the Land of the Two Rivers."

"King of kings?" Herod repeated. "Lord of the Land of the Two Rivers?" He nodded as though mightily impressed. "Ah. Indeed. And what rivers would those be?"

"You don't know?"

"You must forgive me, my friend. I am a mere provincial, a Judaean, even though it was my good fortune to be educated at the court in Rome. Although I was probably taught something about those Two Rivers of yours they seem to have slipped through one of the many damnable holes in my memory, and therefore –"

Gilgamesh had heard such speeches many times before. The Afterworld was full of Johnny-come-latelies.

Coolly he said, "You Romans knew my country by the name of Mesopotamia."

"Oh, *those* rivers!" Herod cried. "Why didn't you say so? King of Mesopotomia! A Parthian, then, is that what you are? Some relative of Mithridates?"

I *will* throw him overboard, Gilgamesh thought in fury.

With great control he said, "Not a Parthian, no. A

Sumerian. We are before the Parthians. Before the Babylonians and Akkadians. Before the Romans as well. *Long* before the Romans."

"A thousand pardons," Herod said.

Gilgamesh glowered and turned away. He peered bleakly into the fire-riven night. The eruption over Brasil was dying down, now. He wondered how much longer it would be before they reached the island. None too soon, if he had to listen to this Herod's maddening jabber all the way across from the mainland.

After a while Herod said, "Do you intend to be king again?"

"What? Why should I?"

"Most kings who come here do."

"Are *you* a king again?" Gilgamesh asked, without turning.

"I prefer not to be. I never found being a king all that fascinating, to tell you the truth. And I like living in Brasil too much. It's the first place that's felt like home to me since I died. But Brasil is Simon's town, and I don't have the urge to try to take it away from him, not that I'd be able to. If he enjoys being boss here, let him do it, is what I say."

"I understand," said Gilgamesh. "You are beyond these ambitions."

"Well, you know the old line about how it's better to reign in the Afterworld than to serve in Heaven. That might be true, though I don't really know much about Heaven. Assuming there is any such place, which I very much doubt. But so far as I'm concerned it feels better to let someone else reign in the Afterworld. My notion is neither to reign nor serve, but just to do my own thing. I suppose that doesn't make much sense to you, does it. If you're like all the rest of the big *goyishe* sword-swingers I've known here, you're itching to get yourself up on a throne again, some throne, any throne –"

"No," Gilgamesh said.

"No?"

"What was that line you used? 'Just to do my own thing'? I like that. *My own thing*. Which was for me, as for you, to be a king; but that was a long time ago, in another life. Here I have no interest in it. What is there to rule, here? This land of trickery and sorcery, where places come and go as though in dreams, and time itself flows fast or slow according to some demon's whim?" Gilgamesh spat. "No, Herod, you mistake me if you think I would be king again! Let me rove freely, let me hunt where I will. And let me find again my one beloved companion, whom I have lost in this land of the Afterworld as I lost him once in the land of the living. Let me be reunited with Enkidu my true brother, the friend of my heart, who is the only one I have ever loved, and that is all I require. Let others be the kings here. While the likes of you and me do our own thing." Gilgamesh grinned and slapped Herod broadly on the back, knocking the little man up hard against the rail. "Eh, Herod? I think we have more in common, you and I, than it seemed at first. Is that not so, King Herod? Is that not so?"

The mainland and the louring fury of all its roaring, sputtering volcanoes dropped away aft and the royal yacht slipped gracefully through the gleaming water toward Brasil. The city stood large before them now. Green ghost-fires danced on its many-towered walls.

Gilgamesh felt a faint flicker of excitement. It was the merest shadow of his ancient curiosity, that world-devouring hunger for knowledge and adventure that in his first life had sent him roving everywhere within the confines of the Land and far beyond it. Once the bards of Sumer and Akkad had sung of him as the man to whom all things had been made known, the secret things, the truths of life and death. They hadn't been so far from wrong, those long-ago singers. He had wanted to know everything, to see everything, to taste everything, to do everything.

Most of that was gone from him now, burned out of his soul in the thousands of years he had spent roving this immense and incomprehensible place after death that was known as the Afterworld. But some fragment of the old vanished Gilgamesh must yet remain alive within him; or else why did he stare so intently at the bizarre island-city that rose glittering before him out of the phosphorescent sea?

"Make ready for landing!" someone shouted. "All hands make ready!"

Herod disappeared below decks. Crewmen sprang from nowhere, half a dozen little oily-looking Levantine types who ran around doing busy things with lines and capstans. Surprisingly, a Hairy Man emerged from the depths of the boat: squat, thick-bodied, heavy-jawed, with hardly any chin and great jutting brows. He was wearing Roman costume. They turned up in the most unlikely places, those harsh-voiced beings out of the dawn of time, from that lost and forgotten world before the Flood. This one appeared to be in the service of Simon, judging by his dress and the gaudy decorations he was wearing.

Simon Magus himself came out next, moving slowly, leaning on Herod's arm. It was plain that the dictator of Brasil was a man much given to the excesses of the body; and yet you could see the force of his spirit within the flab and behind the blotches, you could see the iron strength of soul, the unwavering hunger for power. That hunger had survived Simon's own life. How sad it was, Gilgamesh thought, that a man of Simon's caliber was unable to transcend his own lustful appetites. Gilgamesh knew something about appetite himself, and about lust and excess; but he had never allowed it to show on the surface the way this man did. His body was his temple and throughout his life he had kept it holy. And throughout his long death-life too.

"Ah," Simon said. "The king of Uruk. Well, there's Brasil, just a few hundred yards off our bow. Your first glimpse of my little city. What do you think of it, Gilgamesh?"

"It is not without merit," said Gilgamesh.

"Not without merit? Is that the best you can say of it, king of Uruk? Not without merit?" Simon's red blotches deepened to angry scarlet. Then, in a softer, more diplomatic tone, he said, "But of course my Brasil is as nothing beside your great capital. I understand that."

"Your city is most splendid," Gilgamesh said.

In truth he had almost begun to forget the look of Uruk in all this time. The details of construction and design were going from him; about all he remembered were general outlines, low brick buildings with flat roofs, narrow streets, a temple high upon a platform of whitewashed brick.

This Brasil was a place of narrow spires set with bands of precious stones, parapets that went curving off at improbable angles, boulevards that wound in eye-baffling zigs and zags up the slopes of the lava-rimmed mountain that dominated the island. A strange-looking place indeed, no doubt transformed greatly over time from the simple old Roman town after which it had been originally modeled. Nothing stayed the same in the Afterworld for very long. Not even the mountains and rivers.

Simon said, "My prime minister, the Jew Herod."

"We have met," said Gilgamesh.

So Herod, for all his pious disclaimer of interest in power, nevertheless was prime minister in Brasil? Well, perhaps that was his way of – what was the phrase he had used? – doing his own thing. Let others be the kings here, he had said, but nevertheless he had managed to worm his way into a high enough position among these Romans. Gilgamesh was reminded of that Mongol, Kublai Khan, whom he had encountered while he was wandering the kingdoms of the Outback. The tale was that Kublai in his time on Earth had been one of the grandest of emperors; but here he claimed to have no imperial ambitions and avowed himself quite content to serve as minister of war for Mao Tse-tung's Celestial People's Republic. Which was easier than being an emperor, no doubt: but it was still a position of power.

It seemed that your life on Earth determined the way you lived here. Perhaps it was so. Mountains and rivers might be in constant flux and transition here, but human souls, so it seemed, never really changed. Look at all those Romans and Carthaginians, off there somewhere still fighting and refighting their absurd little Punic Wars. Or that little man Lenin, feverishly launching plot and crazy counterplot in his endless pointless insurrection against whoever it was that claimed currently to be the head of government in Nova Roma. And all the kings and emperors trying to replicate their ancient realms in this other world, Caesar and Mao and Elizabeth and Prester John and the rest. Even those like Herod and Kublai who claimed to have renounced the lust for power tended to turn up somehow among those who gave the orders rather than among those who obeyed them.

No, Gilgamesh thought, no one ever truly changes in the Afterworld. Except me. Except me. I was the king of all the Land, and gloried in my mastery, and made all men bow to me. I conquered cities; I erected temples; I built walls and canals. Here I have done nothing for untold thousands of years but hunt and roam, roam and hunt, and it has been sufficient for me. Whether they will believe it or no, it has been sufficient.

"And this," said Simon, "is my grand mage and high wizard, whose name, of course, I am unable to tell you."

He indicated the Hairy Man.

"Peace and gladness, king of Uruk," said the Hairy Man. Or so Gilgamesh heard him to say. He had never had an easy time understanding the speech of those peculiar folk. Like nearly everyone else here now they spoke English, and before that they had spoken Latin when Latin was the main language of the Afterworld; but whatever language they spoke, they spoke it in a deep, gruff, furry, all but incomprehensible way, as though speaking through a thick stack of oxhides and as though their tongues were attached the wrong way. Perhaps they spoke their own language that way too.

The Hairy Men were mysteries to Gilgamesh. They had no names, or at least none that they would tell to anyone not of their own kind. They worshipped gods without names, too. They looked almost like beasts, covered as they were with dense coarse shaggy pelts of brown – or, more usually, reddish – fur. Enkidu was famed among men for his rough thick-haired body, but even he, shaggy as he was, seemed nearly as hairless as a woman beside a Hairy Man. Bestial though they looked and sounded, however, they conducted themselves as men among men, and when you spent a little time with them you quickly came to see that they were shrewd and wise, with deep cunning and a mastery of many arcane skills.

The tale was that they came from the beginning of time, in those early days before the Flood, when the kingship of men first descended from heaven. Maybe so. But once when Gilgamesh had questioned one about those days, asking him what he knew of Alulim the first king who had reigned at holy Eridu, or Alalgar his successor, or En-men-lu-Anna who had been king after him with his capital at the city of Bad-tibira, the Hairy Man had simply shaken his head.

"These are only names," the Hairy Man had said. "Names are nothing."

"They are kings! Alulim was king for 28,800 years! Alalgar for 36,000! In Bad-tibira En-men-lu-Anna ruled for 43,200 years! Every boy learns of them in school. And you who lived before the Flood, you who come from deepest antiquity – how could you not know the names of the kings?"

"They were not kings to me," the Hairy Man had replied indifferently. "They were never. They were nothing." Or so he seemed to be saying, in his thick-tongued indistinct way. And when Gilgamesh had asked other Hairy Men about the same matters, the answers that he got from them were always the same.

Well, perhaps they had forgotten. It was such a long time, after all. Before the Flood! Or could it be that the Hairy Men were not men at all, but demons native to this other world? Nowhere in the books that Gilgamesh had studied when he was king in Uruk had he ever seen it said that in the days before the Flood men had looked like beasts. A mystery, yes. Maybe while he was in Brasil he would attempt to learn more on these matters from this wizard of Simon's.

Looking shoreward Gilgamesh beheld slaves bustling around at the pier, some waving flags to guide the royal yacht into its slip, others unrolling an astonishingly long magenta carpet for Simon. A trio of gunners detonated bright smoke-bombs, perhaps as a salute to the returning monarch and perhaps just to scare off the evil-looking winged creatures with scaly yellow necks and long glistening fangs that flew in wild circles, flapping and screaming over the harbor.

Simon said, "Magnificent, isn't it?"

"Indeed."

"You've heard of me, have you?"

"In truth, Simon, never at all," said Gilgamesh.

Simon Magus looked displeased, but only for an instant. "You're honest, at any rate. And it's just as well. Most of what you would have heard of me is lies, anyway."

"Indeed?" said Gilgamesh again.

"That I was the father of all heresy. That I went to Rome and performed miracles in front of the Emperor Claudius. That I said I was the Father, the Son, and the Holy Ghost, and that I announced I would be transported to Heaven and was actually in mid-air when Saints Peter and Paul knelt and prayed and brought me down with a smash against the pavement. All lies, you know. Also the one about my having myself buried alive, saying that I would rise on the third day, the way *he* did. All lies."

"I have no doubt of that."

Simon chuckled. "Sorcery, yes. I admit to that. I did magic to a fare-thee-well. But miracles? And heresy? No, Gilgamesh, never. I saw right away that Jesus of Bethlehem had magic better than mine, magic of tremendous power, and I went right over to his side. I was always loyal to him – made sense, you understand, complete and utter sense, throw in your lot with the best wizard and don't try to compete. That was in Samaria, you know – were you ever there? A lovely place, near Jerusalem – but I was never in Rome, not once. Pompeii, yes, I was there, that's why I designed Brasil to look the way Pompeii did. But not Rome, and I never knew Claudius, and he never put up a statue in my honor in the Tiber, or any of that." Shaking his head, Simon said, "They also said that I found Helen of Troy reincarnated in a Roman brothel, and offered her salvation if she would be my mistress. Nothing to it. Do you know Helen, Gilgamesh? Have you ever met her?"

"Never," said Gilgamesh.

"I did, once, long ago, at a place called Theleme. And we had a good laugh over that one. I'd love to find her again someday. But I want you to know, my friend, it was some other Simon who played all those games with false miracles, long after I was dead. I was only interested in power – and therefore sorcery, and religion, since those are the ways to power. Jesus, though –he was the best sorcerer of them all. Next to him I was nothing." Simon, smiling, gestured broadly toward the city they were approaching. "Brasil! There she is! And we'll allow ourselves a few days to rest and enjoy the baths, yes, king of Uruk? A feast, a theatrical show, a circus in your honor with a hundred gladiators. And then we must get down to business, and discuss the expedition to find the kingdom that by rights is yours."

Gilgamesh frowned. "But I covet no –"

Herod nudged him quickly to silence.

"What's that you say, great king?" Simon asked.

He needed no further warnings from Herod. "I said, How good it will be to enjoy your baths, Simon. The feasting, the theatricals, the gladiators."

"And then to search for your city of Uruk, eh?"

Gilgamesh made no reply. Serenely the royal yacht glided into its slip. Swarms of slaves and sycophants rushed forward to greet Simon.

To search for Uruk, Gilgamesh thought. *What* Uruk? Where? Uruk was lost in the swirling mists of time. There would never be another Uruk. What he wanted was Enkidu, carried off or perhaps even slain by whoever it was that had attacked van der Heyden's caravan. He would accept Simon's help in finding Enkidu, yes. But Uruk? Uruk? All that was craziness.

"You will enjoy our circus," said Herod at his side. "In your honor we will send the hundred mightiest gladiators of Brasil to their next lives."

Gilgamesh gave him a sour look. "That matters little to me. Why should a hundred heroes die for my amusement? You Romans and your bloody games –"

"Please," said Herod. "You keep calling me a Roman, but actually I prefer to think of myself as a Jew, you know. Although technically I suppose I could be thought of as a Roman – Julius Caesar did make my great-grandfather Antipater a Roman citizen, after all – but we Jews have a far more ancient lineage than the Romans, after all, and –"

"Do you ever stop running off at the mouth, even for a minute?" Gilgamesh burst out.

"Have I given offense, great king?"

"This chatter of Jews and Romans, Romans and Jews. Who gives a demon's fart about you or your lineage? I was a king when your land was nothing but a swamp!"

Herod smiled. "Ah, Gilgamesh, Gilgamesh, forgive me! Of course your nation is far older than Rome, or even Judaea. But then again, there are others here to whom even grand and glorious Sumer is but a recent event." He looked slyly toward the Hairy Man. "Under the specter of Eternity, Gilgamesh, most of us have been in the Afterworld only an hour or two. Next to *him*, that is. But forgive me. Forgive me. I do speak too much. Nevertheless I urge you to attend the contests in our coliseum. And I bid you welcome to my adopted city of Brasil, King Gilgamesh. Both as Roman and as Jew do I bid you be welcome here."

Eight

In Brasil Gilgamesh took up residence in Simon's palace, a huge rambling building laid out around a courtyard and set in an enormous walled garden. His suite had a bath in the Roman style, a vast circular bed that somehow seemed to float in mid-air, and its own staff of valets, butlers, courtesans, and porters to meet his every need. Just at the moment he felt very few needs, a general austerity having been his mode for more years than he could remember. But it was good to know those comforts were there, he supposed.

Herod came to him in early evening, when the murky glow of the sun was beginning to tint the garden with the deep purples of twilight. He perched casually on a windowsill and said, "Tell me about this Uruk of yours."

"What can I tell? It was a city long ago, where I was born and lived and was king and – died. The River Buranunu ran along its flank. Enlil was the god of the city and Inanna its goddess, and – "

"No. I mean the new Uruk, that is here in the Afterworld."

"I know nothing of any such city," said Gilgamesh.

Herod studied him closely. "Simon thinks you do."

"He does? Whatever I know of the new Uruk, which is very little, I've learned from Simon."

"Ah. I begin to see."

"The first I heard of it," Gilgamesh said, "was when I encountered Simon across the bay in the land of the flaming mountains. There is a city called Uruk in the Afterworld, he told me. He told me that this Uruk is a city much like the city of my life, and there are people of my kin there. This Uruk, he said, is a city of fabulous wealth and enormous treasure."

"Yes. The true picture does come into focus now," said Herod.

"He asked if I would join him in an expedition to Uruk. His soldiers, he said, are bored and seek adventure."

"And also he seeks treasure."

"The treasure of Uruk?"

"Any treasure," Herod said. "Have you looked at the walls and towers of this city? He's encrusted Brasil with emeralds and rubies and sapphires and diamonds. And gems the names of which no one knows, which were never seen on Earth but are found only in the Afterworld. His appetite for fancy baubles is enormous. *Enormous*. Five wizards conjure more stones into existence for him all day long and all the night; but of course those stones last only a short while. He craves the genuine article. If Uruk has great treasure, Simon hungers for it."

"I took him for a wiser man."

"There is much wisdom in him. But this is the Afterworld, Gilgamesh, where the decay of time turns wise men to folly. He loves bright stones."

"There were no stones at all in Uruk," Gilgamesh pointed out. "We built our city from bricks made of mud. We had neither emeralds nor rubies."

"That was your Uruk. Simon means to find the Afterworld's Uruk. He thinks you know the way."

"I told him that I did not."

"He thinks you lie," said Herod amiably.

"Then he's an even greater fool. I've been in the Afterworld twice as long as your Simon, or even longer. Doesn't he think that in all that time I'd have heard of it, if my countrymen had built a new Uruk for themselves here?"

Herod rocked slowly back and forth on the windowsill, smiling to himself. "You two have really screwed each other over, haven't you?"

"What?"

"The valiant Gilgamesh and the shrewd Simon have led each other ass-deep into confusion. He believes you can find Uruk for him. You believe he can find it for you. Each of you thinks the other one holds the secret of Uruk's location. But in fact neither of you knows anything at all about the place."

"I certainly don't, at any rate."

"Neither does Simon. I assure you."

"Then how –"

"Some wandering swindler came to him a little while ago. One Hanno, a Carthaginian, claiming to be a maker of maps. You know how reliable maps are in the Afterworld, Gilgamesh? But this Hanno began telling tales of the treasures of Uruk, and Simon's eyes lit up like the jewels he covets so hungrily. Where can I find this Uruk, Simon asked. And Hanno sold him a map. Then he disappeared. When Romans start buying maps from Carthaginians no good can come of it, I say. The day after Hanno left Brasil, Simon proudly brought me the map and told me the story. Let us plan an expedition of conquest, he said. And unrolled the map. And its lines ran crazily in every direction, so that it would make your eyes ache to follow them, and even as we stared they flowed and twisted about. And then in five minutes the map was blank, just an empty piece of demon-hide. I thought Simon would have a stroke. Uruk! Uruk! That was all he could say, over and over, grunting like that Hairy Man wizard of his. Then off we went to the mainland, where some caravan was supposed to arrive from the Outback, scoundrels and villains of some sort, dealers in stolen gems. Simon had business with them. He's mixed up in all sorts of garbage of that kind. I don't have to pay any attention to it. And what do we hear but that there are two gigantic hulking Sumerians traveling with the caravan, and one of them is Gilgamesh the king of Uruk! Uruk again! The caravan doesn't arrive – hit by bandits in the pass, so the word is – but Gilgamesh does. Which is all the better for Simon Magus. What does the loss of a few caskets of gems matter, if he can hope to loot all of Uruk? Do you see, Gilgamesh? He means for you to lead him to Uruk so that he can plunder it!"

"Sooner would I be able to lead him to Paradise. There is no Uruk here in the Afterworld, Herod."

"Are you certain of that?"

"Who can be certain of anything here? But why haven't I ever heard of it, if it truly exists?"

"The Afterworld is very large, Gilgamesh. There is no one who can claim to have explored it all. Perhaps it grows ever larger each day, so that no one could possibly see every part of it, even if he never rested a moment. I've traveled in it for twice a thousand years and I haven't even seen a tenth of it, I suspect. And you, much older even than I – even you, I wager, are a stranger to much of the Afterworld. You told me yourself that you had never been in Brasil before."

"Agreed. But Uruk – a city built by Sumerians, inhabited

by Sumerians – no. Impossible that it could exist without my knowing of it."

"Unless you knew of it once, and have forgotten that you did."

"Also impossible."

"Is it? You know what memory is like here."

"Well –"

"You know, Gilgamesh."

"But how could I forget my own city? No. No. There is no Uruk in the Afterworld," said Gilgamesh sullenly. "Accept the truth of that or not as you like, King Herod. But *I* know where the truth lies in this matter."

"Merely a fable, then?"

"Absolutely. A phantom of this Hanno's imagination."

"Why would he name his phantom Uruk, after a city which time itself has forgotten, if what you say is true?"

"Who knows? Perhaps he met me once, and I told him where I was from, and the name stuck in his mind. I am well known in the Afterworld, Herod."

"So in truth you are."

"There is no Uruk. Simon deceives himself. If he thinks I know how to lead him there, he deceives himself doubly."

Herod was silent a long moment.

At length he said, "Then answer me this, Gilgamesh. If this Uruk really doesn't exist, why have you agreed to join Simon in an expedition to find a nonexistent place?"

"Because," said Gilgamesh carefully, "the thought came to me that I might just be wrong, that perhaps there is such a place as Uruk after all and it has escaped my memory."

Herod's eyes widened in amazement. "What? You told me the absolute opposite, no more than two minutes ago!"

"Did I?" said Gilgamesh. "Well, then so I did."

"Your way of joking is very odd, my friend."

Gilgamesh smiled. "With all my heart, Herod, I am convinced that this Uruk of Simon's is a mere myth. But this is the Afterworld. Nothing is ever as we expect it to be here. There was Simon, telling me that he has heard wondrous tales of Uruk. It sounded crazy to me, that there should be any such place, but what if I was wrong about that? I must allow for that possibility. As you said, the Afterworld is large beyond anyone's comprehension. For all I know, Uruk does perhaps exist somewhere far off in this incomprehensible place and through some fluke I have never heard of it. Now the powerful dictator Simon is offering me a chance to go searching for it. Why should I say no? What do I have to lose?"

"The only information that Simon has about Uruk is absolute nonsense. He's gambling that you can fill in the blanks on his map for him."

"I wasn't aware of that."

"He means to use you. He'll let you take him to Uruk, if there is any such place, and he'll allow you to help him get his hands on all those strongboxes full of precious gems that Hanno said were there. And in return he'll set you up as Uruk's king."

"As you know, I have no wish to be king of any city. Particularly one that doesn't exist."

"But Simon doesn't know that. He thinks you'd jump at the chance."

"I told you. I want only Enkidu."

"Your missing friend, you mean?"

"My friend. My hunting companion. My true brother. Closer to me than any brother could be."

"And where might he be?"

"Gone. A mystery. Vanished into the sky, it would seem, or into the bowels of the earth. He must have been carried off."

"By whom?"

"I have no idea. The bandits who raided van der Heyden's caravan, I suppose. But I mean to search for him."

"Even though you have about as much chance of finding him as you do of finding Uruk?"

"At least I know that Enkidu exists."

"But he could be anywhere. A million miles away. Ten million. He could be dead. Who knows? You could look for a thousand years and never find him again."

Shrugging, Gilgamesh said, "I have lost him before, and eventually found him. I'll find him again: and if it takes me a thousand years, Herod, so be it. What's a thousand years to me? What's ten thousand?"

"And meanwhile?"

"Meanwhile what?"

"Uruk," Herod said. "What do you plan to do about that, now that you know Simon's been bluffing you? Will you go along with him anyway on this lunatic expedition? With him hoping that you really do know the way – or at least can figure it out somehow – and you absolutely sure that there's no such place, but praying that somehow you'll get to it anyway?"

Herod's waspish buzzing was beginning to bother Gilgamesh again. The little man was constantly probing, pushing, maneuvering. For what purpose?

Gilgamesh walked to the window and loomed over him.

"Why are you so concerned about the Uruk journey, Herod?"

"Because it means nothing but trouble for me."

"Trouble for you? Why for you?"

"If Simon takes off on a crusade to God knows where with you, I'm going to be stuck here running the shop until he gets back. Which could be centuries, and me trying to preside over this madhouse all the while. His viceroy, do you see? The regent, while he's gone. Do you think I'm looking forward to that? Brasil is stacked to the rafters with crazy military types, most of them oversized and mentally underfurnished, who'd like nothing better than to kill me, or you, or each other, and if they aren't enough trouble there are all these sorcerers too, turning the air blue with their incantations, a great many of which unfortunately are quite potent. I'd go out of my mind without Simon here to keep a lid on everything."

"If being regent of Brasil would be such a burden for you, King Herod, you could always come with us to Uruk."

"Fine! Much better! March day and night for a hundred years through the godforsaken wilderness looking for some place that isn't even there!" He shook his head. "*Meshuggenah*, that's what you are. But I'm not."

"And if Uruk is there?"

"And if it isn't?"

Gilgamesh felt himself losing the last of his patience. "Well, then move somewhere else! You don't have to stay in Brasil. Get yourself a villa in Nova Roma, or have one of the Outback princes take you in. You could settle with the Israelis, for that matter. They're Jews like you, aren't they?"

"Jews, yes," said Herod dourly. "But not like me. I don't understand them at all. No, Gilgamesh, I don't want to do any of those things. I like it here. Brasil is my home. I've got a sweet little niche here. I have no desire whatever to live anywhere else. But if Simon –"

The ground rumbled suddenly as if monsters were rising beneath the tiled mosaic floor of Simon's palace.

"What's that?" Gilgamesh asked.

"Vesuvius!" cried Herod. He turned toward the window and stared out into the dusk. The ground shook a second time, more fiercely than before, and there was a tremendous roar. Gilgamesh plucked the little man aside and leaned out the window. An eye-dazzling spear of red flame split the darkness. Another roar, another, another: like the angry growls of some great beast struggling to break free. From the crest of the mighty volcano in the center of the city came cascades of bubbling lava, showers of pumice, choking clouds of dense black smoke: and throughout it all that single fiery scarlet lance kept rising and rising. Fearless though he was, Gilgamesh had to throttle back a reflexive impulse to run and hide.

Hide? Where? Here on the slopes of that dread volcano there was no safety anywhere to be found.

"Let me see!" Herod said, tugging at Gilgamesh's arm. He was panting. His face was streaked with sweat. He forced his way past Gilgamesh's elbow and thrust his head forth to have a better view. There came another world-shaking convulsion underground. "Fantastic!" Herod whispered. "Incredible! This is the best one ever!" There was awe in his voice, and reverence. Slowly it dawned on Gilgamesh that this eruption had aroused extraordinary delight in Herod. He looked transfigured. His eyes were aglow, shining; and there seemed something like a sexual excitement throbbing in him. He seemed almost crazed with ecstasy. "Twice in two nights! Fantastic! Fantastic! Do you see why I could never leave this place, Gilgamesh? You've got to talk Simon out of going off looking for Uruk. You've got to. I beg you!"

Under the cloud-shrouded red light of the dreary sun Gilgamesh made his way through the daytime streets of Brasil. By Enlil, had there ever been a city like this in all the world? There was witchcraft and deviltry everywhere.

Streets that wound in on themselves in tight spirals, like the spoor of a drunken snail. Narrow high-vaulted buildings that looked like snails themselves, ready to pick up and move away. Black-leaved trees with weeping boughs, from which came curious sighs when you got close to them. And everywhere the dry powdery smell of last night's eruption, motes of dark dust dancing in the air, and little sparkling bits of flaming matter that stung ever so lightly as they settled on your skin.

Hands plucked at him as he walked briskly along. Hooded eyes stared from passageways. Once someone called him by name, but he could see no one. Ajax, trotting along at his heels, paused again and again to howl and glare, and even to raise the fur along his back and spit as though he were a cat rather than a dog; but the enemies that Ajax perceived were all invisible to Gilgamesh.

Now and again flying fiery-eyed demons swooped through the city at rooftop height. No one paid any attention to them. Frequently they came to rest and perched, preening themselves like living gargoyles, beating their powerful wings against the air and sending down dank fetid breezes over the passers-by below. Gilgamesh saw one of the winged things suddenly sway and fall, as though overcome by a spell. Little glossy scuttling animals emerged from crevices in the gutter and pounced upon it. They devoured it before Gilgamesh had reached the end of the street, leaving nothing but scraps of leathery cartilage behind.

When he looked off in the distance it seemed to him that there was some sort of translucent wall in the sky beyond the city, cutting Brasil off from the rest of the Afterworld. Its blue-white sheen glimmered with cold ferocity; and it seemed to him that there were monstrous creatures outside, not the usual demon-beasts but some other kind of even greater loathsomeness, all crimson beaks and coiling snaky necks and vast wings that flailed in fury against the wall that kept them out. But when he blinked and looked again he saw nothing unusual at all, only the heavy clouds and the dark glimmer of the light of the sun struggling to break through them.

Then he heard a sound that might have been the sound of a tolling bell. But the bell seemed to be tolling backward. First came the dying fall, and then the rising swell of sound, and then the initial percussive boom; and then silence, and then the dying fall again, climbing toward the clangor of the striking clapper:

mmmmmmoooMMMMNGB! mmmmmmoooMMMMNGB! mmmmmmoooMMMMNGB!

The impact of the sound was stunning. Gilgamesh stood still, feeling the immense weight of time drop away, centuries peeling from him with each heavy reverberation. As though on a screen before him in the air he saw his entire life in the Afterworld running in reverse, the thousands of years of aimless wandering becoming a mad flight at fantastic speed, everything rushed and blurred and jumbled together as if it had happened in a single day, Gilgamesh here, Gilgamesh there, brandishing his sword, drawing his bow, slaying this devil-beast and that, climbing impossible mountains, swimming lakes of shimmering color, trekking across fields of blazing sand, entering cities that were twisted and distorted like the cities one enters in dreams, penetrating the far regions of this place even to the strangest region of all, in the north, where great drifting ivory block-shaped creatures of immense size and unknown nature moved about on their mysterious tasks. Now he was wrestling joyously with Enkidu, now he watched the brawling swarms of Later Dead come flooding in and filling the place with their ghastly noisy machines and their guns and their foul-smelling vehicles, now he was in the villa of Lenin in Nova Roma among Lenin's whole unsavory crew of cold-eyed conspirators and malevolent bitchy queens, and now he sat roistering in the feasting-hall of the Ice-Hunter king Vy-otin, with Enkidu laughing and joking by his side and Agamemnon too, and Amenhotep and Cretan Minos, and Varuna the king of Meluhha, his great companions in those early days in the Afterworld. How long ago that was! And now –

"Great king!" a woman cried, dashing up to him and clutching at his wrist. "Save us from doom, great king!"

Gilgamesh stared at her, amazed. Not a woman but a girl. And he knew her. Had known her, once. Had loved her, even. In another life, far away, long ago, on the other side of the great barrier of life and death. For her face was the face of the girl-priestess Inanna, she whom he had embraced so rashly and with such passion in old Uruk, in the life he had led before this life! During his long years in the Afterworld he had thought more than once about encountering Inanna again, had even once or twice considered seeking her out, but he had never acted on the thought. And now, to blunder into her like this here in Brasil –

Or was he still in Brasil? Was this the Afterworld at all?

Everything was swirling about him. A thick mist was gathering. The earth was giving up its moisture. It seemed to him that he saw the walls of Uruk rising at the end of the street, the huge white platform of the temples, the awesome statues of the gods. He heard the clamor of his name on a thousand thousand tongues. *Gilgamesh! Gilgamesh*! And in the sky, instead of the familiar dull red glaring light, there was the yellow sun of the Land, that he had not beheld in so unimaginably long a time, blazing with all its midsummer power.

What was this? Had that tolling bell lifted him altogether out of this world and cast him back into the other, the world of his birth and death? Or was this only a waking dream?

"Inanna?" he said in wonder. How slender she was! How young! Strings of blue beads about her waist, amulets of pink shells tied to the ends of her hair. Her body bare, painted along its side and front with the pattern of the serpent. And her dark-tipped breasts – the sharp stinging scent of her perfume –

She spoke again, this time calling him by his name of names, the private name that no one had called him in thousands of years, since that day when he was still half a boy and he had put on the mantle of kingship and had for the first time heard his king-name roaring like a flooding river in his ears, *Gilgamesh, Gilgamesh, Gilgamesh.* He himself had forgotten that other name, that birth-name: but as she spoke it the dam of recollection burst in his soul. What wizardry was this, that he should be standing before the girl Inanna again?

"I am Ninpa the Lady of the Scepter," she murmured. "I am Ninmenna the Lady of the Crown."

She reached her hand toward his. As he touched her she changed: she was older now, fuller of body, her dark eyes gleaming with wanton knowledge, her deep-hued skin bright with oil. "Come," she whispered. "I am Inanna. You must come with me. You are the only one who can save us."

A dark tunnel before him – a buzzing in his ears, as of a thousand wasps about his head – a brilliant purple light glowing before his eyes – a mighty roaring, as though Enlil of the Storms had loosed all his winds upon the Afterworld –

And then a fiery pain at his ankle. Ajax, sinking his fangs deep! Gilgamesh stared down at the dog, astonished.

"Careful, Gilgamesh!" Ajax barked. "This is enchantment!"

"What? What?"

The woman held him by the hand. Heat came from her, and it was overwhelming, a furnace heat. And she was changing, again and again; now she had his mother's face, and now she was the round-breasted temple-woman Abisimti who had first taught him the arts of love; and then she was the child-Inanna again, and then the woman. And then she was a thing with a hundred heads and a thousand eyes, pulling him down into the nether pits of the Afterworld, into the yawning blackness that lay beneath the smouldering heart of the Vesuvius volcano.

"I am Ereshkigal of Hell," she whispered, "and I will be your bride."

Down – down – descending a ladder of lights – blinding whiteness all around, and a bright red mantle of copper fluttering in the breeze out of the pit, and demons dancing below. On all sides, lions. From high overhead, golden wine falling from two inverted wine-cups; and the wine was thick and fiery, and burned him where it touched him.

He heard the furious howling of the dog. He felt the terrible pull of the black depths.

"It is enchantment, Gilgamesh," said Ajax again. "Stay – fight – I will get help –"

The dog ran off, uttering terrible wolf-cries as he went.

Gilgamesh stood his ground, baffled, shaking his head slowly from side to side like a wounded bull. If only Enkidu were here! Enkidu would pull him back from the abyss, just as Gilgamesh once long ago had tried to bring Enkidu out of that tunnel of old dry bones that led to the land of the dead. He had failed, then, and Enkidu had perished; but they were older now, they were wiser, they knew how to deal with the demons that surrounded them on all sides –

Enkidu! Enkidu!

"You should not have come to this street alone," a new voice said. "There are many dangers here."

Enkidu, yes! At last! The dog Ajax had returned, and he had brought Enkidu with him to Gilgamesh's side. Gilgamesh felt his soul soaring. Saved! Saved!

Through blurred eyes he saw the powerful figure of his friend: the great muscles, the thick pelt of dark hair, the burning gleaming eyes. Enkidu was struggling with Ereshkigal-Inanna, now. Shoving the Hell-goddess back toward her pit, wresting her cold hands free of Gilgamesh's wrist. Gilgamesh trembled. He could not move. He was helpless to act on his own behalf. In all his years in the Afterworld he had never known such peril, had never fallen so deeply into the power of the dark beings of the invisible world. But Enkidu was here – Enkidu would save him –

Enkidu was freeing him. Yes. Yes. The frightful chill of the abyss which had enfolded him was relenting. The blinding lights had receded. The temples and streets and sun of Uruk no longer could be seen. Gilgamesh stepped back, blinking, shivering. His heart was pounding in dull heavy thuds, almost like the tolling of that backwards bell. Tears were streaming down his face. He looked about for his friend.

"Enkidu?"

Through blurring eyes he saw the shaggy figure. Enkidu? Enkidu? No. The heavy pelt was like a beast's. A reddish color, and coarse and dense, letting none of the skin show through. And the face – that underslung chin, those fierce brooding ridges above the eyes – why, this was not Enkidu at all, but rather the Hairy Man who was Simon's wizard. Or perhaps not, perhaps another of that tribe altogether – it was so difficult telling one Hairy Man from the next –

The very ugliness of the Hairy Man was comforting. The squat bulk of him, the solidity. This creature who had lived when the gods themselves were young, who had walked the earth in the days before the Flood, who had lived fifty thousand or a hundred thousand or a hundred hundred thousand years in the Afterworld before Gilgamesh of Uruk first had come here. Ancient wisdom flowed deep in him. Next to him, Gilgamesh felt almost like a child again.

"Come with me," said the Hairy Man, thick-tongued, husky-voiced. "In here. You will be safe. You will be protected here."

Nine

It might have been some sort of warehouse. A huge dark long room, walls of white plaster, curved wooden ceiling far overhead. A single piercing beam of light cutting through from above, illuminating the intricacies of the rafters and slicing downward to show the sawdust-strewn floor, the rows of bare wooden tables, the hunched and somber figures sitting on backless benches behind them. They were staring straight forward and exclaiming aloud, each in the midst of uttering some private recitation, each ploughing stubbornly onward over the voices of all the others.

"I am Wulfgeat. For chronic disorder of the head or of the ears or of the teeth through foulness or through mucus, extract that which aileth there, seethe chervil in water, give it to drink, then that draweth out the evil humors either through mouth or through nose."

"I am Aethelbald. Seek in the maw of young swallows for some little stones, and mind that they touch neither earth, nor water, nor other stones; look out three of them; put them on the man, on whom thou wilt, him who hath the need, and he will soon be well."

"I am Eadfrith. Here we have rue, hyssop, fennel, mustard, elelcampane, southernwood, celandine, radish, cumin, onion, lupin, chervil, flower de luce, flax, rosemary, savory, lovage, parsley, olusatrum, savine."

In wonder and bewilderment Gilgamesh said, "Why, who are these people, and what's all this that they're babbling?"

"– again, thou shalt remove the evil misplaced humors by spittle and breaking; mingle pepper with mastic, give it the patient to chew, and work him a gargle to swill his jowl –"

"– they are good for headache, and for eye-wark, and for the fiend's temptations, and for night goblin visitors, and for the nightmare, and for knot, and for fascination, and for evil enchantments by song. It must be big nestlings on which thou shalt find them. If a man ache in half his head, pound rue thoroughly, put it into strong vinegar –"

The Hairy Man said, "These are dealers in remedies and spells, and this is the market where such things are sold in Brasil."

"– and also mastic, pepper, galbanum, scamony, gutta ammoniaca, cinnamon, vermilion, aloes, pumice, quicksilver, brimstone, myrrh, frankincense, petroleum, ginger –"

"– that he by that may comfortably break out the ill phlegm. Work thus a swilling or lotion for cleansing of the head, take again a portion of mustard seed and of navew seed and of cress seed, and twenty peppercorns, gather them all with vinegar and honey –"

"– and smear therewith the head, right on top. Delve up waybroad without iron, ere the rising of the sun, bind the roots about the head, with crosswort, by a red fillet –"

Gilgamesh shivered. "I think this place is no better than being in the street. A marketplace of wizards? A hundred mages bellowing spells?"

"No harm can befall you here," the Hairy Man said. "There is such a constant crying-forth of magics in here that each cancels the other out, so there is no peril."

"– the seed of this wort adminstered in wine is of much benefit against any sort of snake, and against sting of scorpions, to that degree that if it be laid upon the scorpions, it bringeth upon them unmightiness or impotence and infirmity –"

"– for ache of loins and sore of the thighs, take this same wort pulegium, seethe it in vinegar –"

"I am Aethelbald."

"I am Eadfrith."

"I am Wulfgeat."

"– this wort, which is named priapiscus, and by another name vinca pervinca, is of good advantage for many purposes, that is to say, first against devil sicknesses, or demoniacal possessions, and against snakes, and against wild beasts, and against poisons –"

"Good sir! Good sir!" It was the one who said he was Aethelbald, waving wildly at Gilgamesh.

"What does he want with me?"

"To sell you something, no doubt," the Hairy Man replied. "Why were you wandering in these streets by yourself?"

"My head was aching when I awoke. From the noise of the eruptions all night long, and, I think, from some prattle of the Jew Herod last evening. So I went out to walk. To clear my head, to see the city. I saw no harm in it."

"– and for various wishes," shouted the one called Eadfrith, "and for envy, and for terror, and that thou may have grace, and if thou hast this sort with thee, thou shalt be prosperous, and ever acceptable –"

"Good sir! Here, good sir, here, if you please!"

"No harm? No harm?" The Hairy Man guffawed, showing huge chopper-like teeth. "No harm playing tag with a mastodon, either, eh, my friend? If you're big enough, I suppose. Walk right up to it, tweak it by the trunk, pull its ears? Eh?"

"A mastodon?" Gilgamesh said blankly. A strange word: he wondered if he had heard it right.

"Never mind. You wouldn't know, would you? Before your time. Never mind. But I tell you, this is no city to be strolling around in unprotected. Nobody warned you of that?"

"Herod said something about wizards and mages, but –"

"Good sir! Good sir!"

"But you ignored him. Herod! That clown!" The small deep-set eyes of the Hairy Man were bright with contempt. "Sometimes even Herod will tell you something useful. You should have heeded his warning. Brasil's a place of many perils."

"I have no fear of dying," said Gilgamesh.

"Dying is the least terrible thing that could happen to you here." The Hairy Man placed a wrinkle-skinned leathery-looking hand on Gilgamesh's arm. "Come. Here. Walk about with me a little, up and down."

"Do you have a name?"

"Names are nothing," said the Hairy Man. "It was a fright for you, what happened outside, eh?"

Gilgamesh shrugged.

The Hairy Man leaned close. There was an odd sweetish flavor about his furry body. "There are places in the streets here where the other worlds break through. That is always a danger, that the fabric will not hold, that other worlds will break through. Do you understand what I'm saying?"

"Yes," Gilgamesh told the Hairy Man. "There was such a place in Uruk. A passageway that ran down from our world into this one. Inanna the goddess descended through it, when she went to Hell to visit her sister Ereshkigal. And during the rite of the Closing of the Gate I dropped my drum and my drumstick into that passageway when a girl startled me by crying out the name of a god." He had not thought of these things in centuries. Recollection, flooding back now, swept him with uncontrollable emotion. "The sacred drum, it was, which Ur-nangar the craftsman made for me from the wood of the huluppu-tree, by which I entered my trances and saw the things that mortal eyes are unable to see. That was how I lost my friend Enkidu, the first time, when I dropped my drum and my drumstick into that dark and terrible hole of cinders and ashes, and he entered the nether world to bring them back."

"Then you know," the Hairy Man said. "You have to learn where these places are, and stay away from them."

Gilgamesh was trembling. Old memories were surging with new life within him.

Enkidu! Enkidu!

Once again he saw Enkidu, gray with dust and snarled in masses of tangled cobwebs, coming forth from that pit in Uruk that led down to the world of the dead; and Enkidu as he came forth was a dead man himself, shorn of all life-strength, who within twelve days would be carried off forever to the House of Dust and Darkness. How great had been the mourning of Gilgamesh! How he had cursed the gods of death for taking Enkidu from him! And then, after Gilgamesh's own time had run its course and he had joined Enkidu in the Afterworld, losing him again – what pain it was, to be reunited with him and then to lose him that second time, when Enkidu had stepped between those quarrelsome Spaniards and Englishmen and caught a bullet meant for someone else –

"And once more he is lost to me," Gilgamesh said aloud. "As though the curse of Inanna follows us even to the Afterworld, and we must find each other and be parted again, and find each other once more, and part once more, over and over and over–"

"What is this you say?" asked the Hairy Man.

"We were on that far shore, Enkidu and I, among a caravan of strangers, of sleazy conniving Later Dead. And while I was gone from the camp, while I was away hunting, there was an attack on the camp, and when I returned I found all of them dead except this brindle dog Ajax; but of Enkidu there was no sign. Brigands must have swept him off, or demons, to torment me by separating us once again. But I will find him, if I must seek until the gods grow old!"

"In the Afterworld there is no finding anyone," the Hairy Man said, "except by accident, or the whim of those dark gods who rule this place. You surely must know that."

"I will find him."

"And if he is dead?"

"Then he'll come back again, as all the dead here do sooner or later. I tell you I will find him."

"Come, now," said the Hairy Man. "Come and walk with me, until your head is clear."

"Wait," Gilgamesh said. He brushed the Hairy Man's hand aside. "Do you think that these doctors here could give me a spell that would help me trace him?"

"They will tell you they can. But in the Afterworld there is no finding anyone, Gilgamesh."

"We'll see about that."

Gilgamesh went toward the rows of wooden tables and benches.

"Good sir, I am Aethelbald," said one of the merchants of spells eagerly.

"I am Eadfrith," said the one beside him, beckoning.

"I am Wulfgeat. I have here a drink that is good for giddiness and fever of the brain, for flowing gall and the yellow disease, for singing in the ears, and defective hearing –"

Gilgamesh impatiently waved them to silence. "Who are you people?"

"We are Angles here," said Wulfgeat, "except for this Saxon beside me, and masters of wortcunning and leechdom are we, and starcraft. Our work is substantial! Our skills are boundless!"

"Wortcunning?" Gilgamesh said. "Starcraft?"

"Aye, and may it be that we have a spell for you! What is your need, good sir? What is your need?"

"There is a man for whom I search," said Gilgamesh after a moment. "A friend whom I have lost."

"A lost friend? A lost friend?" The spell-mongers began to murmur and confer among themselves. "Viper's bugloss?"

suggested one. "The ash of dead bees, and linseed oil?" Another said. "Cammock and thung, wenwort and elder root, steeped in strong mead or clear ale." But the third shook his head violently and said, "It must be done by dreaming. The tokens must needs be induced. To see a well opened beside one's house, or a hen with chickens, or to be shod with a new pair of shoes – aye, those are the tokens, and we must give him the potion that brings on such visions as will be useful, and then the next night –"

"What is this?" a sudden familiar buzzing voice cut in. "What's going on here?"

Herod, pushing and shoving his way through the throng, appeared abruptly at Gilgamesh's side. The Hairy Man scowled and muttered something unintelligible beneath his breath. The merchants of spells looked alarmed, and turned away, gesticulating toward the opposite side of the building and loudly crying out the merits of their wares to those gathered over there.

"Where have you been?" Herod demanded. "Simon's had people looking all over the place for you."

"I thought I would walk through the town."

"Gevalt! And came *here*? Ah. Ah, I think I know why. Shopping for a spell that'll lead you to Uruk, are you? Is that what you're up to? Despite everything I told you last night?"

From afar came the sound of a mighty voice crying, "The Book of the Fifty Names! Who will buy the Book of the Fifty Names?"

"The Hairy Man brought me in here," Gilgamesh said. "I was simply wandering from one street to another when something strange happened to me, a fit, perhaps – in the days when I lived on Earth I was subject to fits, you know, though I thought I was exempt from that in the Afterworld – and I grew dizzy – I saw faces – I saw ancient streets –" Angrily he shook his head. "No, I'm not trying to buy a spell for finding Uruk. I seek only Enkidu. And if these wizards –"

"Marduk! Marukka! Marutukku!" roared the mighty voice.

"These wizards are fishmongers and rabble," Herod said scornfully, making the sign of the horns at Aethelbald and Eadfrith and Wulfgeat. They shrank back from him. "Peasants is what they are. Shopkeepers, at the very best." He drew the six-pointed star in the air before them and they turned from him, pale and shaken. "You see? You see, Gilgamesh? What can they do? Cure an ague for you, maybe? Stop up a sniveling nose? These are foolish men here. They will not find your Enkidu for you."

"Can you be sure of that, Herod?"

A crafty look came into Herod's eyes as he peered up at Gilgamesh.

"King of Uruk, if I show you a true wizard who will give you the answer you seek, will you abandon the idea of taking Simon off on this insane expedition?"

The Hairy Man's yellow-rimmed eyes widened in surprise. "You speak of Calandola?" he asked in his thickest, harshest tone.

"Calandola, yes," said Herod.

The Hairy Man scowled, twisting up his ape-like jaw and lowering his brows until he seemed almost to be winking, and emitted a rumbling sound from deep within his cavernous chest. "This is unwise," he said, after a time. "This is most unwise."

Herod glared at him. "Let Gilgamesh be the judge of that!"

"Asaraludu!" boomed the caller of the Fifty Names. "Namtillaku! Narilugaldimmerankia!"

"And who is this great wizard you offer me?" Gilgamesh asked.

"Imbe Calandola is his name," said Herod. "A Moor, he is – no, a Nubian, or something of each, perhaps. Black as night, terrible to behold. He maintains a temple in the dark tunnels far below the streets of Brasil, and there he presides over the giving of visions. There are those who think he is the Lord of Darkness himself, the Prince of Hell, the Great Adversary, the vast Lucifer of the Abyss: Satan Mephistopheles Beelzebub, the Archfiend, the King of Evil. Perhaps he is; but I think he is in truth only a great savage, who knows the wisdoms of the jungle. In either case he will tell you what you wish to know. The Hairy Men, I understand, consult him frequently."

Gilgamesh looked toward the ancient one.

"Is this true?"

The Hairy Man scowled again, screwing up his face even more bizarrely than before.

"He sees into the other worlds, yes, this Calandola. And he can make others see what he sees."

"Then I mean to go to him," said Gilgamesh.

"There are dangers," the Hairy Man warned.

"So you frequently tell me. But what need I fear? Death? You know that death is a joke to one who has already met it once!"

"Have I not said already that death is the least terrible thing to be feared in Brasil?"

"You have said that, yes. But what you say means nothing to me."

"Then go to Calandola."

"I will do that," Gilgamesh said. He turned to Herod. "How soon can you bring me before him?"

"Do we have a deal? I take you to Calandola, you persuade Simon to abandon the idea of going off in search of Uruk?"

It was maddening to be haggled with this way, as though he and Herod were tradesmen striking a bargain in the marketplace. With difficulty Gilgamesh resisted the urge to pick the little Judaean up and hurl him across the vast room.

"Let there be no talk of favors for favors," said Gilgamesh icily. "I am a man of honor. That should be sufficient for you. Take me to this wizard of yours."

Downward then they went, down into the depths, down into demon country, down into the tunnels of the devils, where the light of the sun never was seen, where this black and monstrous Imbe Calandola had his dwelling-place.

When he was still a boy in Uruk a slave wearing the badge of the goddess Inanna had come to Gilgamesh one day as he practised the throwing of the javelin, and had said to him, "You will come now to the temple of the goddess." And the slave had conducted him to the temple that his grandfather Enmerkar had built on the platform of white brick, and down through winding passageways he had never seen before, into mysterious tunnels that descended beneath the white platform toward the depths of the earth. Past hallways where distant lamps glowed in the subterranean dark, and places where magicians did their work by candleglow, and crosspassages that afforded him glimpses of shaggy goat-hoofed demons silently going about their tasks, until at last he had come to the secret room of Inanna herself, far below the sun-baked streets of Uruk, where the slender priestess waited, cheeks colored with yellow ochre, eyelids darkened with kohl.

That had been long ago, in the days of his first life. It had been his first glimpse of the worlds that lie beneath the world, where invisible wings flutter and the sound of scratchy laughter echoes in dusty corridors. That day the young Gilgamesh had learned that there was more to the world than its familiar surface: that layer upon layer of mystery existed, far from the sight of ordinary mortals. Again and again he had entered that lower world in the course of his kingship.

Now here in the Afterworld, where nothing ever was familiar and mystery was everywhere, Gilgamesh found himself descending once more into a world beneath the world.

He had discovered long ago that the Afterworld had its own subterranean region, a land of tunnels and passageways of unfathomable dimensions and incomprehensible complexity. In the early years of the days of his death he had prowled those tunnels, for then he was still in the grip of the insatiable curiosity that once had driven him to the ends of the earth; but he had quickly lost interest in such explorations, as the aimlessness and passivity of his life in the Afterworld had settled upon him, and this was his first descent into the tunnels in an eon and a half, or more.

There were those who believed that a way out of the Afterworld lay through those tunnels. Gilgamesh doubted that. He did not share the fascination that long had obsessed Enkidu and many others, the dream of finding the way back into the land of the living. To him it was meaningless to speak of a way out of the Afterworld; he was certain, as much as he could be certain of anything in this place, that to those who had come to dwell in it the Afterworld was forever, the Afterworld was eternal. Some, he knew, had gone down into the tunnels and had never emerged. But to Gilgamesh that did not mean they had found a way out, only that they were lost in some doubly nether world, perhaps the House of Dust and Darkness itself, that terrible place of which the priests in Uruk had told, where the dead were clad like birds and sadly trailed their feathers in the dust. Gilgamesh had no yearning to go down into that forlorn land of unending night.

But now – for the sake of finding out where Enkidu had gone this time –

Down. Down. Herod's torch flickered and sputtered. The air was thick and oppressive here. There was the taste of fire in it. In the dimness Gilgamesh saw hideous scenes carved on the tunnel walls, that made his eyes throb and pound. It was all he could do to tear his gaze away from those dreadful pictures.

The tunnels curved and twisted, now plunging almost straight down, now rising in steep ramps. They crossed one another and seemed to blend and meld, and then to split apart again, so that it was all but impossible to remember which path they had originally been bound upon. Herod seemed to know the way, but even he was baffled now and again, and turned to the Hairy Man, who would gesture brusquely with one finger, jabbing the long dagger of his fingernail in the right direction: this way, this, this. No one spoke. They encountered few others in the tunnels. Occasionally demon-sounds reverberated in the distance: cacklings, screechings, hissings, moanings.

And then music: a dreadful barbaric drumming, with the jabbing shriek of flutes or fifes rising above it.

"The house of Calandola lies just beyond," said Herod.

"What must I do as we enter?" asked Gilgamesh.

"Stand upright. Show no fear. Meet him eye to eye."

Gilgamesh laughed. "That will be no great task."

"Wait," Herod said. "Tell me that five minutes from now."

The tunnel swung abruptly to the left, and Gilgamesh found himself staring into a secondary tunnel, long and narrow and lit only by the faintest of star-gleams. The only way to enter it seemed to be through an opening hardly suitable for a dwarf. "In here," Herod said, clambering through. Gilgamesh, crouching, had to shuffle in on his knees, crawling at an angle, first this shoulder, then that one. The Hairy Man followed.

Beyond the single narrow point of light that illuminated the opening, the darkness within was like a night within night: blackness upon blackness, so stark and deep that it struck the eyes like the hammering of fists. Gilgamesh was stunned by the depth of that darkness. He understood now for the first time what it must be like to be blind.

"This way," Herod said confidently. "Follow me!"

And what if a fathomless pit yawned before them on the path, with boiling oil or colossal serpents waiting at the bottom? What if swinging scythes were to reach forth from the sides of the tunnel to disembowel any comers who passed close by? What if swords on tripwires hung overhead, ready to descend and cleave? He could see nothing. He must surrender himself totally to faith.

And yet, and yet, being blind in this fashion, other senses came into play –

He could hear Herod's Roman robe rustling on the heavy air, and the tread of Herod's sandal-shod feet pattering against the ground. The skin of his cheeks and forehead told him of the breeze that Herod's movements created. Like a hunter tracking his prey in the night Gilgamesh read these signs, and more, and followed along without fear or hesitation.

The tunnel narrowed until it pressed like a clammy fist on all sides. The tunnel widened until it became a vast echoing cavern. The tunnel narrowed again. It dipped; it rose; it twisted about and about. And abruptly it delivered them into an immense deep-shadowed room irregularly lit by smouldering torches set in brazen sconces, a room of angles, where ceiling met walls in a manner that oppressed and bewildered the eye. And toward the center of the room there sat enthroned a man of immense presence and authority who could only have been the great sorcerer Imbe Calandola, of whom it was rumored in the Afterworld that he was the Archfiend, the King of Evil, the true Lucifer, the Lord of Darkness.

Gilgamesh saw at once that this was not so. He knew with one glance that this Calandola was neither god nor demon nor devil, but a man of human flesh and blood, such as he was himself, or had been when he had lived. But having perceived that, Gilgamesh perceived also in that same moment that the man before whom he stood was one who was extraordinary in the extreme. Who, mortal though he might have been, might well have the blood of gods in him.

As did Gilgamesh, who had known from childhood that he was two parts god and one part mortal, which was the source of his great stature and the depth of his wisdom. Though none of that had spared him from dying and coming to make his home these long years in the Afterworld.

"Stand and give obedience," a deep rumbling voice commanded out of the shadows behind Calandola's throne. "Yield yourselves, strangers, for you are in the presence of the great Jaqqa, Imbe Calandola."

Gilgamesh stared, and felt an emotion as close to awe as anything he could remember feeling in five thousand years.

The blackness of Calandola was like the blackness of Calandola's tunnel: a blackness upon blackness, the blackness of a void without suns, a blackness so intense that it seemed to suck light from all that was around it. Black-skinned men had not been unknown to Gilgamesh in his life before the Afterworld. In his wanderings in distant places he had seen the flat-nosed thick-lipped woolly-haired sailors of the kingdom of Punt, who came from a land in the south where the air was like fire and darkened the skins of those who lived there. From far-off Meluhha had come other black ones with thin noses and lips, and long straight hair so dark it was nearly blue. And in the Afterworld itself he had encountered many who were black in one of these fashions or another, native to lands whose names meant nothing to him – Nigeria, Ethiopia, Nubia, Mali, Quiloa, India, Socotra, Zanzibar, and many more. Perhaps there were blacks in every part of the world of first life, as also there were yellows and reds and browns, and, for all Gilgamesh knew, blue and green and piebald ones. But he had never seen anyone in either world who was like Calandola.

His skin had the blackness of the people of Punt but his nose was straight and his lips were narrow and harsh, something like the features of the men of Meluhha and India, though they were small men and this Calandola was huge, a giant verging on the great size of Gilgamesh himself. His hair was thick and long and curling and there were sea-shells woven into it, and around his neck was a collar of large shells of a different kind, that stood out like twisted turrets. A strip of glittering copper as long as a man's small finger was thrust through his nose, and two more such strips dangled from his ears. His loins were clothed in a swath of brilliant scarlet cloth, but the rest of his massive body was bare. Red and white designs had been painted down his sides; and where he was not painted, his skin had been cut and carved and otherwise tormented into astonishing raised welts, some sort of monstrous decoration, that had the form of flowers and knots and lines. His skin also was oiled to a high gloss, so that reflections of the torchlight gleamed on him.

And his eyes – !

Gods! Enlil and Enki and Inanna, what eyes!

They were black and bright and deep, pools of utter darkness set in fields of dazzling white. Gilgamesh knew them at once for the eyes of a true king. They were eyes that could seize and hold, eyes that could beat and oppress. Eyes that could charm if they had to, eyes that could kill.

Who was this man? Where had he reigned in life? Why did he dwell now in this cavern beneath Brasil in the depths of the Afterworld?

Calandola rose. Stepped down from his throne, took a few slow steps toward Gilgamesh. There was a curious dark odor about him, a sour reek, which Gilgamesh suspected came from the oil that made his body shine. He moved with extreme deliberation, calm and measured and sure. It became apparent now that Calandola was not as tall as Gilgamesh by half a head; but, then, few men were. His look of great size he owed to the massiveness of his neck and the mighty breadth of his shoulders and the power of his upper arms, which were as thick as thighs.

He nodded in a sniffing way at the Hairy Man, and shrugged at the trembling, fawning Herod. To Gilgamesh he said in a black powerful voice that seemed to rise from some tunnel beneath even this tunnel, "Why have you come to me?"

"I have questions, and they say that you have answers."

"I know where answers may be found, yes. Give me your hand."

And he put forth his own, extending it palm upward. It was dark below and pink in the palm, and its span was enormous, enough to have allowed him to take a man's head in his grasp and squeeze it like a lump of river clay. Gilgamesh, after a moment, placed his hand outspread atop Calandola's, and waited. The outermost two of Calandola's thick black fingers closed in on the sides of Gilgamesh's hand and dug deep, and deeper still, until Gilgamesh could feel a faint stirring of pain, and the bones beginning to move about. A test of endurance? Very well. It was childish, but Gilgamesh would accept it. He withstood the terrible clamping pressure of those two fingers as though he were being stroked with feathers; and when the pain became too intense, he sent the pain from him as one might banish an annoying fly.

A vein stood out now on Calandola's gleaming forehead. The strange ornamentation of raised scars that had been carved upon his skin appeared to rise still higher, and to throb and pulse. The two fingers pressed inward even more fiercely. Unflinching, Gilgamesh looked down with indifference at his hand and Calandola's beneath it; and then, without a word, he slid two fingers of his own along the sides of Calandola's wrist, and returned the pressure with one of his own that was just as powerful.

Calandola seemed not to react. It was as though he felt no pain; or else that he knew how, as Gilgamesh did, to treat pain as unworthy of his notice and dismiss it from awareness.

As they stood locked this way, hand in hand, fingers digging deep, Calandola said, "You are too big to be a Portugal and too dark to be an Angleez. But not dark enough, I think, for an African."

"No. I'm not any of those."

"Then what are you?"

Gilgamesh stepped up the pressure. Still Calandola showed no sign of discomfort. They were unable to hurt one another, it seemed.

"When I lived on the other shore," Gilgamesh said, "my land was known as the Land of the Two Rivers. Or we called it Sumer."

"In Africa?"

"Not in Africa, no." Now and then Gilgamesh had seen maps. He put little faith in them, but other men seemed to live by them; and on the maps, Africa was the name they gave that great hump-shouldered land far to the south of his own where the sky was like fire. "Some called my land Mesopotamia."

"I know nothing of that place."

"Very few do, in these times. But once it was the center of the world."

"No doubt it was," said Calandola, sounding unimpressed. He released Gilgamesh's hand, casually letting go, not in any admission of defeat but merely, it would seem, because whatever test he had imposed had brought him whatever answer he sought. "These Two Rivers of yours: which two were those?"

"The nearer was the Euphrates, as some call it. The other was the Tigris. We said the Buranunu, and the Idigna."

Calandola nodded remotely. Plainly those great names were nothing but noises to him. He seemed lost in private calculations.

"Bring wine," he called suddenly, gesturing to someone in the rear of the cavern.

Gilgamesh saw that a considerable entourage lurked in the darkness behind Calandola: half a dozen black men nearly as huge as their master and perhaps eleven women of the same sort, all of them clad in little more than beads and shells, and their dark skins glossy with oil. One came forward now with a wooden bowl full of some thick sweet-smelling wine. Calandola dipped his fingertips into it, and shook wine out over Gilgamesh's head as if anointing him, and then slowly rubbed the wine deep into his scalp, while murmuring in an unknown language. Gilgamesh submitted to the rite unprotestingly. Then the black giant offered the bowl to Gilgamesh. For an instant the Sumerian wondered if he was supposed to anoint Calandola in return; but no, apparently all he was meant to do was take a drink. He sipped, and found it heavy and almost nauseatingly sweet. Calandola watched him carefully. After a moment's hesitation Gilgamesh reached for the bowl again and took a second draught, draining deep.

Calandola threw back his head and laughed. His mouth was enormous, a great world-gulping hole set about with huge white teeth of formidable size. Four of the teeth were gone, two above and two below, so symmetrical in their absence that it seemed likely to Gilgamesh they had been removed deliberately, perhaps for vanity's sake, or in some witch-rite. And when Calandola's laughter set the men and women of his tribe laughing with him Gilgamesh saw that they too were missing two upper and two lower teeth, in the same pattern.

"You drink like a king," Calandola said. "Do you have a name?"

"I am Gilgamesh the Sumerian, who was king of Uruk."

"Ah. I am Calandola the Jaqqa, who was king of the world." He clapped his hands. "Oil for King Gilgamesh!" he roared.

Two of the black women came forward, struggling with a huge wooden tub that held some sort of dark grease. Dipping his immense hands in it, Calandola scooped up a great gobbet of the stuff and clapped it to Gilgamesh's bare chest; and then, with a surprisingly tender touch, he rubbed it in, chest and back and shoulders and the column of the neck, until the Sumerian gleamed as brightly as any of the Jaqqa folk. The same sharp and sour odor came from the oil that emanated from Calandola himself. Gilgamesh felt it permeating his skin, sinking in deep.

When he was done, Calandola held Gilgamesh a moment in a tight embrace. Gilgamesh sensed the bull-like force of the man, the mountainous mass of him.

Then Calandola let go of him and stepped back. "When you return, King Gilgamesh, perhaps we will seek the answers to these questions of yours."

Calandola flashed his eyes and grinned his gap-toothed grin; and then he turned in clear dismissal and stalked away into the shadows, and his entourage closed in behind him so that Gilgamesh no longer had sight of him.

For a long moment Gilgamesh stood staring, feeling the weight of the sweet wine within his gut and the slippery slickness of the grease with which Calandola had besmeared him. Then he looked about to see what had become of his companions. The Hairy Man leaned against the wall, arms folded across his deep shaggy chest, thin lips clamped in a look of glowering disapproval. As for Herod, he was kneeling in a sweaty heap, eyes fixed in the distance, arms hanging slackly. He looked dazed. It was something of the same look that he had had when he was staring out the window of Gilgamesh's room at the furious outpouring of flame from the erupting Vesuvius.

Gilgamesh poked him with his toe.

"Come," he said. "Get up. I think we have to go now."

Numbly Herod nodded. His eyes were wide. "He gave you the wine!" he murmured. "He gave you the oil! Extraordinary! Astonishing! On the first visit, the wine, the oil!"

"Is that so unusual?" Gilgamesh asked.

Herod was shivering with excitement. "The power of the man! The sheer awesomeness of him! I can't believe he gave you the wine the first time. And the oil. It was as though he looked at you and sized you up in a single glance, and said to himself, Yes, this man and I, we are of the same spirit. My God, how I envy you! To be taken right into Calandola's arms—" He swung around toward Gilgamesh and the Sumerian saw the look of sickening devotion on Herod's face.

In some strange way Gilgamesh felt undeniably impressed by Calandola himself. But not like this. Not like this.

From the shadowy corner the Hairy Man snorted contemptuously. "So much for half a million years of evolution. You lie down with savages and before long you turn into one yourself."

"And what are you?" Herod flared, whirling around in sudden fury. "You animal! You ape! You rug that walks! You half-human thing! You wrap yourself in a toga and you think you're a Roman. But I know what you really are!"

"Come," Gilgamesh said.

"Before Adam ever was," Herod said fiercely to the Hairy Man, "you ran naked in the forests, and lived in holes in the ground, and knew no gods nor language nor civilization, and ate worms and grubs and leaves. Talk about savages! We know what your kind was. Savage is too polite a word. Let me tell you something: You people are just here on a technicality. The Afterworld is for humans. If we have a few of you grunting ape-men here too, well, that's just somebody twisting the rules a little. Maybe certain starry-eyed Later Dead types have fooled themselves into thinking that you're our ancestors, but we both know that that can't be possible. And when you start putting on airs and pretending that you actually are human beings –"

"Enough of this, Herod," Gilgamesh said, more sternly. "Up. Out. Lead me back to the upper city." To the Hairy Man he said apologetically, "He's just overwrought. The air down here, I suppose –"

"He wants to sell his soul," said the Hairy Man. "The trouble is, he doesn't know where to find it. But I take no offense. I'm as accustomed to being called an ape as you are to explaining where your Land used to be. If he needs to think of himself as the crown of Creation, what's that to me? He knows nothing of the life we lived when the gods had not so much as imagined any of you." The Hairy Man laughed and scratched his furry chest. "Ask him, later, what that grease was, that the black wizard rubbed into your skin. Not now. But ask him."

Ten

"– human fat?" Gilgamesh said, feeling his skin beginning to crawl.

Herod moved his head in a quick affirmative. They were in Simon's palace again, by the courtyard fountain.

"But where does he get it?"

"There are plenty of bodies available. Life isn't simply cheap in the Afterworld, you know. It's free for the taking, and who's to say no?"

Gilgamesh knew that well enough. No gods governed this world, and law and order, or the lack of it, was a matter of purely local whim. There were marauding armies everywhere, and freelance bandits, and swaggering bullies, and mere casual random killers; and death was a daily commonplace. But death here was only an irritating annoyance, a bothersome but usually brief interruption of the endless ongoingness of your stay in the Afterworld. There were those who had died three times the same week and came bounding back from it each time, apparently unchanged. Somewhere behind the scenes, unknown and probably unknowable forces reconstructed your body from whatever bits and pieces could be found, and stuffed your soul back into it and turned you loose to live again. Not that he had experienced it himself: so far as he could recall he had died only once in all his thousands of years, and that at the expected time, when his span on Earth had come to its appointed end. But keeping himself from being killed in the Afterworld was only a matter of pride for him. Enkidu had said that of him once, hurling the accusation at him in anger the one time they had quarrelled: "Too proud to die – too proud to accept the decree of the gods –" And Gilgamesh had had to admit to himself that it was true. Because he had been who he had been, he took care to guard himself constantly against attack here, and when he was attacked he saw to it that his strength or his cunning always would prevail. He would not have it that any man might boast that he had slain the mighty Gilgamesh. Yet if by some mischance he did someday die again, he was aware that it would not be for long.

Still and all, to be slaughtering people or hauling in the corpses of those slain by others, and oiling one's skin with the grease of them –!

"Does it disgust you?" Herod asked.

Gilgamesh shrugged. "It is a filthy thing, yes. Who is this Calandola? He said he was a king in Africa. But that means little to me."

"And to me. The Africa we Romans knew was a land of light-skinned folk, just across the water from Rome. He's from deeper down, the dark part of the continent. And of a much later time, they say. He lived by the river Zaire, in the land called Kongo, in the days when the Spaniards and the English and the Portuguese were building empires across the seas."

"Just the day before yesterday, that is to say."

"Yes. His people were known as Jaqqas. Nomads, they were. Warriors who would destroy everything that lay in their path, for the sheer love of destruction. There was something almost religious about it, their fondness for smashing things. Purifying the earth is what they called it."

"And when his army was finished purifying, he'd shine himself up with the fat of the conquered, is that it? A cheerful custom which he takes pleasure in continuing to practise in the Afterworld?"

"Oh, he does worse things than that."

Gilgamesh raised an eyebrow. "Does he?"

"Far worse."

"Such as?"

"Don't ask me to tell you. You'll have to discover the rest for yourself. I'm pledged to reveal nothing. If I break my oath he'll know right away. And cast me out."

"Out of what?"

Herod seemed surprised. "His presence! His fellowship! His – his light!"

Light was an odd term to use, Gilgamesh thought, for one who reigned in darkness and who seemed himself to be the very embodiment of darkness. He stared at Herod in distaste. "You worship him, don't you?"

Herod grinned nervously, "I wouldn't like to think I carry it that far."

"As you wish."

"I'd say that I'm fascinated by him, is all."

"Merely in the way of scholarship?"

"It's more than scholarly," Herod said. "I won't deny that I'm in awe of him. Fascinated to the point of awe, yes. Yes. But so are you. Admit it, Gilgamesh! I was watching you. He's practically as big as you are, and maybe just as strong as you are, and there's something about him, something mysterious and powerful, that draws you in, just as he's drawn in everyone else who ever came near him. Admit it! Admit it, Gilgamesh!"

Herod's high-pitched voice had taken on that buzzing intensity again, and for a moment Gilgamesh had to struggle to keep from swatting him. There were, Gilgamesh had heard, certain poor souls in the Afterworld who had been given the forms of strange insects when they were reborn here, instead of bodies of their own. Well, Herod's body certainly seemed human enough, but it was as if there was something of the insect about him as well. A wasp, a fly, a gnat. He was certainly infuriating.

And this fascination that Herod claimed to feel for Calandola. This awe. There was something sick about it, weak, submissive, ugly. Clearly the black man emanated some magical force that Herod had allowed completely to seize possession of him. Gilgamesh understood now why he had taken so quick a dislike to Herod. The man was looking for some power greater than himself to which he could surrender everything: his identity, his soul, his entire self. If not Simon, then the volcano. If not the volcano, then Calandola. Gilgamesh had never been able to understand the value of surrender of any sort; and certainly he had never held much regard for those who went about searching for it.

"He may be able to see through the mists," Gilgamesh said, "and tell me where Enkidu has gone. That's where my interest in your Lord Calandola begins and ends."

"Not true! Not true! But you won't own up to it."

"You tax my patience, Herod."

"You don't find him – attractive?"

"Attractive? Not in the least. 'Repellent' is the word I'd use."

"I wish I could believe that."

"Do you tell me that I'm lying?" asked Gilgamesh ominously.

"I tell you that you may be hiding things even from yourself," said Herod. "Oh, perhaps not! Perhaps not!" he added quickly, as Gilgamesh glared.

"Oiled in the fat of the dead! I never heard of such a thing in any land, not even the most barbarous. It is a monstrous thing to do, Herod."

"All right, so he's a monster. But won't you at least agree that he's a glorious monster? Larger than life, a monster of monsters. Oh, how my grandfather Herod would have loved him! So big, so dark. Those diabolical eyes. The way his skin is all carved up and covered with bumps and welts. And those four teeth knocked out to make him look prettier – and the way he shines in the darkness, that gleam that he has –"

That gleam, Gilgamesh thought somberly. Yes. The gleam of death.

"A monster, no question of that. I'm not so sure about glorious. The Hairy Man speaks the truth: your Calandola's a savage."

"Of course he is," Herod said at once. "That's what's so wonderful about him! A marvelous overwhelming hideous ghastly frightful savage! But he's a seer, too. You mustn't overlook the reality of his powers. You'll find out. He can open the darkness for you. He'll do the rite of the Knowing with you. And whatever questions you have will be answered."

"Ah, and will they be?"

"Have no doubt of that, Gilgamesh. None at all. All that is secret will be laid bare."

Gilgamesh pondered that. Opening the darkness? The rite of the Knowing? A half-naked savage with a piece of copper thrust through his nose, laying bare all that is secret? Well, maybe. Maybe. The only thing that was certain in the Afterworld was the absolute strangeness of it. What had been invisible on Earth, or nearly so, was made manifest here. On Earth one sometimes caught glimpses of demons out of the corner of one's eye; here they sat down and played at dice with you, or sprawled by the fireside in a tavern, singing curious songs. Witchcraft was everywhere. Gilgamesh had no reason to doubt this Calandola's powers of divination. And if covering one's skin with loathsome grease was the price of finding the path to Enkidu, well, that was not too high a price to pay. No price would be too high for that.

At the far side of the courtyard Simon and his Hairy Man appeared. The dictator beckoned.

"Gilgamesh! Where have you been?"

The Sumerian answered only with a shrug.

"Will you be at the party tonight?" Simon called.

"Party?"

"After the games! Women, Gilgamesh! Wine! Rivers of wine! Don't forget!"

"Yes," Gilgamesh said, without enthusiasm. "Of course." Rivers of wine? Wine meant nothing to him now. Nor women, really. Not for a very long time.

The image of the Jaqqa Imbe Calandola rose up in his mind, soaring like a colossus above him, and then he had a sudden startling view of himself swimming desperately against a terrible current, in a river not of wine but of blood.

"Take," Calandola said. "Drink."

For a second time Gilgamesh, led by a tense and apprehensive Herod Agrippa, had gone down into the tunnels below Brasil. For a second time they had penetrated the torchlit chamber that was the lair of Imbe Calandola and his Jaqqa minions. And for a second time the black wizard-king had offered Gilgamesh the sweet wine and had rubbed his body with the oil of dread origin.

Now some further, deeper rite was about to commence. The room was more crowded than it had been the other time. There seemed to be even more Jaqqas than before, a great shadowy crew of them, thirty or forty or even more, stalking like long-legged goblins through the dim smoky recesses of the cavern performing tasks that not even Gilgamesh's keen vision could clearly perceive. But also there were eight or ten or a dozen other figures in white Brasilian garb, men and women, kneeling in the center of the room like acolytes, like initiates. Some of them were masked with strips of black cloth and others had their faces bared. Like Herod they seemed uneasy: their pale faces were glistening with perspiration and their eyes flickered constantly from side to side. Often during the rite of the wine and the oil they stared at Gilgamesh with great intensity, and sometimes with a strange expression that might have been loathing and fear, or perhaps pity and sorrow: he could not tell. It might even have been envy. Envy? Of what? He felt like one who was about to be sacrificed to an unknown god.

From the depths of the room came music. The Jaqqas were playing fifes that made an ear-piercing shrieking sound, and beating on drums fashioned from the scaly hides of demon-beasts, and also tapping their fingers against thin boards mounted on wooden stakes. Four of the women came dancing across the room in wild cavorting prancing leaps, their oiled breasts bobbling, their gap-toothed mouths wide open in frozen grimaces. Calandola himself, shining and immense, sat astride a small three-legged stool intricately carved with the faces of demons, and rocked back and forth, bellowing in pleasure.

Then he rose and signalled, and two of the Brasilian acolytes sprang to their feet, a man and a woman. Out of the darkness of the cavern's strange-angled corners the man brought a crook-necked flask and the woman fetched a tasseled red pillow on which there rested a cup of strange design, wide and shallow.

The music rose to a feverish frantic pitch. To Gilgamesh it was, like all music, mere irritating noise. The only music he had ever cared for was the delicate flute-music and the light and lively drumming of Sumer, which he had not had the joy of hearing in five thousand years. But this Jaqqa stuff was a noise beyond noise: it was a thunder that thrust itself inside you and occupied all the space that there was within you, so that it threatened to evict your own soul from its housing.

"This is the royal wine," said Calandola in a voice like the dark rumbling of a bear. "It will make the first Opening for you, the Opening that comes before the Knowing. Are you prepared, King Gilgamesh?"

"Give me your wine."

"First your dog, and then you."

"The dog?"

"First the dog," Calandola said again.

"Very well," said Gilgamesh. This was all madness to him; but he saw none of it as any more mad than any other part. The dog? Why not the dog? "If the dog is willing, give the dog the royal wine."

Calandola made a brusque signal with three fingers of his left hand. The woman holding the pillowed cup knelt; the man poured the royal wine from the crook-necked flask.

When the cup was full she turned toward Ajax. The dog uttered a growling sound, but not, so it seemed, in any angry way. He looked up at Gilgamesh and there was an unmistakable questioning in his eyes.

Gilgamesh shrugged. "You are to go first," he said. "That is what I have been told. Drink, Ajax. If you will."

The room grew hushed. The dog drank, lapping quickly at the bowl. Wagging his tail, making little snuffling sounds: the royal wine appeared to please him. Gilgamesh had never known a dog to drink wine. But Ajax was a dog of the Afterworld; there was no reason why the dogs of the Afterworld could not drink wine, or fly through the air, or do any number of other unnatural things. The Afterworld was not a natural place.

At length Calandola signalled again, and the woman withdrew the cup from Ajax. The dog remained motionless. His eyes seemed strange: unmoving and, so it appeared, glowing.

Gilgamesh reached now for the cup.

"No," Calandola said. "Not yet. Your other dog first."

"I have but one dog."

"This one," said the Jaqqa, and pointed with his foot at Herod.

The Judaean prince looked astounded. He had been kneeling beside the other acolytes; now he rose, shaking his head in disbelief, tapping his breast as though to say, "Me? *Me*?" Calandola pointed a second time, making a contemptuous hooking gesture with his outstretched foot to draw Herod forward. Gilgamesh thought the little man would topple over before he had managed to take five steps. But somehow he stayed upright long enough to approach the cup-bearer. She proffered the pillow. Herod took the cup from it, resting it in both his hands and putting his face down and forward, practically into the cup. In long sighing gulps he drank it dry. Then he swayed and shook; the cup-bearer seized the cup before he could drop it; Herod backed away, wearing now the same glazed look in his eyes that the dog Ajax did, and took up his kneeling position once more.

This time Gilgamesh waited to see whether there were any more dogs in the room. But no: at last it was his turn to taste the royal wine.

The man with the crook-necked flask poured. The woman who held the pillow carried the cup to the Sumerian.

"Take," said Calandola. "Drink."

Gilgamesh lifted the bowl as Herod had done, in both his hands. It was cool and smooth, like fine ivory, but irregular of shape beneath. As he stared down into it he ran his fingers over its undersurface and came to realize what sort of thing it was that he held in his hands: beyond any question a human skullcap, with the parts below the eyesockets cut away. Very well, he thought. We drink here from a polished skullcap. Why not? He was beginning to understand Lord Calandola's style of doing things. A skullcap is well suited to be a cup. Why not? Why not?

The wine was dark, not honey-colored like the other stuff, but tinged with red. He took a sip. There was an overpowering sweetness to it: a sweetness like that of the sweetest nectar, or perhaps even more intense. It lay strangely on his tongue, a heavy thick-textured wine. He swallowed it and took another, and suddenly he knew what it was that give the wine its sweetness, and what tinged it with red. This royal wine of Imbe Calandola's was a wine made of blood. Knowing that, he thought his stomach might rebel at it, and hurl it back. But no. No, it slipped down smoothly enough. He had some more.

He drank until the cup was empty, and looked up, and smiled, and handed it back to its bearer.

And waited.

The Opening, this was. That comes before the Knowing.

Well? Why was nothing happening? Why had his eyes not gone glassy, as had the dog's, as had Herod's? Why was he not swaying? Why not dizzy? Was he immune to Calandola's monstrous wine? Was he so lost within the walls of his own self that there could be no Opening for him?

He looked toward Calandola. "There is no effect," he said. "Perhaps another draught of your wine, Lord Calandola –"

Calandola laughed – a strangely drawn-out laugh, that sounded thin and far away, and came cascading down over

Gilgamesh like the tumbling of a waterfall. He made no other reply.

Then came a weird droning voice from somewhere to his left, saying, "Alas, alas, you fall in error, world-striding Gilgamesh! No further wine do you need! The walls are down! The Opening is at hand!"

"What? What?"

"See me revealed! My previous self is what you behold."

The Sumerian gasped. Ajax had disappeared; and in his place a bizarre creature fluttered midway between the floor and the level of Gilgamesh's shoulders. It was something like a wasp, but larger than any insect Gilgamesh had ever seen, and covered with a shining blue incrustation almost like some precious stone. From its rear jutted a cruel-looking green stinger; and its tiny face was the face of a human woman. It buzzed and beat its wings as it hovered beside him.

"You see?" the wasp-woman cried. "In the Opening, much is shown! In my last life I was this, who am come back into the Afterworld now as Ajax the dog."

"Your – last life –"

"As insect, yes. Though even before that did I have human flesh, the same as you. Yet I gave self up to sin, and down I was forced to slip. For my penance was I made insect and greatly did I suffer. But then in later times for loyal service was I granted dog. You see, it is down the ladder and then sometimes up again. I still aspire, beyond dog. I rise again, and be better than dog. Though dog is good. When one has known insect, dog seems good."

Ah. That was it. Gilgamesh understood. His dog Ajax, then, was one of those unfortunates whose fate it was to drift from body to body, from form to form, during their eternal stay in the Afterworld. So it seemed Calandola's wine was doing some work, if he was able to see such things as this. Yes, he was sure now: an Opening of some sort had been achieved, and he was perceiving things beyond the ordinary realm of perception.

"Indeed, dog is good," the wasp-woman was saying. "To have King Gilgamesh as my master is good. I follow the mighty Gilgamesh and he will take mercy on me some day and put me into a woman-body again. Or even a man-body.

What does it matter, man or woman, if only human? Human I would be again, as who would not?"

Gilgamesh smiled. "If I can do it, I will," he said.

Instantly the wasp was a dog again; and Ajax lay flattened by his feet, nuzzling close.

Gilgamesh bent and stroked the beast fondly. Then he rose and turned toward Herod.

"And what of you?" asked Gilgamesh. "You, wasp in human form, what shape do you present now?"

But no outward change had come over Herod under the influence of Calandola's drink. Herod was still Herod, a small bushy-haired quick-eyed man wearing a rumpled white toga, slumped in a kneeling position halfway across the chamber. Yet something was different now. The Herod whom Gilgamesh had come to know in these few days in Brasil was a man of tricks and chatter, fast and flashy of mind, forever swiftly weaving a web of words about himself to keep bigger and more stupid foes at bay. It was a defense that must have served him well in his centuries in the Afterworld; but now it seemed that the royal wine of the Jaqqa king had stripped all that away from him.

Herod was wide open, defenseless: a sad frightened dependent man who was spending the years of his death as he had spent the years of his life, searching for a master. Once it had been the Roman Emperor Caligula, who had turned him briefly into a king. Later – much later, here in the Afterworld – it had been Simon Magus. Now it was this monstrous overbearing creature of darkness, Calandola. It could just as well be Gilgamesh next. Or Lenin, or Mao Tse-tung, or Prester John, or any of the infinite horde of other emperors and princes and demigods and warlords who had set themselves up to rule some little corner of this vast and unknowable realm that was called the Afterworld. Herod needed a master. He would probably be happier as a dog: if only he and Ajax could trade bodies somehow! Look at him, sitting there half slumped. Wishing he had a tail to wag, wishing he had soft brown worshipful eyes that he could turn lovingly upon his master, instead of those beady clever ones of his.

Gilgamesh felt a surge of scorn for Herod, that pitiful and most unkingly king.

But the scorn melted, and gave way to a deep sense of

compassion that swept through Gilgamesh with unexpected force and left him shaken and weak. How could he feel kindness for the dog who had been a wasp and yearned to be a human again, and not for this human whose soul was the soul of a dog? To despise Herod because he was no hero was itself a despicable thing. There was no shortage of heroes in the Afterworld. By the thousands and tens of thousands they swaggered about, replaying in death the dramas they had chosen in life. And if Herod – poor miserable little Herod – could manage nothing better than to find the joy of his life in the shattering outbursts of a volcano and in the barbaric blood-feasts of a nightmare savage, why, it was because he was who he was. He had no choice. No one had any choice. The gods decreed everything.

You, Gilgamesh: you will be a hero of heroes, a man like a god, a king among kings. And it will be your doom to die nevertheless, and to live forever in the Afterworld.

You, Enkidu: you will be a bold hunter and warrior, friend to the great king. And it will be your doom to die again and again, while the king your friend seeks you through all the halls of eternity.

You, Herod: you will be clever and cautious, a mouse in a world of lions. And you will have wit enough to deceive them all and keep your throne and your life, no matter how terrifying the risks of power may be to you.

We are who we are, all of us. The gods determine. We play the parts assigned. Why, then, feel contempt for those who play parts unlike our own? Herod, Simon, Calandola, the Hairy Man, the little scheming quarrelsome Later Dead folk, and all the rest – each was playing his proper part, each was fulfilling the decree of the gods. And each was in his own way the hero of his own drama, doing as it seemed fit for him to do. How could anyone be condemned for that?

Gilgamesh went to Herod's side and bent down to take him by the arm.

"Up," he said gently. "No more crouching, here. You are a man. Stand up like a man."

"Gilgamesh –"

"There's nothing to fear. I am your friend. I will protect you against whatever it is that you fear."

But even as he spoke the words, Gilgamesh realized that the spell was breaking, became aware that the power of the wine was slipping from him. In another moment the warmth and tenderness he felt for Herod faded. The irritation and contempt returned. This sad weak man: why offer to protect him? What was Herod to him? Let him fend off his demons for himself. Let him grovel before Calandola. Let him dance on the rim of the crater of Vesuvius and throw himself into the volcano's boiling heart, if that was where he thought the true home of joy was to be found. Gilgamesh looked down at Herod and shook his head. Released his hold on Herod's arm. Turned away.

"Well, then, it seems to be over," said Calandola, his voice coming as though from a great distance.

Gilgamesh stood blinking and baffled like one who has stepped from midnight darkness into the full noonday blaze of the sun.

"That was it?" he asked. "The Opening?"

"When other souls stand bare before you, yes, that is the Opening, King Gilgamesh."

"And what now? Now the Knowing?"

"No," said Calandola. "Another time. You resisted the wine; you achieved only a partial Opening. Your soul is a stubborn one. It will not yield to forces from outside. Come back another time, King Gilgamesh: and then we will see if you are strong enough to accomplish the Knowing."

"What did I do wrong?" Gilgamesh asked. "Where did I fail?"

"You held back," said Herod. "You were nearly there, and then at the last moment you held back. When the Opening begins, it's necessary to surrender completely to it. You were fighting it."

"Fighting is in my nature. Surrender isn't."

"Do you want the Knowing or don't you?"

"I thought I was yielding to the wine," Gilgamesh said. "I entered the soul of the dog. I saw what he had been in his last life. A wasp-creature, do you know that? With a woman's face and the body of some hideous insect. And then I turned to you – I saw your soul, Herod, I saw the true self within you, I –"

"All right. I don't need to hear about it."

"I saw nothing that would shame you."

"Thanks all the same, but I'd rather not know."

"It was as if the walls that separate us from each other had broken down. And then – then almost at once they were up again. The wine had worn off. Maybe if I had taken more –"

"Maybe," Herod said. "You're so damned big. Maybe Calandola misjudged the quantity. But he's been doing this for centuries. He knows what quantity is right. I think it's you, Gilgamesh. You held back, you kept some part of yourself in reserve. I can understand that. But if you want to learn the answers to your questions – if you hope to discover where Enkidu has gone –"

"Yes. I know."

"Calandola may not allow you to return to him for a week, or even a month. But when he summons you, go. And whatever he asks of you, do it. Or there'll be no Knowing for you. Eh, Gilgamesh?"

"What are you two chattering about?" Simon asked, appearing suddenly beside them. "Hatching a good conspiracy?" The dictator, grinning, clapped one hand to Gilgamesh's broad back and one to Herod's. "It's useless, you know. I have seers who tell me everything. Past, present, and future lie revealed to them. The slightest hint of subversion here will show up instantly as a blip on their screens."

"No need to fear," Gilgamesh said. "I think Herod prefers being prime minister here to any higher responsibility. And surely you know that to rule in Brasil is not a thing that I desire either, Simon."

"I know what you desire, Gilgamesh. Come to me this time two days hence, and we'll study the map of Uruk together. We should be thinking of setting forth soon. What do you say, Gilgamesh? King of Uruk that was, king of Uruk that will be! How does that sound to you?"

"Like music," said Gilgamesh.

Simon laughed and moved on.

Herod, looking troubled, said when the dictator was out of sight, "Is that true? You do want to be king of Uruk again after all?"

"I said Simon's words were like music to me."

"So you did."

Gilgamesh chuckled. "But I am no lover of music."

"Ah. Ah."

"And as for the journey to Uruk – well, let's see what wisdom your great Calandola can offer me, first. When we do the true Opening. And the Knowing that follows it. And then

I'll comprehend whether I am to make this journey or not. Let's wait and see, King Herod."

Eleven

The room of angles in the cavern of the tunnels. The smoldering torches in the brazen sconces. The drums, the fifes, the masks, the dancers. The long-legged black men pursuing unknown rituals in the shadows. The honeyed wine, the shining oil. This was Gilgamesh's third visit to the dwelling-place of Imbe Calandola. Once more now he would undertake to make the Opening; once more he would drink of the second and stronger wine, the thick sweet red beverage. Once more he would see beyond the barriers that divide soul from soul; and this time, perhaps, all the veils of mystery would be stripped away and he would be allowed to know the things he had come here to learn.

"I think you are ready," Calandola said. "For the deeper feast. For the full Knowing."

"Bring me the wine, yes," said Gilgamesh.

"It will not only be wine today," replied Calandola.

In the darkness, chanting and drums. Fires flickering behind the Imbe-Jaqqa's throne. Figures moving about. A sound that might have been that of water boiling in a great kettle.

A signal from Calandola.

The bearer of the wine came forth, and the bearer of the cup. Ajax once again drank first, and then Herod, and then Gilgamesh. But this time Calandola drank also, and drank deep, again and again calling for the cup to be filled, until his lips and jowls were smeared with red.

"Belial and Beelzebub," Herod whispered. "Moloch and Lucifer!"

Gilgamesh felt the strangeness of the Opening settling upon him once more. He could recognize its signs now: an eerie hush, a heightened awareness. Invisible beings brushed past him in the air. There was a deep humming sound that seemed to come from the core of the world. He could touch the souls of Ajax the dog and Herod the Jew; and now there was the formidable presence of black Calandola also revealed to him. Revealed and not revealed, for although Gilgamesh saw the inwardness of Calandola it was like a huge black wall of rock rising before him, impenetrable, unscalable.

"Now will you join our feast," said Calandola. "And the Knowing will descend upon you, King Gilgamesh."

He threw back his head and laughed, and made a gesture with his massive arms like the toppling of two mighty trees. From the musicians came a crashing of sounds, a terrible thunder and a screeching. The throne was drawn aside; and a great metal cauldron stood revealed, bubbling over a raging fire of logs.

Calandola's minions were preparing a rich and robust stew. Into the cauldron went onions and leeks and peppers, beans and squash, pomegranates and grapes, vegetables and fruits of every sort imaginable. The steaming vessel seemed bottomless. Ears of corn and sacks of figs, huge gnarled tuberous roots of this kind and that, most of them unknown to Gilgamesh. Clusters of garlic, double handfuls of radishes, slabs of whole ginger. A barrel of dark wine, of what sort Gilgamesh dared not think. Spices of fifty kinds. And meat. Massive chunks of pale raw meat, flung in whole, still on the bone.

A troublesome feeling stirred in Gilgamesh. To Herod he said, "What meat is that, do you think?"

Herod was gazing at the cauldron with unblinking eyes. He laughed in his oddly edgy way and said, "One that is not kosher, I'd be willing to bet."

"Kosher? What is that?"

But Herod made no answer. A shiver ran through him that made his whole body ripple like a slender tree beset by the wild autumn gales. His face was aglow with the brightness that Gilgamesh had seen in it that time when the volcano had erupted. Herod had the look of one who was held tight in the grip of some powerful enchantment.

By the virtue of the dark wine they had shared, Gilgamesh looked into Herod's soul. What he saw there made him recoil in amazement and shock.

"*That* meat?"

"They say there is no better one for this purpose, King Gilgamesh."

His stomach twisted and turned.

He had eaten many strange things in many strange lands. But never that. To devour the flesh of his own kind –

No. No. No. No. Not even in the Afterworld.

Gilgamesh had heard tales, now and then, of certain races in remote parts of the world that did such things. Not for nourishment's sake but for magic. To take into themselves the strength or the wisdom or the mystical virtue of others. It had been hard for him to believe, that such things were done.

But to be asked to do it himself –

"Unthinkable. Forbidden. Abominable."

"Forbidden by whom?" asked Herod.

"Why – by –"

Gilgamesh faltered and could say no more.

"We are in the Afterworld, King Gilgamesh. Nothing is forbidden here. Have you forgotten that?"

Gilgamesh stared. "And you truly mean to commit this abomination? You want me to commit it with you?"

"I want nothing from you," Herod said. "But you are here in search of knowledge."

"Which is obtained like *this*?"

Herod smiled. "So it is said. It is the gateway, the way of the full Opening that leads to the Knowing."

"And you believe this insanity?"

The Judaean prince turned to face him, and there was a look of terrible conviction in his eyes.

"Do as you please, King Gilgamesh. But if you would have the knowledge, take and eat. Take and eat."

"Take and eat!" came the booming voice of Calandola. "Take and eat!"

The cannibal tribesmen leaped and danced. One who was whitened with chalk from head to toe and wore straw garments that seemed to be the costume of a witch rushed to the cauldron, pulled a joint of meat from the boiling water with his bare hands, held it aloft.

"Ayayya! Ayayya!" the Jaqqas cried. "Ayayya!"

The witch brought the meat to Calandola and held it forth to him for his inspection. From Calandola came a roar of approval; and he seized the joint with both his hands, and put his jaws to it and buried his teeth in it.

"Ayayya! Ayayya!" cried the Jaqqas.

Gilgamesh felt the wine of the cannibals flowing through his soul. He swayed in rhythm to the harsh and savage music. Beside him, Herod now seemed wholly transported, lost in an ecstasy, caught up entirely in the fascination of this abomination. As though he had waited all his life and through his life after life as well to make this surrender to Calandola's foul mystery. Or as though he had no choice but to be swept along into it, wherever it might take him.

And I feel myself swept along also, thought Gilgamesh in shock and amazement.

"Take," said Calandola. "Eat."

Joyously he held the great slab of steaming meat out toward Gilgamesh.

Gods! Enlil and Enki and Sky-father An, what is this I am doing?

The gods were very far from this place, though. Gilgamesh stared at the slab of meat.

"This is the way of Knowing," said Calandola.

This?

No. No. No. No.

He shook his head. "There are some things I will not do, even to have the Knowing."

The aroma from the kettle mixed with some strange incense burning in great braziers alongside it, and he felt himself swaying in mounting dizziness. Turning, he took three clumsy, shambling steps toward the entrance. Acolytes and initiates drew back, making way for him as he lumbered past. He heard Calandola's rolling, resonant laughter behind him, mocking him for his cowardice.

Then Herod was in his path, blocking him. The little man was drawn tight as a bow: trembling, quivering.

Huskily he said, "Don't go, Gilgamesh."

"This is no place for me."

"The Knowing – what about the Knowing –?"

"No."

"If you try to leave, you'll never find your way out of the tunnels without me."

"I'll take my chances."

"Please," said Herod. "*Please*. Stay. Wait. Take the Sacrament with me."

"The Sacrament? You call this a Sacrament?"

"It is the way of Knowing. Take it with me. For me. Don't spurn it. Don't spurn me. We are already halfway there, Gilgamesh: the wine is in our souls, our spirits are opening to each other. Now comes the Knowing. Please. Please."

He had never seen such an imploring look on another human being's face. Not even in battle, when he raised his axe above a foe to deliver the fatal stroke. Herod reached his hands toward Gilgamesh. The Sumerian hesitated.

"And I ask you too," came a voice from his left. "Not to take depart. Not to abandon loyal friends."

Ajax.

The dog was flickering like the shadows cast by a fire on a wall: now the great brindle hound, now the strange little wasp-woman, and now, for only a moment, a hint of a human shape, a sad-eyed woman smiling timidly, forlornly.

"If you take the meat you can set me free," said the dog. "Reach into soul, separate dog and spirit. You would have the power. Send poor suffering soul on to next sphere, leave dog behind to be dog. I beg you, mighty king."

Gilgamesh stared, wavering. The dog's pleas moved him deeply.

"Your friends, great hero. Forget not your friends in this time of savioring. Long enslavement must end! You alone can give freedom!"

"Is this true?" Gilgamesh asked Herod.

"It could be. The rite releases much power to those who have power within them."

"Forget not your friends," the wasp-woman cried again.

For a moment Gilgamesh closed his eyes, trying to shut out all the frenzied madness about him. And a voice within him said, *Do it. Do it.*

Why not? Why not? Why not?

This is the Afterworld, nor is there any leaving of it.

He crossed the room to Calandola, who still held the meat. The cannibal chieftain grinned ferociously at Gilgamesh, who met his fiery gaze calmly and took the meat from him. Held it a moment. It was warm and tender, a fine cut, a succulent piece. Out of the buried places of his mind came words he had been taught five thousand years before, that time in his youth when he was newly a king and he had knelt before the priests in Uruk on the night of the rite of the Sacred Marriage:

What seems good to oneself
is a crime before the god.
What to one's heart seems evil
is good before one's god.
Who can comprehend the minds of gods
in heaven's depths?

"Take," Herod whispered. "Eat!"

Yes, Gilgamesh thought. This is the way. He lifted the slab of meat to his lips.

"Ayayya! Ayayya! Ayayya!"

He bit down deep, and savored, and swallowed; and from the volcano Vesuvius somewhere not far away there came a tremendous roar, and the earth shook; and as he tasted the forbidden flesh the Knowing entered into him in that moment.

It was like becoming a god. All things lay open to him, or so it seemed. Nothing was hidden. His soul soared; he looked down on all of space and time.

"Your friends, Gilgamesh," came a whispering voice from high overhead. "Do not forget – your friends –"

No. He would not forget.

He sent forth his soul into the dog that was the wasp-woman that once had been a human sinner. Without difficulty he distinguished the human soul from the dog-soul and the wasp-soul; and separated the one from the others, and held it a moment, and released it like a bird that one holds in one's hand and casts into the sky. There was a long sigh of gratitude; and then the wandering soul was gone, and Ajax the dog lay curled sleeping at Gilgamesh's feet, and of the wasp-creature there was no sign.

To Herod then he turned. Saw the sadness within the man, the weakness, the hunger. Saw too the quick agile mind, the warm spirit eager to please. And Gilgamesh touched Herod within, only for an instant, letting something of himself travel across the short distance from soul to soul. A touch of strength; a touch of resilience. *Here,* he thought. *Take this from me; and hold something of myself within you, for those times when being yourself is not enough for you.*"

Herod seemed to glow. He smiled, he wept, he bowed his head. And knelt and offered a blessing of thanks.

Gilgamesh could feel the presence of monstrous Calandola looming over him like a titan. Like a god. And yet he seemed no longer malevolent. Distant, dispassionate, aloof: serving only as a focus for this strange rite of the joining of souls.

"Seek your own Knowing now, Gilgamesh," said the Jaqqa. "The time has come."

Yes. Yes. The time has come. Now – Enkidu –?

Where?

Ah: there. There he was, in that narrow high-walled canyon, amidst the people of the caravan, the transporters of stolen jewels. There was the wagon that had fallen over, and now stood upright. Van der Heyden bustling around, giving orders. And now – now two of those whirling noisy flying-machines of the Later Dead, two helicopters, suddenly darkening the sky, descending out of nowhere, fitting themselves with eerie precision between the walls of the canyon. The caravan people shouting, running for weapons. The helicopters hovering, twice a man's height off the ground – guns poking from their sides – the brutal sound of machine-gun fire – the caravan people running, screaming, falling –

Enkidu crouched beside a wagon with an automatic weapon somehow in his hands, firing back –

A figure rising out of the closer helicopter, throwing something down – a fragmentation bomb, it was – a burst of black smoke, screams, caravan people sprawling everywhere, horribly mutilated –

And Enkidu still firing –

"No!" Gilgamesh cried. "Enkidu! No!"

But it was like crying out within a dream. He could do nothing. He was not a god; and this vision, he knew, was sealed already into the irremediable past. Enkidu, rushing wildly toward the closer helicopter as though meaning to tear it apart with his own hands – some man of the Later Dead, with close-cropped yellow hair and hard blue eyes, peering out in amazement, reaching behind him, coming out with a grenade, arming it and tossing it in the same instant – a moment of sudden fierce incandescence, like a tiny sun –

Enkidu caught within it, visible for a moment, staggering, falling –

Falling –

Then there was only nothingness where Enkidu had been. His spirit had been swept away once again to that mysterious place of death within death where those who perished in the Afterworld were sent. Where he would wait in limbo, a year maybe, a thousand years, half of eternity perhaps – there was no predicting it – until it was his turn to be given flesh and breath again, and be sent forth into the death-in-life of the Afterworld.

"Where will I find him?" Gilgamesh asked, numbed by loss.

And a voice replied, "You must seek him in Uruk of the treasures."

Fiercely Gilgamesh shook his head. "There is no Uruk!"

"No? No? Are you sure, King Gilgamesh? Is that what the Knowing tells you?"

"Why –"

He looked. And saw. And the veils of memory dropped away.

Uruk!

It lay glittering upon the breast of a broad dark plain, a white city bright as a jewel. There was the platform of the temples, there were the sacred buildings, there were the ceremonial streets. Uruk. Not the Uruk where he had been born and been king and died, but that other Uruk, New Uruk, the Uruk of the Afterworld, that great Uruk which he –

– had founded –

– had ruled for a hundred years, or was it a thousand –

– he – he – a king in the Afterworld –

He saw himself on the throne. Officers of the court all around him, and petitioners seeking favors, and emissaries from other principalities of the Afterworld. Saw himself issuing decrees, saw himself going over plans, saw himself greeting the generals of his victorious armies. Saw himself being king in the Afterworld as he had been in the world before the Afterworld. Saw it and knew it to be a true vision.

The Knowing came upon him like a torrent, sweeping away all the imagined certainties by which he had been living for so long. Why had he thought he was an exception to the rule that the heroes in the Afterworld must recapitulate the struggles of their life-times? How had he deceived himself into thinking that he and Enkidu had spent all their thousands of years in the Afterworld merely wandering, and hunting, and wandering again, shunning the ambitions that raged like fire in everyone else? Of course he had sought to reign in the Afterworld. Of course he had brought followers together here once upon a time, and built a city, and made it magnificent, and defended it against all attack. How could he not have done such a thing? For was he not Gilgamesh the king?

And then – then –

Then to forget –

He understood now. There was never any trusting of memory in the Afterworld. How often had he seen that! Whole centuries might collapse into a single moment, and be forgotten. Whole empires might rise and fall and go unremembered. There was no history here. There was really no past, only a stew of events that did not form a pattern; and there was no future, and scarcely any present, either.

In the Afterworld everything was flux and change, though beneath the flux nothing ever changed. Gilgamesh had truly thought the lust for power had been burned out of him by time. Perhaps it had. But there was no longer any denying the things he had so long been able to hide even from himself. He knew now why all those little men engaged in conspiracies and revolutions and the other trips of power here in the Afterworld. Without striving, what is there to keep one from going mad in this eternity? He had put striving behind him, or so he thought. Perhaps. Perhaps. But perhaps he was not entirely done with it yet.

He stood stunned and gaping in the midst of Calandola's terrible feast. Within him blazed the forbidden food that had opened his eyes.

Enkidu dead once more. Uruk real. Himself not yet entirely immune to the craving for power.

Now I have had the Knowing, Gilgamesh thought.

He dropped to his knees and covered his face with his hands and let great sobs of mourning rip through his body. But whether it was for Enkidu that he mourned, or for himself, he could not say.

★

"So soon?" Simon asked. "What's your hurry? We need time to plan things properly."

"I mean to set out for Uruk in five days or less," said Gilgamesh. "You may come with me or not, as you please. I have my bow. I have my dog. I am well accustomed to traveling by myself through the wilderness."

Simon looked mystified. "Just a day or two ago it seemed to me very doubtful that you wanted to go to Uruk at all. You didn't even appear to believe the place was there. And now – now you can't wait to get started. What happened that turned you around so fast?"

"Does it matter?" Gilgamesh asked.

"It's your friend Enkidu, isn't it? Some wizard here has told you that he's waiting for you in Uruk. Am I right?"

"Enkidu is dead," said Gilgamesh.

"But he'll be reawakened to Uruk. By the time you get there, he'll be waiting. Right?"

"That could be."

"Then there's no hurry. He'll be there when you get there. Whenever that is. Relax, Gilgamesh. Let's organize this thing the right way. Picked men, decent equipment, give the Land Rovers a good tuneup –"

"You do those things. I don't plan to wait around."

Simon sighed. "Rush, hurry, go off half-cocked, never stop to think anything through! It's not my style. I didn't think it was yours. I thought you were different from all the other dumb heroes."

"So did I," said Gilgamesh.

"Ten days?" Simon said.

"Five."

"Be merciful, Gilgamesh. Eight days is the soonest. I have responsibilities here. I have to draw up a schedule for my viceroy. And there are decrees to sign, materiel to requisition –"

"Eight days, then," said Gilgamesh. "Not nine."

"Eight days," said Simon.

Gilgamesh nodded and went out. Herod was waiting in the hall, cowering by the door, probably eavesdropping. Almost certainly eavesdropping. He looked up, his eyes not quite meeting those of Gilgamesh. Since the last visit to the cavern of Calandola, Herod had been remote, furtive, withdrawn, as though unable to face the recollection of the terrible rite he had led Gilgamesh into.

"You heard?" Gilgamesh asked.

"Heard what?"

"We leave for Uruk, Simon and I. In eight days."

"Yes," Herod said. "I know."

"You'll be the viceroy, I think. I'm sorry about that."

"Don't be."

"You didn't want this to happen."

"I didn't want to be viceroy, no. But I won't be. So there's no problem."

"If you aren't going to be viceroy, who will be?"

Herod shrugged. "I don't have any idea. Calandola, for all I care." He reached out uncertainly toward Gilgamesh, not quite touching his arm. "Take me with you," he said suddenly.

"What?"

"To Uruk. I can't stay here any longer. I'll go with you. Anywhere."

"Are you serious?"

"As serious as I've ever been."

Gilgamesh gave the little man a close, long look. Yes, he did indeed seem to mean it. Leave the comforts and tame terrors of Brasil, take his chances roaming in the hinterlands of the Afterworld? Yes. Yes, that was what he appeared to want. Maybe the experience in the cavern beneath the city had transformed Herod. It was hard to imagine going through something like that and not coming out transformed. Or perhaps the truth was merely that sad little Herod had formed one more attachment that he felt unable to break.

"Take me with you," said Herod again.

"The journey will be a harsh one. You've grown accustomed to ease here, Herod."

"I can grow unaccustomed to it. Let me come with you."

"I don't think so."

"You need me, Gilgamesh."

It was all Gilgamesh could do to keep from laughing at that.

"I do?"

"You'll be a king again when you reach Uruk, won't you? Won't you? Yes. You can't hide that from me, Gilgamesh. I was there when you had the Knowing. I had the Knowing too."

"And if I am?"

"You'll need a fool," Herod said. "Every king needs a fool. Even I had one, when I was a king. But I think somehow I'd do the other job better. Take me along. I don't want to stay in Brasil. I don't want to visit Calandola's cavern again. I might want another dinner there. Or I might *become* dinner there. Will you take me along with you, Gilgamesh?"

Gilgamesh hesitated, frowned, said nothing.

"Why not?" Herod demanded. "Why not?"

"Yes," Gilgamesh said. "Why not?" His own favorite phrase floating back at him. The great unending *Why Not?* that was the Afterworld.

"Well?" asked Herod.

"Yes," said Gilgamesh again. There was some charm in the idea, he thought. He had come to like the little Jew rather more, since they had been in Calandola's cavern together. There was weakness in him, yes, but there was a strong humanity also. And Herod was intelligent, and shrewd besides: a good combination, not overly common. He could be a lively companion, when he wasn't buzzing and chattering. A better companion, very likely, than old wine-guzzling Simon. And possibly Herod wouldn't buzz and chatter quite so much, while they were on the march, out among the rigors of the back country. It might almost make sense. Yes. Yes. Gilgamesh nodded. He smiled. Yes. "Why not, Herod? Why not?"

Twelve

The gritty smear of browns and yellows that was the western coastal desert of the Afterworld appeared to stretch on before Gilgamesh and his companions for a million leagues: past the horizon, and up the side of the sky. Perhaps it actually did. The narrow crumbling highway that they were following was vanishing behind them as soon as they passed over it, as though demons were gobbling up its cracked and pitted paving-stones, and ahead of them the road gave the impression of leading in several directions at once.

"– and surely you would agree, Gilgamesh," Simon Magus said, "that it's better to reign in the Afterworld than to be a slave in it!"

"I think you have that phrase a little wrong," said Gilgamesh quietly. "But never mind. We have lost the thread of our discourse, if ever there was one. Did I mock you? Why, then, I ask your forgiveness, Simon. It was not my intention."

"Spoken like a king. There is no grievance between us. Will you have more wine?"

"Why not?" Gilgamesh said.

Day and night the caravan had been rolling steadily onward across this dismal barren land. They were journeying up the coast above the island-city of Brasil, hoping to find a city whose very existence was at this moment nothing more than a matter of conjecture and speculation.

Gilgamesh drank in silence. The wine was all right. He had had worse. But he could remember, after thousands of years, the joy that had come from the sweet strong wine and rich foaming beer of Sumer the Land. Especially the wine: how many flagons he and Enkidu had quaffed together of that dark purple stuff, in the old days of their life! Indeed it made the soul soar upward. But in the Afterworld there was little soaring, and the wine gave small joy. It was only a momentary tickle upon the tongue, and then it was gone. You expected no more than that, in the Afterworld. Once, at the beginning, he had thought otherwise. Once he had thought this to be a second life in which true accomplishments might be achieved and true purposes won, and true pleasures could be had, and great kingdoms founded. Well, it was a second life, a life beyond life, no question of that. But the wine had only a feeble savor here. As did a woman's body, as did a steaming haunch of meat. This was not a place where real joy, as he remembered it, was to be had. One simply went on, and on and on. The Afterworld was by definition meaningless, and so all striving within it was meaningless also. He had come to that bleak awareness long ago. And it had puzzled him then that so few of these great heroes, these sultans and emperors and pharaohs and all, had learned the truth of that in all their long residence here.

He shook his head. Such thoughts as these were not appropriate for him any more. No longer could he look with contempt on other men's ambitions, ever since he had had the Knowing of his soul at the hands of Imbe Calandola in Brasil.

He reminded himself that he too had dabbled in kingship in the Afterworld: even he, aloof austere Gilgamesh. Had quested for power in this chaotic place and gained it, and founded a great city, and ruled in high majesty. And then had forgotten it all and gone about the Afterworld piously insisting that he was above such worldly yearnings.

It ill behooved him to scorn others for their ambitions and their pride in their achievements. He had forgotten his own, that was all. You could forget anything in the Afterworld. He knew that now. Memory was random here. Whole segments of experience dropped away, thousands of years of hurly-burly event. And then would return unexpectedly, leading you into the deepest contradictions of spirit.

Gilgamesh wondered whether the fever of power-lust that he had claimed so to despise might not seize him again before long. The Afterworld was a great kindler of opposites in one's breast, he knew: whatever you were most certain you would never do, that in time you would most assuredly find yourself doing.

"*Look* at this place!" Simon muttered. "Uglier and uglier. Worse and worse!"

"Yes," said Gilgamesh. "We have reached the edge of nowhere."

Originally there had been seven Land Rovers in the expedition – Simon's gilded bullet-proof palanquin; two lesser vehicles for Gilgamesh and Herod; and four more that carried baggage and slaves. But on the third day the roadbed had gaped suddenly beneath the rear vehicles of the baggage train and the lastmost Land Rover had disappeared amid tongues of purple flame and the discordant wailing of unseen spirits. Then two days later Simon's magnificent motor-chariot had developed a leprosy of its shining armor, turning all pock-marked and hideous, and its undercarriage had begun to melt and flow as if eaten by acid. So now five Land Rovers remained. Simon, disgruntled and fidgety, rode with Gilgamesh in the lead car, consoling himself with prodigious quantities of dark sweet wine.

This supposed Uruk that was their goal, Gilgamesh thought, could be anywhere: to the north, the south, the east, the west. Or some other direction entirely. Or nowhere at all. Uruk might indeed be only a rumor, a vision, a wishful fantasy, a figment of some liar's overheated imagination: mere vaporous hearsay, perhaps. They might spend a hundred years in search of it, or a thousand, and never find it.

So it was probably a foolish quest. But not to undertake it would be folly also. Even if Uruk turned out to be a phantom, they had nothing to lose by looking for it. "Time is money," someone once had said to Gilgamesh – was it that strange old man Ben Franklin, he wondered? Or had it been Sennacherib the Assyrian? *Time is money.* Wrong, Gilgamesh thought. In the Afterworld, time is nothing, nothing at all. And if I stand a chance to find Enkidu this way, and Simon to get the jewels he hungers for – well, why not? The only alternatives were idleness, stasis, hopelessness. At worst they would be disappointed; but if there are no beginnings, there are no fulfilments.

Simon, squirming beside Gilgamesh, said uneasily, "I thought we would be traveling through a region of marshes and lakes, not a desert. This place looks like nothing that was shown on the map the Carthaginian sold me."

Gilgamesh shrugged. "Why should it? The map was a dream, Simon. This desert is a dream. The city we seek is possibly only a dream too."

"Then why were you in such a hurry to set out from Brasil to find it?"

"Even if it may not exist, that in itself is no reason not to search for it," Gilgamesh replied. "And once we are resolved on the quest, searching sooner is better than searching later."

"No Roman would talk such nonsense, Gilgamesh."

"Perhaps not, but I am no Roman."

"There are times when I doubt that you're even human."

"I am a poor damned soul, the same as you."

Simon snorted and handed a fresh flask of wine to a slave to have its cork drawn. "Listen to him! A poor damned soul, he says! Since when do you believe in damnation, or any such Later Dead piffle? And am I supposed to be taken in by that note of sniveling self-pity? A poor damned soul! What hypocrisy! You couldn't snivel sincerely if your life depended on it. Or pity yourself seriously even for half a minute running. You're too damned noble!" Simon accepted the opened flask of wine, took a deep thoughtful pull, nodded, belched. Then he offered the bottle to Gilgamesh, who drank indifferently, scarcely tasting the stuff.

"I did indeed speak sincerely," Gilgamesh said after a time. "We are all damned in this place, though that seems to mean different things to different folk. And we are all poor, no matter how many caskets of treasure we amass, for everything is demon-stuff here, without substance to it, and only a fool would think otherwise."

Simon went crimson, and his blotches and blemishes stood out angrily on his fleshy face. "Don't mock me, Gilgamesh. I'm willing to accept a great deal of your arrogance, because I know you were something special in your own day, and because you have many qualities I admire. But don't mock me. Don't patronize me."

"Do I, Simon?"

"You do it all the time, you condescending oversized Sumerian bastard!"

"Is it mockery to tell you that I accept the fact that the capricious gods have sent me to this place with a flick of a finger – even as they have sent you here, and Herod, and everyone else who ever drew breath on Earth? Do I mock you when I admit that I am and always have been nothing but a plaything in their hands – even as you?"

"You, Gilgamesh? A plaything in the gods' hands?"

"Do you believe we have free will here?"

"Only a simpleton would think otherwise. Look, Gilgamesh: there are some who rule and some who are slaves," said Simon. "Even in the Afterworld, I live in a palace bedecked with rubies and emeralds, and I have hundreds of servants to draw my baths and drive my chariots and prepare my meals. It's a damned better life than I lived in Samaria, or in Rome. Here as once in the other world I'm a leader of men. There I led a sect; here I rule a rich isle. Is that by accident? Or is it by free will, Gilgamesh? By my choice, by my diligent effort, by my hard striving?"

"Those meals you eat: do they have any savor?"

"It is said I set the finest table in this entire region of the Afterworld."

"The finest, yes. But do you get any pleasure from what you eat? Or is the finest not but a short span from the meanest, Simon?"

"Jupiter and Isis, man! Don't be an ass. This is the life after life! We are all *dead*, Gilgamesh. Nobody expects the food to have much taste!"

"Dead? It's only a word. We have died; for reasons the gods alone know, we live again. We breathe, we hunger, we feel pain, we know sensations of heat and cold, of moisture and dryness. This is not some ghostly shadowy life we lead. It is different in nature from the life we led before; but it is a life of its own kind. And not a pleasing one."

"Perhaps not pleasing to you, Gilgamesh. There are some drawbacks, certainly, and some features that aren't exactly ideal. All the same, I make the most of my opportunities. As anybody with any sense would do."

"Yes," said Gilgamesh sardonically. "As you keep insisting, you have free will. Tempered only by a few little inconveniences."

"The inconveniences of this place don't have a demon's turd to do with the question of free will, which in any case is a foolish issue, a lot of gasbag vapor dreamed up by Later Dead idlers. Why are some men kings here and some slaves, if not that we shape our own destinies?"

"We have debated this point before, I think," said Gilgamesh with a shrug. He turned away and stared out at the landscape of the Afterworld.

Mean jagged cliffs that looked like chipped teeth rose on both sides of them. The air had turned the color of dung. The earth was palpitating like a blanket stretched above a windy abyss. Black gaseous bubbles erupted from it here and there. Everything seemed suspended in a trembling flux. A blood-hued rain had begun to fall, but as so often happened, not a drop reached the parched ground. Lean dog-like beasts that were all mouth and fangs and eyes ran beside the highway, leaping and screeching and howling. Far away Gilgamesh saw a dark lake that appeared to be standing on its side. The road ahead still veered crazily, drifting both to the right and left at the same time without forking, and seeming now also to curve upward into the sky. A demon-road, Gilgamesh thought, designed to torment those who dared travel it. A demon-land.

"The Carthaginian's map –" Simon said.

"Was all lies and fraud," said Gilgamesh. "It turned blank in your hands, did it not? Its purpose was to swindle you. Forget the Carthaginian's map. We are where we are, Simon."

"And where is that?"

Gilgamesh gestured with his hands outspread, and leaned forward, narrowing his eyes, seeking to make sense out of what he saw before him.

All was confusion and foulness out there. And, he realized, it was folly to try to comprehend it.

In the Afterworld there was never any hope of understanding distances, or spatial relationships, or the passing of time, or the size of things, or anything else. If you were wise, you took what came to you as it came, and asked no questions. That, Gilgamesh thought, was the fundamental thing about the Afterworld, the particular quality above all others that made it the Afterworld. *You took what came to you.* Simon Magus to the contrary, nobody was the shaper of his own destiny here. If you believed you were, you were only deceiving yourself.

Suddenly all the madness outside disappeared as if it had been blotted out. Thick gray mist began to spout from fissures in the ground and clung close as a cotton shroud, enfolding everything in dense murk. The Land Rover came to a jolting halt. The one just behind it, in which Herod of Judaea was riding, did not stop quite as quickly, and bashed into Simon's with a resounding clang.

Then invisible hands seized the sides of Simon's Land Rover and began to rock it up and down.

"What now?" Simon grunted. "Demons?"

Gilgamesh had already swung about to seize his bow, his quiver of arrows, his bronze dagger.

"Bandits, I think. This has the feel of an ambush."

Faces appeared out of the mist, peering through the foggy windows of the Land Rover. Gilgamesh stared back at them in astonishment. Straight dark hair, dark eyes, swarthy skins – an unmistakably familiar cast of features –

Sumerians! Men of his own blood! He'd know those faces anywhere!

A mob of excited Sumerians, clustering about the caravan, jumping about, pounding on fenders, shouting!

Simon, aflame with rage and drunken courage, drew his short Roman sword and fumbled with the latch of the door.

"Wait," Gilgamesh said, catching his elbow and pulling him back. "Before you get us embroiled in a battle, let me speak with these men. I think I know who they are. I think we've just been stopped by the border police of the city of Uruk."

In a huge dank basement room on the Street of the Tanners and Dyers the man who called himself Ruiz sat before his easel under sputtering, crackling floodlights, working steadily in silence in the depths of the night. He sat stripped to the waist, a stocky, powerful man past his middle years, with deep-set piercing eyes and a round head that had only a fringe of white hair about it.

The work was almost going well. Almost. But it was hard, very hard. He could not get used to that, how hard the work was. It had always been easy for him up above, as natural as breathing. But in this place there were maddening complications that he had not had to face in the life before this life.

He squinted at the woman who stood before him, then at the half-finished canvas, then at the woman again. He let her features enter his mind and expand and expand until they filled his soul.

What a splendid creature she was! Look at her, standing there like a priestess, like a queen, like a goddess!

He didn't even know her name. She was one of those ancient women that the city was full of, one of those Babylonian or Assyrian or Sumerian sorts that could easily have stepped right off the old limestone reliefs from Nineveh that they had in the Louvre. Shining dark eyes, great noble nose, gleaming black hair gathered in back under an elaborate silver coronet set with carnelian and lapis. She wore a magnificent robe, crimson cloth interwoven with silver strands and fastened at her shoulder by a long curving golden pin. It was not hard for the man who called himself Ruiz to imagine what lay beneath the robe, and he suspected that if he asked, she would undo the garment readily enough and let it slip. Maybe he would, later. But now he wanted the robe in the painting. Its powerfully sculpted lines were essential. They helped to give her that wondrously primordial look. She was Aphrodite, Eve, Ishtar, mother and whore all in one, a goddess, a queen.

She was splendid. But the painting – the painting –

Mierda! It was coming out wrong, like all the others.

Anger and frustration roiled his soul. He could not stop – he would keep on going until he finally got one of them right – but it was a constant torture to him, these unaccustomed failures, this bewildering inability to make himself the master of his own vision, as he had so triumphantly been for all the ninety-odd years of his former life.

There were paintings stacked everywhere in the room, amid the ferocious clutter, the crumpled shirts, unwashed dishes, torn trousers, old socks, wax-encrusted candlesticks, empty wine-bottles, discarded sandals, fragments of rusted machinery, bits of driftwood, broken pottery, faded blankets, overflowing ashtrays, tools, brushes, guitars that had no strings, jars of paint, bleached bones, stuffed animals, newspapers, books, magazines. He painted all night long, every night, and by now, even though he destroyed most of what he did by painting over the canvases, he had accumulated enough to fill half a museum. But they were wrong, all wrong, worthless, trash. They were stale, useless paintings, self-imitations, self-parodies, even. What was the use of painting the harlequins and saltimbanques again, or the night-fishing, or the three musicians? He had done those once already. To repeat yourself was a death worse than death. The girl before the mirror? The cubist stuff? The demoiselles? Even if this new life of his was truly going to be eternal, what a waste it was to spend it solving problems whose answers he already knew! But he could not seem to help it. It was almost as though there were a curse on him.

This new one, now – this Mesopotamian goddess with the dark sparkling eyes – maybe this time, at last, she would inspire him to make it come out right –

He had made a bold start. Trust the eye, trust the hand, trust the *cojones*, just paint what you see. Fine. She posed like a professional model, tall and proud, nothing self-conscious about her. A beauty, maybe forty years old, prime of life. He worked with all his old assurance, thinking that perhaps this time he'd keep control, this time he'd actually achieve something new instead of merely reworking. Capture the mythic grandeur of her, the primordial goddess-nature of her, this woman of Sumer or Babylonia or wherever she came from.

But the painting began to shift beneath his hand, as they always did. As though a demon had seized the brush. He tried to paint what he saw, and it turned cubist on him, all planes and angles, that nonsensical stuff that he had abandoned fifty years before he died. *Mierda! Carajo! Me cago en la mar!* He clenched his teeth and turned the painting back where he wanted it, but no, no, it grew all pink and gentle, rose-period stuff, and when in anger he painted over it the new outline had the harsh and jagged barbarism of the *Demoiselles d'Avignon*.

Stale and old, old and stale, old, old, old, old.

"*Me cago en Dios*!" he said out loud.

"What is that?" she said. Her voice was deep, mysterious, exotic. "What are those words?"

"Spanish," he said. "When I curse, I curse in Spanish, always." He spoke now in English. Practically everyone spoke English here, even he, who in his other life had hated that language with a strange passionate hatred. But it was either that or speak ancient Latin, which he found an even worse notion. He marveled at the idea that he was actually speaking English. You made many concessions in this place. Among his friends he spoke French, still, and among his oldest friends Spanish, or sometimes Catalan. With strangers, English. But to curse, Spanish, always Spanish.

"You are angry?" she said. "With me?"

"Not with you, no. With myself. With these brushes. With the Devil. How hellish the Afterworld is!"

"You are very funny," she said.

"Droll, yes, that is what I am. Droll." He put his finger to his lips. "Let me work. I think I see the way."

And for a moment or two he actually did. Bending low over the canvas, he gave himself up fully to the work. Frowning, chewing his cigarette, scratching his head, painting quickly, confidently. The wondrous goddess-woman rose up from the canvas at him. Her eyes gleamed with strange ancient wisdom. But he was helpless. The painting turned, it turned again, always moving away from him: it showed bones and teeth where he wanted robes and flesh, and when he fought with it it took a neoclassical turn, with gaudy late-period slashes of color also and a hint of cubism again trying to break through down in the lower left. An impossible hodgepodge it was, all his old styles at once. The painting had no life at all. An art student could have painted it, if he had had enough to drink. Maybe what he needed was a new studio. Or a holiday somewhere. But this had been going on, he reflected, since he had first come here, since the day of – he hesitated, not even wanting to think the filthy words –

– the day of his death –

"All right," he said. "Enough for tonight. You can relax. What is your name?"

"Ninsun."

"Ah. A lovely name. A lovely woman, lovely name. You are Babylonian?"

"Sumerian," she said.

He nodded. There was a difference, though he had forgotten what it was. He would ask someone tomorrow to explain it to him. Babylonian, Sumerian, Assyrian – all those Mesopotamian peoples, impossible for him to tell apart. This whole city was full of Mesopotamians of various kinds, and yet in the five years he had lived here he had not managed to learn much about them. Five years? Or was it fifty? Or five weeks? Somehow you never could tell. Well, no matter. No matter at all. Perhaps this was the moment to suggest that she slip out of that lovely robe.

There was a knock at the door, a familiar triple knock, repeated: the signal of Sabartes. This would not be the moment, then, to suggest anything of that sort to this priestess, this goddess, this Sumerian witch.

Well, there would be other moments.

He grunted permission for Sabartes to enter.

The door creaked open. Sabartes stood there blinking: his friend of many years, his confidante, his more-or-less secretary, his bulwark against annoyance and intrusion – now, maddeningly, himself an intruder. These days he had the appearance of a young man, with plump healthy cheeks and vast quantities of wild black hair, the Sabartes of the giddy old Barcelona days, 1902 or so, when they had first met. But for the eyes, the chin, the long thin nose, it would be impossible to recognize him, so familiar had the Sabartes of later years become. One of the minor perversities of the Afterworld was that people seemed to come back at any age at all. It was not easy to get accustomed to. The man who called himself Ruiz looked perhaps sixty, Sabartes no more than twenty, yet they had known each other for nearly seventy years in life and some years more – ten? Twenty? A thousand? – in this life after life.

Sabartes took everything in at a glance: the woman, the

easel, the scowl on his friend's face. Diffidently he said, "Pablo, do I interrupt?"

"Only another worthless painting."

"Ah, Picasso, you are too hard on yourself!"

He looked up, glaring fiercely. "*Ruiz*. You must always remember to call me Ruiz. Never Picasso."

Sabartes smiled. "Ruiz. Ruiz. Picasso, no. Ruiz. Ah, I will never get used to that!" He turned and looked with admiration and only faintly disguised envy at the silent, stately Sumerian woman. Then he stole a quick glance at the canvas on the easel, and a sequence of complex, delicate emotions flitted across his face, which after the many decades of their friendship the man who called himself Ruiz was able to decipher as easily as though each were inscribed in stone: admiration mixed with envy once again, for the craftsmanship, and awe and subservience, for the genius, and then something darker, which Sabartes tried in vain to suppress, a look of sadness, of pity, of almost condescending sorrow not unmingled with perverse glee, because the painting was a failure. In all the years they had known each other in life, Ruiz who was Picasso had never once seen that expression on Sabartes' face; but here in the Afterworld it came flashing out almost automatically whenever Sabartes looked at one of his old friend's new works. If this kept up, Picasso thought, he would have to deprive Sabartes of the right to enter the studio. It was intolerable to be patronized like this, especially by *him*.

"Well?" Picasso demanded. "*Am* I too hard on myself?"

"The painting is full of wonderful things, Pablo."

"Yes. Wonderful things which I put behind me a million years ago. And here they come again. The brush twists in my hand, Sabartes! I paint *this* and it comes out *that*." He scowled and spat. "*A la chingada*! But why should we be surprised? This place is a kind of Hell, no? And Hell is not supposed to be easy."

"No one knows if this is Hell, Pablo," said Sabartes mildly. "We know only that it is the Afterworld."

"Words!" Picasso snorted. "Call it whatever you choose. To me it feels like Hell, and the Devil rules here! Once I had only the dealers to wrestle with, and the critics, and now it is the Devil. But I beat them, eh? And I will beat him too."

"You will, indeed," said Sabartes. "What is the name of your new model?"

"Ishtar," said Picasso casually. "No. No, that's not right." He had forgotten it. He glanced at the woman. "*Come se llama, amiga*?"

"I do not understand."

English, he reminded himself. We speak English here.

"Your name," he said. "Tell me your name again, *guapa*."

"Ninsun, who was the Sky-father An's priestess."

"A priestess, Sabartes," Picasso said triumphantly. "You see? I knew that at once. We met in the marketplace, and I said, Come let me paint you and you will live forever. She said to me, I already live forever, but I will let you paint me anyway. What a woman, eh, Sabartes? Ninsun the priestess." He turned to her again. "Where are you from, Ninsun?"

"Uruk," she said.

"Uruk, yes, of course. We're all from Uruk now. But before this place. In the old life. Eh? *Comprende*?"

"The Uruk that I meant was the old one, in Sumer the Land. The one that was on Earth, when we were all alive. I was the wife of Lugalbanda the king then. My son also was –"

"You see?" Picasso crowed. "A priestess and a queen!"

"And a goddess," Ninsun said. "Or so I thought. When I was old, my son the king told me he would send me to live among the gods. There was a temple in my honor in Uruk, beside the river. But instead when I awoke I was in this place called the Afterworld, which does not at all seem to be the home of the gods – and I have been here so long, so many years, everything still so strange –"

"You are a goddess also," Picasso assured her. "A goddess, a priestess, a queen."

"May I see the painting you have made of me?"

"Later," he said, covering it and turning it aside. To Sabartes he said, "What news is there?"

"Good news. We have found the matador."

"*Es verdad*?"

"Absolutely," said Sabartes, grinning broadly. "We have the very man."

"*Esplendido*!" Instantly Picasso felt an electric surge of pleasure that utterly wiped out the hours of miserable struggle over the painting. "Who is he?"

"Joaquin Blasco y Velez," said Sabartes. "Formerly of Barcelona."

Picasso stared. He had never heard of him.

"Not Belmonte? Joselito? Manolete? You couldn't find Domingo Ortega?"

"None of them, Pablo. The Afterworld is very large."

"Who is this Blasco y Velez?"

"An extremely great matador, so I am told. He lived in the time of Charles IV. This was before we were born," Sabartes added.

"*Gracias.* I would not have known that, Sabartes. And your matador, he knows what he is doing?"

"So they say."

"Who is *they*?"

"Sportsmen of the city. A Greek, one Polykrates, who says he saw the bull-dancing at Knossos, and a Portuguese, Duarte Lopes, and an Englishman named –"

"A Greek, a Portuguese, an *Ingles,*" Picasso said gloomily. "What does a Portuguese know of bullfighting? What does an *Ingles* know of anything? And this Greek, he knows bull-dancing, but the *corrida*, what is that to him? This troubles me, Sabartes."

"Shall I wait, and see if anyone can find Manolete?"

"As you have just observed, Sabartes, the Afterworld is a very large place."

"Indeed."

"And you have been organizing this bullfight for a very long time."

"Indeed I have, Pablo."

"Then let us try your Blasco y Velez," Picasso said.

He closed his eyes and saw once again the bull-ring, blazing with color, noise, vitality. The banderilleros darting back and forth, the picadors deftly wielding their pikes, the matador standing quietly by himself under the searing sun. And the bull, the bull, the bull, black and snorting, blood streaming along his high back, horns looming like twin spears! How he had missed all that since coming to the Afterworld! Sabartes had found an old Roman stadium in the desert outside Uruk that could be converted into a *plaza de toros*, he had lined up three or four bulls – they were demon-bulls, not quite the real thing, peculiar green-and-purple creatures with double rows of spines along their backs and ears like an elephant's, but *por dios* they had horns in the right place, anyway – and he had found some Spaniards and Mexicans in the city who had at least a glancing familiarity with the art of the *corrida*, and could deal with the various supporting roles. But there were no matadors to be had. There were plenty of swaggering warriors in the city, Assyrians and Byzantines and Romans and Mongols and Turks, who were willing to jump into the ring and hack away at whatever beast was sent their way. But if Picasso simply wanted to see butchers at work, he could go to the slaughterhouse. Bullfighting was a spectacle, a ritual, an act of grace. It was a dance. It was art, and the matador was the artist. Without a true matador it was nothing. What could some crude gladiator know about the Hour of Truth, the holding of the sword, the uses of the cape, movements, the passes, the technique of the kill? Better to wait and do the thing properly. But the months had passed, or more than months, for who could reckon time in a sane way in this crazyhouse? The bulls were growing fat and sleepy on the ranch where they were housed. Picasso found it maddening that no qualified performer could be found, when everyone who had ever lived was somewhere in the Afterworld. You could find El Greco, here, you could find Julius Caesar, you could find Agamemnon, Beethoven, Toulouse-Lautrec, Alexander the Great, Velasquez, Goya, Michelangelo, Picasso. You could even find Jaime Sabartes. But where were all the great matadors? Not in Uruk, so it seemed, or in any of the adjacent territories. Maybe they had some special corner of the Afterworld all to themselves, where all those who had ever carried the *muleta* and the *estoque* had gathered for a *corrida* that went on day and night, night and day, world without end.

Well, at last someone who claimed to understand the art had turned up in Uruk. So be it. A *corrida* with just one matador would make for a short afternoon, but it was better than no *corrida* at all, and perhaps the word would spread and Belmonte or Manolete would come to town in time to make a decent show of it. The man who called himself Ruiz could wait no longer. He had been absent from *la fiesta brava* much too long. Perhaps a good bullfight was the magic he needed to make the paintings begin to come out right again.

"Yes," he said to Sabartes. "Let us try your Blasco y Velez. Next week, eh? Next Sunday? Is that too soon?"

"Next Sunday, yes, Pablo. If there is a Sunday next week."

"Good. Well done, Sabartes. And now –"

Sabartes knew when he was being dismissed. He smiled, he made a cavalier's pleasant bow to Ninsun, he flicked a swift but meaningful glance toward the covered canvas on the easel, and he slipped out the door.

"Shall I take the pose again?" the Sumerian woman asked.

"Perhaps a little later," said Picasso.

Thirteen

The city was just as Gilgamesh had seen it in his vision, that time in Brasil when Calandola had opened the way for him and given him the Knowing. It was a shimmering place of white cubical buildings that sprawled for a vast distance across a dark plain rimmed by towering hills. A high wall of sun-dried brick, embellished by glazed reliefs of dragons and gods in brilliant colors, surrounded it. Looking down into Uruk from the brick-paved road that wound downward through the mountains, Gilgamesh could see straight to the heart of the city, where all manner of structures in the familiar Sumerian style were clustered: temples, palaces, ceremonial platforms.

It was for him as though the endless years of his life in the Afterworld had fallen away in a moment, and he had come home to Sumer the Land, that dear place of his birth where he had learned the ways of gods and men, and had risen through adversity to kingship, and had come to understand the secret things, the truths of life and death.

But of course this was not that Uruk. This was the Uruk of the Afterworld, a different place entirely, a hundred times larger than the Uruk of his lost Sumer and a thousand times more strange. Yet this place was familiar to him too; and this place seemed to him also like home, for his home is what it was, his second home, the home of his second life.

He had founded this city. He had been king here.

He had no memory of that – it was all lost, swallowed up in the muddle and murk that was what passed for the past here in the Afterworld. But the Knowing that Calandola had bestowed on him had left him with a clear sense of his forgotten achievements in this second Uruk; and, seeing the city before him in the plain exactly as it had looked in his vision, Gilgamesh knew that all the rest of that vision must have been true, that he had once been king in this Uruk before he had been swept away down the turbulent river of time to other places and other adventures.

Herod said, "It's the right place, isn't it?"

"No question of it. The very one."

They were all three riding together in the first Land Rover now, Simon and Gilgamesh and Herod, with their baggage train close behind them and half a dozen of the low, snub-nosed Uruk border-guard vehicles leading the way. Herod was growing lively again, more his usual self, quick-tongued, inquisitive, edgy, nervy. It had given him a good scare when the caravan had been halted by that sudden fog and surrounded by those wild-looking shouting figures. He had been certain that a pack of demons was about to fall upon them and tear them apart. But seeing Gilgamesh step calmly out of his Land Rover and all the wild ones instantly drop down on their faces as though he were the Messiah coming to town had reassured him. Herod seemed relaxed now, sitting back jauntily with his arms folded and his legs crossed.

"It's very impressive, your Uruk," Herod said. "Don't you think so, Simon? Why don't you tell Gilgamesh what you think of his city?"

Simon gave the Judaean prince a cold, sour look. "I haven't seen his city yet, Herod."

"You're seeing it now."

"Its walls. Its rooftops."

"But aren't they the most majestic walls? And look how far the city stretches! It's much bigger than Brasil, wouldn't you say?"

"Brasil sits on an island," replied Simon frostily. "Its size is limited by that, as you are well aware. But yes, yes, this is a very fine city, this Uruk. I look forward to experiencing its many wonders."

"And to getting your hands on its treasure," Herod said. "Which surely is copious. Is that the treasure-house down there, Gilgamesh, that big building on the platform?"

"The temple of Enlil, I think," said Gilgamesh.

"But certainly it's full of rubies and emeralds. My master Simon is very fond, you know, of rubies and emeralds. Do you think they'll mind in this town if he helps himself to a little of their treasure, Gilgamesh?"

Simon Magus said, scowling, "Why are you baiting me like this, Jew? You make me regret I brought you with me on this journey."

"I simply try to amuse you, Simon."

"If you keep this up, it may amuse me to have you circumcised a second time," Simon said. "Or something worse." To Gilgamesh he said, "Does any of it start to come back to you yet? Your past life in Uruk?"

"Nothing. Not a thing."

"But yet you're sure you lived here once."

"I built this city, Simon. So I truly believe. I brought people of my own kind together in this place and gave them laws and ruled over them, just as I did in the other Uruk on Earth. There is evidence of that, all about me, which I'm unable to ignore or deny. But all firm knowledge of it, the memory of works and days, of the actual feel of what I must have done in those days, the solidity and reality of it as embodied in events and incidents, has fled from my mind." Gilgamesh laughed. "Can *you* remember everything that has befallen you in the Afterworld since first you came here?"

"If I had been king of some city before Brasil, I think I would remember that."

"How long have you been here, Simon?"

"Who can say? You know what time is like here. But I understand some two thousand years have gone by on Earth since my time there. Perhaps a little more."

"In two thousand years," said Gilgamesh, "you might have been a king five times over in the Afterworld, and forgotten it all. You could have embraced a hundred queens and forgotten them."

Herod chuckled. "Helen of Troy – Cleopatra – Nefertiti – all forgotten, Simon, the shape of their breasts, the taste of their lips, the sounds they make in their pleasure –"

Simon reached for his wine. "You think?" he asked Gilgamesh. "Can this be so?"

"The years float by and run one into another. The demons play with our memories. There are no straight lines here, and no unbroken ones. How could we keep our sanity, Simon, if we remembered everything that has happened to us in the Afterworld? Two thousand years, you say? For me it is *five* thousand. Or more. A hundred lifetimes. Ah, no, Simon, I have come to see that we are born again and again here, with minds wiped clean, and the torment of it is that we don't even know that that is the case. We imagine that we are as we have always been. We think we understand ourselves, and in fact we know only the merest surface of the truth. The irreducible essence of our souls remains the same, yes – I am always Gilgamesh, he is Herod, you are Simon, we make the choices over and over that someone of our nature must and will make – but the conditions of our lives fluctuate, we are tossed about on the hot winds of the Afterworld, and most of what happens to us is swallowed eventually into oblivion. This is the wisdom that came to me from the Knowing I had of Calandola."

"That barbarian! That devil!"

"Nevertheless. He sees behind the shallow reality of the Afterworld. I accept the truth of his revelation."

"You may have forgotten Uruk, Gilgamesh," said Herod, "but Uruk seems not to have forgotten you."

"So it would appear," said Gilgamesh.

Indeed it had startled him profoundly when the Sumerian border guards had hailed him at once as Gilgamesh the king. Hardly was he out of the Land Rover but they were kneeling to him and making holy signs, and crying out to him in the ancient language of the Land, which he had not heard spoken in so long a time that it sounded strange and harsh to his ears. It was as if he had left this city only a short while before – whereas he knew that even by the mysterious time-reckoning of the Afterworld it must be a long eternity since last he could have dwelled here. His memory was clear on that point, for he knew that he had spent his most recent phase of his time in the Afterworld roving the hinterlands with Enkidu, hunting the strange beasts of the Outback, shunning the intrigues and malevolences of the cities – and surely that period in the wilderness had lasted decades, even centuries. Yet in Uruk his face and form seemed familiar to all.

Well, he would know more about that soon enough. Perhaps they held him in legendary esteem here and prayed constantly for his return. Or, more likely, it was merely some further manifestation of the Afterworld's witchery that spawned these confusions.

They were practically in Uruk now. The road out of the hills had leveled out. A massive wall of red brick rose up before them, and a great brazen gate inscribed with the images of serpents and monsters set in the center of it. It swung open as they drew near, and the entire procession rolled on within.

Simon, far gone in wine, clapped the Sumerian lustily on the shoulder. "Uruk, Gilgamesh! We're actually here! Did you think we'd ever find it?"

"It found us," said Gilgamesh coolly. "We were lost in a land between nowhere and nowhere, and suddenly Uruk lay before us. So we are here, Simon: but where is it that we are?"

"Ah, Gilgamesh, Gilgamesh, what a sober thing you are! We are in Uruk, wherever that may be! Rejoice, man! Smile! Lift up your heart! This city is your home! Your friend will be here – what's his name, Inkibu, Tinkibu –"

"Enkidu."

"Enkidu, yes. And your cousins, your brothers, perhaps your father –"

"This is the Afterworld, Simon. Delights turn to ashes on our tongues. I expect nothing here."

"You'll be a king again. Is that nothing?"

"Have I said I feel any wish to rule this place?" Gilgamesh asked, glowering at the other.

Simon blinked in surprise. "Why, Herod says you do."

"He does?" Gilgamesh skewered the little Judaean with a fierce glare. "Who are you to pretend to speak what is in my mind, Herod? How do you imagine you dare know my heart?"

In a small voice Herod said, shrinking back as though he expected to be hit, "It is because I was with you when you had the Knowing, Gilgamesh. And had the Knowing with you. Have you forgotten that so soon?"

Gilgamesh considered that. He could not deny the truth of it.

Quietly he said, "This city must already have some king of its own. I have no thought to displace him. But if the gods have that destiny in mind for me –"

"Not the gods, Gilgamesh. The demons. This place is the Afterworld," Herod reminded him.

"The demons, yes," said Gilgamesh. "Yes."

They were well within Uruk now and the caravan had come to rest in the midst of a huge plaza. At close range Gilgamesh saw that Uruk was only superficially a Sumerian city: many of the buildings were in the ancient style, yes, but there was everything else here too, all periods and styles, the hideous things that they called office buildings, and the sullen bulk of a power-plant spewing foulness into the air, and an ominous-looking barracks of dirty red brick without windows, and something that looked like a Roman lawcourt or palace off to one corner. A crowd was gathered outside the Land Rover, many in Sumerian dress but by no means all; there was the usual mix, Early Dead and Later, garbed in all the costumes of the ages. Everyone was staring. Everyone was silent.

"You get out first," Simon said to Gilgamesh.

He nodded. A gaggle of what were obviously municipal officials, plainly Sumerian by race, had assembled alongside the Land Rover. They were looking in at him expectantly. They seemed worried, or at least puzzled, by his presence here.

He stepped out, looming like a giant above them all.

A man with a thick curling black beard and a shaven skull, who wore the woollen tunic of Sumer the Land, came forward and said – in English – "We welcome Gilgamesh the son of Lugalbanda to the city of Uruk, and his friends. I am the arch-vizier Ur-ninmarka, servant to Dumuzi the king, whose guests you are."

"Dumuzi?" said Gilgamesh, astonished.

"He is king in Uruk, yes."

"He who ruled before me, when we lived on Earth?"

Ur-ninmarka shrugged. "I know nothing of that. I was a man of Lagash in the Land that was, and Uruk was far away. But Dumuzi is king here, and he has sent me to give you greeting and escort you to your lodgings. Tonight you will dine with him and with the great ones of the city."

Dumuzi, Gilgamesh thought in wonder.

Memories of his first life, so much more clear to him than

most of what had befallen him in the Afterworld, came flooding back.

Dumuzi! That pathetic weakling! That murderous swine! Surely it is the same one, he thought; for in the Afterworld everything that has befallen befalls over and over. And so Dumuzi was king in Uruk once again, the same Dumuzi who in the old life, fearing Gilgamesh the son of Lugalbanda as a rival, had sent assassins to slay him, though he was then only a boy. Those assassins had failed, and in the end it was Dumuzi who went from the world and Gilgamesh who had the throne. No doubt he fears me yet, Gilgamesh suspected. And will try his treacheries on me a second time. Some things never change, thought Gilgamesh: it is the way of the Afterworld. As Dumuzi will learn to his sorrow, if he has new villainy in mind.

Aloud he said, "It will please me greatly to enjoy the hospitality of your king. Will you tell him that?"

"That I will."

"And tell him too that he will be host to Simon, ruler of the great city of Brasil, and to his prime minister, Herod of Judaea, who are my traveling companions."

Ur-ninmarka bowed.

"One further thing," said Gilgamesh. "I take it there are many citizens of Sumer the Land dwelling in this city."

"A great many, my lord."

"Can you say, is there a certain Enkidu here, a man of stature as great as my own, and very strong of body, and hairy all over, like a beast of the fields? He who is well known everywhere to be my friend, and whom I have come here to seek?"

The arch-vizier's bare brow furrowed. "I cannot say, my lord. I will make inquiries, and you will have a report this evening when you dine at the palace."

"I am grateful to you," said Gilgamesh.

But his heart sank. Enkidu must not be here after all; for how could Ur-ninmarka fail to know of it, if a great roistering hairy giant such as Enkidu had come to Uruk? There is no city in the Afterworld so big that Enkidu would not be conspicuous in it, and more than conspicuous, thought Gilgamesh.

He kept these matters to himself. Beckoning Simon and Herod from the Land Rover, he said only, "All is well. Tonight we will be entertained by Uruk's king."

★

Dumuzi, at any rate, seemed to do things with style. For his visitors he provided sumptuous lodgings in a grand hostelry back of the main temple, a massive block of a building that seemed to have been carved of a single slab of black granite. Within were fountains, arcades, so much statuary that it was hard to move about without bumping into something, gigantic figures of gods with staring eyes and plaited tresses in the ancient manner, and towering purple-leaved palm trees growing in huge many-faceted planters of a shining red stone that glistened like genuine ruby. Perhaps it was. Gilgamesh saw Simon fondling one covetously as though contemplating how many hundreds of egg-sized stones it could be broken into.

Each of the travelers had a palatial room to himself, a broad bed covered in silk, a sunken alabaster tub, a mirror that shimmered like a window into Paradise. Of course, there were little things wrong amid all this perfection: no hot water was running, and a line of disagreeable-looking fat-bellied furry insects with emerald eyes went trooping constantly across the ceiling of Gilgamesh's room, and when he sprawled on the bed it set up a steady complaining moan, as though he were lying on the protesting forms of living creatures. But this was the Afterworld, after all. One expected flaws in everything, and one always got them. All things considered, these accommodations could hardly be excelled.

Half a dozen servants appeared as if from nowhere to help Gilgamesh with his bath, and anoint him with fragrant oils, and garb him in a white flounced woollen robe that left him bare to the waist in the Sumerian manner. After a time Herod came knocking at the door, and he too was garbed after the fashion of Sumer, though he still wore his gleaming Italian leather shoes instead of sandals, and he had his little Jewish skullcap on his head. His dark curling hair had been pomaded to a high gloss.

"Well?" he said, preening. "Do I look like a prince of Sumer the Land, Gilgamesh?"

"You look like a fop, as always. And a weakling, besides. At least your toga would have covered those flabby arms of yours and that spindly chest."

"Ah, Gilgamesh! What need do I have of muscles, when I have *this*?" He touched his hand to his head. "And when I have the brave Gilgamesh the king to protect me against malefactors."

"But will I, though?"

"Of course you will." Herod smiled. "You feel sorry for me, because I have to live by my wits all the time and don't have any other way of defending myself. You'll look after me. It's not in your nature to let someone like me be endangered. Besides, you need me."

"I do?"

"You've lived in the Outback too long. You've got bits of straw in your hair."

Automatically Gilgamesh reached up to search.

"No, no, you foolish ape, not literally!" said Herod, laughing. "I mean only that you've been out of things. You don't understand the modern world. You need me to explain reality to you. You stalk around being heroic and austere and noble, which is fine in its way, but you've been paying no attention to what's really been going on in the Afterworld lately. The fashions, the music, the art, the new technology."

"These things are of no importance to me. Fashion? And music? Music is mere tinkling in my ear. It is at best trivial, and usually worse than that. Art is decoration, an insignificant thing. As for this new technology you speak of, it is an abomination. I despise all the inventions of the Later Dead."

"Despise them all you like, but they're here to stay. The New Dead outnumber us a thousand to one, and more of them arrive every day. You can't just ignore them. Or their technology."

"I can."

"So you may think. A bow and a couple of arrows, that's good enough for you, right? But you keep running afoul of things you don't comprehend. You blunder on and on and you get yourself out of trouble most of the time pretty well, but you fundamentally don't know what's what, and sooner or later you'll come up against something that's too much even for you. Whereas I've kept up with modern developments. I can guide you through all the pitfalls. I'm aware, Gilgamesh. I know what's happening. I stay in touch. Politics, for example. Do you have the foggiest notion of the current situation? The really spectacular upheavals that are going on right now?"

"I take great care not to think of them."

"You think it's safe, keeping your head in the sand that way? What happens over there on the far side of the Afterworld can have a tremendous impact on how we operate here. This isn't your ancient world, where it took forever and a half just to carry the news from Rome to Syria. Do you know what a radio is? A telephone? A microwave relay? Like it or not, we're all Later Dead now. You may still be living like a Sumerian, but the rest of the people here are neck-deep in modern life."

"They have my compassion," said Gilgamesh.

"You don't know the slightest thing about the revolutionary movements swirling in half a dozen cities back East, do you? The whole Upheaval? The People's Rebellion against the administration in Nova Roma? What Cromwell is doing, and Lenin, and Frederick Barbarossa? The latest deeds of Tiglath-Pileser? The present status of Metternich? No, no, Gilgamesh, you're out of things. And damnably proud of your ignorance. Whereas I have kept up with the news, and –"

"I have spent time in Nova Roma, Herod. I have seen Cromwell and Bismarck and Lenin and Tiglath-Pileser and Sennacherib and the rest of that crowd putting together their petty schemes. Why do you think I went to the Outback? I wept with boredom after half an hour among them. Their intrigues were like the squeakings of so many mice to me. Whatever they may be planning to do, it will all wash away like a castle of sand by the edge of the sea, and the Afterworld will go on and on as it always has. And so will I. The invisible demons who are the true masters here laugh at the pretensions of the rebellious ones. And so do I. No, no, Herod, I haven't any need of your guidance. If I choose to protect you against harm, it'll be out of mercy, not out of self-interest." He glanced at the watch he wore, a gift from Simon Magus. "It grows late. We should be on our way to the feast."

"The wristwatch you wear is a despised invention of the Later Dead."

"I take what I choose from among their things," said Gilgamesh. "I choose very little. You are not the first to try to mock me for inconsistency. But I know who I am, Herod, and I know what I believe."

"Yes," Herod said, in a tone that was its own negation. "How could anyone have doubt of that?"

Gilgamesh might have pitched him from the window just then; but the servants returned to lead them to the feasting-hall. Simon, waiting for them amid the splendors of the lobby, greeted them with wine-flushed face. He had spurned

Sumerian robes altogether and was decked out in a purple toga and high gilded buskins in the Greek style.

As they moved toward the door Simon caught Gilgamesh by the wrist and said quietly, "One moment. Tell me about this king we are about to meet, this Dumuzi."

"If it is the same one, he succeeded my father Lugalbanda on the throne of Uruk – the first Uruk – when I was a boy, and drove me into exile. He was a coward and a fool, who neglected the rites and squandered public funds on ridiculous adventures, and the gods withdrew the kingship from him and he died. Which made the way clear for me to become king."

Simon Magus nodded. "You had him murdered, you mean?"

Gilgamesh's eyes widened. Then he laughed. This man might be a drunkard but his mind was still shrewd.

"Not I, Simon. I had nothing to do with it. I was in exile then; it was the great men of the city who saw that Dumuzi must go, and the priestess Inanna who actually gave him the poison, telling him it was a healing medicine for an illness he had."

"Mmm," said Simon. "You and he take turns succeeding one another in the kingship of Uruk, here and in the former life. Now it's his turn to rule. And yours may be due to come again soon. Everything revolves in an endless circle."

"It is the way of this place. I am used to it."

"He was afraid of you once. He'll be afraid of you still. There'll be old grudges at work tonight. Perhaps an attempt at some settling of scores."

"Dumuzi has never frightened me," said Gilgamesh, making the gesture one might make to flick away a troublesome fly.

Fourteen

Sabartes said, "Which is it, Pablo, that has you so excited these days? That you have a new mistress, or that we are finally to have a bullfight for you to attend?"

"Do you think I am excited, brother?"

With a sweeping gesture Sabartes indicated the litter of sketches all about the studio, the dozen new half-finished canvases turned to the wall, the bright splotches everywhere where Picasso, in his haste, had overturned paints and not bothered to wipe them up. "You are like a man on fire. You work without stopping, Pablo."

"Ah, and is that something new?" Rummaging absent-mindedly in a pile of legal documents, Picasso found one with a blank side and began quickly to draw a caricature of his friend, the high forehead, the thick glasses, the soft fleshy throat. A little to his surprise he saw that what he was drawing was the old pedantic Sabartes of the last years on Earth, not the incongruously young Bohemian Sabartes who in fact stood before him now. And then the sketch changed with half a dozen swift inadvertent strokes and became not Sabartes but a demon with fangs and a flaming snout. Picasso crumpled it and tossed it aside. To Sabartes he said, "She will be here soon. Do you have anything you must tell me?"

"Then it *is* the woman, Pablo."

"She is splendid, is she not?"

"They were all splendid. La Belle Chelita was splendid, the one from the strip-tease place. Fernande was splendid. Eva was splendid. Marie-Thérèse was splendid. Dora Maar was –"

"*Basta*, Sabartes!"

"I mean no offense, Pablo. It is only that I see now that Picasso has chosen once more a new woman, a woman who is as fine as the ones who went before her, and –"

"You will call me Ruiz, brother."

"It is hard," said Sabartes. "It is so very hard."

"Ruiz was my father's name. It is an honest name for calling me."

"The world knew you as Picasso. All of the Afterworld will know you as Picasso too as time goes along."

Picasso scowled and began a new sketch of Sabartes, which began almost at once to turn without his being able to prevent it into a portrait of El Greco, elongated face and deep-set sorrowful eyes, and then, maddeningly, into the face of a goat. Again he threw the sheet aside. He would not mind these metamorphoses if they were of his own choosing. But this was intolerable, that he could not control them. *Painting*, he had liked to tell people in his life before this life, *is stronger than I am. It makes me do what it wants.* But now he realized that he must have been lying when he said that; for it was finally happening to him, just that very thing, and he did not like it at all.

He said, "I prefer now to be known as Ruiz. That way none of my heirs will find me here. They are very angry with me, brother, for not having left a will, for having forced them to fight in the courts for year after year. I would rather not see them. Or any of the women who are looking for me. We move on, Sabartes. We must not let the past pursue us. I am Ruiz now."

"And you think that by calling yourself a name that is not Picasso you can hide from your past, though you look the same and you act the same and you paint day and night? Pablo, Pablo, you deceive only yourself! You could call yourself Mozart and you would still be Picasso."

The telephone rang.

"Answer it," said Picasso brusquely.

Sabartes obeyed. After a moment he put his hand over the receiver and looked up.

"It is your Sumerian priestess," said Sabartes.

Picasso leaned forward, tense, apprehensive, already furious. "She is cancelling the sitting?"

"No, no, nothing like that. She will be here in a little while. But she says King Dumuzi has asked her to attend a feast at the royal hall tonight, and that you are invited to accompany her."

"What do I have to do with King Dumuzi?"

"She asks you to be her escort."

"I have work to do. You know I am not one to go to royal feasts."

"Shall I tell her that, Pablo?"

"Tell her – wait. Wait. Let me think. Speak with her, Sabartes. Tell her – ask her – yes, tell her that the king's feast is of no importance to me, that I want her to come here right away, that – that –"

Sabartes held up one hand for silence. He spoke into the telephone, and listened a moment, and looked up again.

"She says the feast is in honor of her son, who has arrived in Uruk this day."

"Her *son*? What son?" Picasso's eyes were blazing. "She said nothing about a son! How old is he? What is this son's name? Who is his father? Ask her, Sabartes! Ask her!"

Sabartes spoke with her once again. "His name is Gilgamesh," he reported after a little while. "She has not seen him since her days on Earth, which were so long ago. I think you ought not to ask her to refuse the king's invitation, Pablo. I think you ought not to refuse it yourself."

"Gilgamesh?" Picasso said, wonderstruck. "*Gilgamesh?*"

Motorized chariots painted in many gaudy colors conveyed them the short distance from the lodging-hall to the feasting-place of the king, on the far side of the temple plaza. The building startled Gilgamesh, for it was not remotely Sumerian in form: a great soaring thing of ash-gray stone, it was, with a pair of narrow spires rising higher than any of the fanciful baroque towers of Brasil, and pointed arches over the heavy bronze doors, and enormous windows of stained glass in every color of the rainbow and a few other hues besides. Ghastly monsters of stone were mounted all along its facade. Some of them seemed slowly to be moving. The palace was very grand and immense and massive, but somehow also it seemed oddly flimsy, and Gilgamesh wondered how it kept from falling down, until he saw the huge stone buttresses flying outward on the sides. Trust Dumuzi to build a palace for himself that needed to be propped up by such desperate improvizations, Gilgamesh thought. He loathed the look of it. It clashed miserably with the classic Uruk style of the buildings that surrounded it. If I am ever king of this city again, Gilgamesh vowed, I will rip down this dismal pile of stone as my first official act.

Herod, though, seemed to admire it. "It's a perfect replica of a Gothic cathedral," he explained to Gilgamesh as they went inside. "Perhaps Notre Dame, perhaps Chartres. I'm not sure which. I'm starting to forget some of what I once learned about architecture. I had some instruction in it, you know, from a man named Speer, a German, who passed through Brasil a while back and did a little work for Simon – peculiar chap, kept asking me if I wanted him to build a synagogue for me – what use would we have for a synagogue in the Afterworld? – but he knew his stuff, he taught me all sorts of things about Later Dead architectural design – you'd be astounded, Gilgamesh, what kinds of buildings they –"

"Can you try being quiet for a little while?" Gilgamesh asked.

The interior of the building actually had a sort of beauty, he thought. The sun was still glowing ruddily in the sky at this hour, and its subtle light, entering through the stained-glass windows, gave the cavernous open spaces of the palace a solemn, mysterious look. And the upper reaches of the building, gallery upon gallery rising toward a dimly visible pointed-arch ceiling, were breathtaking in their loftiness. Still, there was something oppressive and sinister about it all. Gilgamesh much preferred the temple in honor of Enlil that he had built, and still well remembered, atop the White Platform in the center of the original Uruk. *That* had had grandeur. *That* had had dignity. These Later Dead understood nothing about beauty.

Dumuzi's servants escorted them to the other end of the palace, where the building terminated in a great rounded chamber, open on one side and walled with stained glass on the other. A feasting-table had been set up there and dozens of guests had already gathered.

Gilgamesh saw Dumuzi at once, sumptuously robed, standing at the head of an enormous stone table.

He had not changed at all. He carried himself well, with true kingly bearing: a vigorous-looking man, heavy-bearded, with thick flowing hair so dark it seemed almost blue. But his lips were too full, his cheeks were too soft; and his eyes were small, and seemed both crafty and dull at the same time. He looked weak, unpleasant, untrustworthy, mean-souled.

Yet as he spied Gilgamesh he came down from his high place as though it were Gilgamesh and not he who was the king, and went to his side, and looked up at him, craning his neck in an awkward way – it was impossible for him to hide the discomfort that Gilgamesh's great height caused him – and hailed him in ringing tones, as he might a brother newly returned after a long sojourn abroad:

"Gilgamesh at last! Here in our Uruk! Hail, Gilgamesh, hail!"

"Dumuzi, hail," said Gilgamesh with all the enthusiasm he could find, which was not a great deal, and made a sign to him that one would have made to a king in Sumer the Land. "Great king, king of kings." He detected a quick flash of surprise in

Dumuzi. But Dumuzi was king in this city, and proper courtesy was due a king, any king. Even Dumuzi.

"Come," Dumuzi said, "introduce me to your friends, Gilgamesh, and then you must sit beside me in the place of honor, and tell me of everything that has befallen you in the Afterworld, the cities you've visited, the kings you've known, the things you've done. I want to hear all the news – we are so isolated, out here between the desert and the sea – but wait, wait, there are people here you must meet –"

Forgetting all about Simon and Herod, who were left behind gaping indignantly, Dumuzi thrust his arm through Gilgamesh's and led him with almost hysterical eagerness toward the feasting-table. It was all Gilgamesh could do to keep from knocking him sprawling for the impertinence of this offensive overfamiliarity. He is a king, Gilgamesh reminded himself. He is a king.

And the desperate bluster behind Dumuzi's effusive cordiality was easy enough for Gilgamesh to see. The man was frightened. The man was scrambling frantically to gain control of a situation that must be immensely threatening to him.

For thousands of years Dumuzi had had the leisure in the Afterworld to reflect on the shameful truth that he had been, in his earlier life, the feckless irresolute interpolation between the two great royal heroes Lugalbanda and Gilgamesh, a mere hyphen of history. Now he was king again, having risen by some mysterious law of incompetence to his former summit. And now here was that same hulking Gilgamesh for whose sake he had been thrust aside once before, materializing like an unwelcome spectre in New Uruk to claim his hospitality.

Of course Dumuzi would be cordial, and effusively so. But all the same it was likely to be a good idea, Gilgamesh thought, to guard his back at all times while in Dumuzi's city. Cowards are more dangerous than heroes, for they strike without fair warning; Dumuzi, tremulous and resentful, might work more harm than Achilles in all his wrath could ever manage.

A moment later these gloomy ruminations went completely from his mind; for a voice he had not heard in more centuries than he could count, but which was so different from any other man's that not even in the Afterworld could it ever be forgotten, came pealing across the room, calling his name.

"Gilgamesh! Gilgamesh! By the Mother, it is truly you! By the Tusk! By the Horns of God! Gilgamesh, here!"

Gilgamesh stared. A man seated near the head of the banquet table had risen and held his arms wide outspread in a gesture of greeting.

Gilgamesh's first thought was that he must be Later Dead, for alone in this great hall this man wore the strange formal costume of the most recent arrivals in the Afterworld, what they called a business suit: tight gray pantaloons that hugged his legs, and a stiff-looking wide-shouldered half-length coat, not exactly a tunic, of the same close-woven gray woollen material, with a white vestment under it, and a narrow strip of blue cloth knotted about his throat and dangling down his chest. He was tall, too, as Later Dead often were – taller by far than any of the Sumerians in the room but for Gilgamesh himself.

Yet there could be no mistaking that voice. It was a voice that came from the dawn of time, from the lost world that had been before the Flood, and it rang through the great room like a brazen trumpet, hard and clear. No Later Dead had ever had a voice like that.

Nor was his lean face that of a Later Dead, clean-shaven though it was. His skin had the burnished gleam of one who has faced the winds and snows of a world without warmth. His cheekbones were broad and strong, his lips were full, his nose was straight and very prominent, his mouth was extraordinarily wide. His eyes were wide-set too, far apart in his forehead, and one of them was missing from its socket: an ancient scar slashed crosswise over the left side of his face.

This man had been king of the cave-dwelling Ice-Hunter people, in that time before time when even the gods were young; and there had been a time in the Afterworld when Gilgamesh had known him well.

Gilgamesh felt a chill of astonishment. How long had it been, he wondered, since they had enjoyed high merriment together in the great windy hall of the Ice-Hunter folk on the northern reaches of the Afterworld – that vast cavern hung with woolly beast-skins where the huge curving tusks of the hairy elephants were scattered like straws on the floor, and the thick mead flowed in rivers, and the smoky fires burned high? A thousand Afterworldish years? Three thousand? It had been in his earliest days in the Afterworld, that simpler, easier time that now seemed forever lost.

"Vy-otin!" Gilgamesh cried. With a whoop he rushed forward, mounting the dais on which the stone feasting-table sat, holding out his arms in a lusty embrace.

"So you have not forgotten," the Ice-Hunter said. "I thought for a moment you had."

"No, by the breasts of Inanna, how could I ever forget you! The old memories are brighter than anything after. Last year is hazy for me, but those old times, Vy-otin, you and I and Enkidu, and Minos, and Agamemnon –"

"Ah, but you looked doubtful a moment, Gilgamesh."

"You confused me with these Later Dead clothes of yours," said Gilgamesh reproachfully. "You, who lived when the world was new, when the great shaggy beasts roamed, when Sumer itself was nothing but a muddy marsh – you, decking yourself out like some tawdry twentieth-century creature, someone out of – what do they call it, *A.D.*?" He made it sound like an obscenity. "I remember a man in fur robes, Vy-otin, and a necklace of boar's teeth around his throat, and armlets of shining bone, not this – this *businessman* costume!"

Vy-otin said, laughing, "It's a long story, Gilgamesh. And I go by the name of Smith now, not Vy-otin. In this hall you can call me by my true name. But in the streets of Uruk my name is Smith."

"Smith?"

"Henry Smith, yes."

"Is that a Later Dead name? How ugly it is!"

"It is a name that no one can remember as long as five minutes, not even me. Henry Smith. Sit with me, and we'll share a flask or two of this wine of Dumuzi's, and I'll tell you why I dress this way, and why my name is Smith now."

"I pray you, Vy-otin, let your story wait a while," said Dumuzi, who had been standing to one side. "There is someone else to whom Gilgamesh owes greetings, first –"

He touched Gilgamesh by the elbow, and nodded toward the other side of the table. A woman had risen there, a magnificent dark-haired woman of splendid stature and regal bearing, who stood calmly smiling at him.

She was a wondrous creature, radiant, beautiful, with shining eyes and the poise of a goddess. It was as if light emanated from her. Plainly, by the look of her and by her dress, she was Sumerian. She wore the robe of a priestess of An the Sky-father. She was within a year or two of Gilgamesh's age, so it seemed, or perhaps a little younger than that. Her face was familiar, though he could not place it. From her size and majesty she seemed surely to be of royal stock, and her features led him to think she might even be his own kinswoman. Some daughter of his, perhaps? He had had so many, though. Or the daughter of his daughter's daughter to the tenth generation, for here in Uruk as everywhere else in the Afterworld there were folk of every era living jumbled all together, and one might meet one's own remote kin at every turning, distant ancestors who seemed to be mere boys, and one's children's children who looked to be in their dotage –

Dumuzi said, "Will you not go to her and show your respect, Gilgamesh?"

"Of course I will. But –"

"You hesitate?"

"I almost know her, Dumuzi. But the name slips from my tongue, and it shames me not to recall it."

"Well it should shame you, Gilgamesh, to forget your own mother!"

"My *mother*?" said Gilgamesh, with a gasp.

"The great queen Ninsun, and none other. Are you addled, man? Go to her! Go to her!"

Gilgamesh looked toward her in wonder and awe. Of course it was plain now. Of course. The years fell away as though they had never been, and he saw his mother's face – the unmistakable features of the goddesslike wife of Lugalbanda, king of Uruk –the face of that great woman who had brought the hero Gilgamesh into the world.

But yet – yet –

What tricks the Afterworld plays on us, he thought. Never once had her path crossed his in the hundred lifetimes of his second life. So far as he could recall, he had not seen his mother since the days of that other world long gone; and he remembered her as she had been in her latter years, still majestic, still regal, but her hair white as the sands, her face lined and seamed; and now here she was in full robust beauty again, not youthful but far from old, a woman in glorious prime. He had been only a child when last she had looked like that. No wonder he had not recognized her.

He hastened to her now, and dropped down on his knees before her, caring nothing for what the others might see or think. He took the hem of her robe and put it to his lips. The thousands of years of his wanderings in this vile harsh land became as nothing; he was a boy again, in his first life, and the goddess his mother was restored to him and stood before him, agleam with warmth and love.

Softly she said his secret name, his birth-name, that no one but she was permitted to utter. Then she told him to rise, and he came to his full height, folding her against his bosom: for, tall as she was, she was like a child beside him. After a time he released her and she stepped back to look at him.

"I despaired of ever seeing you again," she said. "In all the places I have lived in the Afterworld I have heard tales of great Gilgamesh, and never once, never ever, have I been where you have been, unless my mind was tricking me, and in this instance I did not think that it was. I saw Enkidu once, from a distance, in a great noisy mob: that was in New Albion, I think, or the Realm of Logres, or perhaps the place they call Phlegethon, I think. I forget, now. But we were swept apart before I could call to him. And when I asked of Gilgamesh in that place, no one there knew anything of him."

"Mother –"

"And then I came to this new Uruk, knowing you had been king here, and thinking you might still hold your throne – but no, no, they said you had taken your leave of this city long ago, that you had gone hunting with Enkidu and never returned, more years ago than anyone could remember. And I thought, very well, the gods have no wish to let me see my son again, for this is the Afterworld and few wishes are granted here. But then the word came that you were approaching the city. Oh, Gilgamesh! What joy it is to behold you again!"

"And my father?" Gilgamesh asked. "What of the divine Lugalbanda? Surely there is no way he can be here, for he is a god, and how can there be gods in the Afterworld? But do you know anything of him?"

Ninsun's eyes clouded a moment. "He is here too, of that I am certain. For those who were made gods after their lives in

Sumer are gods no longer, and dwell in the Afterworld. You elevated me to godhood, Gilgamesh, do you remember?"

"Yes," he said, only a murmur.

"And you yourself – they ranked you with the gods also. It makes no difference. Those who live as mortals die as mortals, and come to this place."

"You know with certainty that Lugalbanda is here, then?"

"Not with certainty, no. But I think he is. Of him I have heard not one word in all the time I have been here. But some day he and I will find one another again, of that I am sure."

"Yes," Gilgamesh said once more, nodding. It had never occurred to him that his father might indeed be somewhere in the Afterworld, and the possibility aroused excitement and amazement in his breast. "In the Afterworld all things happen, sooner or later. You will be reunited with the king your husband and live by his side as the Sky-father ordained, for you and he were mated for all time and this span in the Afterworld has been but a brief separation; and I –"

An odd look came then into Ninsun's face. For an instant she lowered her eyes, as though abashed. The queenly splendor, the goddess-glow, went from her, and for that instant she seemed to be only a mere mortal woman.

"Have I spoken amiss?" Gilgamesh asked.

She said, "You have uttered nothing that should not have been spoken. But I would have you meet my friend, Gilgamesh."

"Your – friend –?"

Color rose to her cheeks in a curiously girlish way that Gilgamesh was altogether unable to associate with his memories of the regal presence of his mother. She nodded toward a man of considerable years sitting beside her, who got now to his feet.

Standing, he was less than breast-high to Gilgamesh, a short balding man, *very* short, not so tall by half a head as Ninsun herself; and yet as Gilgamesh looked more closely he saw that although he was old there was a strange elemental force about this man, a look of enormous power and commanding strength, that made him seem not nearly as short nor as old as he actually was, made him look, indeed, kingly in size and stance and vigor. It was the depth and breadth of his shoulders and torso that gave him that potent look, Gilgamesh thought:

that and his eyes, which were the most intense that the Sumerian had ever seen, more penetrating, even, than those of Imbe Calandola the mage. Astonishing eyes, they were, dark and glittering, the eyes of a hawk, the eyes of an eagle – no, the eyes of a god, merciless eyes, all-seeing eyes. They blazed like black jewels in his face.

Gilgamesh realized abruptly that this strange and powerful little man must be his mother's lover; and it was a disturbing thought indeed.

Hard enough to find her transformed into a young woman again, beautiful, and for all he knew lusty; but harder still to think of her with a woman's earthy nature, seeking a man's bed, this man's bed, this old man, this man who had no hair, his arms about her, his fingers probing the secret places of her body that only Lugalbanda the king had known –

Fool, he thought. She is your mother, but she is also a woman, and was a woman before she was your mother. She has not seen Lugalbanda for five thousand years, and all vows are canceled in this place. Did you think she would remain chaste for the whole five thousand years that she has spent thus far in the Afterworld? Do you think she should?

Still, why *this* man? – this old man, so short, not even any hair on his head, his leathery skin deeply folded, lined –

"I am called Ruiz," the little man said. "She is your mother? Good. You are a fitting son. She should be the mother of giants, this woman. The mother of gods, eh? And you are the famous Gilgamesh. *Mucho gusto en conocerlo*, Sẽnor Gilgamesh." Ruiz grinned warmly, boldly, and put out his hand in a casual and confident manner, as though they were equals, standing eye to eye, one giant to another. He was the biggest little man Gilgamesh had ever seen.

At the sound of his voice, at the touch of his hand, Gilgamesh began to understand why his mother had chosen this man; or rather, why she had allowed herself to be chosen by him. Choice must have had nothing to do with it. He was like an irresistible force, a river running unstoppably toward the sea.

"Pablo is an artist," Ninsun said. "A painter, a man of pictures. He is making a picture of me." With a little laugh she said, "He will not let me look at it. But I know it will be a very great picture."

"There are difficulties," Ruiz said. "But I will conquer them. Your mother is extraordinary – her face, her presence – I will make such a painting of her as the Devil himself will want to buy. Only I will not sell it to him. And then, after her, you, eh, Gilgamesh?"

"Me?"

"To pose. I will put a mask on you, the head of a bull, and you will be my Minotaur. The finest Minotaur ever, the true man-monster, the creature of the Labyrinth. Eh? Eh? What do you say, Gilgamesh? I like you. You know, this Sunday, *el domingo que viene*, there will be a bullfight in Uruk. You know the bullfight, eh? *La corrida?* You know what it is, to fight with bulls?"

"I know what that is, yes," said Gilgamesh.

"Good. Of course. You will sit with me that day. We will observe the fine points, you and I. You like that? The seat of honor, beside me." The little man's amazing eyes gleamed. "And tomorrow you come to me and we begin to plan the posing, eh? We must begin at once. I will make you great with my painting."

"He is great already," said Ninsun quietly.

"*Por supuesto!* Of course. He is a king, he is a legend, we all know that. But there is greatness and greatness, eh, Gilgamesh? You will be my Minotaur. You know? The son of Minos, but not really Minos's son, but *en realidad* the son of the bull, who I think was Poseidon. Eh? You will pose for me?"

It was only barely a question. This man, Gilgamesh saw, did not regard his questions as questions, but as commands. The curious urgency of his desire to paint him was amusing, and, in its way, compelling. A mere painter, an artisan, a dauber on walls, was all he was, and yet he seemed to think that making a painting of Gilgamesh wearing a bull-mask was a matter of the most supreme importance. Maybe it was. It mattered at least as much as anything else here. To his surprise Gilgamesh found himself liking this little man, and even respecting him. And not even resenting him for having taken possession of Ninsun as apparently he had. He felt an affinity with him that he had felt for very few of the Later Dead. This Ruiz was like someone out of a much older time even than that of Gilgamesh, a time when the distinctions between gods and men had not been as great as they later became. There was about him a demigod's nature. It took only a single glance to see that.

"Yes," Gilgamesh said. "I will pose for you, Ruiz. I will come to you tomorrow, yes."

Dumuzi said then, "To your seats, everyone! It is time for the wine! It is time for the meat!"

Fifteen

It was the hour of first light. They had drunk the night away. Simon Magus was asleep in his seat, snoring. The old sorcerer had been bored and restless throughout the feast, feeling neglected and out of place. Herod sat slouched over a flask of golden wine, the same one he had nursed half the evening; he looked to be frayed and weary, at the last edge of his endurance, but he seemed determined to hang on. He was talking earnestly with a lean, dark, heavily-bearded man in a flowing white robe. Dumuzi, puffy-eyed and pale, was also clearly making an effort at staying awake, though his head was nodding. Across the way, Ninsun looked tired but game, and little Ruiz beside her showed no sign of fatigue whatever; his eyes were keen and gleaming still, and he was scrawling drawings by the dozen on the table napery, on dirty plates, on any flat surface that came to hand.

Vy-otin, still impeccable in his crisp and no doubt miserably uncomfortable Later Dead clothes, came to Gilgamesh's side and said quietly, "Come, let us go for a little walk. The air is fresher outside, and I have things to tell you. Some advice for you, perhaps."

"Yes," Gilgamesh said. "Of course."

Rising, he bowed to Dumuzi – how costly that was to his spirit, bowing to Dumuzi! – and asked to be excused. The king feebly waved his hand. Gilgamesh and the Ice-Hunter chieftain went down the long high-vaulted aisle of the feasting-hall toward the distant doorway.

By early morning light everything had a red glow. The sun

hung low in the sky, a fat distended globe, as though it meant to touch the tips of the Afterworld's mountains before noon.

Gilgamesh said, "How peaceful it is at this hour. Even in the Afterworld, one finds peace now and then."

Vy-otin's wind-tanned face turned stern. His single eye was bright and fierce. "Peace? In other places, maybe, but not here. The only peace you'll find in Uruk is the peace of death. Get yourself out of this city, old friend, as quickly as you can."

"I have only just arrived, Vy-otin. It would be discourteous to leave so soon."

"Stay, then. But only if you're weary of your present life."

"Am I in danger, do you think?"

"Tell me this, and what you tell me will be secret, by our ancient oaths of loyalty: Have you come to Uruk to regain its throne, Gilgamesh?"

The Sumerian halted abruptly, startled. "Do you think that's why I'm here?"

"Dumuzi does."

"Ah, does he? He was ever full of fear."

"And he will have you killed if you remain here," said Vy-otin.

"He will try to, yes. I would expect that of him. He won't find killing me that easy."

"He is king in this city, Gilgamesh."

"And I am Gilgamesh. I will stay as long as I please. No one of Sumerian blood will dare raise a hand against me."

"Not everyone in Uruk is Sumerian," Vy-otin said. "No more than one out of ten, perhaps. There are plenty here who'd like the glory of slaying the famous Gilgamesh. Dumuzi won't lack for assassins."

"Let them come. I can defend myself."

"Indeed. But it's true, then, that you are here to take his throne from him?"

"No!" cried Gilgamesh angrily. "Why does everyone assume that? I don't want his throne or any other. Believe me. I lost my appetite for power a long time ago, Vy-otin. That is the absolute truth. Believe me. Trust me in this. Trust me."

Vy-otin laughed. "That is three or four times in one breath that you call upon me to believe you. It has always seemed to me that only a man who doubts his own words would ask so passionately to be believed."

Gilgamesh, stung, gave the Ice-Hunter a furious glare. "You think I'm lying to you?"

"I think you may be lying to yourself."

"Ah," Gilgamesh said. His hands trembled. He felt rage surging up and down his body – and subsiding. For a long moment he was silent, holding himself utterly still. After a time he said, "Anyone else, Vy-otin, and I would have struck him down for those words. But not you. Not you." He grew quiet again; and then in a very low voice he said, "I will tell you the truth: I no longer know my own soul. I say to myself that I shun power, that I loathe ambition, that I have only scorn for those who scramble for preferment in the land of the Afterworld. And yet – and yet – lately, Vy-otin, there are times when I feel the old fires rising, when I see that I am not as different from other men as I like to think, that I too am driven by that vain urge to clamber to the top of the mountain –" He shook his head. "The truth is as I have already said: I am not at all sure of my own purposes any longer. Perhaps Dumuzi does have something to fear from me after all. But I tell you this, Vy-otin, that I had another reason beside seizing the throne for coming to Uruk."

"Which was?"

"I learned from a sorcerer in the city of Brasil that Enkidu might be here, my dearest friend, the brother of my soul, from whom I have been apart far too often and too long."

"I remember Enkidu, yes. The great hairy roistering man, like a wild bull."

"I came here to find him. Nothing more than that. That is the truth. I swear to you, that is the truth as I believe it."

"Do you have any certain knowledge that he is in Uruk?"

"Only a vision, inspired in me by the wizardry of a black mage. But I think it is a sure vision."

"I wish you joy of the search, then, and all good fortune," said Vy-otin, seizing both of Gilgamesh's hands in his. "By the Horns of God, I will help you in any way I can! But be careful in this city, Gilgamesh. Dumuzi is sly and slippery, and he hates you more than you can imagine. He would send you to the Afterworld a thousand times over if you were not already here."

"I will be wary of him," Gilgamesh said. "I know Dumuzi's ways from the other world."

They walked on for a long while, neither of them speaking. The sullen glow of the sun deepened and climbed and the morning air grew warm. The houses and shops of Uruk began to come to life.

After a time Gilgamesh said, "You have not told me, friend, why you wear this absurd garb of yours."

"I have come to like it," said Vy-otin easily.

"Perhaps so. But it is an odd costume for one who was born at the beginning of time."

"Do I seem that old to you, Gilgamesh? Think of the Hairy Men, who look so near to apes. *They* are truly ancient. Who knows when they lived? It must have been long ago, for they are nothing like us, though they tell us they are our cousins. My time was only ten thousand years before yours. Or perhaps – who can say? – fifteen. I am a man like you."

"Ten thousand years is not a sneeze, Vy-otin. Your time was much before mine. About the Hairy Men I cannot tell you. But you come from a world I never knew, and it was very long before mine. Why, you lived before the Flood!"

"So you like to say." Vy-otin shrugged. "Perhaps so. I know nothing of your Flood. In my time the world was deep in ice. The sun was bright, the air was cool, the wind cut like a knife. The great shaggy beasts roamed the land. It was the grandest of times, Gilgamesh. There were just a few of us, you know, but we were magnificent! You should have seen us, running to the hunt, moving between the dark leafless trees like ghosts! By the Horns, I wish you had been there with us!" In a different, darker voice he said, "I wish I were still there now."

"You made it all live again, that time of cold and great beasts, in your palace in the north," said Gilgamesh. "With the giant tusks on the floor, and the furry skins on the walls, and your people gathered around you. I remember it well, though it was so long ago that I was with you there. Why did you leave that place?"

"You were king in this very city. Why did *you* leave?"

"How can I say? We move about in the Afterworld without understanding anything. I was in this Uruk, and then I was not in Uruk, and I remembered nothing of Uruk. Perhaps I was slain, and awoke somewhere else, Nova Roma, perhaps, or some other city far away. I have no memory of that. Anything could have happened. All I can say is that I was here and then I was not here. The memory of how and why I left has been stolen from me."

"Not from me," said Vy-otin. "I was killed. A stupid brawl, some drunken Egyptians – I made the mistake of getting between them, the usual thing. I went to the darkness that comes between lives and was gone a thousand years, or maybe two, and when I came back I was somewhere else far from any place I knew. Do you know the city of Dis, Gilgamesh?"

"Dis? No."

"On the far side of the White Sea."

"I had no idea there was anything at all on the far side."

"The Afterworld is infinite, friend. I lived in Dis a long while, and then I crossed the sea, and now I live in Uruk. My people are scattered and no one remembers the palace in the north. Everything changes, Gilgamesh, and not for the better."

"And you decided to dress as Later Dead in the city Dis, is that it? Why?"

"So they wouldn't know I was prehistoric. For that is what they call me, *prehistoric*, as though I were some kind of animal."

"They? Who?"

"The scholars," Vy-otin said. "The philosophers. The archaeologists. The dull prying boring Later Dead folk. Let me tell you what happened, Gilgamesh. In Dis I fell in with a man of the Later Dead, short and ugly, but strong, very strong, a musician: Wagner was his name. And his friend, who was called Nietzsche, if you can think of that as a name, and another one, a Jew like your Herod, but older, with a white beard, and sharp staring eyes. He was named Freud. We sat up drinking all night, the four of us, just as you and I have done here tonight, and when dawn came they asked me my name and I told them that it was Vy-otin, and that I was of the old Ice-Hunter folk, that I had lived in a cavern during the cold times and lost my eye in a battle with a tiger of the snows. And I told them a thing or two more of what my first life had been like. Suddenly this Wagner cried out, 'Wotan! You are Wotan!' And Nietzsche said, 'Yes, the very man.' And old Freud began to laugh, and said that it was quite possible, that there could be no question that myth has its roots in reality and that I might well be the myth in the flesh."

"I have trouble understanding all this," said Gilgamesh.

"This Wotan, who also is called Odin, was a god, long after your time and mine, a one-eyed god of the cold northern lands. Those three, they were convinced that I was the model from whom he was created, the ancient original of this Odin, this Wotan, do you see? That in the years after my death I went on to become a legend, the wise one-eyed king of the snow-country, and over thousands of years the people of the north had come to worship me as the father of the gods."

"And if that is so? Time has turned many kings and warriors into gods. What is that to you? Why would it trouble you?"

"Only that those three foolish men were dancing with joy, to know that they had the original of a great myth right there at the table with them. That was fine for them, but where did it leave me, the real me, the man who lived and was? It swept me away, Gilgamesh, it robbed me of all that was real! I said I am no myth, I am who I am; and they brushed that aside. Who I was was of no importance to them. They thought I was quaint, a primitive, a savage. A beast. I think they were amazed that I was capable of speech at all. It was what they wanted me to be that excited them: the archetype. That was what they called me, the archetype. I asked them what an archetype was and they spent hours explaining it to me, when one word would have done. It means the original. I am the original Wotan, if you can believe those three. All the great myths, they said, come down out of the prehistoric dawn of mankind, and here was a man out of that dawn sitting right there with them in the tavern, and it made them delirious with a fever of the mind. *Wotan!* Wagner cried, and he wanted to know if I had had any daughters. Freud, though, asked if I had sons. And Nietzsche wanted to know if I believed in God. Ah, those three, Gilgamesh! One of them had written operas about Wotan – you know what an opera is? Singing and noise, and costumes – and one had written philosophy, and the third one claimed to know more about the way of life of my times than I knew myself. They each saw their own reflections in me. And they asked me ten thousand thousand questions, and called others to see me, scientists and thinkers, and made such a fuss and a bother that I would have given them my other eye to let me alone. By the Mother, they drove me crazy! I fled from them finally. I am no god, Gilgamesh, and I am no archetype. I am only a simple man of the Pleistocene, and –"

"The what?"

"It is what the scholars call the time when I lived. The time when ice covered everything and the shaggy animals were still alive." Vy-otin laughed. "*Pleistocene.* You see? Their silly words infect me. *Prehistoric.* Do you think we thought of ourselves as prehistoric? Mere grunting beast-men? That was not what we were. We had poetry. We had music. We had gods. *Aurignacians*, that is their name for us. It means nothing to me, that name. *Archetype.*" Vy-otin shook his head. "I fled, and I hid from them. And now I call myself Henry Smith, and I pretend I am Later Dead, so that the scholars can't annoy me any longer – the deep thinkers, the philosophers who would tell me what I am. Let them study someone else. Let someone else be prehistoric for them. Let someone else be an Aurignacian archetype."

"You don't *look* Later Dead, Vy-otin."

"No?"

Gilgamesh smiled. "Not to me. To me you look like a one-eyed Ice-Hunter chieftain dressed up in Later Dead clothing. A barbarian just like me. You look – Pleistocene. You look – what is it? – Aurignacian. Definitely an Aurignacian. You look like an archetype, Vy-otin. Do I say the word correctly? An archetype."

Vy-otin smiled also, but without much warmth. "Be that as it may," said the Ice-Hunter, sounding a little testy. "I will not play their game. And woe betide you, my friend, if you should find yourself some day among a pack of philosophers. They'll give you no peace; and by the time they're done with you you won't be sure of your own name."

"Perhaps so," said Gilgamesh. "In the Outback once I met a poor crazy man of the Later Dead who mistook me for one Conan, an ancient warrior, who he said was something called a Cimmerian – not Sumerian, *Cimmerian* – and wanted to worship me, or worse. What a sad fool he was! It was more of that archetype business, I think."

"They are all such fools, these modern men," Vy-otin said.

"But foolishness was not invented yesterday," said Gilgamesh. "We had our share of it in my time. Possibly so did you."

"Indeed," said Vy-otin.

Gilgamesh stared thoughtfully at his old friend, and suddenly found himself wondering about his own gods, Sky-father An and Enlil of the storms and Enki the compassionate and all the rest. Had they once been only men themselves – warriors, priests, kings – and been turned by time and human gullibility into these lofty remote creatures, these archetypes? If he wandered the Afterworld long enough, would he find the true originals of the gods of Sumer the Land gathered in some tavern in the City of Dis, drinking deep and laughing lustily and telling each other tales of the good times before the Flood?

That was not something that he cared to think about.

In silence once more they walked back toward the feasting-hall.

Gilgamesh said, "So this is the advice that you had for me? That I should keep away from philosophers?"

"That, and being on your guard against Dumuzi."

"Yes. Yes, that too. But I should fear the philosophers more, if your experience is to be any guide. Swords and daggers I can handle. But buzzing men of words? Pah! They madden me as much as they do you!" He saw Herod now, coming out of the feasting-hall looking much the worse for his night's carouse. The little Judaean leaned woozily against the intricate reliefs of the hall's dark facade and drew breath again and again, and rubbed his eyes, and ran the back of his hand across his lips. His white Sumerian robe was stained with wine, his skullcap was askew. "Do you see that one?" Gilgamesh asked. "He travelled with me from Brasil. Words, all words! Give him an ear and he'll buzz at you for hours. No more courage than a flea. And yet he claims he was a king once too."

"Gilgamesh?" Herod called, shading his eyes in the glare. "There you are, Gilgamesh!" Walking in an uncertain way, as if he expected his ankles to give way at any moment, he came toward the Sumerian and said, "Been looking for you. Can I talk with you?"

"Go on."

Herod glanced uneasily at Vy-otin. He said nothing.

"What is it?" Gilgamesh said.

Herod said, still uneasy, "I've managed to pick up some information this night. A few things that ought to interest you."

"Speak, then."

"Your mother's friend? The man who wants to paint you?"

With mounting impatience Gilgamesh said, "Well, what about him?"

"He goes by the name of Ruiz here. But do you know who he really is, Gilgamesh? He's *Picasso*!"

"Who?"

"Picasso. Pablo Picasso!" Herod, bloodshot and stubble-faced as he was, seemed almost apoplectically animated. "He's trying to hide from some ex-wife or ex-girlfriend, that's why he's going under another name. But one of Dumuzi's courtiers told me who he actually is. Isn't that fantastic? Of course you'll let him paint you, won't you? He'll turn you into a masterpiece the likes of which the Afterworld has never –" Herod paused. "You aren't impressed. No, you aren't, not at all. You don't even know who Picasso is, do you? Only the greatest Later Dead artist who ever lived! I've studied these things, you know. Later Dead art, music, architecture –"

"Is it not as I told you?" Gilgamesh said to Vy-otin. "An endless buzzing. A torrent of words."

"All right, you don't care," said Herod sulkily. "Let him paint you anyway. I thought you'd be glad to know who he was. But that wasn't the most important thing I wanted to tell you."

"Of course not. You save what is important for last. How considerate. Well, speak, now!"

But again Herod was still, and looked uncertainly toward Vy-otin.

"This man is my dear friend and brother Henry Smith," said Gilgamesh. "I have no secrets from him. Speak, Herod, or by Enlil I'll hurl you as far as –"

"Enkidu is in Uruk, just as the Knowing foretold," Herod blurted hastily.

"*What?*

"The big rough-looking man, the one you seek. Your friend, the one you call your brother. Isn't that Enkidu?"

"Yes, yes!"

"The courtier told me – an Assyrian, he is, name of Tukulti-Sharrukin, very drunk. Enkidu appeared here last week – perhaps the week before, who can tell? Anyway, he showed up in Uruk and went right to the palace, because he had heard a rumor you were here, or had had a dream, or – well, whatever. He thought you might be at the palace. But of course you weren't. He kept asking, Where is Gilgamesh, where is Gilgamesh? He should be here. Dumuzi became very upset. He didn't like the idea that you might be anywhere in the vicinity."

Gilgamesh felt a thundering of excitement within his breast. "To Hell with Durnuzi. Where is Enkidu now?"

"The Assyrian wasn't sure. Still here somewhere. A prisoner somewhere in Uruk, that's what he thinks. He promised to find out for me and let me know tomorrow."

"A prisoner?" Gilgamesh said.

"By the Tusk!" Vy-otin bellowed. "We'll find him! We'll free him! By the Mother! By the Horns of God! A prisoner? Enkidu? We'll tear down the walls of the place where he's kept!"

"Gently," Gilgamesh said, putting a hand to Vy-otin's shoulder. "Stay calm. There are ways and ways to go about this, Vy-otin, my friend."

"You told me his name was Henry Smith," said Herod softly.

"Never mind about that," Gilgamesh snapped. To the Ice-Hunter he said, "Haste would be wrong. First we must find out if Enkidu is truly here, and where he is, and who guards him. Then we approach Dumuzi, carefully, carefully. He is a weak man. You know how one must deal with weak men, Vy-otin. Firmly, directly, taking care not to send them into panic, for then they might do anything. If he slays Enkidu out of fear of me I could be another thousand years finding him again. So we must move slowly. Eh, Vy-otin? What do you say?"

"I think you are right," the Ice-Hunter said.

Gilgamesh turned to Herod. A pitiful little man, he thought. But a clever and a useful one.

"A good night's work," he said, smiling warmly. "Well done, King Herod! Well done!"

"This will be your mask," Picasso said. "Here. Here, put it on."

He moved about the big, ugly underground room like some chugging little machine, rearranging the heaps of clutter, kicking things out of his way, pushing them aside. Gilgamesh looked at the mask that had been thrust into his hands, puzzled. It was as ugly as everything else in this room: a massive bull-snout of papier-mâché, with huge black nostrils and great jutting square teeth. There was one staring red eye along the left side and another on top. Short sharp curved horns made of wax protruded at peculiar angles. Clumps of thick crinkly black fur were glued to it everywhere. A sour smell rose from the thing. He was supposed to fasten it, apparently, by tying the cord that dangled from it around his throat.

"You want me to wear *this*?" Gilgamesh asked.

"Of course. Put it on, put it on! You will be my Minotaur!" Picasso waved his hands impatiently. "I made it today, especially for you."

Only a day had gone by since Dumuzi's feast. The mask, hideous though it was, was highly elaborate, surely the product of many days of work. "How is that possible?" Gilgamesh said. "That you could have made this so quickly?"

"Quickly?" Picasso spat. "*Cagarruta!* What do you mean, quickly? That mask took me more than an hour!"

"You are a sorcerer, then."

Picasso laughed, and went on clearing space in the studio.

Gilgamesh put the mask aside and wandered around the room, peering at the paintings stacked against every wall. They were horrifying. Here was a woman with two faces on one head, and it was impossible to tell whether she was looking straight at you or showing you the side of her head. Here was a picture that was all little boxes, that made your eyes jump around until you wanted to weep. Here were three monsters with mocking faces. Here, a woman with three breasts and teeth between her legs.

The shapes! The colors! No one had ever seen such scenes, not even in the Afterworld. Surely there was some witchcraft being practised here. In old Uruk, Gilgamesh thought, he would have ordered these paintings to be burned, and the painter to be driven from the city with whips. And yet he found himself beguiled despite himself by these works. He could sense the little man's powerful and playful mind behind them, and his formidable strength of will.

"Are you a sorcerer?" Gilgamesh asked.

"*Por favor.* The mask. Put it on."

"A demon of some sort?"

"Yes," said Picasso. "I am a demon. The mask, will you?"

"Show me the picture you have made of my mother."

"It is not finished. It keeps changing. Everything keeps

changing. I will put the mask on you myself." Picasso crossed the room and snatched it up. But he was too short; Gilgamesh rose above him like a wall. "*Dios!* What a *cojonudo* monster you are! Is there any need for you to be so big?" He shoved the mask upward toward Gilgamesh's chin. "Put it on," he said. "*Ahora a trabajar*. It is time for us to work, now."

He said it quietly, but with great force. Gilgamesh slipped the mask over his face, nearly gagging at first at the stink of glue and other things. He tied it behind his neck. There were slits through which he could see, though not well. Picasso beckoned him to a place under the bright, intense electrical lights and showed him how he wanted him to stand, arms upraised as if ready to seize an onrushing enemy.

"All these other pictures, you have painted using models?" Gilgamesh said, his voice muffled and rumbling inside the mask. "They are things you have actually seen?"

"I see them in here," said Picasso, tapping his forehead. He lit a cigarette and stepped back, staring at Gilgamesh so unwaveringly that the power of that keen gaze felt like the pressure of cold knives against the Sumerian's skin. "Sometimes I use models, sometimes not. Lately more often than not, because of the difficulties. I tell myself that the models will help, though they do not, not very much. This place, this Afterworld, it is shit, you know? It is *mierda*, it is *cagada*, this whole place is *un gran cagadero*. But we do what we can, eh, King Gilgamesh? This is our life now. And it is better than the great darkness, the big *nada*, eh? Eh, king? Hold your arms up. The legs apart, a little. Thrust forward from the hips, as though you are going to stick it into her, eh, just as you stand there." He was painting already, swift broad strokes. Gilgamesh felt a quiver of uneasiness. What if this really was some kind of sorcery? What if Picasso could capture his soul and put it on that canvas, and meant to leave him locked up in it forever?

No, he told himself. That was nonsense. The little man was just what he said he was, a painter. A very great painter, if Herod could be believed. There might be a demon inside him, but it was the same kind of demon that once had been in Gilgamesh, that had driven him onward to go everywhere, see everything, learn everything, devour everything. I understand this man, Gilgamesh thought. He and I are very similar.

The difference is that in the Afterworld I have grown quiet and easy, and this one still burns with the restlessness and the hunger.

"You were always a painter?" Gilgamesh asked.

"Always. From the cradle. Don't talk now, eh?"

How casually he orders a king around, Gilgamesh thought. Just a little bald-headed man wearing only a pair of ragged baggy shorts, sweat running down the white hair of his chest, a cloud of cigarette smoke surrounding him, and he has no fear of anyone, of anything. It was not hard now to see how he had captured Ninsun. This man, Gilgamesh thought, could probably have any woman he wanted. Even a queen. Even a goddess.

"Do you know?" Picasso said, after a long while. "I think this time it will work. The painting holds. The others, they turned in my hand. This one holds. It is the charm of the Minotaur, I think. The bull rules in the Afterworld! I am a bull. You are a bull. We are in the arena all the time. I could not become a matador, so I became a bull. The same with you, I think. It makes no difference: the power of the bull is in us both. In your city, did they fight the bull?"

"I fought one once," Gilgamesh said. "Enkidu and I. It was the Bull of Heaven, with the power of Father Enlil in him. He was let loose in the city by the priestess Inanna, and ran wild and slew a child; but Enkidu and I, we caught him, we danced with him, we played him, we fought him down. Enkidu wearied him and I put the sword in him."

"Bravo!"

"But it angered the gods. They took Enkidu's life, by way of revenge. He wasted away and died. That was the first time I lost him; but I have lost him again and again here in the Afterworld. I am doomed to search for him forever. It is our fate never to be together very long. That man is my brother; he is my other self. But I will find him again, and soon. They tell me he is in Uruk, a prisoner. You may have seen him, perhaps – he is just as tall as I am, and –"

But Picasso did not seem to be listening any longer. He was lost in his work, and in some private distant dream.

"The bullfight on Sunday," he said, as though Gilgamesh had not been speaking at all. "How you will love it! We will sit together in the seat of honor, you and I. Sabartes has found a matador of whom I know nothing, but perhaps he will be good, eh? It is very important that the matador be good. Mere butchery, that is shameful. The *corrida* is art. Lift the arms, yes?"

He has not heard a word of what I said to him about Enkidu, thought Gilgamesh. His mind went elsewhere when I spoke of killing the Bull of Heaven. He hears only what he wants to hear. When he wants to hear, he listens, and when he wants to talk, he talks. But in his soul he is the only king. No matter, Gilgamesh thought. He is a great man. His greatness shines about him like the light from a polished shield. And Herod is probably right: he is a great painter also. Even if the only things that he paints are monstrosities.

"It goes well," Picasso said. "The image holds true, you know? The power of the bull. No cubism today, no blue, no rose." His arm was moving so quickly now that it seemed to be not a single arm but three. His eyes were ablaze. Yet he gave no appearance of haste. His face was fixed, still, expressionless. His body, but for that one unceasing arm, seemed totally relaxed. Gilgamesh ached to see what was on that canvas.

The mask was hot and stifling now. The Sumerian felt that if he kept it on much longer he would choke. But he dared not move. He was caught in the little man's spell. Sorcery, yes, definitely sorcery, Gilgamesh thought.

"Do you know why I paint?" Picasso asked. "I say, each time, What can I learn of myself today that I don't know? The paintings teach me. When it isn't me any more who is talking, but the pictures I make, and when they escape and mock me, then I know I've achieved my goal. Do you know? Do you understand? No?" He shrugged. "Ah, it makes no difference. Here. Here, we can stop now. Enough for today. It goes well. *Por dios*, it goes well!"

Gilgamesh lost no time working himself free of the mask. He gasped for fresh air, but there was none. The room was heavy with the scent of sweat.

"Is it finished?" he asked. He had no idea how long he had posed, whether it had been ten minutes or half a day.

"For now," said Picasso. "Here: look."

He swung the easel around. Gilgamesh stared.

What had he expected to see? The picture of a tall muscular man with a bull's hideous face, gaping mouth, swollen tongue, wild red eyes looking in different directions, the face that was on the mask. But there were two naked men in the picture, crouched face to face like wrestlers poised to spring. One was huge, black-bearded, with powerful commanding features. Gilgamesh recognized himself in that portrait immediately: it was a remarkable likeness. The other man was much shorter, stocky, wide-shouldered, deep-chested. Picasso himself, plainly. But his face could not be seen. It was the short man who was wearing the mask of the bull.

Three assassins were waiting for him when he stepped out into the Street of the Tanners and Dyers. Gilgamesh was neither surprised nor alarmed. They were so obviously lying in wait for him that he hardly needed them to draw their weapons to know what they were up to.

They were disguised, more or less, as Uruk police, in ill-fitting khaki uniforms badly stained below the arms with sweat. One, with a big blunt nose and a general reek of garlic about him, might have been a Hittite, and the other two were Later Dead, with that strange yellow hair that some of them had, and pathetic straggly beards and mustaches. They had guns.

Gilgamesh wasted no time. He struck one of the Later Dead across the throat with the edge of his hand and sent him reeling into a narrow alleyway, where he fell face forward and lay twitching and croaking and puking. On the backswing Gilgamesh rammed his elbow hard into the Hittite's conspicuous nose, and at the same time he caught the other Later Dead by the wrist and twisted the pistol free of his grasp, kicking it across the street.

The Later Dead yelped and took off at full speed, arms flailing wildly in the air. Gilgamesh drew his dagger and turned to the Hittite, who had both hands clapped to his face. Blood was pouring out between his fingers.

He touched the tip of his dagger to the Hittite's belly and said, "Who sent you?"

"You broke my nose!"

"Very likely. Next time don't push it into my elbow that way." The Sumerian said, with a little prod of the dagger, "Do you have a name?"

"Tudhaliyash."

"That's not a name, it's a belch. What are you, a Hittite?"

Tudhaliyash, looking miserable, nodded. The blood was flowing a little less copiously now.

"Who do you work for, Hittite?"

"The municipality of Uruk," said the man sullenly. "Department of Weights and Measures."

"Were you here to weigh me, or to measure me?"

"I was on my way to the tavern with my friends when you attacked us."

"Yes. I often attack strangers in the street, especially when they come in groups of three. Who sent you after me?"

"It would be worth my life to say."

"It will be worth your life to keep silent," said Gilgamesh, prodding a little harder. "One shove of this and I'll send you on your way to your next life. But you won't get there quickly. It takes a long time to die of a slash in the guts."

"Ur-ninmarka sent me," the Hittite murmured.

"Who?"

"The royal arch-vizier."

"Ah. I remember. Dumuzi's right hand. And who were you supposed to kill?"

"G-G – G-Gil –"

"Say it."

"Gilgamesh."

"And who is he?"

"The former k-king."

"Am I Gilgamesh?"

"Yes."

"I am the man you were told to kill?"

"Yes. Yes. Make it quick, Gilgamesh! In the heart, not the belly!"

"It wouldn't be worth the trouble of having to clean my blade of you afterward," said Gilgamesh coolly. "I will be merciful. You'll live to belch some more."

"A thousand blessings! A million blessings!"

Gilgamesh scowled. "Enough. Get away from me. Show me how well you can run. Take your puking friend over there with you. I will forget this entire encounter. I remember nothing of you and I know nothing of who it was who sent you upon me. You didn't tell me a thing. You understand? Yes, I think you do. Go, now. Go!"

They ran very capably indeed. Gilgamesh leaned against the

wall of Picasso's house and watched until they were out of sight. A nuisance, he thought, being waylaid in the street like that. Dumuzi should show more imagination. Persuade some demons to have the pavement swallow me up, or drop a cauldron of burning oil on me from the rooftops, or some such.

He looked around warily to see if anyone else lay in ambush for him. There was a faint ectoplasmic shimmer on the building across the way, as though some diabolic entity were passing through the walls, but that was nothing unusual. Otherwise all seemed well. Briskly Gilgamesh walked to the end of the street, turned left into a street calling itself the Street of Camels, and went onward via the Corridor of Sighs and the Place of Whispers to the great plaza where he was lodged.

Herod was there, bubbling with news.

"Your friend is indeed a prisoner in Uruk," he said at once. "We've found out where he's being kept."

Gilgamesh's eyes widened. "Where is he?" he demanded. "What have they done to him? Who told you?"

"Tukulti-Sharrukin's our source, the Assyrian courtier who likes to drink too much. Your friend is fine. The Assyrian says Enkidu hasn't been harmed in any way. He's being held at a place called the House of Dust and Darkness on the north side of the city. The House of Dust and Darkness! Isn't that a fine cheery name?"

"You idiot," Gilgamesh said, barely containing his anger.

Herod backed away in alarm. "What's wrong?"

"Your Assyrian is playing jokes with you, fool. Any man of the Two Rivers would know what The House of Dust and Darkness is. It's simply the name we used in the old days of Sumer for the place where dead people go. Don't you see, we're *all* in the House of Dust and Darkness!"

"No," Herod said, edging still farther back as Gilgamesh made menacing gestures. "I don't know anything about Sumer, but that's what the building is actually called. I've seen it. The name's written right over the front porch in plain English. It's just a jail, Gilgamesh. It's Dumuzi's special upscale jail for his political prisoners, very nice, very comfortable. It looks like a hotel."

"You've seen it, you say?"

"Tukulti-Sharrukin took me there."

"And Enkidu? You saw him?"

"No. I didn't go inside. It's not *that* much like a hotel. But Tukulti- Sharrukin says –"

"Who is this Assyrian? Why do you have such faith in what he tells you?"

"Trust me. He hates Dumuzi – something about a business deal that went sour, a real screwing, he and the king going partners on a land-development scheme and the king goniffering up the profits. He'll do anything to stick it to Dumuzi now. He told me all about it the night of the feast. He and I hit it off like *this*, Gilgamesh, just like *this*. He's a member of the tribe, you know."

"He's what?"

"A Jew. Like me."

Gilgamesh frowned. "I thought he was an Assyrian."

"An Assyrian Jew. His grandfather was Assyrian ambassador to Israel in King David's time and fell in love with one of David's nieces, and so he had to convert in order to marry her. It must have been one devil of a juicy scandal, a royal niece not only marrying a *goy* but an Assyrian, yet. David wanted to murder him, but he had diplomatic immunity, so the king had him declared *persona non grata* and he was sent home to Nineveh, but somehow he took her with him and then the family stayed kosher after he got back to Assyria. You could have knocked me over with a straw when he said he was a Yid, because he's got that mean Assyrian face with the nose coming right out of the forehead, you know, and the peculiar curly beard they all wear with the tight ringlets, but when you listen for a little while to the way he speaks you won't have any doubt that he's –"

"When I listen for a little while to the way *you* speak," said Gilgamesh, "I feel like strangling you. Can't you ever keep to the point? I don't care who this ridiculous tribesman of yours did or did not marry. What I want to know is, will he help us to free Enkidu or won't he?"

"Don't be an anti-Semite, Gilgamesh. It doesn't look good on you. Tukulti-Sharrukin promises to do what he can for us. He knows the guy who runs the main computer at the House of Dust and Darkness. He'll try to bugger up the software so that Enkidu's name gets dropped from the prisoner roster, and maybe then we can slip him out the back way. But no guarantees. It isn't going to be easy. We'll know in a day or two whether it's going to work out. I'm doing my best for you, you know."

Gilgamesh closed his eyes and breathed deeply. Herod was a colossal pain in the fundament, but he did get things done.

"All right. Forgive me my impatience, Herod."

"I love it when you apologize. A minute ago you had that I-suffer-no-fools-gladly gleam in your eye and I thought you were going to knock me from here to Nova Roma."

"Why *should* I suffer fools gladly?"

"Right. But I'm not all that much of a fool." Herod grinned. "Let's get on to other things. You know that Dumuzi has a contract out on you, don't you?"

"A contract?" said Gilgamesh, baffled again.

"Zeus! Where did you learn your English? Dumuzi wants to have you killed, is what I'm saying. Tukulti-Sharrukin told me that too. Dumuzi's frightened shitless that you're going to make a grab for power here, and so –"

"Yes, I know. Three buffoons tried to jump me as I was leaving Picasso's. One of them admitted that he was working for Dumuzi."

"You kill them?"

"I just damaged them a little. They're probably halfway to Brasil by now, but I suppose there'll be others. I'll lose no sleep over it. Where's Simon?"

"At the baths, trying to sober himself up. He and I have an audience with the king in a little while. Simon wants to set up a trade deal, swap Dumuzi a couple dozen of his spare necromancers and thaumaturges and shamans for a few barrels of the diamonds and rubies and emeralds that he's convinced Dumuzi possesses by the ton."

"Even a fool could see there is no great abundance of diamonds and rubies in this city."

"You tell Simon that. I'm only an employee. He's four hundred percent convinced that this city is overflowing with precious gems, and you know how he salivates for precious gems. He'd sell his sister for six pounds of sapphires. *Meshuggenah. Goyishe kup.* Well, he'll find out. How did things go with you and Picasso?"

"He made me wear a strange mask, a bull's face. But when he painted me, he was in the painting too, and the mask was on him. I could not understand that, Herod."

"It's art. Don't try to understand it."

"But –"

"Trust me. The man's a genius. Have faith in him. He'll paint a masterpiece, and who gives a crap which one of you has the mask? But you don't understand these things, do you, Gilgamesh? You were great stuff in your time, they all tell me, a terrific warrior and a splendid civil engineer, even, but you do have your limits. After all, you have a *goyishe kup* too. Although I have to admit you manage all right, considering your handicap."

"You use too many strange words. *Goyishe kup?*"

"It means you have Gentile brains."

"Gentile?"

"That means not Jewish. Don't be offended. You know how much I admire you. Do you and Picasso get along all right?"

"We find each other amusing. He has invited me to sit with him at the bullfight on Sunday."

"Yes, the bullfight. His grand passion, watching skinny Spaniards stick swords into big angry animals. Another *meshuggenah*, Picasso. Him and his bullfights. A genius, but a *meshuggenah.*"

"And a *goyishe kup*?" Gilgamesh asked.

Herod looked startled. "Him? Well, I suppose so. I suppose. But a genius, all the same. At least he makes great paintings out of his bullfights. And everyone's entitled to a hobby of some sort, I guess. An obsession, even."

"And what is yours?" said the Sumerian.

Herod winked. "Surviving."

Sixteen

It was one of those nights that went by in a moment, in the blink of an eye. That often happened in the Afterworld; but they were balanced by the days that seemed to last a week or two, or a month. Gilgamesh had been here so long that he scarcely minded the Afterworld's little irregularities. He could remember clearly enough how it had been on Earth, the days in succession coming around at predictable intervals, but that seemed unreal to him now and woefully oppressive. Sleep meant little here, meals were unimportant: why should all the days be the same length? What did it matter?

Now, by common consent, it was Sunday. The day of the bullfight. The calendar too fluttered and slid about, no rhyme, no reason. But the bullfight was to be held on Sunday, and the bullfight was today, and therefore today was Sunday. Tomorrow might be Thursday. What did it matter? What did it matter? Today was the day he would be reunited with Enkidu, if all went well. That was what mattered.

The night, brief as it was, had been enlivened by a second attempt on Gilgamesh's life. Nothing so crude as a team of thugs, this time, but it was simple-minded all the same, the old snake-in-the-ventilating-shaft routine. Gilgamesh heard slitherings in the wall. The grille, he discovered, had been loosened, probably by the maids who had come in to turn down the bed. He pushed it open and stood to one side, sword at the ready. The snake was a fine one, glossy black with brilliant red markings and eyes like yellow fire. Its fangs had the sheen of chrome steel. He regretted having to chop it in two; but what alternative, he wondered, did he have? Trap it in a bedsheet and call room service to take it away?

The same motor-chariots that had transported Gilgamesh and his companions to the royal feasting-hall a few nights before were waiting out front to bring them to the stadium that morning. The bullfight, evidently, was the event of the season in Uruk. Half the city was going, judging by the number of cars travelling in the direction of the arena.

Herod rode with Gilgamesh. The driver was a Sumerian, who genuflected before Gilgamesh, trembling with obvious awe: no assassin, not this one, unless he was one of the best actors in the Afterworld.

The bullfight was being held well outside the city, in the sandy hill country to the east. The day was hot and overcast. Some long-fanged bat-winged demon-creatures, purple and red and green, soared lazily in the hazy sky.

"It's all arranged," said Herod in a low voice, leaning toward Gilgamesh. They were near the stadium now. Gilgamesh could see it, tier upon stone tier rising from the flat desert. "Tukulti-Sharrukin will try to spring Enkidu from the House of Dust and Darkness just as the bullfight's getting started. We'll have half a dozen of Simon's men posted nearby, with three of the Land Rovers. Everybody knows what to do. When Enkidu comes out of the jail building, he'll get into one of the Rovers and all three will take off in different directions, but they'll all head out this way."

"And Vy-otin?"

"Smith, you mean?"

"Smith, yes!"

"He'll be waiting just outside the stadium, the way you wanted. When the Land Rovers show up, Smith will meet the one with Enkidu and bring him in, and lead him to the box where you and Picasso will be sitting, which is right next to the royal box. Dumuzi will have a stroke when he sees him."

"If not when he sees him, then when I embrace him before the entire town," Gilgamesh said. "The hero Gilgamesh reunited with his beloved Enkidu! What can Dumuzi say? What can he do? Everyone will be cheering. And after the bullfight –"

"Yes?" Herod said. "After the bullfight, what?"

"I will pay a call on King Dumuzi," said Gilgamesh. "I will speak to him about the unfortunate error of judgment that led his officials to imprison my friend. I will do it very politely. Perhaps I will speak to him also about the state of law and order in the streets of his city, and about proper maintenance of the ventilating systems of his hostelry here. But that will be afterward. First we will enjoy the pleasure of the bullfight, eh?"

"Yes," said Herod glumly. "First the bullfight."

"You don't look pleased."

"I never even liked to go to the gladiators," the Judaean said. "And they deserved what they did to each other. But a poor dumb innocent bull? All that bleeding, all that pain?"

"Fighting bulls is an art," Gilgamesh replied. "Your great genius Picasso the painter told me so himself. And you are a man of culture, Herod. Think of it as a cultural experience."

"I'm a Jewish liberal, Gilgamesh. I'm not supposed to enjoy cruelty to animals."

"A Jewish what?"

"Never mind," said Herod.

The chariot pulled up in a holding area in front of the stadium. At close range the circular structure was enormous, a true Roman coliseum on the grand scale, five or perhaps six levels high. The topmost tier was partly in ruins, many of its great stone arches shattered; but the rest of the building seemed intact and splendid. There were throngs of people in colorful holiday garb walking around on every level.

As he got out of the car Gilgamesh caught sight of Vy-otin, in slacks and a loose short-sleeved shirt, waving to him from a point near one of the ticket booths. The long-legged Ice-Hunter chieftain stood out clearly above the short, square-hewn, largely Sumerian crowd all about him.

He came over at once. "There's trouble," he said.

"Enkidu?"

"You," Vy-otin said. "One of my people overheard something in a washroom. Dumuzi's putting snipers on the top tier. When things start getting exciting and everybody's yelling, they're going to open fire on Picasso's box. The prime target is you, but they're likely to hit Picasso too, and your mother, and anyone else who's close by. You've got to get out of here."

"No. Impossible."

"Are you crazy? How are you going to guard yourself against shots from the sky? Someone your size will be the easiest target in the world."

"How many men do you have here?" Gilgamesh asked.

"Nine."

"That should be plenty. Send them up on top to take out the snipers."

"There'll still be a risk that –"

"Yes. Maybe there will. Where's your warlike spirit, Vy-otin? Have you truly become Henry Smith? Dumuzi can't have put a hundred sharpshooters up there. There'll be two or three, is my guess. Five at most. You'll have plenty of time to find them. They'll be easy enough to spot. They won't be Sumerian, and they'll be looking nervous, and they'll have rifles or some other cowardly Later Dead armament. Your men will locate them one by one and push them off the edge. No problem."

Vy-otin nodded. "Right," he said. "See you later."

★

Picasso closed his eyes and let memory come seeping back: the old life, the thyme-scented tang of dry Mediterranean air in the summer, the heat, the crowds, the noise. If he didn't look, he could almost make himself believe he was eight or nine years old, sitting beside his tall sandy-bearded father in the arena at Malaga again where the bullfights were the finest and most elegantly conducted in the world. Sketching, always sketching, even then, the picador on his little bony blindfolded old horse, the haughty matador, the mayor of the city in his grand box. Or he could think this was the bull-ring of La Coruña, or the one at Barcelona, or even the one at Arles in southern France, an old Roman stadium just like this one, where he would go every year when he was old, with his wife Jacqueline, with his son Paul, with Sabartes.

Well, all that was long ago in another world. This was the Afterworld, and the sky was murky and the air was thick and acrid, and the crowd around him was chattering in English, in Greek, in some Mesopotamian babble, in just about everything but good honest Spanish. In the midst of the hubbub he sat motionless, waiting, hands at his sides, silent, solitary. There might well have been no one else around him. He was aware that the priestess-woman Ninsun was beside him, more splendid than ever in a robe of deep purple shot through with threads of gold, and that her giant son the warrior Gilgamesh sat beside him also, and the faithful Sabartes, and the little Jewish Roman man, Herod, and the other Roman, the fat old dictator, Simon. But all those people had become mere wraiths to him now. As he waited for the *corrida* to begin he saw only the ring, and the gate behind which the bulls were kept, and the shadows cast by the contest that was to come.

"It will not be long now, Don Pablo," Sabartes murmured. "We have been waiting for the king. But you see, he is in his box now, *el rey*." Sabartes gestured toward his left, to the royal box just alongside theirs. With a flicker of his eye Picasso saw the foolish-looking king waving and smiling to the crowd, while his courtiers made gestures instructing everyone to cheer. He nodded. One must wait for the king to arrive, yes, Picasso supposed. But he did not want to wait any longer. He was formally dressed, a dark blue business suit, a white shirt, even a necktie: the *corrida* was a serious matter, it demanded respect. But in this humidity he was far from comfortable. Once the fight started he would no longer notice the weather or the pinching at his throat or the sweaty stickiness along his back. Just let it start soon, he thought. Let it start soon.

What was this? Some new commotion close at hand?

The huge Sumerian was up and prancing about and shouting like a lunatic. "Enkidu! Enkidu!"

"Gilgamesh!" bellowed a newcomer, just as enormous but twice as frightful, shouldering his way into the box. "My own true brother! My friend!"

This one was a Sumerian too, by the look of him. But he was strange and shaggy, almost like a beast, with a fiery, smouldering look about him and black hair tumbling into his eyes and a beard so dense it hid most of his face. Another Minotaur, Picasso thought: an even truer one than the first. They were embracing like two mountains now, Gilgamesh and this other, this Enkidu. Gilgamesh was like a child in his excitement. Now he clapped Enkidu on the back with a blow that would have felled a dragon, and now he dragged him over to meet Ninsun, before whom Enkidu fell in a pose of utter devotion, kneeling and kissing her hem, and now Gilgamesh was nodding toward Dumuzi's box and both men began to laugh. "And this," said Gilgamesh, "this is the painter Picasso, who is a great genius. He paints like a demon. Maybe he *is* a demon. But he is very great. This is his bullfight, today."

"This little man? He will fight bulls?"

"He will watch," Gilgamesh said. "He loves that more than anything, except, I think, to paint: to watch the bulls being fought. As was done in his homeland."

"And tomorrow," said Picasso, "I will paint you, wild one. But that will be tomorrow. Now the bulls." Out of the corner of his mouth he said to Sabartes, "Well? Do we ever commence?"

"Indeed, Don Pablo. Now. Now."

There came a great flourish of trumpets. And then the grand entry procession began, the *cuadrillas* coming forth led by a pair of mounted *alguaciles* in eye-dazzling costumes. Everyone crossing the great arena, the banderilleros, the picadors riding demon-horses that looked almost like the horses of the other world except for their red blazing eyes and stiff lizard-like tails, and then finally the matador, this Blanco y Velez, this Spaniard of the time of Charles IV.

Sabartes had organized everything very well, Picasso thought. It all looked as it was supposed to look. The men, the subordinates, moved with dignity and grace. They understood the grandeur of the moment. And the matador showed promise. He held himself well. He was a little thicker through the middle than Picasso had expected – perhaps he was out of shape, or maybe in the time of Charles IV the style had been different, matadors had not been so slender – but his costume was right, the skintight silken trousers, the richly embroidered jacket and waistcoat of satin embroidered in gold and silver, the hat, the cape, the linen lace shirt-waist.

The procession halted before the two boxes of honor. The matador saluted the king, and then Picasso, who was the president of the bullfight today. The king, who had been staring at the newly arrived Enkidu as though he were some sort of demon that had materialized in Picasso's box, and whose face now was as dour and foul as bile, acknowledged the salute with an offhand flick of his hand that Picasso found infuriating in its discourtesy. "*Puerco,*" he muttered. "*Hijo de puta.*"

Then Picasso rose. As president he carried the keys to the bull-pens. With a grand swing of his arm he tossed them out to one of the *alguaciles*, who caught them nicely and rode over to release the first bull.

"And so we commence," said Picasso quietly to Sabartes. "*Al fin*, we commence."

He felt himself settling into the inviolable sphere of concentration that always enveloped him at the bullfight. In a moment he would feel as though he were the only one in the stadium.

The bull came galloping forth.

Madre de dios! What a horror! That was no bull! That was an evil monster!

Sabartes had told him what to expect, but he had never quite grasped it, apparently. This could have been something out of one of his own paintings. The creature had six many-jointed legs, like some giant insect, and two rows of terrible spines on its back that dripped a nasty fluid, and great flopping ears. Its skin was green with purple blotches, and thick like a reptile's. There were horns, short and curved and sharp and very much like a bull's, but otherwise this was pure hell-creature.

Picasso shot a venomous look at Sabartes. "What have you done? You call that a bull?"

"We are in the Afterworld, Pablo," said Sabartes wearily. "They do not send bulls to the Afterworld, only human beings. But this will do. It is much like a bull, in its way."

"*Chingada!*" Picasso said, and spat.

But they were making a brave attempt down in the arena. The banderilleros were dancing around the bull, striving to plant their little lances in the beast's neck, and sometimes succeeding. The hell-bull, maddened, charged this way and that, going for the horses of the picadors, who warded it off with thrusts of their pikes. Picasso could see that these were experienced men out there, who knew what they were doing and were doing their best, though plainly the hell-bull puzzled them. They were trying to wear it down to make it ready for the Hour of Truth, and by and large they were achieving that. Picasso felt the bullfight slip around him like a cloak. He was wholly engulfed in it now. He saw nothing else but the bull and the men in the ring.

Then he looked toward the matador, waiting his moment to one side, and everything turned sour.

The matador was frightened. You could see it in his nostrils, you could see it in the angle of his chin. Perhaps he had been a master of his art back there in the time of Charles IV, but he had never fought anything like this thing, and he was not going to do it well. That was plain. He was not going to do it well.

The trumpets sounded. It was the moment.

Blanco y Velez came forward, holding out the *muleta*, the little red silk cape, and the *capote*, the big work cape. But he moved stiffly, and it was the wrong stiffness, the stiffness of fear rather than the stiffness of courage. The picadors and the banderilleros saw it, and instead of leaving the ring they withdrew to one side, exchanging uneasy glances. Picasso saw it. The hell-bull saw it. The matador's moves were awkward and hesitant. He didn't seem to know how to use his capes – had the art not progressed that far, in the time of Charles IV? – and he had no grace and he took quick, mincing steps. He led the bull around and around, working closer and closer to him, but that should have been beautiful and it was merely depressing.

"No," Picasso said under his breath. "Get him out of there!"

"He is our only matador, Pablo," Sabartes said.

"He will die. And he will die stupidly."

"He looked better when I saw him yesterday. But that was with a heifer."

Picasso groaned. "He will die now. Look."

There had been a shift of equilibrium in the ring. Blasco y Velez was no longer working the bull; the bull was working Blasco y Velez. Round and round, round and round – the bull seeming not angry now but amused, playing with him, dancing around, picking up speed – the picadors trying now to intervene, Blasco y Velez backing away but now finally putting a brave face on things, trying a desperate *veronica*, a *farol*, a *mariposa*, a *serpentina*, a *media-veronica* – yes, yes, he knew his work, he understood the art, except that he was trying to do everything at once, and where was his control, where was his stillness, where was his art? The bull, passing him, snarled and nipped him in the shoulder. Blood flowed. Blasco y Velez jumped back and went for his sword – forbidden, to use the sword in mere self-defense – but the bull knocked it from his grasp with a contemptuous whirl, and swung on past, throwing down a picador's horse and goring it, and coming back again toward the matador –

"No!" came a tremendous roar from Gilgamesh's shaggy friend, the huge Enkidu.

And then the second Sumerian giant leaped from the stone bench and vaulted down into the arena.

"*Enkidu!*" Gilgamesh cried.

Picasso gasped. This was becoming crazy, now. This was turning into a nightmare. The big Sumerian picked the hapless matador up and tossed him aside to safety as though he were a doll. Then he came toward the bull, caught it by the double rows of spines, swung himself up easily on to the beast's back, and began to throttle it.

"No, no, no!" Picasso muttered. "Clown! Butcher! Sabartes, stop this idiocy! What is he doing? *Riding* the bull? *Strangling* the bull?" Tears of rage crowded into his eyes. His first *corrida* in who knew how long, and it had been a dreadful one from the start, and now it was dissolving into absurd chaos. He stood on his seat, bellowing. "Butchery! Madness! For shame! For shame!"

★

Enkidu was in trouble. He was on the bull and had made a brave beginning of it, but now the bull's anger was rising once again and its strength was in the ascendant, and in another moment the creature was going to roll over and kill him by falling upon him, or hurl him loose and fall upon him with its hooves. Enkidu's peril was great and it was immediate. That was the one thing Gilgamesh saw, and nothing else mattered to him. To have won him back once more, and then to lose him again so quickly in this craziness of a bullfight – no, no, it could not be.

It was like that time in the other life when the Bull of Heaven was loose in old Uruk, and Enkidu had mounted it and seized it by its horns and tried to force it to the ground. It had taken both of them to slay the bull that time. It would again.

Gilgamesh snatched up his sword. Herod saw him and grabbed at his arm, crying, "Gilgamesh! No! Don't go out there!" The Sumerian swatted him aside and clambered down over the edge of the box. Enkidu, holding on with difficulty now atop the plunging, bucking monster, grinned to him.

The whole stadium seemed to be going insane.

People were up, some of them screaming, others just milling about in excitement. Fist-fights were breaking out everywhere. Dumuzi was on his feet, eyes wild, face purple, making frantic gestures. Glancing upward, Gilgamesh had a quick glimpse of struggling figures outlined against the rim of the arena. Dumuzi's snipers, fighting with Vy-otin's men? And farther up, a flock of demon-birds circled in the sky, ghastly things with gaping beaks and long shimmering wings.

The bull, lurching from side to side, was trying to shake Enkidu free. Gilgamesh rushed forward and took a spew of the bull's sweat in his face. It burned like acid. He drew his sword, but the bull backed out of range, and twisted itself so violently that Enkidu nearly was flung from its back.

Yet he showed no fear at all. He held tight, thighs gripping the bull's back just in front of the spines, and took a firm hold on the thing's diabolical horns. With all his great strength he fought to force the bull's head downward.

"Strike, brother, strike!" Enkidu called.

But it was too soon. The bull had plenty of fight left in it. It whirled wildly around, and the rough scaly skin of its flank caught Gilgamesh across the ribs and drew blood. It leaped and bucked, leaped and bucked, slamming its hooves against the ground. Enkidu flailed about like a pennant flapping in the breeze. He seemed about to lose his grip; then he called out in his most confident tone and rose again, rearing high above the creature's razor-sharp back. He regained his grip on the horns and twisted, and the bull yielded and weakened, lowering its head, turning so that the nape of its neck was toward Gilgamesh.

"Strike!" Enkidu called again.

And this time Gilgamesh drove the blade home.

He felt a quivering, a shudder, a powerful movement within the creature. It seemed to resist its death a long moment; but the blow had been true, and suddenly its legs collapsed. Gilgamesh extended a hand toward Enkidu as he sprang free of it and came down beside him.

"Ah, brother," Enkidu said. "Like the old days, yes?"

Gilgamesh nodded. He looked outward. On every level of the stadium there was frenzy, now. Gilgamesh was amazed to see that Dumuzi had left the royal box and had leaped into Picasso's. As though fearing for his own safety, the king had one arm tight around Ninsun's waist and held Picasso with the other arm around his throat, and was dragging them from the box, struggling with his two hostages toward the exit.

"Your mother," Enkidu said. "And your little painter."

"Yes. Come on."

They rushed back toward the stands. But suddenly Ninsun twisted about and reached toward one of the guards in the box adjoining. When she swung around again a dagger was in her hand. Frantically Dumuzi attempted to shove Picasso against it, but as Gilgamesh stared in amazement his mother pivoted away with the agility of a warrior, reached around, drove the dagger deep into Dumuzi's side. In the same instant Simon, coming from the rear, put his sword through the king's middle. Dumuzi fell and was swept under foot. Picasso stood unmoving, eyes focused far away, as if lost in a dream. Ninsun looked at the hand that still held the dagger as though she had never seen her hand before.

"Up here!" Vy-otin called to Gilgamesh, not from Picasso's box but from the royal one. "Quickly!"

The Ice-Hunter extended a hand. Gilgamesh jumped upward beside him. Vy-otin pointed.

"On the royal bench. Fast!"

"What?"

"Dumuzi's dead. He panicked when the snipers didn't open fire, and tried to escape with Picasso and your mother as hostages, and –"

"Yes. I saw it."

"You're the king here now. Get up there and act like one."

"King?" Gilgamesh said, struggling to comprehend.

Vy-otin shoved him. Gilgamesh caught hold of the edge of the royal bench and pulled himself up on it, and turned and looked upward toward the many tiers of the arena. The sky had darkened and was full of screeching demons. Surging mobs were boiling back and forth. Everyone seemed to have gone berserk.

He extended his arms. "People of Uruk!" he cried, in a voice like an erupting volcano. "Hear me! I am Gilgamesh! Hear me!"

"Gilgamesh!" came the sudden answering roar. "Gilgamesh the King! Gilgamesh! Gilgamesh!"

"You're doing fine," Vy-otin said.

He felt figures close around him. Herod, Simon Magus, Vy-otin – Enkidu – Ninsun – Picasso –

He turned to them.

"By Enlil, I swear to you I did not come here to make myself king," Gilgamesh said angrily.

"We understand that," said Herod.

"Of course," said Simon.

"Keep waving your arms," said Vy-otin. "They're starting to settle down. Just tell them to take their seats and stay calm."

"Gilgamesh!" came the great roar again. "Gilgamesh the King!"

"You see?" Vy-otin said. "You're doing just fine, your majesty. Just fine."

Yes. Yes. Despite himself he felt the rush of oncoming power now, that sense of strength and righteous force that the word *majesty* summed up. Perhaps he had not come here to make himself king, but now he was king all the same, king of Uruk in the Afterworld as once he had been king of Uruk in Sumer the Land. He gestured and felt the crowd in his grasp. "People of Uruk! I am your king! Take your seats! All of you, take your seats!"

They were obeying now. He saw them standing frozen, staring, and then beginning to return to their places. The shouts and hubbub turned to a low murmuring, and then to stillness. An eerie hush fell over the stadium.

Enkidu said, "Have them send out another of those bulls. You and I will fight it, Gilgamesh. We'll fight all the bulls they can throw at us. Yes? Yes?"

Gilgamesh glanced at Picasso. "What do you say? Shall we continue the bullfight?"

"Ah, *compañero*, that is no way to fight a bull, the way you two do it. It is not what I came here to see, this jumping on the bull's back." Then the little man laughed. "But that is no bull, eh, King Gilgamesh. So why must it be fought according to the Spanish way? Go. Go. Commence your reign with a *corrida* in the Uruk style. Show us what you can do, my friend. I will sketch you as you work."

Gilgamesh nodded. To Herod he said quietly, "Get the late king out of here, will you? And have the arch-vizier and the rest of the court officials rounded up." With a gesture to Enkidu to accompany him he leaped down again into the bull-ring. He shouted to the *aguaciles* across the way and the gate opened and a second hell-bull came charging forth. Calmly the new king of Uruk waited for it with Enkidu at his side.

Seventeen

Altogether they dispatched five bulls that day. Each encounter began in silence, the crowd awed, puzzled, astonished as much by this strange new sport, so it appeared, as by the tumultuous transfer of royal power that had taken place before their eyes. But as the banderillos and the picadors went about their tasks, and the angered bull snorted and reared and brandished its claws, the excitement and noise would grow, and when the two robust heroes entered the ring for the fifth time to bring the contest to its triumphant end the arena echoed with a great constant roaring, a bedlam of shouts, that did not diminish until the last thrust had gone home and the bizarre bull-monster lay sprawled on the floor of the dusty coliseum.

Picasso, sketching away with astounding manic zeal, beckoned Gilgamesh on to one more *corrida*, and one more after that. And Ninsun, presiding in majesty over the now kingless royal box, looked on with warm pride, smiling, nodding in satisfaction each time her son drove his blade home.

After the third one Herod and Simon Magus began to look troubled, as though they found it unseemly for a king to be slaughtering strange creatures for amusement in front of his subjects, or – more likely – that they feared Gilgamesh would perish if he continued to risk his life in the bull-ring this way, and the city would be engulfed by chaos before they could make a safe escape. But Gilgamesh shook off their worried gestures, and when Herod sent him a folded note he cast it aside without looking at it. This was joyous work, this bullfighting, the closest thing to high pleasure that he had experienced in longer than he could remember, and he meant to make the most of it. When he left the arena joy would cease and responsibility begin: he was in no hurry for that. He braced himself and called for the next bull.

But at last the bull-pens were empty and the sky was streaked with the dark violet and scarlet of oncoming night. The wondrous day of combat was at its end. Gilgamesh and Enkidu stood side by side in the blood-streaked arena, sweaty, bloodied somewhat themselves, but unharmed.

"Come, brother," Enkidu said. "To the palace, now!"

"To the palace, yes," said Gilgamesh.

It seemed to him as he left the arena with Enkidu that they moved through the throng as if contained within a globe of impenetrable stillness. Royal guards who only this morning had protected the person of King Dumuzi preceded and followed them, flourishing ornate staffs of office, but such displays scarcely seemed necessary. The people of Uruk held back, wide-eyed, uncertain, as their new king passed by; and only when he had gone his way did the cries of "Gilgamesh!" and, sometimes, "Enkidu!" rise in the distance behind them.

In the vast and somber palace that had been Dumuzi's, Gilgamesh held his first royal levee that night, seated on Dumuzi's ponderous high throne and holding the thick, intricately worked golden sceptre of Uruk indifferently on his lap. Enkidu stood to his left, Ninsun to his right, Herod and Simon Magus in the shadows by the wall, and Vy-otin near them in his strange suit of Later Dead cut, as the ministers and officers of the dead king came forward one by one to pay their homage. Little Picasso was there too, scribbling sketches of everyone and everything as fast as his hand could move.

For Gilgamesh all this felt like a dream more vivid and intense than reality itself. It was as if thousands of years had dropped away in an instant, and he was living the life of his first life again. Once more he was newly come to Uruk out of exile and wanderings; once more he had taken the crown from the weak and hated Dumuzi, just as he had when he was young. And once more Dumuzi's viceroys and chamberlains, his overseers and stewards, his tax-gatherers and governors, came in procession to bend the knee before Gilgamesh the king.

That other time it had seemed inevitable to him that he would be king. He had been born to it. But he had never expected this. How often the Gilgamesh of the Afterworld had insisted to all who would listen that this was something he did not want, this grandeur, this pomp, this pageantry! How Caesar would mock him now! How Bismarck would laugh, or Lenin! "I crave no kingships," he had said so often. "The quest for power in the Afterworld is folly and madness."

Yet he was ensnared. One thing had led to another, and another, and another, and here he sat enthroned, feeling kingship rolling in upon him like an unstoppable torrent and bringing with it a loneliness more keen than anything he had known in his solitary years in the Outback.

"The chamberlain of the sash of Enlil! The master of provisions! The steward of the Ubshikkinakku sanctuary! The overseer of the royal splendor! The governor of –"

They filed by, on and on, somber-looking minor potentates in elaborate robes, looking desperately to the new king for confirmation of their continued high rank. And he nodded, glassy-eyed, waving his crowned head at this one and that and that, and it seemed to him that the noose of kingship drew tighter and tighter about his throat with each new moment.

Would it never end, this procession?

Enkidu reached across and touched his arm and winked.

"Show some cheer, brother Gilgamesh! Show some joy! After this comes the feast! And after that –"

Enkidu leered and clutched himself down the middle, and wriggled voluptuously and thrust his hips forward three or four times.

Despite his growing gloom Gilgamesh managed a grin. It had always been Enkidu's gift, to be able to rescue him from his prevailing sin of overseriousness. He gestured to the line of officials, speeding them along. From his place in the dimness of the far aisle Herod nodded his approval. He made a tiny circling movement of his hand as if to indicate that Gilgamesh could hurry the ceremony even more. Simon Magus, beside him, seemed asleep on his feet.

To Enkidu Gilgamesh said, "How many more are there?"

"The line goes outside the palace and halfway across the plaza."

"Here," said Gilgamesh, pushing his scepter into Enkidu's hands. "Go down there among them and hold this up before them, and tell them that they are all reconfirmed in their posts, or we'll never get on to the feasting. We can get rid of most of them later, when we've had a chance to find out how this place really works." He shook his head. "Gods! What did Dumuzi need all these officials for?"

But afterward, when the interminable ceremony finally had wound down and he moved from the hall of the throne to the adjacent feasting-hall, he found himself thinking that most of these people probably did have real functions of some sort, and would be useful to him. Chaotic though the Afterworld might be, its cities still required governance, and it was not kings who kept a city running, but those who worked beneath the king at the daily toil of administration. That much he remembered from his own earlier days of power, both in the other world and in the first days of rule in this Uruk of the Afterworld, memories of which now were coming flooding back to him.

"Is it too heavy for you, brother, the crown?" Enkidu asked.

"It presses very close," said Gilgamesh. "But no, no, I will wear it happily enough."

"I never thought I'd see you enthroned again."

"Nor I. I thought I had done enough of this for one lifetime, or even two. But I can hide from crowns only so long, and then they find me, eh?"

"So it seems, brother. A king is what you must be," cried Enkidu. "But it's not so bad, I think. All the wine we can hold, and women, and fine robes, and a warm place to sleep – not so bad, brother, not so bad!" And slapped him lustily on the shoulder, and they laughed together as they entered the great hall of feasting, where fat barrels of wine stood ready, and huge sides of meat were roasting on half a dozen spits. "Not so bad!"

Not so bad, no. But Gilgamesh was beginning to remember, also, that there was more to kingship than pomp and pageantry. Once – in the brief wink that had been his first life – he had found salvation at a troubled time in the knowledge that the wise wielding of responsibility was the true reward of the throne. The things that went with kingship, the palaces and women and fine robes and rich wines and shining jewels and such, were mere trifling ornaments, insubstantial as air. Only a fool sought power simply to have such things, and such fools, though they might wear a crown and sit upon a throne, had no quality of kingliness about them. A fool could wear three crowns at once, and still be a fool. Kingliness lay elsewhere than in outward show or private pleasure, Gilgamesh knew. To sustain and enhance the security of the realm was the king's inward purpose and highest joy and fullest salvation.

Perhaps such salvation could be his again, he thought, even in this mad place that was the Afterworld.

And, thinking such things, Gilgamesh felt less trapped by the royal grandeur that had overtaken him in this seemingly accidental way. For it had been no accident, this coming to the kingship once more. There were no accidents, he knew. It was his destiny, and how can one's destiny be deemed a trap, or an accident, since it is the will of the gods? Though he had tried to turn his back on that destiny, there had been no escaping it, and so be it. This was what he had been meant for: to rule, and to rule wisely. In shunning that in the Afterworld he had been shunning, all the while, the essential truth of his own nature. But now he had found himself again.

In the dawn hours, when the feasting was at its end and sated sleepers lay like discarded cloaks everywhere in the hall, Gilgamesh and Enkidu, still restless, prowled the dark corridors of Dumuzi's palace together. They wandered along the long sides of the place, peering into some of the many rooms that opened off the aisles – most of them were empty, though some held statuettes and other ritual objects – and going on upward by way of a narrow, winding stone staircase to the galleries above, where more chambers were to be found like the cells of a honeycomb in the cavernous walls of the huge building.

"This is a wondrous ugly place," Enkidu said, after a time. "Why would he seek to build such ugliness?"

"There are those who find it beautiful," said Gilgamesh. "Herod the Jew told me that it is a copy of some famous holy temple of the Later Dead."

Enkidu shuddered "This? A temple? Gods forbid!"

"When I first saw it, I said to myself that if I am ever king in this city, I would tear it down as my first deed. But now the kingship has come to me and my mind begins to change."

"You'll *keep* it?"

"The light is very beautiful when it shines through those windows of colored glass. And the high ceilings – those strange pointed arches – the carvings on the front – the great buttresses outside that hold the place up –" Gilgamesh shook his head. "Gradually I come to admire what I hated on first sight. I think I will keep it, yes. Perhaps I'll build a palace of my own, something more like what we're accustomed to, but I think to rip this one down would be wrong."

Enkidu laughed. "Do you remember, Gilgamesh, when first I came to Uruk – the other one, the old one – and you showed me the Enmerkar temple, the one your grandfather had built, thinking I'd be awed by it? And I had never seen any sort of temple before, so I wasn't impressed at all, I was expecting much more –"

"Yes – yes –"

"– so I looked at it and shrugged and said, 'It's very small and ugly, is it not?' And you were very upset. But afterward you tore it down and built your great temple in its place."

"The Enmerkar temple was old and badly in need of repairs. But I never realized that until you said what you did."

"It was a wonderful temple that you built, brother."

"Are you saying I should rip this palace down the way I did the Enmerkar temple, simply because you don't care for it?"

"Not at all," replied Enkidu. "What I'm saying is that perhaps I'll see this place through your eyes, and come to admire it as you have, just as once you saw the Enmerkar temple through my eyes, and came to see it as it really was."

"Ah," Gilgamesh said. "I understand now."

They walked on, until they reached the loftiest of the galleries. Looking over the edge, Gilgamesh saw the feasting-hall floor, far below, and some of the sodden sleepers beginning at last to rise as morning light entered the palace windows.

"Tell me," he said after a time. "What was it like, that day in the canyon when I went hunting and the caravan was attacked?"

"I was slain," said Enkidu.

"I know that. I saw a vision of it, that a black wizard conjured for me in the city of Brasil, by a means that I hesitate to speak of even with you. The helicopter attack, the bandits, the grenade –"

"Then you know," Enkidu said in a brusque way.

"I know what happened. But will you speak to me of the moment of your dying, brother? For it is a thing that I have a great curiosity about."

Enkidu looked strangely at Gilgamesh. There was a somberness about him that Gilgamesh had rarely seen, or never: for Enkidu was a rough and earthy man, forever laughing, untroubled by moments of the darkness of the spirit, and that was one of the things Gilgamesh loved him for. But now – now –

"It was nothing," he said finally. "As it always is when we die here. An end, and sometime afterward another beginning. There was heat, there was noise, there was, I suppose, an instant of great pain, and then it all ended. And when next I knew anything, I was whole again and I was in this city of Uruk, which I had not seen for more years than I could count. Well, that was not the worst thing that might have befallen me, to awaken in Uruk, so I was pleased. I thought you might be here too, and I went about asking after you, until Dumuzi grew uneasy and had me imprisoned. And then you came. The rest you know."

Gilgamesh said, staring, "So you knew about this Uruk of the Afterworld?"

"Of course."

"I mean this one, and not the Uruk of our first life."

"This one, yes, Afterworld-Uruk, which you yourself built long ago, and ruled over for I could not tell you how many hundreds of years. With me by your side all those years, in this very place, Gilgamesh."

Gilgamesh felt his mind whirling. "The whole time we wandered together in the Outback, you were able to remember that we had once lived here, that I had been king here?"

"Of course. Of course."

"And never spoke a word about our life here to me?"

Enkidu looked mystified. "But I did. Often. Many times did we recall the good times of Afterworld-Uruk to one another, Gilgamesh, as we sat about the campfire late after a day's hunting. Many times."

"Could this be so? I remember nothing of it."

"Do you say it never happened that we spoke that way?"

"I say I have no memory of it."

"That you have no memory of it is not the same as that it never happened, brother."

"Perhaps you never spoke of it with me."

"But I did! I did!" Anger began to gleam now in Enkidu's eyes. "Gilgamesh, what do all these questions mean? What is troubling you? I tell you, we spoke many a time of Afterworld-Uruk, and wondered who was ruling here now, and whether he was just, and much more in the same vein."

"I have forgotten all of that."

"What?"

"I tell you I remembered nothing of this Uruk, or my time as king here, until just a little while ago," said Gilgamesh, holding a hand to the side of his head, where it had begun to ache. "Or that we ever spoke of it during our Outback years. In Brasil, Simon Magus invited me to go in quest of Uruk, and I said, What Uruk? There is no Uruk in the Afterworld. After a time I had some evidence that I was wrong about that, but still I doubted it, and went on doubting it until I was actually here. Now it begins to come back to me, yes. But all those years away from here it was gone from my mind."

"Gone from your mind, brother? Well, and that is how it often is, in the Afterworld," said Enkidu, shrugging. "It is a place of devilish tricks."

"So it is indeed."

"I see now that it must have greatly troubled you, then,

when Simon began to speak of this city here and you knew nothing of it." Enkidu gave him a close look. "Can that be why, brother, you asked me about the manner of my death? Have you forgotten also what death is like here?"

"How could I forget that which I haven't experienced? I have never –"

He saw the glint in Enkidu's dark eyes, and halted.

"Do you say I have died also in the Afterworld?" Gilgamesh asked, after a long tense pause.

"You ask, so you must not know the answer."

In a hard steady voice Gilgamesh said, "I have died only once, brother, and that was in the other world, when I was old and heavy with years, and the kingdom was great about me, and darkness came to me in my sleep. But here – no, Enkidu, never here, not even once."

Enkidu looked amused. "Not even once? In thousands of years of dwelling amidst the many dangers of this place?"

"You say that I have?"

Gilgamesh was trembling now.

"Yes, brother," said Enkidu softly.

"When?"

"When? How would I know when? Who can keep the count of the years here? Ah, but let me think a bit. There was the time when the earth turned to quicksand beneath you, when we were in Santo Domingo, that is one. And when the mountain of ice fell, in the Great Borealis, for another. And in Estotiland Isle, when the beast came up out of the sea –"

Gilgamesh swayed. The paving-stones seemed to be melting away beneath his feet. There was nothing substantial in this world, no reality that could be trusted.

"Gods! What are you saying? How many times has death had me here?"

Enkidu turned his palms upward. "This is hard for me. Five? Ten? I could not count them. I never counted very well, brother. But it was often enough. You know, it happens again and again to us all."

"I remember no such things," said Gilgamesh, his voice barely rising above a whisper.

"There must be much that I have forgotten also, brother. No doubt of it. The slate is cleared again and again. What does it matter? We live, we die, we live, we die – it is the way of this place. If we had to bear all our memories in our minds all at once, we'd be no more than madmen. Though sometimes I think we are madmen even so."

"Deaths – so many deaths –" Gilgamesh muttered.

He stared into the air and saw himself toppling again and again, like a great tree that somehow could be felled over and over. He saw himself lying lifeless on a barren plain, and by the edge of a stormy sea, and on the crest of some wolf-haunted mountain. And each time awakening, and beginning anew, and remembering nothing. It stunned him that he could forget so much, that the extent of the Afterworld's treachery was so far-reaching. His face blazed with shame. And with scorn, too, for the petty pride that had led him to pretend that he was invulnerable here, and for believing his own pretence.

"Gilgamesh?" Enkidu said.

"A moment. This bewilders me."

"No, brother, let it slide easily from you!"

"If only I could."

"Ah. You were ever haunted by death, weren't you?" said Enkidu. "But it comes so easily. It should be dismissed just as easily."

"Yes," Gilgamesh said. "You speak the truth."

"Then dismiss it. Dismiss it!"

Gilgamesh nodded, and looked away.

But he could not shake himself free of the darkness that Enkidu's words had wrapped about him. One by one all his illusions had been stripped from him, since those days of innocence when he roamed the Outback, and it was a hard and painful thing to withstand. He stood motionless, gripping the stone rail of the high gallery as though he feared plummeting to the floor below if he were to let go. Desperately he struggled to regain his equilibrium.

"Come, brother!" Enkidu leaned close, laughing, pummeling Gilgamesh lightly now with his fists, as if to sting him from his brooding this way. "What does a death or two mean? It happens to everyone. But we are alive now, are we not, and you are a king again, and all is well! All is well, brother! All is well!"

A few days afterward Simon Magus appeared before Gilgamesh in the audience-chamber, smelling of wine and looking more seedy than ever, and said, "I will be leaving for Brasil in a short while."

"You know you may remain as my guest as long as you wish, Simon."

"I'm grateful for your generosity. But I've been away from my city long enough. Who knows what's been going on back there while I've been here in Uruk?"

"Surely your wizards have everything in your Brasil under careful control," said Gilgamesh.

"Yes. That is my hope."

There was an uncomfortable silence. It seemed to Gilgamesh that there was more on Simon's mind than mere leave-taking, something of considerable import, but Simon simply waited, his small cold eyes narrowed expectantly, his blotches and blemishes looking more fiery than usual on his soft sagging face.

"Will you have some wine?" Gilgamesh asked finally.

"Wine is always welcome, yes."

Gilgamesh signalled. A servant fetched an ewer of the rich dark wine of Uruk.

Simon said, drinking deep, spilling a few drops on a toga that already bore purple stains, "So you have your kingship now, Gilgamesh."

"Indeed."

"The kingship that you insisted you didn't want."

"It came to me. It would have been wrong to refuse it."

"Wrong indeed," said Simon. "There is a fundamental rightness that must be obeyed, and we know it when we encounter it. It is one power, divided between above and below, self-generating, self-increasing, self-seeking, self-finding, being its own mother, its own father, its own sister, its own spouse, its own son, mother, father, the root of all things."

Gilgamesh blinked and frowned and stared.

"What you say is very hard to follow, Simon."

"It seems clear enough to me."

"No doubt it does," said Gilgamesh. "But you are a mage and a sorcerer. You are full of strange philosophies and mazy words. I am only a warrior."

"And a king."

"And a king, yes."

"A very noble king."

Gilgamesh ordered Simon's wine-glass refilled. Impatience rose in him.

"Enough of this dance. What is it you wish to ask of me, Simon?"

"I remind you that we came here together, as partners. You to regain your Uruk and your Enkidu, and I – I –"

"You to plunder the jewels of Uruk, yes."

"Yes."

Gilgamesh smiled. "There are no jewels here, Simon."

"Do you know that?"

"There are more jewels set into one arm's-length of your palace wall in Brasil than I have seen in all of Uruk."

"Ah, but you're wrong."

"Am I? Tell me, then."

Simon moved nearer and said in a low voice, "There's plenty here. I have ways of obtaining information. I haven't forgotten all my craft of sorcery, Gilgamesh. Call your court officers together and ask them what they know about Dumuzi's treasure, and you'll be greatly surprised."

"I am growing accustomed to great surprises," said Gilgamesh.

"Well, you'll have one more. There's treasure here, even as the tales maintain." His color deepened. His lips and jowls worked with covetousness, like those of a hungry glutton. "We had an understanding, Gilgamesh! Do you mean to go back on our understanding? We came here as partners, I remind you, Gilgamesh – I remind you –"

The Sumerian held up a hand and nodded. But Simon would not be pacified by that.

"I want my share! Without me you'd never even have known about this place! I remind you – I beg you, Gilgamesh, don't deny me what I seek! I beg you."

"You have nothing to fear, Simon," said Gilgamesh calmly. "I will deny you nothing, so long as it's within my means to grant it. But first let me find this treasure that you say is here. I have only your word that it exists; and so today I can give you only words. But when I have the jewels, ah, Simon, then you'll have your full share. I pledge you that."

"Is it so?"

"Upon my mother's soul I pledge it."

"Very well, then, Gilgamesh. But soon. Soon!"

"Soon, yes."

Simon departed then, in apparent satisfaction, after one last draught of wine and a long, cool, searching look at Gilgamesh. Gilgamesh stared after him, baffled by the depth of Simon's greed. For what? For mere shining stones? That made even less sense to him than the lust after power for power's sake that had driven so many men, and not a few women, into vast and empty exertions. Here was Simon, an intelligent man, a philosopher, even, quivering and sniveling for pretty baubles with childish eagerness, which was repellent in one who was so very far from being a child. Hovering before Gilgamesh, hinting and maneuvering and finally simply begging for the trinkets he craved.

Well, if there were jewels here for Simon to have, he could have them. They were of no use to Gilgamesh. Summoning the overseer of the royal splendor, a bald rotund eunuchoid Sumerian who called himself Akurgal, he said, "Does custody of the crown treasure fall into your sphere of duty?"

"It does not, majesty."

"Doesn't treasure qualify as royal splendor?"

"My responsibilities are the robes and personal articles of your majesty, majesty."

"But there is a treasure here? Jewels, and such?"

"So there is, majesty."

"Who looks after it?"

Akurgal pondered that. "The guardian of the Ereshkigal shrine, perhaps. No, it may be the Inanna master-at-arms. But no – no, that hardly makes sense – they would never let *him* deal with anything so weighty – let me think another moment, majesty, just one moment more –"

"I could get quicker answers from a string of sausages!" said Gilgamesh, his face darkening.

"I'm thinking, majesty – thinking –"

"You'll be a string of sausages yourself if you don't tell me what I ask."

"The chamberlain of the sash of Enlil!" Akurgal gasped desperately.

"Indeed?"

"The chamberlain of the sash of Enlil, yes. Yes, truly, majesty. He's the one!"

"Fetch him for me."

"At once, majesty. At once."

Akurgal trotted away, arms churning, robes flapping. Gilgamesh laughed. In minutes there came a second functionary, lean and hatchet-faced, with a stark Assyrian look about him, though he had a Sumerian name: Ur-Namhani. When Gilgamesh indicated his wishes, Ur-Namhani stared at him a long while, as though negotiating with himself about whether to comply. After some time he said with great dignity and some show of irritation, "The treasury is in the shrine of Enlil. Shall I have it brought here or will you accompany me to it?"

"We'll go there," said Gilgamesh.

None of Simon's frenzied fantasies had prepared the Sumerian properly for what awaited him in the dark, dank, chilly vaults beneath the temple of the father of the gods. Producing a chain of keys, Ur-Namhani ostentatiously opened gate after gate as they proceeded through a series of narrow tunnels until they had reached the innermost storeroom, and there, when the lights had been turned on, Gilgamesh found himself confronted with a surfeit of splendors beyond all imagining. Wherever his eye came to rest there were bags, chests, casks, satchels, strongboxes, overflowing with all manner of precious things, and the hint of even more in the shadows beyond, on and on into an immeasurable maze of caverns.

There were bricks of gold piled higher than a man's head, and bangles by the barrel, necklaces, bracelets, rings, pins, brooches, armlets, all of the finest yellow glitter. There were lavalieres, torques, pendants, chains. There were necklets, stickpins, circlets, solitaires. There were bags of pearls. There were gold coins in vast heaps; Gilgamesh scooped some up, and saw on them the heads of emperors and kings, and fierce gryphons and dragons on the other side. He saw horseshoes of gold, and daggers, and belt-buckles, and trinkets in the shape of towers, bridges, carriages, castles. There were golden toothpicks set with rubies, and little golden spoons with jade handles, and boxes of gold that contained shimmering diamonds, and strings of diamonds threaded on gold. Raw jewels spilled from taut-stretched burlap sacks hard pressed to contain them: they gleamed in every color, red and green and yellow and blue and radiant white and a dozen more, and Gilgamesh, dipping his hands in, came up with streaming arrays of rubies, emeralds, sapphires, opals, amethysts, of jasper and carnelian, of chrysoberyl and moonstone, of turquoise, amber, coral, jade. There was no end to it. No wonder Simon Magus had yearned to conquer this city. For a long while Gilgamesh explored these marvels in silence. Then he turned to the waiting Ur-Namhani.

"Are these things real?" he asked.

"Real?"

"Sorcerer-stuff, or actual gems?"

"Oh, they are real, majesty, most definitely real," said Ur-Namhani in a lofty, condescending way. "Gathered by Dumuzi from every part of the world, for the glory of Enlil. Not a year went by but another fortune in treasure was laid up in this vault, equal to any king's ransom."

Gilgamesh nodded. "I had no idea there were enough bandits in this city to collect so much plunder, even in a thousand years. It is a very impressive haul. Very impressive." Rising, he tossed a double handful of shimmering treasure back into the nearest barrel. His head was throbbing. The vastness of this hoard left him stunned, even he, for whom such a gross welter of wealth offered no delight. The very abundance of it was oppressive, and yet the power of its mass could not be denied. "Very well. I will send Simon Magus to you – my guest, the fat drunken monarch of the isle of Brasil. You know who I mean?"

Ur-Namhani inclined his head curtly in assent.

"Give him anything from this room that he wants," said Gilgamesh.

The chamberlain of the sash of Enlil gasped. "*Anything?*"

"Let him have his fill."

The eyes of the chamberlain of the sash of Enlil bulged alarmingly. "But – majesty – do I understand you correctly? – I ask you to consider –" Ur-Namhani took a deep breath. "What if he asks for it all?"

"Then he will have a very slow journey of it back to Brasil, with only his five cars to carry this much and his other baggage as well."

"Majesty – majesty –"

Gilgamesh smiled. "I doubt somehow that even Simon will have the gall to ask for everything. But let him have whatever he wants. Probably only the jewels will interest him, I think. He can have the gold, too, if that catches his fancy. We have no need for this stuff here."

"These are sacred things, majesty! This is the treasure of Enlil!"

"Enlil is the father of us all," said Gilgamesh. "If he can create the world and the Afterworld as well, he can surely create himself another six storehouses just as rich as this one. These things do nobody any good locked away down here. Simon, at least, loves them, and will bedeck his palace with them, or perhaps his entire city. It makes no difference to me. Give him his fill, Ur-Namhani. Do you hear? Give him his fill."

Eighteen

"The vizier Herod is here, majesty," the major-domo said.

Gilgamesh sighed. "Let him enter."

Herod came in, carrying an immense print-out, which he unrolled in front of the throne as though it were some precious scroll of far Cathay. Gilgamesh regarded it sourly.

"Well? More data, Herod?" He made *data* sound like an obscenity of obscenities.

"The civil service roster," Herod said. "Arranged by departments and order of seniority."

"Seniority? Seniority?"

"It's very important here, you know. They've got strong unions and a string of tough labor codes longer than your – well, your arm. Do you want me to go over this with you now, or should we save it for some other time?"

"Some other time, I think," said Gilgamesh. Then he shook his head. "No. No. Enlil's eyes, let's see it now!" And with as much patience as he could muster he set to work.

Gilgamesh found it surprising, though perhaps he should not have, that ruling over Uruk was so complex and time-consuming a job. There were rituals to perform, appointments to confirm, knotty decisions to make, building projects to initiate and oversee, ambassadors to greet, even the occasional insurrection to quell – for the Afterworld was an untidy place and self-appointed kings were as common as lizards, popping up constantly to lay claim to the nearest throne. His royal presence was required, too, at theatrical events and games, most particularly the bullfights that now became a regular Sunday feature, under Picasso's enthusiastic direction, of life in Uruk. Gilgamesh no longer took part in the *corrida* himself – the occasional matador did get killed, and Gilgamesh, now that he had knowledge of his own vulnerability, felt that it would be shirking his sacred kingly duties to run the risk of being sent onward in so frivolous a way. But he attended nearly every one. Enkidu was always the main attraction, dealing with two or sometimes three bulls before the afternoon was out.

The kingship, Gilgamesh thought, certainly hadn't been nearly this much work in the ancient days of Sumer the Land, nor, he suspected, in the time of his first reign in Afterworld-Uruk; but he was willing to believe that he was deceiving himself in that. He knew all too well, now, how little he could trust his memory of these matters.

But even if there was more now to do than ever there had been before, he did not seriously begrudge it. He had had enough of the solitary wandering life for a long while; and there was high satisfaction in doing a king's job and doing it well. It was plain to see that this Uruk had been misruled under Dumuzi just as the first Uruk had been in the other world, and Gilgamesh took fierce pleasure once more in undoing Dumuzi's senseless self-serving decrees and in repairing that which Dumuzi had allowed to fall into decay.

He named his old Ice-Hunter friend Vy-otin his chief minister. Herod was another useful source of advice. He had preferred to remain behind in Uruk with Gilgamesh when Simon Magus, glutted with the jewels of Uruk's royal treasury, returned to Brasil. Ninsun too, prudent and loving, was a valuable counsellor. There was always Enkidu for diversion and close companionship and earthy, heartfelt wisdom. And after he had been in office some time Gilgamesh acquired another adviser, a strange and unexpected one, none other than the Hairy Man out of deepest prehistoric antiquity who had been Simon's chief mage in Brasil.

He arrived without warning, appearing on foot outside Uruk one day during a season of hard black weather, of apocalyptic bellowing storms and torrential floods. Gilgamesh was toiling along the walls of the city when he came, struggling under a merciless iron sky to prop sandbags against the ramparts of baked brick, which were threatened with undermining in half a dozen places. Just about anyone who could carry a load was out there working that day, with the king himself setting the example. Mocking demon-creatures with long scaly yellow necks and bright green wings wheeled and screeched overhead. In the upper sky were flickering lightnings, bloody streamers, fiery comets. The rain was inexorable, an ocean falling upon the city in strands thick as cables. The king was standing thigh-deep in mud, or nearly, catching the sandbags that Enkidu threw him from above and propping them with furious haste against the base of the wall, when a strangely familiar harsh voice came to him out of the storm, speaking in thick frost-edged phrases that were all but impossible to comprehend.

"What?" Gilgamesh roared. "Who's there? What'd you say?"

"That perhaps this is the great Flood, of which you make so much, returning to drown your land again," said the other, speaking more slowly now and with an effort at precision.

Gilgamesh glanced behind him. By thundercrack and demon-light he saw the Hairy Man, short and stocky and bestial of face, as casual in the storm as though it were nothing but a gentle spring zephyr. He wore a Roman toga, white edged with crimson, through which his heavy reddish pelt was visible, made dense and matted by the rain. Beneath his massive brows his dark eyes gleamed with a strange primordial fire. This was a creature, Gilgamesh knew, who had lived in the world when the gods were young.

"The Flood, you say?" Gilgamesh grunted.

"The Flood, yes, that came after my time and before yours, or so you told me, King Gilgamesh. Coming again, to end this world and begin a newer one. Here. Let me assist you." He strode forward into the flowing mud, and, picking up a sandbag that Enkidu had tossed from the rim of the wall to a point beyond the reach of Gilgamesh, pushed it carefully into place.

Gilgamesh stared. "Who are you?"

"Why, you knew me in Brasil."

"Simon's high wizard?"

"The same. Peace and gladness, king of Uruk."

Far above them, Enkidu peered down, frowning. He called something that was lost in the howl of the wind, and tossed another sandbag, which strayed too far to the side. The Hairy Man reached forward to catch it and deflect it into its proper place, and beckoned for another. Gilgamesh eyed him. Well, he supposed, it probably was the same one as before. They all looked alike, the Hairy Men. No wonder none of them had any names. Like shaggy wraiths they wandered their own paths through the Afterworld, these mysterious creatures from the dawn of time, and one was so much like another that they might just as well all be the same one. But as Gilgamesh stared closely at the Hairy Man he decided that something about him seemed familiar, though he did not know what it could be. This must indeed be the one he had known before in Brasil, the one who had guided him through the diabolical streets of that city, the one who had led him to Calandola.

"And what are you doing here?" Gilgamesh asked.

"Simon sent me. I am a gift, to live at your court and be of service to you."

"A *gift*, did you say?"

"To be your chief sorcerer. Simon thought you might need one."

Gilgamesh felt a momentary stab of suspicion. Had Simon sent the mage as a spy, perhaps? No, no, he decided. That was too blatant, that was too obvious.

Enkidu yelled again, and another sandbag fell from above. This time Gilgamesh caught it and heaved it into its place.

The Hairy Man went on, "I am sent also as a reward to you for your generosity. Simon felt that he should do something for you in return for the jewels of Uruk, so great was his gratitude for the great treasures which you gave him. When last I saw him he was bathing in them: lying in an alabaster tub, and having the emeralds and rubies poured over him in a great cascade."

"He is a man of simple pleasures," said Gilgamesh drily. Thunder resounded again, sharp and fierce, like the crack of the last trump. It was a sound potent enough to bring forth monsters in the air, a swarm of things with many heads, and grasshopper wings, and the yellow eyes of toads. Perhaps the Hairy Man was right, that this was the Flood all over again, in which case he might be wiser hastening to build a new Ark than wasting time striving to bolster this doomed wall. But no one had prophesied a Flood for the Afterworld, not ever. To the Hairy Man Gilgamesh called, "And are you serious? Do you think this is a new Deluge?"

The Hairy Man uttered a sound that seemed to be a laugh, and shook his heavy thick-necked head, and spoke furry words that were swept away by the wind. Gilgamesh hoped that what he had said was that he was only jesting, that this was no Flood, but only some new Afterworldish prank, a storm that before long would pass without destroying all that lay before it.

They worked on in silence, stolidly placing the sandbags. Hundreds were toiling nearby along this section of the wall, a host of able-bodied men and more than a few women also. The rain seemed to abate a little now. But still came the fierce awesome thundercracks, the showers of streaming lightning, the buzzing thrumming swarms of airborne monsters. The plain surrounding the city was a desert no longer, but now a shining sea. Far off it appeared that a great dazzling blue-white glacier floated in the sky, its jagged edges shining with an inner light, and on its flanks danced stags with human faces, bull-headed men, and strange and frightening behemoths of uncertain shape. The little man Picasso should see these things, Gilgamesh thought, and set them down in drawings. Picasso, though, was safe indoors just now: he did not have much love for this sort of stormy toil, he had said, and would not come out. Well, Picasso could call forth monsters enough from his own teeming brain, Gilgamesh told himself. He had no need to see these.

"If you are a true wizard," said Gilgamesh to the Hairy Man, "don't you know some way to bring a halt to this miserable downpour?"

"Wizards far greater than I have sent it, king. There are no spells that will halt it."

"And will we all drown? Tell me, will we?"

"We will live to die another day, I think," said the Hairy Man.

Indeed the rain subsided a few hours later, for which the Hairy Man took no credit, and the walls of the city were spared. When the sun returned Gilgamesh walked the rampart with

Enkidu and Vy-otin, looking out in wonder at the flooded plain, the tangle of great trees lying up-ended, the debris of scattered villages and drowned beasts that had washed up out of the lowlands. But Uruk itself was intact, if somewhat waterlogged. There was not to be a second Deluge this time. Perhaps it had been only some war of demons, far overhead, Gilgamesh thought, that had brought this devilish cataclysmic rain upon the city.

It pleased and surprised him that Simon had sent the Hairy Man. There was great wisdom in those ancient beings who had lived before mankind was, and their aid was something much to be prized. Surely Simon had had the short end of the transaction, giving up this age-old sorcerer, this worthy mage, in return for nothing but a few sacks of coloured stones. But it had been a truly kingly gesture, showing that there was more to Simon than mere debauchery and greed. Or maybe the wily old wine-soaked tyrant had not cared; maybe he saw his next death already looking him in the eye, and no longer was concerned with anything but to surround himself with the shining pretties he so deeply loved. Whatever the reason – and Gilgamesh doubted that there was anything sinister at the bottom of it – he was glad to have the strange being at his court.

Gilgamesh provided the Hairy Man with a suite of choice rooms in the royal palace, by a cloistered courtyard where he could sleep out of doors if he chose: creatures of his sort preferred no roofs over their heads by night. In the daily workings of the court Gilgamesh kept him close at hand, both for conjuring and wizardry and for plain consultation in matters of diplomacy and statecraft, for he was a very useful counsellor.

The pace of court life was unrelenting. Every day new envoys arrived from other principalities of the Afterworld, now that word was beginning to get around that the puissant hero Gilgamesh had come to power again in Uruk, and state receptions had to be held for them. They came stumbling in, often frayed and shaken by the random intricacies of their journeys across the vastness of the Afterworld, bearing gifts and praises, and other oily suasions. They all wanted the same thing: alliance with the Sumerian against some actual or potential enemy, or else Gilgamesh's cooperation in some elaborate and costly scheme designed to aggrandize themselves at the expense of their neighbors.

The stacks of ambassadorial accreditations grew like dunes driven before the wind. Gilgamesh shook his head in irritation over the unruly mounds of them heaped high in his throne chamber. "The Perfect Aryan Republic – the New Ottoman Sultanate – the Glorious Proletarian Kingdom – the Realm of Free Spirits – the Invincible Amazon Empire – the Grand Dionysian Realm – the Rolling Acres Country Club –" He looked up at Vy-otin. "Is that supposed to be a nation too? The Rolling Acres Country Club?"

"A very wealthy land, they tell me, with splendid green lawns and fine houses, ruled over by a committee of eighteen kings."

"A committee of kings! Madness!"

"They say it works very well for them."

"And this scroll – from Her Serene Greatness, the Artemis of New Crete – and this, from His Transylvanian Excellency, Vlad the Fifth – and here's another, on vellum, no less, from – what does it say? Do you call this stuff writing? Jigme Phakpa Chenrezi the Totally Compassionate, High Lama of –" Testily Gilgamesh pushed the stack aside and said, "Who are all these kings and queens and sultans and lamas, anyway? Where do their territories lie? Does anyone who can find five fools to follow him proclaim himself a monarch nowadays? I don't believe all these places exist! Bring me a map! Show me where these ambassadors come from!"

"Surely you haven't forgotten, Gilgamesh, that there are certain problems inherent in the use of maps," Herod pointed out. "They provide very untrustworthy information, to say the least."

Color rose in the Sumerian's face. In his fury he had forgotten just that.

"Well, yes, perhaps some maps do," Gilgamesh growled. "But there have to be some that are more reliable. And even an untrustworthy map is better than no map at all. Find me Mercator, and have him draw me a chart."

"Who?"

"Mercator, he was called. I knew him a hundred years ago, or two, in Persepolis Khaikosru, where he was in the service of the Shah, and spent all his days sitting in a tavern and scrawling maps on strips of leather. Or there was another one, a Greek, Herodotos, talked from morning to night without stopping, but at least he told marvelous stories, and he had traveled in every land there is. Maybe you can find him. If not them, someone else. Send out the word through Uruk for a mapmaker."

Mercator could not be found, nor Herodotos; but in a few days' time Herod brought Gilgamesh a certain disreputable-looking dark little man with a lame leg and bleak, ferocious eyes, a Later Dead but dressed in an old-fashioned way for a Later Dead, very somber. He gave his name as Ferno de Magalhaes, a Portuguese, known to the Spaniards, he said, by the name of Magallanes, and he said he knew something of geography.

"Are you a mapmaker, then?" Gilgamesh asked.

Magalhaes gave him a smoldering look. "I was a user of maps, not a maker of them. A mariner, a man of the sea, a captain. I sailed around the world once, or nearly."

"Around this world?" Gilgamesh said, eyebrows rising.

"Around this world there is no sailing, for it never ends. The one I spanned was the true one," said Magalhaes. "Across its belly from end to end, even if God did not allow me to go the whole way, even though others finished the voyage after I was slain; but the glory was mine. The idea was mine; the plan was mine; the execution was mine; the leadership was mine. The achievement was mine."

His eyes blazed. Perhaps he is a little unbalanced, Gilgamesh thought. But falling just short of encompassing so great a goal might unhinge anyone. To sail around the world! There was real strength in the man, no question of that. Besides, most people he had met in the Afterworld struck him as unbalanced. Gilgamesh still could not quite understand how sailing around the world might be accomplished, considering the problems that one would encounter when one came to the edge; but if this man said that he had done it, well, then very likely he had.

"Can you sketch me a map?" he asked.

"Of the true world?"

"Of this one," said Gilgamesh.

Magalhaes scowled. "Much good it will do you. This is a damnable place where no latitude will hold, and the compass is only a toy."

"I know that. Nevertheless, I have need of a map. To show me the general outlines of the world and the many kingdoms within it, even if the specifics are not quite right, or if they change beneath my gaze."

"You'd do as well navigating by the lines in the palm of your hand," said Magalhaes. "But yes, yes, I'll sketch a map for you, if that's what you want. Here – here, give me a pen, give me a scroll of leather –"

Muttering to himself, he set swiftly to work on a stretched hide, drawing great swirling arcs that surged boldly out to right and left. "Here," he said, "here we have the White Sea, and this is the black one, and over here the land of Dis. This is what we call the Great Unending, down here, where you can sail forever and never see land. Many brave men have been lost there, and many fools. Of course, it is sometimes hard to tell one from the other. And this here" – a sweeping flourish of his pen – "this is the central continent, where we find ourselves now. Sometimes it has other shapes, but this is how I knew it when I went along its coast the entire length with the Norseman Harald, some many years back. Here: this is Nova Roma, here, by the far coast. And this is the Crystal Peninsula, and this, the Strait of Ghosts, as narrow and cold and evil as that strait I found in the frozen southern ocean of the other world, long ago. And here – here – here –" Magalhaes drew mountains, and rivers, and enormous lakes. He sketched in the vast dry reaches of the Outback, and the isle of Brasil, and Uruk itself, up in the top corner beyond the Outback's western edge. He put in the names of other cities: Cambaluc, Novo Lisboa, Niemals Nunca, Tintagel, New South Brooklyn, Ciudad Meshugah, Akhetaten, Valhalla.

"The Perfect Aryan Republic," Gilgamesh said. "Where is that?"

"Here, I think."

Gilgamesh nodded. At last he was beginning to get some grasp of the shape of the other territories of this world with which he would have to deal.

"And the New Ottoman Sultanate?"

Magalhaes pointed to the southern reaches of the Outback. "Here, very likely."

Gilgamesh consulted his stack of ambassadorial documents. "And the Rolling Acres Country Club?"

Magalhaes was silent. After a long moment's thought he tapped the scroll and said, "Here, so I recall. Close by Adonai Elohim. But is it to the east of it? No, the west – definitely the west – let me see, I was journeying from the coast, and I came first to Adonai Elohim, and then –" He closed his eyes. "The places move about. There is no certainty." Rage flared up suddenly in him. "This map I have drawn for you is worthless, King Gilgamesh!"

"No," Gilgamesh said. "It may have some flaws, perhaps, but it gives me a far better idea of –"

"Worthless! Worthless!" Magalhaes was trembling. He could barely contain his wrath. "Do you know what a curse it is for a man like me, to travel back and forth upon the face of the world and never twice to know where I have been, nor where I am going? To try to set my course by the stars, and see them shaping themselves into mocking faces above me? To have the sun rise here one day, and on the other side the next? There is no sense to it! There is no honor!"

Quietly Herod said, "Would you like a little wine?"

"It would help, perhaps," said Magalhaes.

He was calmer after drinking. His map, he said, did not look so bad to him after all. It would do. There were doubtful things in it, and things that were maddeningly imprecise, and things that he had once known to be true that he suspected were true no longer; but, all in all, he said, he had done the best he could, considering the obstacles, and he doubted that Gilgamesh would find the job done any better anywhere else.

"So I feel also," said Gilgamesh. "It is a splendid map, my friend. Now, if you would just mark in the location of New Crete, and the Grand Dionysian Realm –"

After the rains came a long dry period of searing heat, when the sun scarcely seemed to set at all, and the fields around Uruk shriveled and turned brown. The air itself seemed to burn, and when Gilgamesh rode out beyond the walls with Enkidu to hunt they found no beasts out there except scrawny pitiful lurking things, all bones and mange. But there was wheat stored in the granaries of Uruk against such a time of hard times, and no one went hungry, though Vy-otin reported that the people were grumbling a little over the tight hand that Gilgamesh kept on the supplies of food.

"Let them grumble," Gilgamesh said. "Those who don't think they're getting enough to eat can move on to greener fields, if they can find any. Let them go to the Amazons. Let them go to Rolling Acres."

"Let them eat cake," Herod said.

"What? But we have no cake for them! Where would we find cake, when we barely have bread?"

"Never mind," said the Judaean. "It was only a joke."

Gilgamesh shook his head. "A joke that makes no sense. Cake? What's funny about cake?"

"I can explain it later," Vy-otin offered.

"You? How would you know what he means? Is this something you two picked up from your Later Dead friends? I expect no more from Herod, but you, Vy-otin, you –!"

Herod sputtered, "By the Mass, Gilgamesh, I tell you it was only –"

Just then Enkidu entered the royal chamber. Brusquely waving Herod into silence, Gilgamesh turned to him and said, "Cake, Enkidu. Let them eat cake."

"What?"

"It is the newest joke. It comes by way of Herod."

Enkidu blinked. "Am I missing something? Let them eat cake? That doesn't sound like a joke to me."

"It is Later Dead, and too subtle for the likes of us."

"For the love of Allah, Gilgamesh!" Herod cried. "Will you let me tell you the story, so you'll understand? There was a queen in France – France is a Later Dead kingdom, in Europe, near what they call Germany and Spain – and things were very troubled in France in this queen's time, most of the populace was going hungry, and –"

Enkidu said, "Tell it to us afterward, Herod. I have news for the king. There is an army just outside the city."

"An army?" Gilgamesh asked, eyes going wide. "What kind of army?"

"A very ragged and weary one, brother. Four or five hundred men, and some women, and from the looks of them they're on their last legs. Some farmers drilling for water found them a couple of hours ago, half dead of thirst and starvation. They're camped a couple of leagues out in the desert and they ask permission to enter."

"This is not an army," said Gilgamesh. "This is merely a band of harmless pitiful stragglers, I think."

"Unless they've got a Trojan horse with them," Herod said.

"A what? Is this another of your Later Dead jokes?"

"Not Later Dead, Gilgamesh," Vy-otin said. "What Herod's talking about is older stuff than that – one of Homer's stories this time. When the Greeks were laying siege to the city of Troy, they realized they could enter the city only by deception, and so they built a giant horse of wood, which –"

Gilgamesh gave the one-eyed man a peculiar look. "Wait a minute. You're supposed to be – what is the word? – *prehistoric*. You are – am I right? – *Pleistocene*. How do you know so much of Greeks and their war with Troy? All that was long after *my* time, let alone yours!"

"But this is the world I live in. The other one was only a moment very long ago, and this one is forever. Therefore this is the world that is real to me, and the other was like a dream. I've kept up with things. Should I not know something of the history of the people I have to deal with every day, Gilgamesh? Shouldn't you?"

"Go easy on him," Herod murmured. "History comes and goes in all our minds, like a fever. He's having a forgetful time of it just now."

"Ah," said Vy-otin. "Yes. Of course."

Gilgamesh said, annoyed, "Is the point of all this that we are supposed to fear treachery from this raggle-tag bunch of strangers?"

"That was Herod's notion, not mine," Enkidu said. "From the information I have, they're in very bad shape and not likely to make any trouble for us."

"Except that they come to a city that's already in the midst of a drought and a famine," Herod said. "Do we need to take them in? Five hundred more thirsty throats? Five hundred more empty bellies?"

"We are civilized here," said Gilgamesh coldly. He nodded toward Enkidu. "Take a hundred border patrolmen, brother, and find out who these people are and what they want. And whether they have brought any wooden horses with them."

"Sir Walter?" Hakluyt whispered. "D'ye be awake, Sir Walter?"

Cautiously Ralegh opened his eyes. It was a painful business: the lids were tender as a babe's, blistered from the sun and the glare off the endless sand. His armor lay discarded beside him; he wore only a jerkin and felt-trimmed leggings. He raised his head. That was a painful business too. This whole expedition has been a painful business, he thought.

"What is it, Richard, you damnable whoreson baboon?"

The little geographer was flushed with excitement. He was bobbing and jigging giddily about, and waving something wildly. "The map, Sir Walter! It can be read again!"

"*What?*" Ralegh sat up abruptly, awake and attentive all at once. "God's ears, Hakluyt, if you're deceiving me –"

"Look. Here." Hakluyt held up the thing he had been waving, a worn, tattered, all-too-familiar scroll of rolled-up leather, and undid its laces. With quivering hands he pushed it forward, practically into Ralegh's face. "It's being this close to Uruk that did it, I think. The map has regained its vitality from proximity to the city, perhaps owing to some spell that Dr Dee laid upon it before we left, and –"

"*Dee!*" Ralegh cried, and spat. "May his lungs turn to water! May his beard grow inward upon his lips, that dastardly sorcerer! Assuring me that this map was a perfect one, that he had witched it so that it would never lead us astray –"

"But look at it," Hakluyt said.

Ralegh peered at the scroll, squinting and shading his eyes, straining to make out the markings it bore. He was surprised that Hakluyt had kept the villainous thing at all, after all the months – or had it been years? – since it had faded in a moment and gone perfectly blank. But in truth it did seem to be covered once again with some sort of writing now. Some new diabolical deception? Or the true map that once had been? So it seemed to be, the true original, as well as he could recall it. Yes, there it all was again, miraculously restored, pale red ink on dark brown leather: the entire track that they had followed in this foolhardy adventure, which had seen them marching in circles for year after year, more years than he had kept certain count of, searching for something that probably did not exist. There was Her Majesty's domain proudly outlined in the north, and grim old King Henry her father's territory not far from it, and the dread sprawl of the Outback, Prester John's kingdom and the one of Mao Tse-tung and all the rest of the dominions of those frantic little princelings of the desert, and at the far western edge an eerie scarlet glow emanating from the leather to mark the isle of Brasil, where the traitorous magician Dr Dee claimed it would be possible to find the route that led to the land of the living.

Anger throbbed in his breast. The return of the map gave him no pleasure. It was simply one more reminder of the monstrous soul-breaking capriciousness of this place.

Bad enough was it that in the old life he had known such an unending series of heart-rending reverses, the Roanoke disaster and the humiliating attack on Cadiz where he had fought so foolishly, and the catastrophic folly of his quest for El Dorado in Guiana, which had cost him his son and his health and his fortune and, ultimately, even his head. He could blame those misfortunes on bad luck, perhaps, or an excess of enthusiasm leading to bold premature ventures which would be carried off more successfully later by more cautious men; but surely those were not grave sins, to be unlucky, to be overeager. Here, though, where he found himself condemned to trek back and forth across the face of a land that defied all reason, where his maps themselves mocked him as he studied them – no, no, it was too much. Out of love for Her Majesty he had come this far and had suffered this much; but now Ralegh was beginning to think he had suffered enough for Elizabeth's sake, and for his own insatiable nature. Where had it got him, all his vaulting ambition, all his courage, all his buoyant unconquerable will? To lands of cannibals and monsters, and men whose heads do grow beneath their shoulders, and places where there was nothing to drink but sand and nothing to eat but leafless twigs. He stared gloomily at the three broken-down jeeps across the way, the last pathetic rusting reminder of the hundred and fifty shining vehicles with which this expedition had so grandly begun, what seemed like a century ago.

If ever I get out of this barren land alive, he told himself, I mean to settle down and never roam further. By the Rood, I will wander no more, not for the Queen's sake nor mine own nor that of any man! Jesu Cristo, I will not, I do vow it!

"Well, so we have our map again," he said sourly. "Shrive me, Hakluyt, what good is that? Can we drink the map? Can we eat the map? We have been in this desert fifty times as long as Moses, and does it ever end? You said that beyond the

Outback there were green fields, and a sea, and a way to the land of the living –"

"It was Dr Dee that said that, Sir Walter."

"Well, you, Dee, whichever one it was, what boots that now? Beyond the Outback was only another desert, nor are we likely to be quit of it, map or no map. God's wounds, d'ye think I have the strength to go on? Do you?"

"But we are near to the city of Uruk, and if they take us in and give us drink, we can continue on thence to the isle of Brasil, where peradventure –"

Ralegh threw up his hands. "Peradventure yes, peradventure no, hunger and thirst and sore feet all the while. And utter surety of sorrow and weariness. What is this place called Uruk, anyway?"

"A great city of the Sumerians, Sir Walter, famous for its wealth and power."

"And who are they, these Sumerians of yours? Saracens, d'ye mean? Paynim villains?"

"They are a Babylonish race," Hakluyt said, "very ancient, who write with little sticks on soft bricks of clay. It was they who built Babel's tower in Nimrod's time, which was before Abraham's."

"So they are not Saracens? They know not Mohammed, then?"

"I think they have the look of Saracens, Sir Walter, but Saracens they are not."

"Not Christians either, though. And they'll be glad enough to let us leave our bones bleaching in the sand, I trow."

"The ones we spoke with were kindly folk," said Hakluyt. "Farming people, they were, inoffensive, without guile. They will return with assistance for us within the hour, I wager, and our sufferings will be at an end."

"And what will you wager, Richard? Your reading spectacles? Your boots, with the toes sticking through? One of your manuscripts of geography, perhaps? Yes, and I'll stake my tin drinking cup, or my tobacco-pipe that has no tobacco, or mayhap my –"

"Sir Walter? Sir Walter!" a voice called suddenly in the distance.

"Who's that?" Ralegh asked, blinking into the sun.

"Helen, I think," Hakluyt murmured.

"Ah. Yes, that trollop! What is she screeching about now, I wonder?"

"Sir Walter! Sir Walter!"

"I hear you, girl," Ralegh said. "What is it?"

She came running up before him, white-robed, dark-haired, smooth-skinned, flawless. She seemed as untouched by her ordeal in the desert as if she had been bathing in musk and ointments of Araby all the while.

"Girl?" she said, with a little laugh. "Do you call me a girl, and I with three thousand years of lusty life behind me? Ah, Sir Walter –"

"Don't misconstrue me. It was only a word," said Ralegh irritatedly. She looked as excited as Hakluyt had been over the map, all flushed and fluttering. And beautiful, too, in her dark Turkish way. He had never been much taken with her famous beauty, really – she was too swarthy for him, give him a good fair English wench and none of these sultry Eastern tarts, and there was something remote and unreal about her besides, too perfect, a waxworks woman, no life to her – but now the spark seemed to have been re-awakened in her, and she was as radiant as an empress. The face that launched a thousand ships, Ralegh thought, not for the first time: well, if only she could launch a ship this very moment that would sail them to some more kindly place! "What rouses you this way, Helen?" he asked.

"The Sumerians! They've come to rescue us, with a fleet of Land Rovers!"

"They're here?" Ralegh struggled to his feet, swaying dizzily, and looked about for his armor. "How many? Where?"

"Fifty or a hundred of them. Armed like Achilles, every one of them, to the teeth. But they seem friendly."

"Did I not tell you?" Hakluyt said.

Helen said, "They'll bring us to their city. They'll feed us and give us to drink. All this by order of their king, whose name is Gilgamesh."

Ralegh shrugged. "Never heard of him. Is he here too?"

"He has sent his deputy," she said. "A giant of a man, Enkidu by name, most amazing for his strength and beauty."

"His beauty?"

"Oh, yes," she cried. "Yes! A true Heracles, he is. Achilles is nothing compared with him. Paris, Menelaus, Agamemnon – even Hector – they are all nothing to him! Nothing! Oh, Sir

Walter, we're saved, saved, saved!" She looked then at Hakluyt, who as usual was studying her in his dry, indifferent, scholarly way, but yet with a sort of bloodless fascination, not as though she was the most celebrated seductress who had ever lived but rather some rare manuscript, or other such clerkish treasure. To him she said, "There must be something in your archive, is there not, Dr Hakluyt, about this Enkidu? Tell me what you discover. Tell me everything. I want to know all that is to be known about this man. I want to know it right away."

Nineteen

"I have heard," said Gilgamesh, sprawling back comfortably on the throne, "that what you have come to these parts to seek is nothing less than the gateway to the land of the living."

There was a flicker of surprise, only the tiniest flicker, on Ralegh's face. But he said calmly enough, "They tell many strange and fabulous stories about me, your majesty. I would that I had a shilling for each one of them."

"Are they all lies, then?"

"Not at all. I have indeed done a few of the things that are attributed to me. But only a few."

Gilgamesh chuckled. "I know how that is. Once the poets and romancers get hold of you, there's no end to it, is there?"

"And the envious, majesty. Don't forget them. The little petty negligible people whose lives are measured only by dreams and lies, and whose tongues wag foolishly day and night, conjuring up deeds for their betters that they wish they themselves had the daring to undertake – they turn all truth into falsehood merely by touching it."

"It is so," said Gilgamesh.

The Sumerian was silent a moment, staring through the smoky candlelit dimness of the throne chamber at this bold and confident man whom Enkidu had hauled, parched and withered and more than halfway to starvation, out of the badlands just a little while before. Behind Ralegh stood the other Englishman, the mild bookish one, Hakluyt, and behind him was the dark sleek woman Helen, the Greek, she who claimed to be the one called Helen of Troy. She had eyes only for Enkidu, so it seemed, and he only for her. There was a hot erotic force bristling and crackling in the air between them like ghostly fire: you didn't need to be a mage to feel it. Her eyes were slits, her nostrils flared, her tongue licked over her lips like a serpent's; and as for Enkidu, he stood rigid, with hands tautly cupped, as though her breasts were already in them. Gilgamesh winked at him, but it seemed to go unnoticed. When Enkidu had come to him with the news that the leader of these ragged wanderers was the Englishman Sir Walter Ralegh, and Gilgamesh had said that Ralegh was known to have been searching for a way into the land of the living on behalf of Elizabeth his queen, Enkidu had been all afire with eagerness to know what luck he had had. "Ask him, brother, ask him and make him tell," he had said. But from the moment Helen had clamped herself to him, such matters as the way to the land of the living and all other things had seemed to lose all urgency for Enkidu. There was nothing in Enkidu's eyes now but the reflection of Helen, Helen, Helen, Helen. And she all aglitter and aglow with him. Perhaps this time, Gilgamesh thought, Enkidu has met a woman who can match him appetite for appetite. That would be interesting to see.

All the same, he had given Enkidu his promise that he would question Ralegh, and so he would do.

To the Englishman he said, after a bit, "And the gateway to the land of the living, Sir Walter, for which supposedly you have been searching? Is that one of the strange and fabulous stories also, or is there something to it?"

"Ah," Ralegh said, smiling broadly. "On that subject I can tell you nothing useful. For all the true knowledge I have of this purported gateway, your majesty, it might have no more substance to it than the myths and fables of the Greeks, or the tales of the Round Table."

Gilgamesh smiled also. The way Ralegh had twisted the discourse about was admirably deft. Saying that he knew of no proof that the way to the land of the living existed did not mean, after all, that he had not been looking for it. Or that he had not been on the verge of finding it when his provisions and strength had run out. Plainly this man had spent a long time close to those who wielded great power, and understood the art of withholding information without actually uttering lies. To lie to a king can be dangerous. But so, too, can telling the truth be.

It was clear that Ralegh did not mean to speak of his expedition's purpose, nor of the land of the living, nor of any gateways that might lead to it. Well, so be it, Gilgamesh thought. This was beginning to grow wearying. He would not press him for the information too seriously, at least just now. One more attempt, perhaps, and then he would drop it. All this mattered much less to him than it did to Enkidu, after all; and Enkidu seemed to be greatly preoccupied with other interests at the moment.

Certainly the Englishman was putting a brave front on things, for one who had been in such grim straits so recently. He was an impressive man, thoughtful and courtly, with a high shrewd forehead, keen eyes, a beard carefully trimmed to a fine point. He was clad in what no doubt were his finest garments, elegant splendid raiment of silk and velvet, bedecked with many a magnificent piece of glistening silver jewelry. Yet there were ineradicable blemishes and stains on the fine fabrics where the rigors of the Outback had marked them, and his finery hung poorly on him where his flesh had grown lean, and his face was gaunt and sun-blackened, and there was a darkness and a bitterness in his deep-set eyes that spoke of great hardships endured and greater ones anticipated. Gilgamesh felt oddly drawn to him. Ralegh seemed no ordinary man.

"I have heard of you, you know," Gilgamesh said.

"Have you, indeed?"

"Our paths nearly crossed once. There was a time when I was at the court of Prester John, and word came that you were traveling with an army of exploration across the southern boundary of his territory."

"That was quite some long time ago, your majesty, when I was in Prester John's country."

"So it was. It amazed me greatly to hear that you and your troops had continued on the march all this while since."

"That was not our intention," said Ralegh, and shot a bleak look toward the clerkish man Hakluyt, as though to say that he had served as the expedition's guide, and had served none too well. "We lost our way. Our map proved to be useless."

"Indeed. They often are."

"It has been a hard journey for us. I am no stranger to hard journeying, but this one has been a burden to me of an unusual severity. We are more grateful for your kindness than can easily be put in words. But I assure you we will make no long demand on your hospitality. A few days to rest, if we may, and then –"

"Stay as long as you wish," said Gilgamesh, with a gracious wave of his hand. "It would be an unmannerly thing to send you on your way before you were recovered from your toil." He heard Herod coughing and muttering behind him. Thinking of the depleted granaries, no doubt. Gilgamesh glared at him. To Ralegh he said, at last making his one final effort at returning the discussion to the point Enkidu had urged him to pursue, "When I was at the court of Prester John two men were there from King Henry's land, ambassadors to Prester John, who said that your queen – what is her name?"

"Elizabeth, majesty."

"Elizabeth, yes. Your Queen Elizabeth, they said, who is King Henry's own daughter, desired greatly to find the gateway to the land of the living. It was their belief that she planned to create an English settlement at that place, if it existed, and extract a tariff from those who wished to travel through it to whatever lies beyond."

"They imagined such a thing, did they?" Ralegh said casually, as though the idea were the wildest fantasy.

Shrugging, Gilgamesh said, "So I remember it, though it was only something I happened to overhear. There was some discussion of it at court between the ambassadors and Prester John in my presence. Their King Henry had sent them to raise an army from Prester John that was to intercept you before you could find what you sought."

Ralegh looked toward Hakluyt. "Do you hear, Richard? The treacherous vile old caitiff pig!"

"Sir Walter!"

"I can call him whatever I please, Richard. He was never king of mine in the other life, and I owe him no love here, which is not England, and if it is, it is Elizabeth's England, not Henry's, to me." To Gilgamesh he said, "Well, the scheme miscarried, majesty. No army of Prester John's ever gave trouble to us."

"No," Gilgamesh said. "Prester John was distracted, just then, by an attack from another quarter, a rival Outback prince, some Chinese king."

"Mao Tse-tung," said Ralegh. "The Celestial People's Republic."

"The very one, yes."

"A clever devil, this Mao. My queen speaks highly of him. He sends her gifts of silks and ivories, and scrolls of his poetry, and many volumes of his own books on the art of governance – I read one once, and could make no sense of it, but perhaps the fault was mine –" Ralegh shook his head. "Well, and did Mao's army destroy that of Prester John, then?"

"I have no idea. I left the court as the battle was impending, and never heard another thing of it. My travels took me far away from that place, as far as the isle of Brasil –"

At the mention of that name Ralegh caught his breath short between his teeth, as if he had been pricked by a needle.

"You know of Brasil?" Gilgamesh asked.

"I've heard of it," said Ralegh in an oddly vague and distant way. "A place of witchcraft, and sorcerers, and much else of that sort, is it not?"

"Very much. And strange to behold, also, looking like no other city I've seen."

"I hope to visit it one day," Ralegh said. "Perhaps when I leave here. It has long been of great interest to me, the isle of Brasil."

"The Hairy Man my chief mage lived there many years," said Gilgamesh. "As did my vizier here, Herod the Jew. They might be able to tell you the way."

"I would be most grateful for that, yes," said Ralegh.

As the audience came to its end and those in attendance began to stream from the hall, Enkidu felt the woman Helen catch hold of his arm, digging her fingers fiercely into his flesh. In a low harsh tone she said, "Come with me!"

"But the king –"

"The king can wait. Come!"

He nodded. He was helpless before her. His throat was dry, his heart was hammering wildly in his breast. Far off in the dimness he saw Gilgamesh still enthroned, conferring with Vy-otin and Herod; and perhaps it was his duty to be there too. But there was no resisting Helen. Her face was bright with the heat of lust and Enkidu could see her nipples rising against the thin fabric of her robe. Gilgamesh would forgive him. She tugged eagerly at his arm, and though she stood scarcely rib-high to him and seemed to weigh no more than a cloak of feathers, Enkidu let himself be pulled along by her, onward into the flow of those who were leaving the chamber.

When they were outside she led him swiftly into a dark deserted corridor paved with smooth cobbles and roofed in a pointed arch, and pressed him against the wall. Her eyes were bright as jewels. Her breath was hot and sweet. Take her now, he wondered? Right here in the hall, pull up her robe, stroke the smoothness of her belly, seize her behind her thighs and hoist her to him just like that? He hesitated, though his yearning was strong. In the old days he would not have waited: against the wall, or on the paving-stones, or in a window-ledge, or wherever, take what is offered and take it swiftly. But they had pumped too much civilization into him over the centuries. And yet was it not foolishness to hold back? There she was, hot and ready.

Well, if that was so –

But no, he was reading her wrong, she seemed to want to talk. Even as his hands moved toward her there was some sort of change in her look: the glow was still there, but the heat was not, as if she could turn the furnace on and off to suit the moment, and this was not the moment to be ablaze. She baffled him. He felt clumsy, impossibly ponderous, bewildered, as if hypnotized by her.

"Are you the king's brother?" she asked.

"His friend, only."

"Yet you call each other brother."

"It is because our friendship is so close."

"Ah," she said.

The way her eyes sparkled was maddening to him. There was the unmistakable look of invitation in them, but also something meant to keep him at a distance, at least for a little while longer. Enkidu's trembling fingers hovered about her, but still he did not dare to touch. How easy it would be to seize her and take her. But no, he realized: not easy at all. She held him off with a glance, with a smile. She forced him to wait. This was new to him, this waiting, this holding back for the proper moment. But he had never known a woman like this before, either.

There must be sorcery in this, Enkidu thought. How did she come to hold such power over him? This must be enchantment.

She said, "I was the wife of a king, once, who had a greater king for his brother, and no end of trouble came of that. But it was a long while ago. Do you know who I am?"

"Your name is Helen."

"Helen of Troy!"

"I ask your pardon. Perhaps I should know that name, but I must confess –"

"You are Early Dead?"

"Of course."

"Egypt? Assyria?"

"Sumer the Land, my lady. Between the rivers Idigna and Buranunu, it is."

"Can you speak Greek?"

"I could once, I think. It was long ago."

"Never mind," she said. "You must be very ancient. You know of the Trojan War, do you?"

Enkidu thought a moment. "It is all so mixed together. But yes, yes, Homer's war, that is what you mean: it was Achilles, Agamemnon –"

"I was the wife of Agamemnon's brother Menelaus. The war started over me. Or so it is often said, though others say that it was about trade routes. But I know that it was over me, because I had left the king my husband and gone to live in the land of Troy, where Paris my lover took me, and Menelaus could not abide that insult, nor Agamemnon his brother."

"Indeed. Yes," Enkidu said.

He could understand that, wanting to start a war over this one. Those eyes, that skin, her breasts, the hair dark as a moonless night, the fire of her that he could feel throbbing so close by him – yes, she was maddening. Maddening. Here she was close in front of him, almost in his grasp, in his grasp if he wanted. And yet not so. It still seemed to him that she was alive with the same yearnings that he felt, but she was able somehow to hold them, and him, at bay.

He thought of all the women he had known in all his years in this world and the other one, trying to remember whether there had been any with hair as fragrant as this Helen's, with limbs as pale and enticing, but he found that he could not recall any of them now in any separate way: they were a smoky blur, a vague dark smudge in his mind. And this one, who was just beyond his reach, was crystalline and bright and hot, burning like a fiery diamond, clear and glittering and perfect.

"And now you are the wife of this Ralegh?" he asked.

She laughed, a growling lioness-laugh. "Him? No, though I could do worse. But we simply travel together. He thinks I'm impure, he thinks I'm unclean. And worse. A succubus, he calls me. The whore of Babylon, he calls me, though I've never seen Babylon in my life. I am not English, that's his problem. He wants only English women, this Ralegh."

"Yet he keeps you with him?"

"I was a damsel in distress. He found me abandoned in the Outback – I was traveling with another Englishman then, a Lord, very sweet, a little strange – Byron was his name, a poet, he was writing a new *Iliad* about me, he said, but he was massacred by a band of dervishes. Our whole company was. I alone escaped, and Ralegh found me and took me in, because he is so gallant, though he despises me. And I stayed with him, because I hoped he would come upon the way to the land of the living, which he seeks."

"The land of the living?"

"I'm tired of the Afterworld, Enkidu. I want to be real again."

"We are real here, lady."

"You know what I mean. I want to live in a place where things make some sense, where the rivers don't run uphill when they feel like it, where cities don't move about like boats on a lake."

"Yes," Enkidu said. "I do know what you mean. And I have the same wish. I would go to the land of the living myself, if I could find the way."

"We could find it together, Enkidu."

"What? How?"

"Do you know where Brasil is? The magic isle?"

He nodded uncertainly. "Down the coast some considerable way, I think."

"You've not been there?"

"Not I, though I was near it once. But Gilgamesh has."

"The way to the land of the living is in Brasil."

Enkidu stared. "Do you know that?"

"So Ralegh was told, in good faith, by one who seemed to know. I have seen it marked on his map, with a mark like a flame. He was heading that way when our provisions ran out. Well, he has lost the desire to go that way, now. But I have not. You and I, Enkidu, you and I – we could find Brasil, we could penetrate its mysteries, we could enter that gateway –"

"You think so?"

"I know it," she said. She leaned upward toward him, and slyly ran her tongue over her lips, and laughed, not a lioness-growl this time, but something more like a purr. "We could find it, you and I. That I know." He felt the heat of her again, now. She had turned the furnace back on. "Well, Enkidu?"

This time he did not hesitate. His hands went to her breasts. She covered them with her own. The purring grew in his ears until it was a roaring; and she swept upon him like an avalanche of fire.

No one remained with Gilgamesh in the audience chamber but Vy-otin and Herod, and a couple of guards. He would have kept Enkidu with him also, but Enkidu had gone sweeping out at Helen's side before Gilgamesh could catch his notice, and he had not had the heart to summon him back. But he did send for Magalhaes, and the Hairy Man.

"Well?" he said, while waiting for them to arrive. "What do you think of this Ralegh?"

"An unusual man," said Herod. "Intelligent and deceitful. A great leader and a great liar, is what I believe."

"No greater a liar than he needs to be," Vy-otin said. "I spoke with him before he came in here. It was the nature of his country that great men ran great risks, unless they had nimble tongues. This Elizabeth he seems to worship was a dangerous woman in the first life, forever cutting off the heads of her favorite courtiers, though Ralegh managed to keep his. But the king who followed Elizabeth to her throne put him in prison for a dozen years or so, and finally *did* have him slain."

Gilgamesh frowned. "Why do that? It seems an enormous waste."

"The reason was something about an expedition that miscarried at heavy expense to the nation, and talk of conspiracy with some other country's king, which this Ralegh denied to me with very strong oaths. But in truth it seems the king slew him out of general resentment, I think, of his brilliance and cockiness."

"But to kill a man of his quality for that – they must have been a barbarian tribe, those English," Gilgamesh said.

"We Pleistocene folk," said Vy-otin, with a wicked grin, "were the last true civilized folk. We Aurignacians, we archetypes. There's something about living in an ice age among the glaciers and the woolly mammoths that makes you humane and decent. It's all been downhill for the human race ever since. The species began to spoil like rotten fruit when things started getting too warm, do you see?"

Herod laughed. "How can we argue with you?" he asked. "You have the perspective of twenty thousand years. But perhaps our friend the Hairy Man would say that *his* people were the pinnacle of creation, and yours just a bunch of fur-wearing hatchet-wielders with runny noses. What do you say to that, Henry Smith? What do you say?"

With a pleasant nod Vy-otin said, "Of course they were civilized, the Hairies. And so were we. By the Tusk and the Horns of God, it's all you latecomers, you Sumerians and Babylonians and Greeks and Romans, who don't deserve to be called –"

"And Jews," Herod said. "Don't forget about the Jews. "We're the worst villains of all. We're such barbarians that you wouldn't ever have been able to get us to eat mammoth meat."

"Why not? Have you ever tried it?"

"Buddha forbid!" Herod cried, and crossed himself. "Mammoth meat? That's not kosher! Our god commands us never to touch such stuff!"

"Why, then that explains why I encountered no Jews in the Pleistocene," said Vy-otin. "You all must have starved to death in a condition of great sanctity. There was nothing else to eat then, you know. The occasional saber-tooth, and maybe the odd rhinoceros, but mammoth was the thing, lad, the fine old rumbling fellows with the red woolly hides –" He laughed and looked toward Gilgamesh. "What are you planning to do with this Ralegh? Keep him around?"

"For a little while. For Enkidu's sake."

"Enkidu's?"

"The gateway to the land of the living, that supposedly Ralegh was searching for: it fascinates Enkidu greatly, that gateway. Perhaps Ralegh can tell us something about it."

"Is there such a thing?" Vy-otin asked. "For a hundred centuries have I heard tales of it. But nobody has ever seemed to find it, nor have I ever encountered anyone who even had a clear idea of where it might be."

"Nor have I," said Gilgamesh. "But I want at least to try to learn whatever Ralegh may know of it. Although getting anything out of him isn't going to be easy."

"Is that really Helen of Troy he's traveling with, do you think?" Vy-otin said.

"She claims she is. I'm willing to believe her."

"She's impossibly beautiful," Herod said. "Doesn't look real."

Vy-otin laughed. "Enkidu seems to think she's real enough."

"He is possessed by her, yes," said Gilgamesh. "Not in thousands of years have I seen him like this over a woman. But it will do him good. He has always been restless when he is without a woman, and when Enkidu is restless trouble often follows. This Helen may be able to calm him for a little while."

"Just the opposite, I'd think," said Herod. "But you know him better."

The door at the far end of the hall opened. "Magalhaes is here," said Vy-otin.

The mariner came limping in, and stood before the throne. "You asked for me, majesty?"

"Yes," said Gilgamesh. "I did. You know all the venturers and seafarers, Magalhaes. What can you tell me of this Walter Ralegh who has come among us now? Did you have dealings with him, ever, in the other world?"

"After my time, he was. Fifty years or more."

Gilgamesh laughed. "Fifty years? What's that?"

"In the other world, majesty, it is everything. I was long gone before he was born. But I have heard of him here. Draco has told me tales of him."

"Draco?"

"Francisco Draco the pirate," said Magalhaes. "Another English, well known to Ralegh in the other world."

"Sir Francis Drake, he means," Vy-otin explained.

Gilgamesh nodded. "Thank you. You are ever the expert on these Later Dead details, old friend." To Magalhaes he said, "Very well. And what did your Drake, your Draco, tell you about Ralegh?"

"A genius, he said. But unpredictable and unreliable, as most geniuses are. Wonderful projects, always, that he could never quite bring to fulfilment."

"Such as trying to find the way to the land of the living?"

"That would be this Ralegh's kind of scheme, yes."

Bending toward the little Portuguese, Gilgamesh said quietly, "And what do you know on that subject? Is it possible that such a gateway exists, do you think?"

"It is a fable," replied Magalhaes at once. "The land of the living is unreachable. I think so, and Draco thinks so, and Cook thinks so, who is another great mariner. These are men I know and trust, Draco and Cook, they both sailed around the world as I did, and one who makes a voyage such as that can never be like ordinary men again. What he sees, he sees truly."

"Perhaps so."

"Draco has sought it, so he has told me. So has Cook. They have been to the Afterworld's farthest corners, even into the Great Unending. Would they still be here, if they had found the way to the land of the living? Yet I saw Draco only the other month, and Cook barely five years back, and they said nothing to me of gateways, or of other worlds, though they would surely have told me. If they have not found it, it is not there. Trust me on this, majesty."

"If that is the case –" Gilgamesh began, but just then there was a commotion in the hallway outside the throne chamber – a thumping sound, a volley of discordant singing, lusty laughter, some heavy-handed clapping, the usual signs of Enkidu's approach – and then Enkidu himself came rollicking into the room, flushed and sweaty, his long rank hair unkempt, his robe rumpled. The scent of Helen's perfume came in with him.

"My lord Gilgamesh!" he roared. "I have it! The great secret – I've found it out!"

"Why, I could have told him," Herod murmured, "and I've never so much as spoken with the woman. It's simple: one breast on either side of her chest, that's how she's built, and down below there's a patch of dark hair where her legs meet, and she makes a little soft sound when you touch –"

Gilgamesh hissed sharply at the Judaean to be silent.

"What secret is this, brother?" he called, as Enkidu strode toward him, swaying as he walked, the way a sailor would as he walked on deck.

"The way to the land of the living! I know where it can be found!"

Gilgamesh frowned and glanced at Magalhaes, who merely shrugged.

"This mariner here has been telling us that there is no such gateway anywhere in the Afterworld."

"This mariner is wrong. I have the location of it on good faith, and let any man deny it and he will have to answer to me for calling me a liar."

Magalhaes, looking unworried, turned to stare up at Enkidu, who stood towering over him, seemingly twice his height. "I said only that I think the gateway to be a fable, before you entered here. Those who wish to believe in its existence may go on doing so, and it will not matter to me, nor will I call them liars. There are those who say that the world is flat, and they are not liars either. They are telling the truth as they believe it. One does not have to be lying in order to be speaking that which is not true."

"Who is this little man?" Enkidu bellowed, clenching both fists and raising them. "Why is he here, and why do you allow him to mock me? By Enlil, I'll –"

"Peace, both of you," said Gilgamesh, signalling to Vy-otin to step between them. He waited a moment for Enkidu to grow more calm; and then he said, "All right, brother. Tell us what you have learned."

Enkidu looked about sullenly. "In front of –?"

"Herod, Vy-otin, yes. Why not?"

"*Him?*" He indicated Magalhaes.

"He is a great seafarer, a man who knows much concerning the routes of this world and the other one. He is in our service now. We trust him. You can speak, Enkidu."

"Well –" Enkidu shook his head. "It was the woman Helen who told me this, she who came here with Ralegh –"

Herod snickered.

"Are they all going to mock me today?" Enkidu cried.

"Be quiet, Herod. Go on," said Gilgamesh. "What Helen told you –"

"She and Ralegh, as we know, have been roaming the Outback under commission from Ralegh's queen, Elizabeth by name, who seeks the way to the land of the living. Ralegh carries a map, or rather the little man Hakluyt who is his guide carries it, and Helen has seen it. It shows plainly where the opening into the other world is located."

"And that place is?" Gilgamesh asked.

Once again Enkidu hesitated, glowering at Magalhaes.

"Go *on*, Enkidu! Where is it?"

"Brasil," said Enkidu.

"Brasil?"

"The isle of Brasil, yes, Simon's city, where you had the Knowing that led you here, brother."

Gilgamesh stared. "I thought Ralegh did indeed look surprised, when I told him that I had once been in Brasil. I merely mentioned the place, and his breath came short, and his eyes went wide. But no, Enkidu, no: how can it be? I have been there. Surely I would have heard."

"Did you ask?"

"Why would I have asked about that? The thought of the land of the living scarcely crossed my mind when I was in Brasil."

"You see? You see?"

Gilgamesh looked toward Herod. "You lived many years in Brasil. What can you say of this? Is the way to the land of the living to be found there, or not?"

"Well, there were tales, yes," Herod said in a vague way. "That the tunnels below the city might lead there, and other such fables. I never paid much attention to them. I never believed a tenth part of the fantastic-sounding stories which circulated in that city. Maybe not a hundredth part."

Gilgamesh peered into the distance. The image of those dark tunnels beneath Brasil, where Calandola and his band of cannibals lurked, awakened in him at Herod's words. He too had heard, more than once, yes, that somewhere in those tunnels could be found the path to the land of the living. He recalled that now. But there were age-old tunnels under many of the cities of the Afterworld, tunnels under Nova Roma, under Elektrograd, under Nibelheim, perhaps even tunnels under Uruk, for all he knew. In those cities, too, it was often whispered that one might find a way out of the Afterworld through one of the tunnels. But because a thing is whispered does not make it true. No one remembered who had built the tunnels, or why. They were mere dank caverns, dusty, sinister, dismal, abandoned long ago. Gilgamesh saw no reason to think that they had any magical import. There have always been those who hate the light of day, he thought, and prefer to burrow in the bowels of the earth. Why, though, should he believe that these labyrinths created in antiquity by the forgotten diggers of the Afterworld would lead anywhere except in futile circles?

He said, after a time, "Where is the Hairy Man? We will ask him about this."

"He is in the outer hall," Herod reported.

Enkidu said, "Would it not be a grand thing to see the land of the living, brother? Let us set out for it, brother! You and me – and Helen."

"And Helen, eh?"

"She will go with us, yes. She will lead the way, and all obstacles will fall before her." Enkidu's eyes were gleaming. "Oh, Gilgamesh, my brother, you have never known a woman like this one! She is a miracle! She is a goddess!"

"I have embraced goddesses, brother," said Gilgamesh drily, thinking of his first life, when he was king in the true Uruk and each year was obliged to enter into the Sacred Marriage with the divine Inanna. That had been a stormy thing, his dealings with Inanna, whose envy and love of power had nearly cost him his life far before his time. "They do not always make comforting bed-companions, let me remind you. But look – look, the Hairy Man –"

"I am here at your command, King Gilgamesh," the ancient creature said.

"We are speaking here of the path to the land of the living," Gilgamesh said.

"Ah." The Hairy Man's amber eyes burned like lanterns in his fur-shrouded inscrutable face.

Gilgamesh said, "Word has come to us just now that the entrance to that land is known, and that it is to be found in the isle of Brasil."

"Why do you tell this to me?" asked the Hairy Man coolly, in that thick-tongued way of his that made Gilgamesh lean forward to catch every word.

"Everything that is in Brasil, both in the city and in the tunnels beneath it, is known to you, I think. Therefore you should be able to say if it is so that the gateway to the land of the living is in that city."

The Hairy Man was silent for a time.

"No," he said, at last. "No, such a gateway is not to be found there. Not in the city, not in the tunnels."

Enkidu uttered a hissing sound of disappointment and fury.

"Are you certain of that?" Gilgamesh asked the Hairy Man.

"This palace of yours is a palace of stone, King Gilgamesh, and to enter the palace one must pass through a gateway. This city of Uruk is surrounded by a wall of brick, and to enter Uruk one must also pass through a gateway. But the land of the living is not entered the way your palace is entered, or the way the city of Uruk is entered, that is, through a gateway that one can step through, crossing from one side to the other, from a place outside to a place within. You will go up and down the face of the Afterworld and you will not find any such gateway."

Enkidu hissed again, more fiercely than before, and turned away, clenching his great fists and banging them against each other again and again.

Gilgamesh said, "Then is it only a foolish tale, that we can reach the land of the living from this world? A dream, a fable, an idle fantasy?"

The Hairy Man paused again a long while; and when he spoke he said something so indistinct that Gilgamesh could make out only a broken syllable here and there, and the rest of the lengthy speech was lost in the Hairy Man's beard.

"What was it you said?" Gilgamesh asked. "Tell it to me again, if you will."

"I said, O king, that the land of the living can indeed be reached. But the path that takes one there is not a path as you understand paths, and it is entered by a gateway that is not a gateway. The path is nowhere and everywhere, it is in Brasil and it is not in Brasil, it is in Uruk and it is not in Uruk, it is in the desert and it is not in the desert."

Scowling, Gilgamesh said, "Such words make no sense to me. To me a thing is somewhere or it isn't. A place can be reached or it can't be. No, you say. You say that there's a way to get there, all right, but you have to take a path that isn't a path, and the path is here but it isn't here, and –" Gilgamesh shook his head. "I understand you not at all."

The Hairy Man said, "These are not easy matters to understand. The path is not an easy path to find. Without the help of one who knows the way, you will never find it at all."

"And where can we find one who knows the way?"

"You have already found one, O king. I can put you on the path you seek."

"You? How can you do that?"

"If you truly wish to visit the land of the living," the Hairy Man said, "I can send you there. Do you not believe me? There is a way to open the path, and that way is known to me."

Enkidu, with a gasp, turned suddenly around again. He seemed to swell to twice his ordinary size. His eyes were wild and blazing.

"You hear?" he cried, pointing furiously at Magalhaes. "Do you hear?" And to Gilgamesh he said, trembling, "Brother, make him tell us the secret this minute! We must go there, you and I! We must find the way and follow it to its end! Or would you rather sit and grow fat in Uruk for another ten thousand years? Eh, brother? Eh?"

Gilgamesh stared at the Hairy Man in confusion. "You never said anything to me about this. Why is that, that you never said a thing?"

Something almost like a smile crossed the Hairy Man's bestial face.

"Ah, King Gilgamesh! You never asked!"

Twenty

It was a long somber night, punctuated by quick, abortive coppery-red sunrises and the dancing of unfamiliar yellow moons in the sky. Gilgamesh wandered alone in the streets of Uruk. A sharp, sour wind was blowing. For a time it brought with it gusty squalls of something much like snow, which dusted the white roof-tops with short-lived white flecks; when he picked up a handful of the stuff it was hot against his skin, like fine ash blown from a volcano's heart, or a delicate pumice.

Fragile but horrifying night-creatures, as filmy as dreams, fluttered about him in swarms, baring long gleaming teeth that dripped a pale venom. He batted them away as though they were mosquitos. A squat stubby tree with leaves like long greasy feathers seemed to be laughing at him. Doorways opened before him in mid-air, but there was nothing behind them. The paved streets undulated like the surface of a stormy sea.

One thought, and one only, went through his mind as he roamed the dark city:

You will be separated from Enkidu yet again, or else you must surrender the throne of Uruk. If you give up the throne you will never regain it. And if you lose Enkidu this time, you will never find him again.

There had come a time in the old life, Gilgamesh recalled, when Enkidu had become bleak and downcast, and sat scowling and sorrowing all day long; and Gilgamesh went to him and said to him that he knew what troubled him, which was that he had grown restless in their soft life of citified ease, and weary of dallying in idleness in Uruk, and longed to go forth into adventure, into danger, into mighty deeds that would raise up his name before mankind.

"Yes," said Enkidu, "that is so, brother."

And Gilgamesh had said that it was the same with him, that

there was something unsleeping in him also, forever questing, forever unsatisfied. The gods had played a jest on him, said Gilgamesh, fashioning him in such a way that he would yearn always for a peaceful life but never would be satisfied when he had attained it.

Enkidu laughed then, and said, "We are like two overgrown boys, casting about forever for new diversions."

That was the time when they went off into the Land of Cedars to bring back the fine wood that grew in the forest there, and encountered the demon Huwawa, and slew him in his fiery lair, and returned in triumph to the city of Uruk, as joyous as though they had conquered six kingdoms.

But all that had been in the other life, the old one long ago, before the first of the many deaths that they were destined to die. Now here was Enkidu once again restless for new adventure, and here was Gilgamesh king in Uruk again, settled in his tasks. What was it Enkidu had said, when he had urged Gilgamesh to come away on this quest with him? *Would you rather sit and grow fat in Uruk for another ten thousand years?* But this time Gilgamesh was uncertain of his way. There was a part of him that yearned to go with Enkidu in search of the land of the living – that part that was forever restless, forever seeking, and which was not yet entirely dead within him – but also there was another aspect of him that had grown within him during his time in the Afterworld, which said, *Stay, stay, rule your city, do the tasks that you alone were meant to do*. And that voice was as strong in him, or nearly, as the other.

And yet –

Stay? For what, he wondered? To play out yet again all that had happened before, in this world and the one that had preceded it? Was there no more to this existence of his than an eternal cycle of wielding power and then renouncing it, of governing and wandering, governing and wandering? Had nothing any end? Had nothing any purpose? When would he ever simply rest?

He heard the beating of mighty wings overhead, though there was nothing there. He saw the great hill beyond the city's north wall stirring and slowly beginning to move, lifting itself like the humped back of an awakening dragon. The air grew blood-red and very heavy, and a thick insistent buzzing came from it, as if from a million million angry flies.

A voice that spoke without speaking aloud said, "This is your kingdom, Gilgamesh of Uruk. How deeply do you love it?"

And the buzzing air echoed, "Do you love it? Do you love it? Do you love it?"

Ninsun said, "So you will go, then."

"I must, mother. He leaves me no choice."

She shook her head. "It seems a great mistake to me, this journey."

"And to me also," came Vy-otin's ringing voice from the far side of the hall. "How can you say you have no choice? Are you and he like twins who are joined by a band of flesh at the waist, that you have to follow him wherever he goes?"

Gilgamesh stared sadly at the Ice-Hunter a long moment.

"Yes, Vy-otin. That is exactly what we are."

"Then tell him you won't go. He'll have to give the idea up."

"He will go anyway," said Gilgamesh.

"Ah," said Herod. "Then you're a Siamese twin, but he isn't? How very peculiar."

"No," said Gilgamesh. "To enter the land of the living is something that he wants more than anything else. Such a need severs all bonds. He died his first death when he went down into the House of Dust and Darkness to bring back the drum that I had lost, the drum that the craftsman Ur-nangar made for me out of the wood of the huluppu-tree – do you remember, mother? That was the drum by whose beating I could send my spirit free to rove in strange realms of gods and monsters, and when I lost it he gave up his life that I could have it back. Ever since that time, I think, he has sought to regain the thing he lost that day. And he is certain now that the Hairy Man's witchcraft will help him find it."

"Then let him go and look for it," Vy-otin said. "But why must you –"

"Because I must," said Gilgamesh.

Herod laughed. "There's no reasoning like circular reasoning, is there?"

Gilgamesh whirled on the little Judaean with such wrath that Herod jumped back five paces. "You understand nothing of this! Nothing!"

"Forgive me, Gilgamesh," said Herod in a chastened voice. "But couldn't you simply forbid Enkidu to do it, if doing it causes you such grief?"

"I could, yes."

"But would he obey?"

"He'd obey me, yes. If I told him that I wouldn't go with him because of my duties here, and that I couldn't bear his going without me. But how could I ask that of him, Herod? To give up something for which he has yearned so long, simply because I –"

"But he asks that of you," Herod said.

"No. How does he do that?"

"By putting you in a position where you have to choose between your friend on the one hand and your city, your entire world, on the other."

"He has done nothing of the sort," said Gilgamesh, though without much conviction.

"If you make the crossing into the land of the living," Ninsun asked, "will you ever be able to return to the Afterworld again?"

"I have no way of knowing that. Perhaps the Hairy Man can tell me. But I came here once from that place. I should be able to do it again, if I wanted to."

"By giving up your life again, you mean?" she said.

"Yes."

"But if you return a second time, will you ever be able to find Uruk, do you think?"

"I suppose that I could. Or perhaps not. How can I say?"

"There is no way of knowing that, is there?" Ninsun said. "If you returned, you might come into the Afterworld anywhere. You might arrive a thousand years from now, and a thousand thousand leagues from this place. Everyone you had known here before would have been scattered to the seven corners of the world. You would be alone, Gilgamesh."

He gave her a long sorrowful look. But when he spoke there was renewed firmness in his voice.

"I have been alone before, and have been reunited somehow with those I love. You and I, mother, we were separated for thousands of years, and we found each other again, did we not?"

"And now you're proposing to head off to God knows

where, even though you may never see her again!" Vy-otin cried. "Leaving your mother, leaving your friends, leaving all you've built here in Uruk, leaving every single thing that you know and love – no, Gilgamesh! It's not right!"

"Let him be, Vy-otin," Ninsun said. "He has made up his mind, can't you see that?"

"The Hairy Man," Herod murmured.

"Peace and gladness, king of Uruk," the ancient one said, entering the throne room. He made a quick, offhand gesture of respect. "I have fetched the materials I need from Brasil," he said. "Have you decided?"

"You've obtained everything already?"

"Yes, all that I need."

Gilgamesh gaped at him. "How can you have brought anything from there so quickly? What has it been, one day, two? To get to Brasil and back takes weeks – months –"

"Sometimes less, King Gilgamesh. I tell you, I have all that I need."

More witchcraft, Gilgamesh thought. This creature of time's dawn was beyond his understanding.

"So be it," he said, shrugging.

"You will make the journey?"

"I will. And Enkidu. And the woman Helen of Troy."

"Helen also?"

"Enkidu wishes it."

The Hairy Man was silent a moment.

"Simon Magus is aware that she is here," he said, after a time. "It is the wish of Simon Magus that Helen of Troy be sent to him, O king."

"Ah, is it?"

"Very much so."

"Does Simon think that she's mine to bestow, like a casket of rubies?"

"They were lovers once. He wishes to see her again."

"If Helen had to be shipped back to everyone she'd been lovers with every time one of them snapped his fingers, she'd be whizzing around the Afterworld like a comet," Herod said, laughing.

Gilgamesh signalled him angrily to be quiet. To the Hairy Man he said, "I regret having to disappoint so powerful a wizard as Simon Magus."

"You will not send her to Simon?"

"No," Gilgamesh said. "She wants to go with Enkidu. Enkidu wants her to go with him. Why should I separate them? Simon's had his jewels from me, hasn't he? That should be enough for him."

The Hairy Man seemed unperturbed. "As you wish, O king. But you should know that no one goes from here to the land of the living with anyone else. Those who go, go alone."

"What does that mean?"

"It means what it means."

"Only one of us can go?"

"You all may go. But each goes separately and arrives separately. It is the only way."

"Enkidu and I won't be together when we get there?"

"You will make the journey alone and you will arrive alone."

"But we'll be able to find each other once we're there?"

"Perhaps."

Gilgamesh drew a long breath. "You aren't sure?"

"I have not been to the land of the living myself, King Gilgamesh, in more years than there are hairs on your head. How can I say what will happen there? But come: come, now. Everything is ready for the journey."

"Wait a little," Gilgamesh said. He glanced around the great dark hall. "Where's Enkidu?"

"I'll get him," Herod said, and went from the room.

He returned after a while, with Enkidu behind him like a walking boulder, and Helen radiant at Enkidu's side. Gilgamesh said at once, "The Hairy Man's been to Brasil and back already, don't ask me how. He has the things he needs to open the way to the land of the living."

Enkidu grinned; but quickly his face grew solemn. "And will you be joining us in the crossing, brother?"

The room was very still.

"I will," said Gilgamesh quietly.

"By Enlil! By Sky-father An! I knew you would! I always knew –"

"Wait," said Gilgamesh. "There are other things you need to know. He says that Simon wants Helen sent to him as a gift."

"He says *what*?" Enkidu roared. A menacing rumbling sound came from him and he started toward the Hairy Man.

But Helen, stilling him at once with no more than a touch of her hand to his wrist, said lightly, "Rest easy. It will not be."

"It had better not be," said Enkidu.

She smiled. "Simon's a sweet man, in his way. But if he wanted his chance with me, he should have taken it when we met long ago at the Abbey of Theleme." To the Hairy Man she said, "Tell him he's a thousand years too late. I'm going wherever Enkidu goes."

Gilgamesh said, "The Hairy Man informs me also that we'll be separated when we make the crossing, and we won't necessarily be able to find each other afterward."

Enkidu's eyes blazed. "What is this?" he boomed. "Are you sure you heard him right?"

"There is no doubt that that is what he said."

Enkidu wheeled around to confront the Hairy Man, who crossed his wrists in a strange gesture that might have been one of indifference, and looked off into the distance.

Helen said, turning to Enkidu, "Is it true? That we will lose each other in the crossing?"

"Do you mean to change your minds about making the attempt?" the Hairy Man asked placidly. "If that is so, let me know now, so that I may halt the preparations before –"

"No!" Enkidu cried. "This is some trick, that's all. Something that Simon told him to say, to discourage us if Helen refused to go to him. He was Simon's man before he was yours, brother. He's still Simon's man now."

"What do you say to this?" Gilgamesh demanded.

With unruffled calmness the Hairy Man said, "The journey will be the way the journey must be. The terms are the terms. I have no power to alter them."

"That is no answer at all," said Gilgamesh.

Helen said, trembling and looking suddenly very small, "This frightens me. To go off into the unknown not knowing whether or not we'll find each other on the other side –"

"We will find each other!" shouted Enkidu defiantly. "Somehow we will, that I know! You must believe that!" He looked down at her. "We found each other once, and we will do it again. You must believe it. You must." And pulled her close against him. "What do you say?"

"Yes," Helen murmured. Her eyes brightened, color came to her face. "Yes, I think we will. Yes. I have no doubt of it, Enkidu."

"And you, brother? What do you think? Are you still with us?"

Gilgamesh looked about. Enkidu, Helen, the Hairy Man. Behind them Herod. Farther away, Vy-otin, Ninsun. They all were silent. That silence crashed upon him like the waves of a furious sea. A strange indecision gripped him: he felt immobilized by it, as though he were frozen.

He had decided to undertake this journey, perilous and mystifying though it was, only for the sake of remaining by Enkidu's side. The Hairy Man offered no guarantee of that. And if what Enkidu said was true, that the Hairy Man meant to work some vengeance on them in Simon's name, to show Simon's displeasure over the withholding of Helen – but no, that would not be like Simon, nor had the Hairy Man ever showed treachery before –

"Well, brother?" Enkidu asked.

Gilgamesh stared at the Hairy Man. But that grizzled shaggy face was inscrutable. He looked toward Herod, but Herod only shrugged and looked away. He looked to Vy-otin, and found no answer in the Ice-Hunter's single fiery eye. To Ninsun, then –

She was smiling. She was nodding.

"Mother?" he said.

"When did you ever turn away from risk before, my son?"

"You want me to go?"

"You want to go," Ninsun said. "Why, then, do you hesitate?"

"But you said –"

"Of course I want you to stay. I would speak a lie if I told you anything else. But I see you are bound on this course, and no one could or should stop you. You are Gilgamesh: you do as Gilgamesh will do. Besides, Enkidu is right. You will find each other, somehow."

"Yes," Gilgamesh said, and it was like the breaking of a dam within him. "You have never spoken other than the truth, mother. How can I doubt you now?"

The Hairy Man said, "This is the salve. Rub it on your cheeks, and on your throats, and above your eyes. Then make your minds calm, and wait."

"So it is a drug that sends us there, then?" Gilgamesh asked. "The same one by which Calandola opened us to the Knowing?"

"It is nothing like that," said the Hairy Man.

He set three white porcelain pots out before them. They were in one of the loftiest rooms of the palace, a bare stark room with mere slits for windows, through which only the faintest trickle of light could enter, and a wisp of hot wind. Gilgamesh glanced at Enkidu, who already held his pot in his hand and was vigorously rubbing the stuff on his face. Helen, too, was beginning to bedeck herself with it. Yet he himself held back from taking up the salve. It surprised him, that at this late moment he would find himself holding back. That he still hesitated, Gilgamesh knew, was a measure of the changes that had come over his spirit in this latest life of his: he who once had hesitated at nothing now stared at the little white porcelain pot as if it held some dire poison that would burn the flesh from his bones.

To the Hairy Man he said, "Tell me only –"

"Tell me, tell me, always tell me! No more questions, King Gilgamesh. Just go. Go!"

"Yes, brother!" Enkidu called. "We must all depart together!"

"Yes," said Gilgamesh. "So we must."

He picked up the pot. It was warm, and a powerful fragrance came from it, which was like honey and wine and the oil of roses, but which had in it also some sharp fierce spice that stung his nostrils, and something else, a troublesome heavy aroma, dark and musty and strange. The other two were nearly done with their anointing now. Gilgamesh scooped some of the salve on to his fingers and brought it to his face. He thought for a moment of that time when Calandola had anointed him with a strange oil, and given him a stranger wine to drink, and then a frightful meat to eat, and he remembered all that had come from that ominous rite. Well, so be it: come now what may, he was bound on this adventure, he would not hold back from it any longer. He smeared the ointment on his cheeks, and felt it sting, but not painfully, and rubbed it on his throat, and on his forehead, until the pot was empty, and the fragrance of the stuff was rising to his nose and traveling deep down into his lungs.

Almost immediately he felt a dizziness, and a constriction of the throat. He swayed and steadied himself, and swayed again. There was a great stillness in the room. He had expected rustlings and hissings and dronings, dream-sounds, witch-sounds, some sinister music in the air, the beating of bat-wings, the cries and howls of monsters. But there was nothing. Nothing. Only a weird clarity of perception, and a mighty silence that might have been the silence of the moon.

He looked across to Enkidu and Helen. They stood apart from one another, staring as though gazing into an endless nothingness. Of the Hairy Man there was no sign.

"Brother?" Gilgamesh called. "I feel myself leaving, brother. Will you follow me?"

But he could not hear the sound even of his own voice, nor did Enkidu respond.

Now he no longer saw the others at all. He was alone on some barren plain under an empty sky. To his back was a single enormous rock, mountain-high. Before him yawned the abyss, the fissure that lies between the worlds. And on the rim of the abyss rose a tree of incomprehensible height that had no leaves, only bare rigid branches that were themselves each the thickness of a tremendous tree, jutting from it like the rungs of a ladder.

He knew what this tree was. It was the *axis mundi*, the world pole, the Tree of Life about which all else revolves, with its roots at the core of creation and its branches rising beyond the roof of the sky. And he must climb it to reach the land of the living.

Seizing the lowest branch, he swung himself upward.

It was easy enough at first. Reach up, catch the branch just above, pull yourself to it, pause a moment with both arms hooked over it, then a stretch and a heave and one leg up, and then the other, and halt a moment and go on, up and up and up. Climb and climb and climb, until you have climbed beyond this world into the one that adjoins it.

Up. Up. Up.

But as he rose he found himself also descending. The tree seemed to go in both directions at once, so that each upward move – and now he saw the North Star shining with a cold savage light far overhead – carried him downward as well, into the dark airless abyss, into the great mother-vault of the cosmos. He did not try to comprehend it. At the axis of the world who could understand anything? If the way out was also the way in, so be it. So be it. He continued to climb, rung after rung after rung. The wood was smooth and cold against his hands. Now he could no longer tell in which direction he was going; he was in a cleft of the earth, a twisted subterranean passage, and at the same time he was far above the ground, high overhead in a star-seared region of chill winds and eternal night.

It was a time outside a time, a space outside of space. He was deep in the womb of the world. He was close to the roof of the sky.

He knew that he was making the crossing now from one world to another.

There was brightness ahead. The tree was no longer bare here: it was blossoming wildly, a burst of blood-red blooms, and when he looked down Gilgamesh saw the ground beneath the tree carpeted in red by the fallen petals, as though a blood-sacrifice had taken place there. He moved more swiftly in this zone of the tree, where the branches were not as thick and he could grasp one entirely in his hand. Scarlet petals fluttered all about him, clinging to his hair, his face, his shoulders, cloaking him.

He could climb no higher now. He could delve no deeper.

For an instant that stretched until it encompassed all of eternity, the world was still with a stasis that went beyond that of death itself.

Then the silence suddenly broke, and about him all was a storm of noise and light and motion and vibration. So stunned was he by the fury of it all, coming as he had from that eerie realm of stillness, that his first impulse was to crouch down and cover himself and wait for the onslaught of sensation to sweep over him and go past. But he forced himself to stand and stare and gape.

He thought in that first dazzled moment that he had emerged somehow in Nova Roma, that bustling lunatic city which had embodied for him all the worst that the Later Dead had brought with them to the Afterworld. But no, no, this place was far more dreadful even than Nova Roma. Nova

Roma was an isle of tranquility next to this. He was in some nightmare land. He had passed through the portal of worlds only to come forth into some place of terrible frenzy and turmoil, hideous beyond belief, a hellish realm that looked like no city he had ever seen.

Twenty-one

All about him were colossal jutting buildings, no two alike, that swept upward into the sky like mighty palisades. They were so tall that Gilgamesh could not understand how they could stand without toppling, and as he stared in disbelief toward their distant summits it seemed to him that in another moment they must come thundering down.

The air was thin and harsh, with a knife-like edge to it, and the first few breaths he took were nauseating before he grew accustomed to its flavor. The sky was a pale murky iron-gray, what little could be seen of it between the lofty building-tops. He was on some broad, straight boulevard, choked with swiftly moving traffic. To his right and left he saw lesser streets, crossing the main one at right angles in a constricted, obsessively rigid way, as though they had been put there by some maniacal mathematician. The ground shook, perhaps under the impact of the astounding phalanxes of loud smoky vehicles that went roaring by without a halt. He seemed to be wearing some sort of Later Dead garb, close and chafing and awkward.

Swarms of people clad in grotesque Later Dead costumes similar to his rushed past him like desperate soldiers late for battle, shouting in ragged voices, gesturing furiously, jostling him, pushing their way around him as he stood frozen in the midst of the flow.

He looked about. The building just behind him, one of the tallest, appeared to be made of plates of some sheenless white metal, rising in stepped stages, tower growing out of tower. That was strange in itself, a metal building. The dull pallid plates that formed the hide of the thing, which seemed so flimsy that he could put his finger right through them, were stamped all over with repetitive ornamentation in low relief, not in any way pleasing – tawdry, in fact. There was no true gateway, only a cavernous opening that led to a wide hall. Angry hordes of hard-eyed people were rushing through it toward smaller entrances within, or into glass-walled shops at ground level that displayed sleek, incomprehensible Later Dead merchandise.

Beyond this building were others, of metal of every color, of stone, of glass. He saw one a few streets away, broad and not so tall as the others, that might have been a temple or a palace: it was of pale gray stone, and not too different in design from the structure that Dumuzi had erected for himself in Afterworld-Uruk, with great arched doorways and twin spires rising above its intricate facade. Beyond that was another tower of shimmering burnished bronze, or so it seemed, so massive that surely the gods themselves would be angered by its size. And beyond that, another, almost as huge, and another, and another –

There was a fierce roaring in his head.

Why did they have to build everything so close, and so high? He could never have imagined a city landscape of such brutal intensity. Not a bit of grass in sight, not a tree. And the noise, the frenzied pace, the bleak harried faces he saw all about him –

Could this place truly be the land of the living? Or had he been deceived, and was this the Pit, the Depths, the Ultimate Abyss, that he had landed in?

– "Jesus, will you look at the *size* of him!"

– "You got the time, mister? Hey, mister? You there, mister?"

– "For Christ's sake, don't just *stand* there blocking the whole fucking street –"

– "You want Walkmans, half price? Brand new, still in the original package. We got wristwatches, genuine Rolex, you wouldn't believe the price, right here – maybe a portable TV, Sony 2-inch screen –"

– "Mommy? Mommy?"

– "A little spare change to help the homeless?"

– "Excuse me –"

– "Excuse me –"
– "Hey, you big bozo, get outa the fucking *way*!"
– "Kosher dog? Polish sausage? Falafel?"
– "Please take one. All the news of the coming Messiah, and may God bless you –"
– "Mommy?"
– "All I need is half a buck for a subway token, maybe you could help out a little –"
– "Christ, don't just *stand* there –"

If he could, he would have sought out the tree that grows between the worlds, and clambered back down into the familiar realm he had so rashly left behind. But there was no sign of that tree here, nor of any other. Whatever this place might be, Gilgamesh saw no immediate way of escaping from it. Nor either of the companions with whom he had made the crossing.

He stared into the swarming throngs all about him.

"Enkidu?"

Nothing.

"Enkidu? Can you hear me? Enkidu? Enkidu?"

That it was another world he had no doubt. Very likely it was indeed the land of the living, transformed beyond all recognition by the passing of the thousands of years since last he had walked it, and not merely some nightmare vision brought on by the Hairy Man's salve. The sun was yellow, as he remembered it to have been in the other world of his first birth, and not reddish. The vehicles in the street were much like those he knew from the cities of the Later Dead in the Afterworld, although subtly different in style, which was only to be expected. Everyone here was dressed in the same way, more or less: there was none of the wide range of costume and appearance and manner, that random mixture of every era and every nation, that one saw everywhere in the cities of the Afterworld. Above all, everything that was not in motion seemed solid, leaden, fixed securely in its place. The facades of the buildings did not shift about with that dreamlike mutability that he associated with the Afterworld, the streets did not seem likely to alter their paths, everything was firm, rigid, steady.

Nor did he see any of the demon-creatures, great and small, that flew and slithered and crawled and leaped and danced all through the Afterworld, both in the cities and the countryside. The only animals here seemed to be dogs – dogs of strange breed, nothing much like those he knew from the Afterworld – which, tethered on leashes, accompanied some of the passers-by in the streets. One of them, a great dark hound with stiff upturned ears, paused to growl at Gilgamesh and paw the pavement in sudden motiveless rage, and it was all Gilgamesh could do to keep himself from springing at the beast and slashing its throat with his knife.

But he had no knife. Nor did he have his bow. He was altogether unarmed, he realized; and it made him feel worse than naked.

The great strange tree had been easier to climb than Helen had expected. Looking up at it, she had thought it would be beyond her strength to clamber from one immense branch to the next, but once she began the ascent she found it almost like floating.

Very odd, to be floating higher and higher, and yet to seem at the same time to be going down and down some immense staircase –

Well, it was done. And here she was. No Enkidu, no Gilgamesh – just throngs of ugly little Later Dead people, rushing about in the busy street like madmen. And the air was chilly, with a biting wind blowing. It was windier here even than in Troy, and the air was filthy, too, carrying with it a burden of dust and dirt that she feared would scour and score her skin if she stayed out in it much longer. But the huge buildings were impressive, at any rate, vast shining towers that looked like the dwellings of gods. And she liked the excitement of the place, the tempo, the hard throbbing beat of it. She knew she would be all right here.

But first she had to find Enkidu, somehow –

The building nearest her looked like a government house of some kind, or perhaps a holy building. It was a wide low structure of grey stone, rising at the corner of two large avenues on a high plaza-like pedestal set with broad steps. Despite the cold, people were sitting on the steps, reading or talking or simply staring at the passing crowds in the street below. At either side of the plaza she saw stone statues of two idols, lion-gods, mounted on low pedestals of their own.

Perhaps in here she could find local officials, explain her plight, arrange shelter for herself –

Someone sitting on the steps called out to her.

"Hey, baby! Don't you know you need a coat in this weather?"

She gave him a quick glance. Poorly dressed, youngish, stringy yellow hair, pale blue eyes, drooping mustache: nobody. But he seemed friendly, at least.

She said, "Can you tell me – what is the name of this building here –"

"You got to be kidding. You don't know the 42nd Street Library?" He rose slowly and ambled toward her. "What planet you from, anyway?"

Helen smiled. "I've – just come to town –"

"Well, let old Georgie help you out, then." He stared at her, almost hungrily. His eyes were chilly, glinting. Whistling softly, he murmured, "Hey, what a fox you are, huh? You ought to be in movies, you know? What's your name?"

"Helen. I –"

"Helen. Yeah. Come here, will you? I just want to lend you my jacket, okay? Come on, we can go someplace warm and –"

He was moving closer to her. Nobody around them seemed to be paying attention.

"Let me alone," she said, in the voice that she had used when she was Queen of Sparta.

He stared. "Oh, fiery, huh! I like that. Come here. Come here."

"Keep away from me."

He seized her arm. Pulled her close, slipped one arm around her shoulders and up to grasp her breast. He held a pocket-knife in his other hand, the tip of the blade barely visible. The people around them on the steps were simply looking away from them. She could not understand that, the way they were ignoring what was happening.

"Let – me – go!"

"Oh, baby. Baby, baby, baby!"

After a time, growing weary of being buffeted by the crowds hurrying past him as he stood before the metal-jacketed building, Gilgamesh began to walk. The sun was visible in front of him, pale and low on the horizon, in the opening that the street made between the buildings. That and the chill of the air told him that the season was late autumn or winter, and so he must surely be heading south, but beyond that he had no idea of where he might be going, or why.

Crowded though the street was, people stepped out of his way as he approached. Perhaps it was because of his size, he thought. Or perhaps he looked as strange and disturbing to them as they, so fierce and frantic, did to him.

He became aware, after a time, that he was hungry. There were metal carts here and there along the streets, and he stopped at one and pointed to a bin of sausages steaming on a metal plate.

"One of those," he said.

"With mustard and sauerkraut?"

"I don't understand."

"What language you like me to talk? Mustard, sauerkraut, onion, tell me what you want, okay?"

"Just give it to me," said Gilgamesh.

"Sure, buddy. Sure." The vendor put the sausage in a kind of folded roll and handed it brusquely to the Sumerian, who began at once to eat. Four bites and it was gone.

"Another one," he said.

"That's one ninety-five," the vendor said.

"Yes. Another one," said Gilgamesh.

The vendor stared. "You hear me? One ninety-five!"

"I don't understand that. But I am very hungry."

"I'm sure you are, buddy. But you pay me for that one first."

"Pay – you –?"

"Pay me, that's right. You understand. You spikka da English very nice." He held out his hand. "Come on, schmuck! Buck ninety-five, and stop crappin' around or I'll call a cop!"

Gilgamesh understood now.

"Ah, you want money. But I have no money!"

"Jesus H. Christ! What are you, something that escaped from the circus? Officer! Hey, officer! Officer, this guy here don't wanna pay for the hot dog –!"

Plainly there was going to be trouble. Gilgamesh saw a man

in a peaked cap and coarse-looking dark blue clothing unlike that of anyone else nearby looking at him from farther up the street. A street guardian of some kind, most likely. He began to move away at a steady pace, without looking back.

The sausage vendor continued to yell, and the guard called out something too. People were staring. After twenty paces Gilgamesh paused and glanced over his shoulder past the heads of the thick crowd behind him to see the man in blue make what seemed like an angry beckoning gesture, then shake his fist at him, and turn away, shrugging. He heard the vendor's angry cries a moment more, and not again.

Too much trouble, probably, to pursue him in this crowd over the price of a sausage. But Gilgamesh, moving on swiftly down the street, knew he would have to be careful. Of course they were going to want payment for food here. Yet there was nothing in his pockets that seemed to be the currency of the place. It seemed that the Hairy Man had sent him here unprepared, unskilled in the ways of this other world, forced back on whatever wit and inner resourcefulness he could summon.

He wondered how adept he was likely to be at coping with the intricacies of this place. He had lived aloof too long, stalking his lonely path through the wilderness; and when he had finally come forth to live among men and women again, it had been as a king. A king does not need to know the skill of buying sausages in the streets. Enkidu, rough boisterous Enkidu, was probably a great deal better suited for making his way here than he was, Gilgamesh realized.

But how was he to find Enkidu, in this teeming multitude of strangers?

He walked onward. There were signal-posts at every corner, flashing lights that marked off the time when the cars could go, and when the people. Red light, wait. Green light, go. It was a sensible system – for here, at any rate. But Gilgamesh doubted it would work well in the randomness that was the Afterworld, where the signals most likely would flash both red and green at once to the same side, or green to both sides, or some other colors entirely.

Vendors selling food out of carts were everywhere. The aromas that came from them put him into an agony of hunger. He was famished; but he forced himself to keep walking. Until he had figured out how to obtain food properly here, he wanted no more dealings with these difficult, snarling-voiced folk.

Ahead of him now lay a significant-looking intersection, where a second major road crossed the one he was following. On the far side, he saw an imposing building somewhat like the one he had seen a dozen or so streets behind him, stone-gray, set back somewhat from the street, much less monstrous in height than those all around it although it was itself of great size and bulk, and approached by a wide staircase rising upon a plaza. This one had no towers and its facade was not so intricately carved as the other, which must, he thought, have been a holy building, what Herod would call a cathedral. There were two statues in front of it, lions, not particularly ferocious-looking ones: symbols of the local king's strength and benevolence, perhaps.

This might well be the palace of government, Gilgamesh supposed. If so, then the thing to do was go inside, explain to one of the viziers that he was the king of a distant land, transported here suddenly by enchantment, and ask for the hospitality of his brother monarch in this place. Doubtless they would not have heard of Uruk here, but all the same he was confident that the court officials were bound to receive him favorably. Surely they would take him seriously, he thought, so kinglike was he in manner and bearing, so sure of himself. And certainly he would be able to obtain warmer clothing from them, a little coinage of the kingdom, the king's assistance in finding his Enkidu –

Yes. Yes.

He started up the steps.

When he was a little less than halfway up he noticed something odd taking place not much farther up. A dark-haired woman, very lightly dressed for so cold a day, was struggling with a shabbily-dressed man. He seemed to be trying to drag her away. Her robe was torn, and she was shrieking angrily and cursing. She had one arm free and was beating him with it, but to very little effect, for he was laughing and talking to her even as he pulled her across the steps.

The strangest thing was that although there were many people seated on the steps, some of them quite close to the man and the woman, no one was paying the slightest heed to their struggle. Perhaps it was the custom in this land for men to rape women on the steps of public buildings. But did the custom also decree that no one must go to the victim's aid? Strange. Strange. Gilgamesh paused for a moment, staring, outraged by what he was seeing but uncertain of the appropriate response.

Then he heard the woman cry out, "Enkidu! Wherever you are, help me, Enkidu, help me!"

By all the gods! That was Helen!

Gilgamesh broke instantly into motion, crossing the steps in a moment, seizing the man by one arm, yanking and twisting, pulling him away from Helen with one quick tug.

He whirled, glaring furiously at Gilgamesh. "Hey, what the fuck –"

"Gilgamesh! He's got a knife!"

"I see it, yes."

The blade flashed. Gilgamesh saw the thrust coming as the knife drove upward toward the center of his chest, and caught the other man's wrist before the weapon could touch him. He bent his attacker's hand backward. There was a sharp cracking sound and the knife fell. Helen snatched at it and tossed it down the steps. The man did a weird sort of dance in front of Gilgamesh, muttering in pain and astonishment and spitting out a string of incomprehensible curses. Disdainfully Gilgamesh swatted at him as one would swat an annoying insect. The blow lifted the man and sent him tumbling and sprawling down the entire course of steps to the bottom. His head struck the last of the steps above the left-hand lion statue, and he fetched up like a heap of discarded rags against its pedestal. He moaned for a moment and grew still.

Gilgamesh turned to Helen, who was staring, white-faced, wide-eyed, shivering.

"Are you all right?" he asked. "Did he hurt you?"

"Frightened me, only. The dirty presumptuous peasant – putting his hands to me, me who was a queen, for whom the greatest war that ever was was fought –" She shook her head. "I don't know what he was going to do with me. Drag me off to his hut, I suppose. Did you kill him, do you think?"

"I doubt it. Not that he'd be much of a loss. Is Enkidu with you?"

"No," she said. "I thought he might be with you." All at once her queenly rage seemed to go from her, and she was just a small chilled woman in a rumpled torn robe. "Where are we, Gilgamesh? What are we going to do?"

"We are in the land of the living. And Enkidu must be close at hand somewhere. Perhaps if we simply stand here and wait, he'll come along. Once the three of us are together again, we can –"

"Oh, look, Gilgamesh. Down there."

A crowd was gathering at the foot of the stairs, where Helen's assailant still lay. Gilgamesh saw one of the blue-clad street guardians kneeling next to the man, and another talking with people in the crowd. They were pointing up toward Gilgamesh and Helen. One of the guards gestured to him.

"What are you going to do?" Helen asked.

"Go down and talk to him, I suppose. I've done nothing wrong. And these officers may be able to help us find food and shelter."

"He's got a gun, Gilgamesh!"

The Sumerian nodded. "So I see. But I mean him no harm. I'm unarmed, and he's bound to realize that."

"Be careful. Be careful!"

"You, there!" the man in blue clothing called. "Come down from there, slowly. No funny stuff. The woman down here, too."

Gilgamesh nodded.

When he was closer, the guard indicated the man on the ground and said, "You the one threw him down these stairs?"

"That man attacked me," Helen said fiercely. "I'm a stranger in this city, and I asked for directions, when suddenly that man grabbed me – you see how my clothing is torn – and if my friend hadn't come along just in time –"

"Easy, lady. Easy. Let him speak, okay? We can hear from you in a minute." To Gilgamesh the guard said, "Well? You the one flung him down?"

Gilgamesh struggled to keep his temper. The strident voices of these coarse little Later Dead folk, their insolence, even the way they framed their words, maddened him. Hovering around him, buzzing and droning, offering no respect, plaguing him with their incomprehensible lingo. "I slapped him, yes, when he began screaming at me, and he fell. But I never had any intention of – it was not my purpose to – you must believe that I was not – by Enlil, he is trash! He is nothing but trash! Let me be. I have done nothing. I have done –"

"Hey! Hey, stay cool, big guy!"

"Cool?" Gilgamesh said. "Cool?"

The guard nodded. "Right, keep your cool and you'll be okay. We aren't going to book you. We got plenty of witnesses here to the whole thing, and they all say you were helping the lady out and he pulled a knife on you. But we still got procedures to follow here, you understand?"

Gilgamesh frowned. "Procedures?"

"First thing I need to know is your name, okay?"

"Of course," said Gilgamesh grandly. He drew himself up to his full heroic height. "Be it known that I am Gilgamesh, son of Lugalbanda, king of Uruk. The woman who is with me is Queen Helen of Sparta, once wife to Menelaus, famous throughout this world and the other by the name of Helen of Troy –"

"Hinky?" Gallagher called. "Hey, Hinky! It's for you. Phone call."

"Coming," Enkidu said.

He uncoiled himself from the narrow couch where he had been trying unsuccessfully to nap and went to the door of the dressing room at the back of the club that Gallagher had given him. Gallagher, drink in hand, was leaning against the wall just outside in the hall.

"Phone's right down that way," he said.

"Is it the police?"

"Anybody else know you're here?"

"Nobody," Enkidu said.

"Must be the police, then."

"Have they found my friends?"

"Look," Gallagher said, "*I* don't know. Call's for you. You go and talk to them, you find out what's what."

"Right," Enkidu said. "Right." He started down the hall. When he had gone a few paces he paused and said, "Will you get on the extension, the way you did before, Bill? In case I don't know the words to say. You can cut in, you can keep me from sounding dumb."

"Yeah," Gallagher said. "Yeah, I better do that."

They went down the hall to the telephone together.

This was the third day that Enkidu had stayed here, in the little room in the back of the Club Ultra Ultra on West 54th Street. Gallagher had found him wandering around in the place they called Times Square, looking for Helen and Gilgamesh. Gallagher was a small, agile-looking man with thick curling sandy-colored hair that grew close to his scalp, and the hardest, coldest blue eyes Enkidu had ever seen. He had lost no time opening a conversation.

"In from out of town, are you?"

Enkidu had smiled. "How can you tell?"

"It isn't really very hard. You a wrestler?" Gallagher asked. "Ex-football player, maybe? You wouldn't happen to be looking for a job, would you?" His frosty eyes sparkled like polished marble. "Big guy like you, I could have some work for you if you wanted it."

There was something about Gallagher's blunt, direct manner that appealed to Enkidu. And he was alone and more confused than he wanted to admit, even to himself, in this strange hectic city.

Carefully he said, "What kind of work?"

"Doorman. Nightclub. Bouncer, is what I'm saying."

"Bouncer," Enkidu repeated, not understanding a thing. "Nightclub. Ah."

"Six fifty a week. Payable in cash, if that's how you like to go. Sunday and Monday nights off. Free drinks, up to a point. You can probably snag all the nooky you like, backstage, if nooky is what you like." Gallagher grinned. "You're interested, huh? Yeah, you're interested, all right. What's your name?"

"Enkidu."

"Hinkadoo? What kind of name is that? Pakistani? Israeli? No, wait, I got it: you're Iranian. Right? All that thick black hair, that thick black beard. Jesus, I didn't know they made Iranians big as you. What are you, six-seven, six-eight? Something like that for sure. Come on, let's go over to the club, okay? Ten blocks, but who the fuck can get a cab around here this time of day? Well, you can walk. I know you can walk. Come on. My name's Gallagher, Bill Gallagher. Only half Irish, but it's the half that shows. The rest is Polish, believe it or not. Some combination, a Mick and a Polack, huh? I knew an Iranian once, name of Khalili, Aziz Khalili – maybe you knew him too, little guy, half your size, big beard, very sad eyes, dealer in fake antiquities, had a shop over on 57th, always used to say, 'I am not Iranian, I am Persian' – I think they sent him back, some trouble about a visa –"

Enkidu stared, saying nothing.

He had learned long ago, in another world entirely, that the less you said the better, when you were in an unfamiliar place where you barely knew what they were talking about. Here they spoke English, it seemed, though with an accent very different from anything he remembered from the Afterworld, and spoke it so quickly it was almost impossible to follow them. But even where he understood, he didn't understand, not really. It might almost be another language. In two minutes this Gallagher had said fifty or a hundred things that made no sense at all to Enkidu. The wise thing was to keep quiet, nod a lot and shrug a lot, let Gallagher do all the talking.

The Club Ultra Ultra turned out to be a dark, smoky place where people came to drink and dance, and where, every hour or so, girls came out and took their clothes off to music. Enkidu's job was to stand at the door and make sure that no one who was drunk or disorderly went inside; and when someone became drunk and disorderly *after* he was inside, Enkidu was supposed to go in and get him, and encourage him to leave quietly. It didn't seem like terribly difficult work. And it provided him with a place to stay, and with a useful ally who knew his way around this mysterious world that he had landed in.

Before Enkidu went on duty the first evening, Gallagher came to him with a sheaf of papers to fill out. They were tax forms, he said, and employment department forms, and other official things, standard new employee stuff, strictly regulation. But when he asked Enkidu where he lived, Enkidu said that he didn't live anywhere, at the moment, and when Gallagher asked him what his last name was, Enkidu was silent for a long while and finally said simply that his name was Enkidu. Gallagher gave him a strange look. "Hinkadoo Hinkadoo, that's your name? And you don't live anywhere. And of course you're not an American citizen, no, so you don't have a driver's licence or a social security card or a passport or any goddamned kind of I.D., right? Right. Somehow I didn't think you did. A green card? I should save my breath, asking. And no papers from wherever it is you come from, either, right? Right." He shook his head. "You know, Hinky, I could get into the most humongous kind of trouble with the state liquor board, and the immigration service, and the I.R.S., and Christ knows who-all else. Man drops in from Mars and I just find him in the street and hire him to be my doorman, just like that, no papers at all, no scrap of I.D., won't even tell me his fucking last name, right?" Enkidu stared, comprehending almost none of this. Gallagher went right on. "They could close this place down. I got to have my head examined. But I like you. I like you. And I need somebody who can keep the fucking drunks under control. I dragged you in, now I might as well keep you. All right, you get the job, but you stay off the books, clear? Anybody looking official comes around and asks you if you work here, you say no, no, you just stopped by for a visit. And you better stay out of trouble, too, and if you get into any, well, I never saw you in my life. *Capisce? Farschtey?* You understand me?" Gallagher took a deep breath. "I got to be fucking crazy, doing this. Tell me one little thing, okay, Hinky? Will you do that? Just tell me what you're doing in New York in the first place."

"Trying to find my friends," Enkidu said. "Gilgamesh who is like a brother to me. And Helen. They are here in this city somewhere. Somewhere."

"Somewhere. It's a pretty big city. You don't know where?"

"We were separated as we came here. That was – yesterday, I think. He is very tall, like me. She is very beautiful, with dark hair. I must find them."

"You try the police?" Gallagher laughed. "No, of course you didn't try the police. Well, look, we'll do that now. What's his name?"

"Gilgamesh."

"He's Iranian too?"

Enkidu shrugged. "We are Sumerian."

"New one on me, Sumerian. But all right. We'll try it. We want a missing-persons report on a big Sumerian named Gilgamesh. You know how to use the phone, don't you?"

"I'm not sure. They are different where I come from."

"Well, I'll show you. You call up, ask for Missing Persons, maybe that'll work – that's how they do it on television, anyway. They'll switch you around until you hit the right department. Tell them you're his brother – friend isn't good enough, they won't give a shit about that, but a brother, maybe – and the girl, she's your fiancée, right? You understand what I'm saying? You can't just ask them to trace any girl you might want to find, but your fiancée, yeah, they'll help you with that, especially if you sound foreign the way you do and act a little confused, which you are anyway. Come on, let's go make the call, okay? Okay?"

That had been two days ago, when Enkidu told the police that he and his fiancée and his brother had become separated from one another on their first day in New York – with Gallagher on the extension phone, prompting him whenever he didn't know the right thing to say – and here he was now, two days later, on the phone again, listening to a rasping New York voice telling him, "Look, the tracer on your brother just came through, okay? Report out of Bellevue, guy calling himself Gilgamesh who fits the description, bearded, extremely tall and brawny, foreign accent, brought in for observation, girl named Helen, neither of them any I.D. at all, involved in an incident on steps of 42nd Street Library – unidentified drifter seriously injured, attempting rape on the girl, Gil broke it up and hurt the guy, no charges pressed but looks like a psycho case, they say –"

Enkidu, utterly lost, signalled frantically. Gallagher cut in: "I'm Mr Hinkadoo's friend and representative, William Gallagher. How can we go about arranging the release of Mr Hinkadoo's brother and fiancée into our custody?"

"You might try getting yourselves down to Bellevue, for starters."

"Is there any sort of case number that we –"

There was a click at the other end. Gallagher scowled and put down the phone. To Enkidu he said, "You follow any of that?"

"They have found them, right?"

"Right. Some sort of fracas outside the library, police took them in for storage at Bellevue on account of no I.D. and generally off-center behavior, I guess."

"What is this I.D. everyone talks about, that we have none of?"

"Identification, it means."
"Ah. And this Bellevue?"
"It's the local funny farm."
"Funny farm?"
"You know. The bughouse."
"Ah. The bug house. But why would they put Gilgamesh in a house for bugs?"
"Because –" Gallagher put his hands over his eyes. "They ought to put *me* in a bughouse, you know? But of course you wouldn't understand. Of course." He said, peering through his fingers at Enkidu, "It's a psycho ward, a loonybin, a place for the insane. Does any of that make sense to you? Yes? No. Never mind. Let's go down and get them out of there, that's all. Remember that he's your brother, not your friend. Your name is Hinkadoo Khalili, and you come from Iran, and so does he, and so does the girl, and you all came here seeking political asylum if they ask, but let's hope they don't ask, and you left your passport in your hotel room, and if they ask you what hotel let me do the answering, and in general don't say any more than you have to."
"She is Greek," said Enkidu.
"Look, today she's from Iran, okay? It's simpler if all three of you came from the same place, even if you don't come from there." He rubbed his scalp, carefully, thoughtfully. "I should have my head examined. I should have my fucking head examined. Come on, put your shoes on and let's get going."

Gilgamesh looked in bewilderment from Enkidu to Helen to the little hard-faced blue-eyed man, and back to Enkidu. Enkidu made a quick and barely perceptible gesture that said, *Just keep quiet and let this man handle everything.*
Fine, Gilgamesh thought. In the Afterworld he might be a hero among heroes, but in this foul despicable sumphole of a world he was hopelessly lost. This man whom Enkidu somehow had found seemed to know the right things to do and say here. Fine. Fine. Just get me out of here, is all I ask.
The other little man, the one in the soiled white coat who had been asking him so many absurd questions these past two days, said to the new one who had arrived with Enkidu, "You're William Gallagher?"
"That's right, doctor."

"What's your relationship to these people?"

"It's my sister Marie, actually. She works for the Iranian-American Friendship League, which has an office up on Morningside Heights, you know, and she asked me to pick all three of these people up and deliver them to some address around West 112th Street where they'll be looked after. They're political refugees. Unfortunately there was a mixup out at the airport and they got separated boarding the bus that was going to take them to the West Side Terminal, where I was supposed to meet them, and –"

"All right," the one in the white coat said. "I assume you're authorized to sign for their release on your sister's behalf, or will she have to come in?"

"I can sign. My God, she'll be so glad to have them show up, finally! She's been practically beside herself since Gil and Helen disappeared. Marie is such a wonderfully *concerned* woman, you know – so dedicated to helping the unfortunate –"

The doctor scribbled things in a notebook. Then he looked up and nodded toward Gilgamesh. "Speaking of help, does your Iranian Friendship League have any sort of arrangements for mental health programs? This man needs treatment very badly."

"Is that so?" said the one called Gallagher in a solemn voice. "My sister will need to know that. Can you be more specific, doctor?"

"I'll give you the print-out on him. But it'll be evident to you after just a moment or two of listening to what he says how profoundly disturbed he is. The Helen of Troy fantasy, the Gilgamesh fantasy, quite massively worked out in truly obsessive detail – is Gilgamesh really his name, by the way? It is? Well, obviously that's had some influence on the nature of his disturbance. Basically, it's a delusional psychosis, a classic case, very deeply rooted. He seems to be living in some other world entirely, which so far as I've been able to judge in the day or two that he's been under observation here he seems to have developed with extraordinary depth and conviction. If I weren't so hellishly overloaded I'd want to do a paper on him. But of course, the press of daily work here, the press of routine work –" He nibbled the end of his pen a moment. "Actually, it makes one wonder how he got into the country at all, considering how badly deranged he is. Refugee or no refugee, one would think that there would have been difficulties in obtaining a visa, considering the provisions of the Immigration Act of –"

"A compassionate exception was made," Gallagher said. "As I understand it, these men were considerable heroes of the underground resistance, and in recognition of their extraordinary services both of them were granted entry. What you see here in Gil is a man who withstood the worst that the Ayatollah's torturers could throw at him, with the inevitable tragic result. He's supposed to be in his brother Hinkadoo's custody at all times, you understand, but because of the unfortunate mixup at JFK –"

"I see. I see," said the doctor, still scribbling.

Gilgamesh, frowning, looked toward Helen, who was nestling up against Enkidu. She seemed to be working hard to smother a laugh. He felt his anger rising. First to put up with hour after hour of interrogation by these dwarfs, these buzzing little insects – and now this, all these lies and fantasies, this longwinded dispassionate discussion of him as though he were nothing but a pitiful madman –

Well, it was all simply a maneuver designed to get him out of this place, he saw that quite clearly, but nevertheless – nevertheless – how humiliating, to have to sit here like a sheep while all this nonsense about him was being spilled forth –

Be silent, he told himself. Let this Gallagher say whatever he must say.

But it was too much. Why did he have to pretend to be insane to win his freedom? He could keep quiet no longer. The words came bursting from him despite all his efforts. "This chatter begins to offend my ears. I ask that an end be made of it and that we be released at once without further foolishness."

"Ah, brother, brother!" Enkidu said, in a syrupy voice that one might use in addressing a child. "It is all right, brother! You will leave here very soon." Gilgamesh felt a quick sharp kick against his ankle. "There are just a few little formalities, which Mr Gallagher will handle – and then you will be taken from here, to an extremely nice place where you'll be very comfortable, where Mr Gallagher's sister will give you everything you need, where you will have help for the things that torment you – a soft bed, a quiet room, medicines to soothe your troubled mind –"

You shaggy bastard, Gilgamesh thought in fury. I'll make you pay for this afterward!

But then he caught the playful twinkle in Enkidu's eyes, and his anger melted, and his heart overflowed with love for his friend who had come here to save him, and laughter began to well up in him with such force that he had to struggle fiercely to throttle it back.

Night had begun to fall by the time they were finally out of there. A cold wind was coming off the river behind them, and lights were glowing like a million little suns in the towering buildings that rose all about. There was noise everywhere, an unbelievable cacaphony of screeching and honking. Gilgamesh felt a savage pounding behind his forehead. This world that Enkidu had brought him to was like a joke, a very bad joke that went on and on, that threatened never to end.

If this is the land of the living, he thought, give me the Afterworld. He wondered what would happen if he jumped under one of those onrushing vehicles. Perhaps he would die in an instant and return to the place where he belonged. Or perhaps not. Perhaps once you left the Afterworld you could never return, and he was condemned for his impiety to spend the rest of eternity here. That would be Hell indeed. They would patch him together and send him out into this ghastly hateful land of the living again, and again and again, forever and ever, world without end.

Is it my fate, he thought, always to be restless and discontented, whichever world I may find myself in? Will I never know peace again?

Gallagher said, "Well, here we are, free as birds. It only took five times as long as it needed to, getting you guys sprung." He shook his head. "Shit, half past four, now, and we're way the hell over here on First Avenue, and pretty soon I've got to start opening up the club –"

Who is this man, Gilgamesh wondered, whom Enkidu has found?

Gallagher was still talking, not seeming to care whether they were listening, or understood anything he said. "Well, so we open a little late today. At least your friends are loose,

Hinky, and that's the important thing. Scared the crap out of me when that wimp of a psychiatrist started in wanting to know my sister's phone number right at the end when I thought we were all done, and the address of the Iranian-American Friendship League –"

"But you gave him the phone number," Enkidu said.

"My sister lives in Los Angeles. That was the number of a girl I used to know, graduate student at Columbia."

"What about the address you gave him?"

"Of the Iranian-American Friendship League? Christ, I don't even know if such an outfit exists. I made it all up. But what the hell, Gil, you're out of there, and that's what counts." Gallagher thrust out his hand. "I'm pleased to have been of service. Any friend of Hinkadoo's a friend of mine. I'm Bill Gallagher, manager of the Club Ultra Ultra on West 54th."

Gilgamesh accepted the handshake.

"Gilgamesh, son of Lugalbanda," he said. "Formerly king of Uruk."

"Very nice to meet you, Gil. And this is Helen of Troy?"

"My name is Helen, yes."

"A real pleasure, Helen. Here, let's turn west on 34th. We're never going to find a cab, this hour, but maybe we have a better chance here than the little streets." Gallagher laughed. "Just one illegal alien wasn't enough for me, I guess. Hell with it. Listen, all three of you can stay at the club for a while, if you like, but I've only got the one room for all three of you, so you'll need to get a hotel pretty fast, or something, okay? And some kind of jobs. We don't really need two bouncers at the club, but maybe you two could take turns at it, Gil, Hinky, day on day off, and the other one can help out in back, maybe. Won't anybody get out of line, with a couple of guys the size of you two on the premises. Is that all right with you, Gil, Number Two bouncer at the Ultra Ultra?"

"Is he speaking to me?" Gilgamesh asked.

"They speak very quickly here," said Enkidu. "But I am starting to understand what they say." He turned to Gallagher. "He will be pleased to have the job, yes, Bill. Very pleased."

"Good. And you, Helen – you need some work too. Can you do topless, you think?"

"Topless?"

"You know. Strip. Show the skin. Bare the boobs."

Helen looked at him. "Do I understand? You mean, take my clothing off in front of others? This is what you mean by topless?" She laughed. "In the poem they wrote about me, it was the towers that were topless, not me."

"What?"

"The towers. The topless towers of Ilium."

Gallagher said, "Help me out, Hinkadoo. What's she talking about?"

Helen said, "You know. 'Was this the face that launched a thousand ships –'"

"Oh. The poem," said Gallagher doubtfully. "It's about you, is it?" He thought a moment. "'Was this the face that launched a thousand ships –' The poem's talking about Helen of Troy?"

"Yes."

"And you are –"

"It is a joke," Enkidu said. "She likes to pretend to be Helen of Troy. Just as my Gilgamesh pretends that he is Gilgamesh the king, who ruled long ago in Sumer. A joke, do you see, Bill? Only a joke."

"Right," Gallagher said.

How easily Enkidu picks up the way of speaking here, Gilgamesh thought. How glibly he tells the lies!

It is all noise, he thought. Everything that is said and done in this world is mere noise without meaning. And the noise was growing more intense every moment. The roaring, the booming, the honking, the screaming – he thought his heart would burst from the utter madness of it. Yet Enkidu took no notice of it, nor Helen. They went babbling merrily on and on, speaking with this Gallagher, saying things he could not understand and speaking so quickly that the words themselves became a blur of noise. He gave Enkidu a desperate look, but Enkidu merely smiled, and went on talking. Gilgamesh trembled. There was a drumming now in his ears, in his head, in his chest. The lights of the big buildings were blinking crazily, like beacons gone berserk. Voices rose and fell all about him, now thundering like waterfalls, now dropping to a sinister, oily whisper. Strangers in the street were pointing at him, nudging one another, laughing.

I am going mad, Gilgamesh thought.

Gods, is there no way I can depart from here? I have had enough. It is time to move on. I must escape this place or perish. I will fall down and do obeisance – yes, I will pray for my deliverance –

Once he had wanted to live forever, and that had been denied him, for at the end of his time in the first Uruk he had died, full of years and beloved by his people; but that death had led only to a new birth, in a world where indeed it did seem that he would live forever, and when he had attained the life eternal that he had sought so badly it seemed to lose its savor for him, and he could not remain content. Whereupon he had chosen to return to the land of the living. And here he was. But, he told himself, if only he could be discharged of his voyage, he would be restless no longer, he would gladly be still, he would make an end of his questing and seeking. Yes. Yes.

Now prayer rose and coursed in him like a river. He who had not prayed in the thousands of years of his life after life now humbled himself before the gods he once had worshipped.

Enki, spare me! Enlil, great one, set me free.

Lugalbanda – father – grant me peace!

For an answer there was only the lunatic cacophony of the traffic, and the vile fumes that choked the air, and the buzzing chatter of Gallagher and Enkidu and Helen.

Once again he closed his eyes and made entreaty to the great gods of Sumer and to the god his father, Lugalbanda. And opened his eyes again, and looked out without hope into the squalid ugly jumble that was the land of the living.

Then he beheld something before him that kindled a great strangeness in his soul, as though the earth were about to erupt and explode, and everything whirled about him. He blinked and caught his breath. And said, pointing down the street, "Enkidu? Do you see that man there?"

"Which, brother? There are so many."

"The one with the red face, the big chest, down there. Surely we've seen him before – in the Afterworld –"

"I'm not sure which one you –"

"There. There. He was at the court of Prester John, do you remember? The ambassador from King Henry, he was. He and the other one, the one with the strange long face – Howard was this one's name, I remember now, Robert Howard –"

"Here? How can it be? This is the land of the living, brother."

"I tell you, he is the man," said Gilgamesh. "Or else his twin."

Shaken, he looked off into the deepening dusk. Could it be? Perhaps his eyes were deceiving him. How could the man Robert Howard possibly be here, possibly be on the very same street he was, of all the teeming myriad chaotic streets of this city in this teeming chaotic world? A trick of the darkness, he thought. Or of his memory.

But no – no – the red-faced man was pointing, too, staring, looking dumbstruck at Gilgamesh – running wildly toward him, now, pushing people aside –

"Conan!" he cried. "By Crom, it is you, Lord Conan! Here – here!"

Twenty-two

Gilgamesh stood still, scarcely even breathing. Everything seemed quite different, suddenly. The street about him was growing misty and insubstantial. The towering buildings were wavering and flickering like the frail plants that grow beneath the water and dance in the current. The frantic noise of the traffic died away. He could barely see Gallagher now, and even Enkidu and Helen seemed remote and indistinct.

The strange red-faced man Howard kneeled before him as he had done once before long ago in the Outback, sobbing and babbling.

Then the other one appeared, the lantern-jawed one, gaunt and pale – Lovecraft was his name, Gilgamesh remembered, King Henry's other ambassador. Putting his hand on Howard's shoulder, he said gently, "Up, Bob. You know that this is not your Conan. This is Gilgamesh the king."

"So he is. Yes. Yes."

"Come. Let him be."

"Why are you here?" Gilgamesh asked. "Is this not the land of the living?"

"We all came to visit you," a new but familiar voice said. Gilgamesh glanced to his side and saw Herod of Judaea, clad now not in Roman robes but in a suit of Later Dead style. Vy-otin was with him, majestic in a bulky overcoat and a narrow-brimmed hat pushed down low over his forehead on the side where the eye was missing. They were smiling at him. The buildings were all but invisible, now. The cars that still streamed by in the street were ghost-cars, silent, mysterious. Herod slipped an arm through one of Gilgamesh's, and Vy-otin took the other.

"You two should be in Uruk," Gilgamesh said uncertainly. "I left you in charge of the city."

"The city can look after itself for a while," Vy-otin said. "This was more important. Let's go, Gilgamesh."

"Wait," he said. "Enkidu – Helen –"

"Come on," Herod said. "This is New York! We have to live it up! First the Natural History Museum – Vy-otin wants to show us the mammoth bones, and some paintings his friends did a long time ago – and then maybe I ought to stop in the synagogue for the services – it's Friday night, you know – but you can come along, they won't mind –"

"And the Museum of Modern Art," said Picasso, stepping out of the mists. "The Metropolitan. You should not forget those. He has much to learn about the great painters. Let him see Cézanne. Let him see Velasquez. *Y pues, carajos*, let him see Picasso!"

"Are all of you here?" Gilgamesh said softly. "Every one of you?"

Yes. All of them. There was that kindly old German doctor – Schweitzer, was he? – smiling and twisting the ends of his immense mustache. There was Simon Magus, holding out a flask of wine. And there? Caesar, was that? Yes. And Walter Ralegh, in full gleaming armor, making a courtly bow? Yes. Yes. Baffled, amazed, Gilgamesh took a few stumbling steps toward them. The city around him had all but vanished, leaving nothing but a radiant glow stretching far toward the horizon. It seemed to him that he was in Vy-otin's ancient feasting-hall now, the palace of the Ice-Hunters where the bones of the great beasts lay strewn about as they had in the early mists of time. And all about him were unexpected figures, coming to him from the other world, crowding close – Prester John saluting him now, and limping little Magalhaes, and Belshazzar, Amenhotep, Kublai Khan, Bismarck, Lenin –

That was Calandola standing apart from the others, like a massive column of black stone, grinning, his eyes blazing like beacons – and the Hairy Man – and Dumuzi – Ninsun – Minos – Varuna of Meluhha –

They were all here, everyone he had ever known. A horde of faces ringing him around, people nodding, smiling, waving, winking, laughing –

"What is this?" Gilgamesh asked. "What is happening to me?"

He wondered if he might be dying at last. The third and final death, the true death, after he had died from this world into the other one and died from that one back into this, and now was going onward into oblivion, into the ultimate sleep. Could that be it? So at last, then, – was it peace at last? Sleep? Eternal rest? An end to wandering, an end to kingship, an end to Gilgamesh?

He understood nothing. Nothing.

"Herod? Mother? I beg you – tell me – please, tell me –"

It was growing even darker. The glow was fading from the sky, and the figures around him were mere shadows, faceless, indistinguishable. No longer did he see the Ice-Hunter hall. Now it seemed to him that he was in Uruk again, the first Uruk, the city of his birth – in the great palace of the king, that formidable place of fortified towered entrances and intricately niched facades and lofty columns, where the walls were a brilliant white and the ceilings of rich black wood from far-off lands.

"Enkidu? Where are you, Enkidu? Vy-otin? Simon, are you there? Or your Hairy Man?"

"Come to me, Gilgamesh," a great voice called in the darkness, a voice that he did not know.

"I can't see you. Who are you?"

"Come to me, Gilgamesh." And then the voice used another name, that secret one, his birth-name that no one must ever speak, conjuring him by it, urging him forward.

The vast rolling tones came to Gilgamesh like the tolling of a colossal bell. He took an uneasy step, another, another. He was in utter blackness now. "Come to me," the voice said. "Come. Come. Come."

There was sudden light, as if a new sun had been born that instant.

Before him in the void there rose a mighty figure, a man who seemed as high as the highest of towers, before whom Gilgamesh stood as though before a god. He wore nothing but a flounced woollen robe of the sort that the men had worn in Sumer the Land, which left him bare above the waist. His shoulders were as broad as a mountain, his chest was as deep as the sky. His skin was smooth and dark from the sun, and his scalp was shaven clean, and his beard was thick and black, falling in curling folds.

Most wondrous of all were his eyes: dark and bright and enormous, so large that they seemed almost to fill his whole forehead. Gilgamesh knew those eyes. He had seen them before, and he could never forget them.

"Father?"

"Yes. I am Lugalbanda."

Gilgamesh went to his knees. Yet it seemed to him that he was floating forward into the vast pool of those eyes, that he would be lost within his father's soul forever.

"How splendid you are, my son," Lugalbanda said. "Come to me. Closer. Closer."

"Father –"

Lugalbanda smiled. His voice rolled down from high above. "Ah, Gilgamesh, Gilgamesh, you were only a boy when I went away. Though I could see even then that you would be kingly one day. I would have wished to be with you, to watch you grow into manhood. The gods took me too soon for that."

"Yes. I was six."

"Six, yes. And even before I died I saw you so rarely. There were so many wars to fight. And the pilgrimages afterward, the shrines that had to be visited –"

"You promised that there would be time later," said Gilgamesh. "When you and I could hunt lions together, and you would teach me all the things of manhood."

"But that could not be," said Lugalbanda.

"After you died I still thought you would come back," said Gilgamesh. "Perhaps I spent my whole life thinking that, that I would find you again some day."

"I am here now."

"Am I dead, father?"

"Dead? Yes, yes, of course. We are all dead."

"I mean, will I sleep now? Will I go into the great darkness and never awaken?"

"Ah," said Lugalbanda, "but our spirits are eternal. Have you not learned that, in all your seeking?"

Gilgamesh was silent, staring at the immense form that filled the void before him. After a time he said, "Sometimes I think I have learned nothing at all, father."

Lugalbanda smiled and stretched forth one enormous hand.

"Come closer, Gilgamesh. Put your hand in mine."

"Yes, father."

"Here. Yes." Their hands touched. Through Gilgamesh went a surge of power so intense that he nearly fell to his knees a second time; but he kept himself upright, receiving it, absorbing it. The vastness and majesty of Lugalbanda were overwhelming. The eyes of Lugalbanda were like suns before him. I know my father at last, Gilgamesh thought. And he is a god.

Quietly Lugalbanda said, "I tell you only this, Gilgamesh my son, that which you have already learned, though you think you have forgotten it: there is no death. There is no death. There is only change, and change leads only to rebirth and renewal. Your soul goes ever onward, in joy and wonder, through all that will come; and when everything has come, it will come again, and again and again, everlasting and unwaning. We are indestructible, though we die and are scattered to the winds, for we will be brought together again and renewed. That is the truth of the world, Gilgamesh. That is the only truth: there is no death. Do you see, Gilgamesh? Do you see?"

"I think I see, yes, father."

"Good. Go, then, and take my blessing."

It seemed to Gilgamesh that the figure of Lugalbanda wavered, and began to grow dim.

"Father? Father, will I see you again?"

"Of course."

"Father! Father!"

"Go," said Lugalbanda. "Everything awaits you."

He tried to hold tight to his father's hand, but no, there was no substance to it, there was only shadow, and then just the shadow of a shadow, and then nothing at all, and he stood alone, blinking as sudden brightness came pouring down upon him. Jagged green lightning danced on the horizon. A wind came ripping like a blade out of the east, skinning the flat land bare and sending up clouds of gray-brown dust. He held a bow in his hand, his bow of several fine woods, the bow that no man but he was strong enough to draw, he and Enkidu. He knew this place. Indeed, he had been here before. This was the Afterworld. This was the Outback where he had hunted so long. He narrowed his eyes and stared into the distance. A figure was coming this way across the plain, a man, robust and vigorous, a man he knew as well as he knew his own self. Enkidu, it was. Enkidu, smiling, waving. "Brother!" he cried. "Hail, brother!" And Gilgamesh, smiling, waving also, called out in joyous response, and began to walk toward him.